BAD BILLIONAIRES 2

ELISE FABER

BAD BILLIONAIRES 2
BY ELISE FABER
Newsletter sign-up
This is a work of fiction. Names, places, characters, and events are fictitious in
every regard. Any similarities to actual events and persons, living or dead, are
purely coincidental. Any trademarks, service marks, product names, or named
features are assumed to be the property of their respective owners, and are used
only for reference. There is no implied endorsement if any of these terms are
used. Except for review purposes, the reproduction of this book in whole or part,
electronically or mechanically, constitutes a copyright violation.

BILLIONAIRE'S CLUB

BILLIONAIRE'S CLUB CAST OF CHARACTERS

Heroes and Heroines:

Abigail Roberts (*Bad Night Stand*) — founding member of the Sextant, hates wine, loves crocheting

Jordan O'Keith (*Bad Night Stand*) — Heather's brother, former owner of RoboTech

Cecilia (CeCe) Thiele (*Bad Breakup*) — former nanny to Hunter, talented artist

Colin McGregor (*Bad Breakup*) — Scottish duke, owner of McGregor Enterprises

Heather O'Keith (*Bad Husband*) — CEO of RoboTech, Jordan's sister

Clay Steele (*Bad Husband*) — Heather's business rival, CEO of Steele Technologies

Kay (*Bad Date*) — romance writer, hates to be stood up

Garret Williams (*Bad Date*) — former rugby player

Rachel Morris (*Bad Hookup*) — Heather's assistant, super-powers include being ultra-organized

BILLIONAIRE'S CLUB

BILLIONAIRE'S CLUB CAST OF CHARACTERS

Heroes and Heroines:

Abigail Roberts (Bad Night Stand) — founding member of the Sextant, hates wine, loves crocheting

Jordan O'Keith (Bad Night Stand) — Heather's brother, former owner of RoboTech

Cecilia (CeCe) Thiele (Bad Breakup) — former nanny to Hunter, talented artist

Colin McGregor (Bad Breakup) — Scottish duke, owner of McGregor Enterprises

Heather O'Keith (Bad Husband) — CEO of RoboTech, Jordan's sister

Clay Steele (Bad Husband) — Heather's business rival, CEO of Steele Technologies

Kay (Bad Date) — romance writer, hates to be stood up

Garret Williams (Bad Date) — former rugby player

Rachel Morris (Bad Hookup) — Heather's assistant, super-powers include being ultra-organized

Sebastian (Bas) Scott (Bad Hookup) — Devon Scott's brother, Clay's assistant

Rebecca (Bec) Darden (Bad Divorce) — kickass lawyer, New York roots

Luke Pearson (Bad Divorce) — Southern gentleman, CEO Pearson Energies

Seraphina Delgado (Bad Fiancé) — romantic to the core, looks like a bombshell, but even prettier on the inside

Tate Connor (Bad Fiancé) — tech genius, scared to be burned by love

Lorelai (Bad Text) — drunk texts don't make her happy

Logan Smith (Bad Text) — former military, sometimes drunk texts are for the best

Kelsey Scott (Bad Boyfriend) — Bas and Devon's sister, engineer at RoboTech, brilliant

Tanner Pearson (Bad Boyfriend) — Bas and Devon's childhood friend, photographer

Trix Donovan (Bad Blind Date) — Heather's sister, Jordan's half-sister, nurse who worked in war zones, poverty-stricken areas, and abroad for almost a decade

Jet Hansen (Bad Blind Date) — a doctor Trix worked with

Molly Miller (Bad Wedding) — owner of Molly's, a kickass bakery in San Francisco

Jackson Davis (Bad Wedding) — Molly's ex-fiancé

Kate McLeod (Bad Engagement) — Kelsey's college friend, advertiser extraordinaire, loves purple and Hermione Granger

Jaime Huntingon (Bad Engagement) — vet, does excellent man-bun

Heidi Greene (Bad Bridesmaid) — science, organization, and *Twilight* nerd

Brad Huntington (Bad Bridesmaid) — travel junkie, dreamy hazel eyes, hidden sweet side

Additional Characters:

George O'Keith — Jordan's dad
Hunter O'Keith — Jordan's nephew
Bridget McGregor — Colin's mom
Lena McGregor — Colin's sister
Bobby Donovan — Heather's half and Trix's full brother
Frances and Sugar Delgado — Sera's parents
Devon Scott — Kels and Bas's brother
Becca Scott — Kels and Bas's sister in law
Cora Hutchins — Kels' friend since childhood

BAD HOOKUP

BILLIONAIRE'S CLUB BOOK 4

ONE

Rachel

RACHEL WATCHED her boss dance with her second husband—or maybe husband twice over was a better description?—and gave a little sigh of happiness.

Yes, Heather was technically her boss, but she was also her friend.

And her friend deserved a happily ever after.

The party was just getting started, friends and business associates spilling out onto Heather's back patio that had been decorated with twinkly lights, an abundance of flowers, and plenty of portable heaters.

Only the Sextant—herself, Abby, Bec, Seraphina, CeCe, and Heather—along with Jordan and Colin, Abby and CeCe's husbands, respectively, and of course, Clay, knew that the surprise wedding they'd celebrated that night was technically a *second* wedding.

The rest of the guests just thought Heather had pulled a fast one on Clay.

Rachel smiled as she remembered the way the couple had

come down the stairs, both of their eyes a little damp, but love emanating from every fiber of their bodies.

The vows had been beautiful and—

Ugh. She was getting a little too sappy.

Wiping the tears away before they could escape—and heaven forbid, ruin her mascara as Abby was always so worried about—Rachel blew out a breath and set about making sure the food the caterers had delivered was arranged properly.

Soon the cocktail hour would be over, and then the group of fifty-plus—okay, so she knew it was exactly fifty-*seven* guests, because she was damned good at her job—would descend like locusts on the food tables.

Everything needed to be ready.

So, she went down her mental checklist. Appetizers. Check. Several types of salad. Blegh, but check. Entrees. Pasta, chicken, and vegetarian. Check. Check. Check. The cake was also ready, perched at the end of the table and waiting to be cut.

"This little shindig your doing?"

Rachel froze, all her nerve endings going on alert.

She knew that voice.

She knew if she turned around, she would see *him*.

Him.

Tall, much taller than her, but lean when compared to her curves. Still, all that lankiness hadn't meant a lack of strength. He'd been all sorts of hard and hot as he'd pinned her against the door and pounded into her.

Rachel cleared her throat but didn't rotate to face him. "Not my doing. I just helped out."

A long pause, probably because normal people usually looked each other in the eyes when they conversed.

"Well, from what I've seen, you've done *a lot* of helping out." He put a hand on the table next to her, and she shifted away, shivering. She remembered what those fingers could do, how they'd traced over her skin, slipped between her legs, slid *inside*.

Shuddering, she smoothed out a wrinkle on the tablecloth.

"For a last-minute surprise wedding, everything is beautiful," he said, no doubt waiting for her to say something semi-coherent.

She didn't.

Instead, Rachel shrugged and began fussing with the placement of the warming dishes.

The man didn't take the hint. He didn't leave.

Why won't he leave?

She dropped her chin to her chest.

"So," he finally said after another lengthy—and silent—moment. "Gay, taken, or not interested?"

"Oh my God," she moaned, one hand coming up to push her bangs off her forehead. "This is *not* happening."

"I—" A beat then his voice was incredulous. "I *know* that moan." Warm fingers grasped her wrist, tugged until she could see him in all his yumminess.

Her moment of weakness. Her hookup because she'd been feeling desperate and lonely and—

"It's you," he said softly.

Yes, it was *her*. Rachel, the good girl who didn't sleep around, who *certainly* didn't hook up with random strangers in a bar.

Rachel, who *had* hooked up with a stranger.

The sex had been damned good. Incredible, actually.

But it had been just that. Sex. And she hadn't been able to let go of the guilt. She'd now slept with a grand total of two men in her life, and one of them was her husband.

"I—" She tugged at her wrist. "I need to go."

Heather and Clay chose that exact moment to saunter over.

Why universe? Why?

"Rachel," Heather said, closing the distance between them and hugging her tight. "I told you not to work so hard on the wedding. This"—she swept her hand around the deck—"is all too much."

"You deserve to have a beautiful wedding," Rachel murmured to her boss and gave her a quick squeeze before she stepped back.

Heather shook her head, but she was smiling. "Thank you."

"Yes, thank you," Clay said. "For all of it. I know it was a lot of work, but we appreciate—*Oh, good*"—he wrapped an arm around her shoulders, turning her to face Sebastian fully—"I was going to introduce you two, but I guess you've already met my assistant, Sebastian."

Sebastian's expression flickered with shock—no doubt mirroring her own—but luckily, Clay and Heather were too lost in each other and the moment to recognize just how big of a bomb Clay had just dropped.

After a few more words, their bosses moved on to talk with a business associate, and Sebastian's blue-gray eyes darkened. His stare, all heat and desire and sex appeal, was what had undone her the first time they'd met.

But it was his words, the hint of a growl edging into his voice that made her insides tremble in *that* moment.

"I'm *really* looking forward to working with you, Rachel."

She tipped over a bowl of salad dressing.

TWO

Sebastian

HER NAME WAS RACHEL. Somehow the name fit her perfectly.

She was absolutely gorgeous, but in an understated way, with olive skin and deep chocolate brown locks. That hair had tumbled over his hands in long silken waves as he'd sent them both skyrocketing to completion. Pouty pink lips had matched him kiss for kiss, slender fingers had gripped his shoulders tightly as he'd slid home.

She'd been cute in the bar but unbelievably beautiful in the throes of an orgasm.

Sebastian hadn't been able to get her out of his mind since that night.

But she hadn't come back to the bar—or at least, she hadn't returned when he'd been there. And he'd been back to Bobby's *a lot*. There was also the complication of not knowing her name. He couldn't stalk her on Instagram or Facebook, couldn't even look for her on Tinder.

And now she was here, elbows deep in ranch dressing.

"Shit," she muttered, scooping up the mess with practiced efficiency, shifting a plate this way, a bowl that way until the stain had disappeared. Her heels clicked on the composite deck boards as she rounded the table and bent to peak under the floor-length tablecloth.

Fuck him senseless.

Her ass—

Rachel glared at him as she straightened, a fresh bowl and a bottle of salad dressing in her hands. "You're a pig," she snapped.

He raised a brow as she stormed past him. "You don't wear a dress like that"—his gaze trailed down the tight red number, plumping up her breasts until they threatened to spill from the deep V, clinging to her narrow waist, her hips and ass on full display—"and—"

"And what?" She filled the bowl, stomping over to return the bottle back underneath the table, though without the mouth-watering bend this time. "I'm asking to be ogled?"

Sebastian, rather intelligently, he thought, opted not to answer that particular minefield of a question. "You're beautiful," he replied instead. "And freakishly efficient."

Her shoulders, which had been hunched somewhere in the vicinity of her ears, relaxed. "I don't know about the first, but I'm definitely trying for the second."

"You're succeeding."

She pressed her lips together, drawing his gaze to her brightly painted mouth—crimson today instead of pink. Fitting, given her dress, but not helping his concentration. He wanted to kiss it off her.

"So," he said when she went back to ignoring him. "Are we going to talk about it?"

Her hands clenched into fists. "No."

He leaned a hip against the table, rattling the carefully

arranged bowls, but before he could move, she was in front of him, yanking him back a pace.

"So help me God, if you mess this up for Heather and Clay—"

And that was enough.

Sebastian wrapped his fingers around Rachel's arm and began leading her to a private corner of the deck. He'd scoped it out earlier, knowing that this type of socialization was important for his future in the business world, but also just as easily understanding that small talk was taxing for a guy like him.

A guy who had to work for it. Who was naturally awkward and unfunny.

A guy who'd prefer to be the quiet observer rather than the center of attention.

But he wanted to be successful, dammit, and that meant he needed to learn how to play the game. Sebastian just considered himself lucky that Clay thought him smart and talented enough to be willing to teach him the rules of the game.

He would be learning from the master.

Well, the *two* masters, since his boss was lucky enough to be married to one Heather O'Keith. It could be said she was an even more successful businessman than his own boss . . . and that was really saying something.

Rachel's heels skidded on the deck, and he cursed under his breath before slowing his pace.

He'd been warring with himself, thinking only of getting her out of sight in order to kiss that lipstick from her mouth and demanding, coaxing, pleading, okay, *begging* for another night.

He knew he'd fucked up.

But just one more night.

He'd make it good for both of them.

Shit.

Because Sebastian knew he couldn't bring up any of those

appeals. Heather and Clay were the keys to his future. He needed to learn from them, not piss Heather off by screwing with her assistant. Clay was loyal, but he was also pragmatic.

If Sebastian made Rachel angry and then that got back to Heather? Well, Sebastian had no doubt he'd be packing up his corner office at Steele Technologies.

Wife trumped assistant any day of the week.

"Sorry," he said and loosened his grip, gently tugging her around the side of the house so they were out of sight of any of the wedding guests.

The noise of the party muted and shadows danced around them.

This was a bad idea.

Rachel's chest rose and fell rapidly. Her breasts. *Fuck*. He wanted her to breathe just a little deeper, prayed for one of her dusky nipples to pop free. His mouth actually watered for it.

She stepped back, crossed her arms over said breasts. "Not going to happen," she snapped. "They're taped in."

His lips curved. "Well, that's a damn shame."

"What do you want . . ." Her chin lifted, but he knew she scrambled for his name. "What do you want?" she asked, more firmly that time.

"Sebastian," he said. "My name is Sebastian."

A huff. "I *knew* that."

"Did you?"

Olive skin dusted with the slightest hint of pink. "Yes. So why did you drag me over here?"

He hesitated, warring with himself. "Why did you go home with me that night?"

Her eyes flashed to his. "I—"

"I still remember the feel of you coming against my tongue, sweetheart. I can *still* feel—"

Her fingers came up to his mouth, pressed firmly to stop his words.

"We have to work together," she said. "This can't—"

"I know," he said and let himself rub one strand of her hair between his fingers. It was silk, just like he remembered. "*I know*. But that night was . . ."

Her chin dropped to her chest, tugging the lock from his grip. "I can't do this."

"Why?" he asked, suddenly brightening as the obvious occurred to him. They could work together. Their bosses were married, for Christ's sake. "Heather and Clay are—"

Brown eyes flashed up to meet his, regret in their depths. "I'm married."

THREE

Rachel

"I'M MARRIED."

Okay, that was pretty much a technicality at this point, but Sebastian didn't need to know that.

Except, he somehow knew she wasn't telling him the truth.

Or the whole truth anyway.

"There's something you're not telling me," he said, moving closer. Near enough that she could smell the spicy scent of his aftershave, the slightly bitter tang of pine from his hair gel.

She'd nuzzled against that throat, ran her hands through his hair over and over, taking the scent home with her on her fingertips. The smell had teased her for hours and yet she hadn't been able to wash her hands.

Hadn't been able to wash away his scent.

Or maybe she was the one who had actually stepped closer —damned pheromones or hormones or—

"What is it you're not telling me?" His voice had softened, but she wasn't fooled by the quiet tone. There was something ruthless about the statement, almost warning her to not explain herself, to disobey him and see what might happen.

The thought of what *might* happen made her shiver.

"*Rachel.*"

"Nothing." Unfortunately, she squeaked her reply. Literally *squeaked* it out.

And such was her voice on Sebastian.

Her response made his brows yank down, made his stormy blue-gray eyes darken, as if a squall were raging just beneath his surface. And based on the step he took in her direction, the way he reached for her, it wasn't a tropical depression.

It was a category-four hurricane heading straight in her direction.

Shit and *Oh boy* flashed through her mind in equal measures.

"Rach—" Heather's voice cut off as she no doubt took in the cozy little scene in front of her.

Or rather, Rachel seconds from launching herself into Sebastian's arms and forgetting the shame she'd felt after the night they'd shared, the imprudence of having a relationship with someone she worked with, the fact that almost every man on the planet was a giant egotistical asshole.

But, thankfully, Heather's interruption managed to jump-start Rachel's brain.

"Go away," she said, thinking quickly and waving a hand to shoo Heather back in a fashion that was more friend than boss . . . but that was how they rolled these days. Still, Rachel forced herself to keep her tone light, not wanting to alarm either friend or boss. Not when she was barely saving the situation as it was. "Sebastian and I are trying to figure out how to squeeze two more days for your honeymoon from the Berlin trip."

Heather's expression transformed from perplexed and slightly concerned to satisfied. "I knew you two were going to be the ultimate tag team for our quest to take over the world." She rubbed her hands together, evil genius style.

"Oh Lord," Rachel said. "You're too much. Now go. Enjoy the party and leave the plotting to us."

Heather smirked. "Don't work too hard."

"Pot meet kettle," Rachel replied with a roll of her eyes.

"Just remember that playtime is part of the fun."

Rachel felt her cheeks heat. The last time she'd hung out with their group of friends, the Sextant had made it perfectly clear that they thought Rachel was in serious risk . . . of re-growing her hymen. "I remember."

Sebastian raised a brow but didn't say anything as Heather left with a chuckle.

"Playtime?" he asked after they were alone. "Or maybe the more important question is if you're really married then why in the fuck did you sleep with me?"

Now wasn't *that* the question of the hour?

"It doesn't matter," she snapped.

"Like hell, it doesn't." Sebastian was close enough that she could smell the whiskey he'd been drinking on his breath. "You—"

"Fuck. Off," she gritted out. "My life. My vagina. My fucking business. And it doesn't matter because it is never happening again. Got it?"

Okay, so maybe she shouldn't have poked him in the chest.

But, Rachel didn't do too well with men ordering her around.

Not anymore.

He gripped her biceps, holding her still as he glared at her. "It matters because I don't sleep with married women."

"Congratulations," she said, dislodging his hands. "I'll send you a goddamned medal."

He caught her wrist.

"Let me go."

"We're not done here."

Four words that made her temper explode. Admittedly, it had already been fraying at the edges, but she'd heard that particular phrase too often over the last seven years.

Too often to ignore it. Again.

Too often to acquiesce. Again.

Too often to cower. Again.

"Let. Me. Go." She twisted, yanking her wrist from his grasp and executing a breakaway she'd practiced repeatedly.

And then she was free.

Her anger faded almost as quickly as it had come on, transmuting to shocked awareness.

It had worked.

It had actually worked.

Sebastian lifted his hand—

Rachel might have been training in taekwondo and jujitsu for the last eighteen months, might have been working her ass off, learning how to be strong and safe and—

Eighteen months didn't change twenty-six years.

A man lifted his hand and . . . she cringed back.

Silence. Taut and edgy and uncomfortable.

Sebastian dropped his hand and bent to meet her eyes, and she had to force herself not to recoil away from him, from that blue-gray stare that saw too much. "I wasn't—" he began. "The tape— I was just going to fix your dress."

She swallowed, eyes stinging now. "Yeah."

More silence.

Her arms were aching now, and Rachel was mortified to realize they were curled next to her head, protecting her brain, her face. She'd been taught that . . . just not from her karate instructor.

She'd been trained to cover her face from her father, from her husband.

Otherwise she ended up with bruises that were difficult to explain away.

But no more. It was why she'd finally summoned the courage to leave. It was why she worked for Heather O'Keith, the biggest, baddest female CEO around. If Rachel just took one percent of what Heather did and said to heart, then she might one day find herself normal and complete.

Not the half alive being that had slipped from her Iowa home in the middle of the night with just the clothes on her back and hadn't looked back.

"I don't hit women."

She forced her arms down to her sides. "I wasn't worried you would."

Lie.

"I—" He shook his head. "Fix your dress."

She glanced down at the bodice of her dress, saw that fashion tape or not, she was dangerously close to a wardrobe malfunction. Sebastian averted his eyes as she tugged everything in place.

"Thanks," Rachel said once all her body parts were safely stowed.

Her embarrassment was growing with every passing moment. She wanted to go home, wanted to get away from Sebastian, from the careful way he now looked at her.

She'd ruined all her progress with a single cringe.

How humiliating.

"I'll squeeze those two extra days out for the bosses' honeymoon," he said. "You can go."

Saw. Too. Much.

She lifted her chin. "I'm fine."

"No," he said, shaking his head. "No, you're not."

Rachel opened her mouth to argue. Pointlessly, since obviously, he was right. She *was* seriously fucked up. "I—"

He sighed. "See you at the office."

And then he was gone, taking her pride, dignity, and confidence with him.

Another lie. Because she'd lost that particular trifecta many years before.

FOUR

Sebastian

SEBASTIAN PROPPED himself on the fringes of a circle of chatting wedding guests. Close enough that he could appear to be involved in the conversation, but distant enough that no one was going to try to draw him in or force him to actually contribute to the dialogue.

He didn't know anyone aside from Clay and Heather, and even his boss's wife could hardly be considered more than an acquaintance at this point.

Normally, he would have made himself put on the charm, practice some of the skills he was learning and honing due to Clay's help, but today he just wanted to be invisible for a little while longer.

Plus, he couldn't focus on holding his own when Rachel—

There.

She emerged from the corner of the house, dress straight, expression placid.

Her stride in those sexy-as-fuck heels was steady and her smile when she reached her group of friends was wide.

Of course, it was also fake as hell.

Which he definitely shouldn't know, but he'd seen her real smile, experienced it firsthand that night in the bar a few months before. And he remembered it because the simple quirk of her lips had elicited a very *not* simple response in him.

Heart pounding. Hands clenching. A yearning deep inside—

And fuck him, now he sounded like a romance novel.

But he had this hole inside of him, an aching emptiness that never seemed to be filled, no matter how hard he worked or how many contracts he snagged or how many hours he spent at the office.

He was empty.

Except that night, he'd almost felt full.

A woman with bright red hair wove her arm through Rachel's and tugged her more firmly into their circle. Sebastian knew the woman was Cecelia Thiele—or formerly Thiele, anyway, as she had married Colin McGregor, Heather's business partner.

He watched and waited as her friends laughed and talked a mile a minute, but he didn't relax until Rachel joined in, finally gracing the group with a real smile.

Then he breathed.

Finally.

He slipped free of his group before heading toward the back door, ready to escape. No one was paying him any attention and it was easy to bypass the pockets of conversation, to slip inside. His neck prickled as he moved further in, becoming surrounded by the dim light of the kitchen.

He glanced back.

Lights twinkled over the deck, little pockets of bright that competed with the setting sun as it shone through the windows.

Sebastian was fully in the shadows, but the awareness didn't leave him.

Not when he could see Rachel through those plates of glass, observe her watching the house with unmasked concern. There was no way she could see him inside since the windows were all tinted with UV reflective coating. Clay had arranged, or rather Clay had paid and Sebastian had coordinated the installation on Heather's windows when one of their new business investments had recently perfected the process. The coating was said to reduce energy loss by almost ninety percent.

In other words, Clay had invested in another soon to be billion-dollar corporation.

The man was a fucking genius.

Rachel watched the house for nearly a minute until one of her friends said something that drew her attention back to their group.

Her gaze flicked toward the house only once more and he didn't have to be a fucking genius to see that she was beyond relieved he hadn't stepped back out.

Shaking his head, he headed down the hall and out the front door.

He'd go back to the office. At least he could make heads or tails of things there.

Fuck. She'd actually thought he was going to hit her. The look in her eyes as she'd cowered—pleading mixed with the purest form of fear he'd ever witnessed. And then her expression when she'd realized what she'd done. Disgust, humiliation.

As beautiful as she was, he hadn't been able to look at her, not when she so obviously hadn't wanted to reveal that side of her.

Not when she was so vulnerable and hating every goddamned second of it.

He'd looked away.

And now he wished he hadn't. Why couldn't he have told

her it wasn't her fault? That *no matter what*, no one should have—

He unlocked his car and slid inside. She didn't want him to wax poetic on what was right or wrong. She certainly didn't want him nosing further into something that was obviously so painful.

Nothing he said would change what had happened to her.

"Fuck!" he yelled and punched the steering wheel hard enough to make his hand ache. "Fucking hell," he said, softer, after spending a minute staring out the window and trying to make sense out of the whole fucked up scenario.

She was married.

The bastard hurt her.

Sebastian had slept with a married woman.

For the first time in years, he'd felt whole. Because Rachel was gorgeous and amazing and sweet and shy and so fucking responsive. She'd been out of place in the bar—sophisticated, kind, and funny in a sea of normal. He'd considered himself so fucking lucky when she'd invited him back to her hotel room.

But then Clay had called with an emergency and he'd had to go into the office to sort it out.

It had been a doozy, a mix-up with an intern sending the wrong documents to a prospective investor and nearly torpedoing all hope of a deal. Sebastian had fired the intern then had personally flown to L.A. with the proper documents in order to rescue it.

He'd been on the plane, heading home at nearly one in the morning before he realized that he'd forgotten to leave a note.

Or find out Rachel's name.

But he'd gone back to Bobby's every chance he got, hoping to run into her again, hoping to make it up to her all while assuming she'd been in town for a business trip or quick vacation—hello, hotel room—and had gone back home.

Little did he know that this was Rachel's home.

So why the hotel room?

And why hadn't he gotten her name?

It had been a funny little joke between them, a shared smile when some pathetic excuse for a man had tried to pick her up. She'd dismissed him and he'd taken a chance by chiming in from the other side.

"Don't worry, my name doesn't rhyme with cock, I promise." She'd turned and he'd nearly swallowed his tongue. Model beautiful, but skeptical eyes.

They had softened upon meeting his. "Luckily for me, mine doesn't either."

Then they'd spent the next hour talking about bad pickup lines in bars, favorite movies—*Pride and Prejudice* for her, *Die Hard* for him—books, and Netflix.

When she'd invited him back to her place, fuck if he'd been prepared to decline. The most beautiful woman he'd ever met, who'd kept him laughing with snarky comments about bar scenes and cheesy Netflix documentaries—Who knew that Flat Earthers were a thing?—had wanted him to leave with her.

Sebastian would have had to be stupid not to accept.

He was a lot of things, but stupid wasn't one of them.

Rachel was incredible and . . . someone had hurt her.

He started his little Toyota, carefully navigating through the minefield of a driveway filled with Mercedes and Land Rovers and Bugattis, and pulled out onto the highway.

His rage barely contained, he forced himself to keep the pace safe, forced himself to drive carefully to the office. If there was one thing he was good at, it was control. He'd control himself for the time being, channel this fucking anger into something productive.

But he damn well was going to find out who hurt Rachel.

And then he was going to kill the son of a bitch.

FIVE

Rachel

"HE'S GONE," CeCe whispered.

Rachel straightened, tried to play it cool. "Who's gone?"

One red brow raised. "The yummy slice of man meat who disappeared with you around the corner not too long ago."

"Nothing happened." Her cheeks felt hot even though it was the truth. Nothing *had* happened, that day anyway. And she also wasn't counting her . . .

Well, she could say with all sincerity that cowering before him was much more humiliating than sleeping with the man. He might have fucked and run, but that was what she got for picking him up in a bar, no matter that she'd thought Sebastian different.

So yeah, she was going to excise the memory of her cringing before a man when she'd promised herself that she would never, *ever* do that again, and she was just going to pretend it hadn't happened.

Rachel was really good at that.

"We know nothing happened," Seraphina said, all blond

and buxom and gorgeous. She was also incredibly kind and had taken Rachel under her wing in recent months, extending dinner dates and movie nights when the other girls were busy with their husbands or in Bec's—another one of their friends—case, being too swamped with work to hang out.

"Yup," Bec chimed in. "Lips not swollen. Hair in perfect, shiny, bouncing"—a glare from the high-powered attorney—"curls. Bitch, you'd better share your fucking secret. My frizz is real."

"Humidity is not your friend, especially in Iowa during the summer. I had to learn fast." Rachel forced herself to keep her tone light even though the mere mention of her home state caused her heart to pound.

She'd promised no more hiding.

Not now that the divorce was almost finalized.

"Ugh," Bec said. "You're so"—she swept a hand up and down—"beautiful."

Sera snorted.

"And you," Bec added, "have no room to talk. It's like the two of you were vomited up from a shampoo commercial. Oh look, I'm so gorgeous and bouncy and—"

"That's twice she's mentioned bouncy," CeCe said, lips twitching.

"Oh, Bec." Sera patted her arm, affecting an overly sympathetic tone. "You're emotional from the wedding, aren't you? Poor thing. So many feelings."

Bec glared. "Shut it, you."

"That's more like it," CeCe said.

"What's more like it?" Abby, their ringleader and Heather's sister-in-law, swept into the circle with her son, Carter, on her hip. "What'd I miss?"

Sera grinned. "Bec has *feelings*."

Rachel's lips twitched and Abby couldn't hold back her hoot

of laughter. Bec narrowed her eyes at them, but then Carter reached for her and she backed up in panic.

"Oh, no." She raised her hands up. "This is Armani. It doesn't do babies."

Rachel rescued her by snagging Carter as he almost leapt from Abby's arms in an effort to get to Bec. She smiled down at him then made a silly face. "Aunty Bec is just a big ol' scared baby, huh?" She glanced up. "They're like cats, you know? They sense weakness and pounce."

Abby's hazel eyes danced with amusement. "Did you just call my son an animal?"

She pointed down at the onesie Carter was wearing. It was emblazoned with the words, "Party Animal."

"Case in point." Her eyes flicked back to Bec, who, speaking of pouncing, looked ready to circle around and jump back on the fact that Rachel had emerged from a shadowed corner of the deck only minutes after Sebastian.

Or maybe that was just her imagination.

Regardless, Rachel wasn't about to let the conversation come back to her.

Down that path led madness.

Or perhaps retribution, she thought after she'd raised Carter's arm and pointed it in Bec's direction, saying, "Let's go back to why Bec has feelings."

Considering the death stare her friend shot her, Rachel had a *feeling* that payback would very much be in her future.

───────────

THE EMAIL CAME LATE that night.

Mission accomplished.
-S

Rachel sat on the couch of her new apartment, a lovely little space just a few blocks from RoboTech's San Francisco offices. It was above a bookstore, which if she were truly being honest, would have been enough to sell her on the place, lovely original wood floors and slightly larger than a postage stamp kitchen aside.

She even had managed to squeeze in a washer and dryer, which after living in her previous crappy apartment for almost a year, was a luxury she reveled in.

No longer would she need to haul her unmentionables down the street to the laundromat. Hell, she could wash her bras in the comfort of her pajamas with Netflix streaming in the background.

Which she'd been about to do, albeit with a much-earned glass of wine, when her inbox had pinged with a message.

Rachel had opened it immediately.

Heather might have gotten better about the sheer volume of her work hours, thanks to the addition of Clay, but she'd been a demanding boss for too long for Rachel to ever risk shutting off her phone.

Though, she should have realized that even Heather wouldn't be emailing Rachel on her wedding night.

Smiling at the thought of Clay banning Heather from her phone instead of pondering how to respond to Sebastian, and it *was* Sebastian, she reasoned, seeing that the address it came from was sebastianscott@steeletechnologies.com, Rachel opened and closed the foldable stand on the back of her cell.

It popped in and out. In and out.

She wondered what Clay's expression would be when he saw the lingerie the Sextant had picked out to kick off their married life, round two. It had even made Bec blush, and Bec was about as hard ass as they came.

Hard. Ass.

Snort.

Oh dear Lord, she was getting to be as bad as the rest of them.

And . . . none of this was helping her email reply.

She could just say, "Thanks" and leave it at that. But simple gratitude was also a little boring, and she didn't want Sebastian to think she was boring.

So, what to say?

"Awesome, see you soon!"

Blegh. That was way too chipper.

"Well done."

Not his boss, so could be read as condescending.

"Nailed it."

What, was she a nine-year-old?

In the end, she didn't have to come up with anything. Her inbox pinged with another message that made her heart skip a beat when she read it.

I can smell the smoke from here. Don't worry. I've included the details below so you can review and approve. I hope this Saturday night finds you safe and with a serial killer documentary streaming in the background.

-S

P.S. Yes, this is Sebastian

P.P.S. I won't bring up what happened . . . any of it.

P.P.S.S. But I still wish you'd never experienced what-ever it was that put that much hurt in your eyes. Your smile lights up the room.

Rachel blinked back tears.

Fuck. Why did he have to be nice?

And this addendum to his previous message brought her no

closer to the light, witty response she'd been attempting to come up with.

Ugh. Why was she overthinking this?

Uh, because he'd seen her at her absolute weakest and she didn't know how to make his impression of her go back to how it was before. If she could only come up with something funny or clever enough, maybe he'd forget that she'd been cowering like a pathetic—

No.

She wasn't weak or pathetic. Not anymore. She'd left Iowa and come to California to make a new life in a place that she'd always dreamed of living.

That took big ol' lady balls.

Rachel was the current owner of giant lady balls. *See.* That meant something. She could come up with a humorous little email. No problem. Of course, she could—

Her inbox chimed again.

No response needed. Good night, and enjoy your doc.
-S

Okay, seriously?

The man did not play fair.

I haven't started it yet. The Killer Chronicles, join me if you dare.
-R
P.S. This is definitely Rachel, mainly because my name is in the email.

Ha.

Beat that Sebastian Scott.

Unfortunately, or maybe fortunately for her, he did.

SIX

Sebastian

SEBASTIAN GLANCED AT HIS PHONE, read Rachel's response, and smiled.

Considering what he'd found out during the last few hours, he shouldn't be smiling, shouldn't be feeling amusement, but Rachel had struck again and he somehow found himself grinning at the pert email she'd sent.

Rachel Morris was technically still married.

But what she had neglected to tell him, in what was both an extremely quick-thinking and wholly effective way to keep him at a distance, was that she was not so much married as nearly divorced.

As in the divorce paperwork had all gone through, both parties had had their say—or at least their lawyers had—and the date of finalization was less than a month out.

So, married.

But just barely.

Which begged the question of why she'd told him at all and had him circling back to the notion that she'd done it to push him away. Sleeping with a married woman would tend to make the average guy back off.

Except Sebastian didn't consider himself average.

Ego, much? he imagined his sister Kelsey saying.

Okay, yes. But he'd worked hard to become the person he was, had put in hours transforming himself from the quiet nerd who'd been too afraid to chime into a conversation into a confident businessman.

So a little ego was warranted, at least as far as he was concerned, *and* Rachel being married for just twenty-six more days didn't particularly concern him.

Not when he considered how she'd reacted to him lifting his arm, not when she'd thought he was going to strike her. He'd seen dogs cower the same way, knew it took many instances for their reactions to be so honed and instinctual.

Someone had hit Rachel, and it had been more than once.

Also, it didn't take a genius to figure out that her former husband, Preston Johnston, was the likely culprit. He'd had a multitude of police reports filed against him for assault, but no formal charges brought by the local Iowan DA from the town that Rachel had grown up in.

Hardly any effort had been required to hack into the police department and the district attorney's records and even less to track down the records mentioning Rachel. From there, his source had discovered Rachel's husband's name.

Despite Mr. Preston Johnston acting the part of a good church-going man and reveling in his roles as a pillar of the community, Sebastian had dug up plenty on Rachel's ex.

Sixteen reports of assault and battery from a variety of sources—former employees, restaurant staff, even several former girlfriends—but the instances that had made his blood really boil were the five reports filed by Rachel.

They'd come with pictures.

Of Rachel bloodied and bruised, with busted lips and blackened eyes that had been so lacking in emotion, she could have been a corpse.

And considering some of the injuries, especially those from the final report, Sebastian was half surprised she *wasn't* dead.

Preston had beaten the shit out of her. He'd also never paid the price for it.

Sadly, it had taken Sebastian longer to find the two extra honeymoon days they'd promised their bosses in the Berlin trip's itinerary than for his source to access the records that were supposed to be private. It had only taken one call to the former Steele Technologies employee, who now specialized in doing exactly the kind of research that was just shy of being illegal, but which many business owners relied on to make sure their investments and prospective employees had been vetted properly.

It was beyond inappropriate that he'd used those services on Rachel, but Sebastian couldn't find that he gave a shit.

He'd needed to know the truth of why she'd reacted as she had and . . . he was going to find some way to make Preston Johnston pay.

No one should ever be allowed to do what he did and get away with it.

His phone buzzed with an incoming email.

Too scared, Bas? Afraid this little documentary about a guy who killed and then ate his victim's corpses will give you nightmares?

Well, put it that way.
He rolled his eyes and typed back.

I am man, hear me roar. I'm not scared of no kill-or.

Oh fuck, that was bad. But the thought of his horrible attempt at a rhyme making Rachel laugh or even just smile a little bit, had him pressing the send button.

Yes, it was horrendous.

No, he didn't care, so long as it made her burden a little lighter.

Also, that—wanting revenge upon her ex, wanting to make Rachel happy—was going to be a huge problem. He knew it, he could foresee it disrupting all his carefully laid out plans, but he couldn't stop himself from skipping down that particular path with a bucket of daisies held in his hands.

And *that* particular metaphor was going to stay firmly locked in his skull.

Her reply came only a few seconds later, in the form of a GIF with a hysterically laughing baby tipping backward under the force of its laughter.

His own lips tipped—up, not backward.

He also couldn't resist trying his hand at adding another line to his poem, which he gave a perfectly horrible name.

Men who Roar . . . or Maybe Purr
I am man, hear me roar. I'm not scared of no kill-or.
I am man, hear me purr. I'm only scared of a dude using
my skin like fur.

And . . . send. Sebastian imagined her bursting into laughter, the sparkling sound that had made his night so much better in the bar. He anxiously awaited her email in response. Something pert about him being terrible? Another GIF?

But he waited long minutes and nothing came through.

Score zero for his rhyming abilities—

Ping.

I am woman, hear me roar. I need to eat ice cream-a-four?
Clearly, I'm even less talented than you at rhyming. I'm pressing play on my murderer doc in thirty seconds.

Sebastian sank onto the couch and cued up the movie. He had a shit ton of work he should be doing—emails that didn't involve horrible poems to return—research to complete for his proposal to Clay, logistics to solve with his boss being out of the office for an extended amount of time.

But instead, Sebastian put his feet up and hit play just as his internal counter passed thirty seconds then he pulled out his phone and sent:

You'll have to explain all the big words to me.

Rachel's reply didn't disappoint.

I am woman, I'm not scary. I can be your dictionary.

SEVEN

Rachel

MONDAY MORNING FOUND her back at the office.

Saturday night, well also the wee hours of Sunday morning, should have been a distant memory.

That poem.

Lord. They'd added so many horrible lines to that poem.

And yet, as they'd finished the first documentary and moved onto a second and then a third, Rachel couldn't remember the last time she'd had so much fun with a man.

Not ever, if she were being truthful.

Her father had been a terrifying creature, only bringing pain and fear for the three months out of the year he'd been home. Something that she'd considered a blessing then as well as now. She'd at least been able to escape him *sometimes*.

Of course, without a mother and having a father who'd been gone three quarters of the year, meant she'd stayed with family.

With her grandparents.

Her father had hit her, had pushed her around more than a

few times, but it was her grandparents who'd seriously damaged her psyche.

They'd been there day in, day out.

And they'd been determined that they stamp out any lick of her "whore of a mother."

The church and religion had been their weapon.

They'd wielded it masterfully.

Rachel blinked, realized that she'd been sitting in her office, staring at her computer screen for at least ten minutes. She was losing it. Seriously. But between the divorce and Sebastian and all the feelings he invoked, she was losing her freaking mind.

It was the timing of it all. Everything was still so fresh and confusing. On one hand, she was relieved to be almost free of Iowa and Preston and her family and the memories. On the other side, she had friends at home that she missed.

The church community had been both a blessing and a curse.

Just because her husband and grandparents had used religion as a way to control and punish her, didn't mean that the rest of her church had been bad. She'd had so many of the members bring her meals when she'd been "sick" as Preston had declared to the congregation. They'd given her so much of their generosity—cleaning her house, doing her laundry, filling her fridge with food.

But they hadn't helped her get out.

For the longest time, she'd held that against them.

Now, she understood they didn't know how much of a snake Preston was.

She'd been fooled during their courtship, and of course, they had been fooled as well. They didn't live with him. They didn't experience the unpredictable violence of his mood swings. They didn't—

A knock at her office door. "Rachel?"

Luckily, she'd gone back to staring at her computer screen, rather than out the window, when the interruption made her jump. At least she'd given the appearance of doing *something*.

"Yes?" she said, swiveling her chair so she faced the intruder.

Her arch tone made Brian, their newest intern, pale. "I-uh —" He swallowed hard, and she took pity on him.

"Come in and sit down." She gestured to the chair in front of her desk. "What's going on?"

He walked in slowly and sat. "I'm—uh—"

Okay, she understood he was new and that he was probably nervous and wanting to do a good job, but the kid seriously needed to finish that sentence.

Her brow lifted when no further words came. "Today, please."

"I wanted to know if I could take Friday off?"

Rachel pressed her lips together in an effort to stop her sigh from escaping. She'd been two seconds from diving straight into crisis mode, and Brian wanted to take a day off?

"You have PTO days," she said. "Use them. Just make sure to finish the rest of your work before you take off."

He nodded and relief made his shoulders relax. "Thanks. I know I'm new here, but the snowpack is looking really good this time of year and I want to—"

She raised a hand. "Too much information." He shut up. "Now please make sure the Pearson, the GloGlobal, and the Cruz reports are finished and on my desk by ten."

"But it's eight thirty now," he said.

Rachel pointed to the door. "So, I guess you'd better get moving."

Brian's head went full on bobblehead as he all but ran for the door. On the threshold, he hesitated then said, "Oh. I forgot to mention, someone from Steele Technologies is here to see you. I think he said his name is . . . Sebastian?"

Shit.

She was woman, hear her run. She couldn't bear to see that particular some*one*.

Double shit.

She couldn't face Sebastian. Not today.

Flicking her eyes back to her computer screen, she waved a dismissive hand. "Tell him I'm busy."

"I—uh—"

There those words went again. Brian really needed to remember how to use them.

But the next voice stole her words right alongside Brian's.

"Not going to get rid of me that easily, Morris."

Her gaze shot up, and she saw Sebastian leaning against her open door, arms crossed casually, one foot resting over the other. A smirk teased his lips.

"Speechless?" he asked. "Didn't think that was possible with you."

Brian shifted, clearly wanting to escape.

"Move, Bas," she said. "Brian has work to do."

"Invite me in, why don't you?" Sebastian walked past Brian and sank into the chair in front of her desk.

"Shut the door," she told Brian as he all but sprinted from her office. It clicked closed a second later.

"Bas?" Sebastian asked, all sexy male and though he was confined to the chair, it somehow didn't do anything to lessen his presence in her space. His scent trickled through the air, teasing her senses with hints of pine and spice. She'd thought him rangy before, teetering toward lean, but occupying the same area that Brian had just vacated indicated how wrong she'd been about his size.

He wasn't bulky, but he also wasn't small in the least. He

filled out his suit remarkably well, and the phrase that kept popping back into her mind was that he had a quiet strength.

There wasn't any tumult radiating beneath the surface, no mean streak lurking, *waiting* for the right opportunity to lash out at her.

Or . . . he hid it really well.

"Sebastian is too long," she said, glaring when his lips twitched. "Don't take it too deep."

His brows rose, a snort escaped. "Long? Deep?"

She groaned and leaned back in her chair. "You're not serious, are you?"

"It made you smile."

Rachel felt her cheeks creasing into said smile and realized he was right. "You're a juvenile." A beat. "And why would you want to make me smile, anyway?"

He went very still in the chair, and quiet stretched between them as he studied her. Finally, he relaxed back and crossed his arms over his chest. "You're beautiful when you smile."

She froze. "I . . ."

"And, for the record, I like when you call me Bas." He pulled out his phone, holding it in her direction and adding quickly, "I know you're busy, but I'm here to exchange numbers and coordinate calendars."

Rachel forced herself to focus—on the calendars, not the fact that she'd had to play off the fact that she'd given Sebastian a nickname without even realizing it . . . and that she hadn't even played it off very well.

"How do you want to manage them?" she asked instead of commenting on the fact that he liked her calling him Bas. "Keep their separate calendars for each of them but add one joint calendar that we'll both have access to?"

"Works for me." He made a note in his phone. "Do you handle all of Heather's scheduling?"

She nodded. "For now. She wants to move me over eventually to help coordinate some specific projects so I don't get stuck in the administrative assistant track."

Not that Rachel would have minded.

She enjoyed organizing things, tucking them all away into their proper cubbies, fitting in meetings, streamlining her boss's day so Heather could accomplish more in a shorter amount of time. Work smarter, not harder, and all that.

Though Heather could hardly be accused of not working hard.

"What about you?" she asked Bas—*Sebastian*. "Do you want to remain Clay's assistant?"

Because she was curious and wanted to learn more about him, okay?

It was stupid, but she wanted to know what made him tick. Things like—did he often meet up with chicks in the bar and go back to their places? Or maybe, why had he disappeared without a goodbye?

That last one had hurt most of all. But it did make more sense after discovering that he worked for Clay Steele.

She, herself, had dropped many a plan when something desperate had come up with Heather.

But that night had been—

Well, it had been the first time she'd really put herself out there since her marriage.

She'd taken a risk and been burned.

Rachel had been celibate for so long and even before that, sex had been a control tactic for her soon-to-be ex, for her grandparents. They'd controlled what she'd read, watched, even what she'd worn, and the slightest hint of cleavage or a shortened hemline had invoked all types of lectures about her fall into whore-dom.

There had been no personal expression.

And then Preston.

God. He'd seemed like her savior at first. So charming, so sweet. Oh, there had been many red flags, but she'd been desperate to get away from her father, from her grandparents.

She'd jumped from the pan into the fire.

He'd controlled it all and even with sex he'd decided when and where, how long, whether or not he'd bring her pleasure or . . . well, if there would be pain instead.

But that had been the past and she'd been determined to move on. So, when Bec and Sera had invited her to meet up with them for a drink at Bobby's, owned by Heather's brother, who was aptly named, Bobby, she'd gone when normally she wouldn't have.

Bobby's had two rooms—a back bar area for the "older" crowd and a front space filled with the youngsters. Her gorgeous friends had been inundated the moment they'd stepped into that first room. Of course they had, Sera was stunningly beautiful and too kind to reject even the creepiest soul, but Bec had stayed by Sera's side, de facto wingman, and had waved Rachel into the back room.

Which was where the really cool kids hung out.

Or at least where she and her posse of grown women who laughed at inappropriate jokes like twelve-year-olds and teased each other relentlessly tended to congregate.

He'd been there that night, sitting on a stool pulled close to the worn wooden bar, a glass with amber liquid in his hand.

And for some reason—*okay*, because he'd drawn her in even then—she hadn't gone into the Sextant's usual booth.

She sat at the bar.

"God no," he said and she snapped out of her memories and scrambled to remember what they'd been talking about.

He'd asked and then she had—

Oh. She'd asked if he enjoyed being Clay's assistant.

"I like Clay, a lot," he said. "And I don't mind the role for now. He's taught me so much. But"—he sighed—"I want to be doing more, you know? Find something that I can really sink my teeth into."

It was the sigh that did her in. He just looked so earnest yet unsure that her heart went full squish.

He was sweet. He was one of the good ones.

She stood and crossed to the front of her desk, leaning back against it. A lock of his blond hair had fallen across his forehead and her fingers itched to push it back into line.

Instead, she said, "You want something that isn't flight schedules and hotel points?"

He watched her, blue-gray eyes as soft as her heart felt. There was something about this man, about them together that just made sense. Like they were old souls or reincarnated, or lovers in a former, okay, in *this* life.

But draw or not, attraction or not, one glorious night of multiple orgasms or not, she was married—

Excuse.

Fine. Almost not married.

It didn't make a difference. She was damaged goods. Rachel had a past that made her, if not suspicious of the opposite sex, then at least not open to a relationship with one.

Yes, there were good men out there—Jordan, Clay, Colin, and despite his disappearing act, even Sebastian—but she . . .

She what?

Didn't deserve one?

That was bullshit.

Everyone deserved to feel safe and loved and cared for.

But . . .

Her throat tightened.

No one had ever really loved her. What if there was something, not wrong exactly, but what if she was broken or missing something that normal people had?

Or what if she was just unlovable?

Fingers on her cheek made her jump.

"I'm going to kill him."

Her eyes flashed open.

Sebastian was on his feet, expression furious.

She almost did it, almost scuttled backward in fear.

But then she remembered his poem and somehow, somehow, her mouth curved up into a smile. "I am man, hear me roar. The only thing I fear is your dirty, dirty underwear." She bent over, ridiculous, inappropriate laughter bursting out of her.

Bas wouldn't hit her.

She didn't know *how* she knew, just that deep down in her heart of hearts, she understood that he was one of the good ones.

But then she remembered what he'd said.

She straightened. "You're going to kill who?"

Guilt swept across his face.

Wobbly legs took her around her desk, managed to line her ass up with her chair before they gave way. The cushion of cool leather did nothing to calm her temper.

"Sebastian Scott, you did *not* background check me."

EIGHT

Sebastian

OKAY, so he'd fucked up.

Sebastian winced. "It's not like you think—" he began.

"So, you *didn't* background check me?" Rachel stood again, hands plunking onto her desk as she leaned toward him.

Pink colored her cheeks and those brown eyes had darkened to espresso.

Fury absolutely radiated through every line of her body.

It was a beautiful thing to witness.

If only *he* hadn't been the one on the receiving end of that death glare.

"Well . . ." He hesitated.

"That's not a no," she gritted out and straightened, crossing her arms over her chest. The motion plumped her breasts and drew his gaze. Literally, he couldn't *not* look there. "When did you—" She snapped her fingers. "Eyes up here, Sebastian."

He blinked but dutifully raised his gaze. "I'm sorry," he said, already sad about the fact that she stopped calling him Bas.

"For what?" she asked, lips pressed together. "For the background check or the inappropriate looking?"

"There isn't really a good way for me to answer that question." He rose to his feet, crossing around the desk to stand next to her. "You're beautiful, and I think I made it clear that I wouldn't turn down another night with you."

Rachel's chin lifted. "I thought I made it clear that I would."

"Ouch." Sebastian risked touching her shoulder, a gentle brush of his fingers that was as much of an apology as his words. "I shouldn't have done the background check. I knew it was wrong, but I still did it anyway."

She retreated a step. "So why?"

"Because you said you'd been married and then behind the house . . ." He clenched his hands into fists, wanting to reach for her, to tug her close and hold her tight, to make her ex a distant memory.

And he didn't have that right.

So, he told the truth instead. "I was worried that you were still in danger."

There. He'd said it, and if she were still mad at him about the invasion of privacy, then he'd accept her rage as well earned.

But Rachel didn't get mad.

Nope. She burst into tears.

She bent in half and sobs wracked her body. And finally, Sebastian didn't think any longer, didn't resist. Instead, he crouched down and pulled her close. He sank to the floor and rested back against her desk, holding her tight as she cried.

"Aw, baby," he murmured. "Don't cry. I'm sorry I did that. It was wrong of me. But you also don't have anything to be ashamed of. Your ex is a disgusting excuse for a human being who deserves to have his entrails torn from his body and—"

She sniffed and shook her head. Her sobs changed to slightly hysterical laughter. "I'm sorry," she cried. "I just—I had the inappropriate thought that you've been watching too much *Game of Thrones*."

His lips twitched and he leaned back enough to meet her eyes, to wipe the tears trailing down her cheeks. "I really am sorry."

Rachel bent and wiped her face on his shirt.

He grimaced but figured it was penance for his overstep.

"Oh damn," she muttered, straightening again and wincing at the wet spot on his button-down. "Sorry. I didn't think. I'll pay for your dry cleaning. I—"

"It's fine," he told her. Snot aside, he kind of liked that she wasn't thinking about her interactions with him, that she was just reacting. "I didn't like this shirt anyway."

She snorted.

"Are you—" Sebastian hesitated to bring up the background again but figured it was best for both of them to clear the air completely. "Are you okay with . . .?"

She sighed. "I wasn't—I'm *not* crying because of the check. Or, I guess I am. I mean . . . I am pissed about that. But"—she tilted her head up toward the ceiling—"I guess I'm crying because no one has ever cared that I was in danger before."

His brows pulled together.

"It wasn't just my ex who was abusive. It was my dad, my grandparents." When she glanced back down at him, her smile was fragile. "You don't even know how big of a treasure trove of fucked up you've stumbled upon."

"Rach—" he began when she pushed up from his lap.

"No." She raised a hand when he reached for her. "Might as well make it clear, yeah? My mom left. My dad was a real asshole, but lucky for me only home for a few months out of the year. My paternal grandparents raised me and while they didn't hit me like dear old Dad did, they managed to fuck my head up so much that I married Preston, thinking he was my safe way out." A brittle laugh. "And Preston was worse than all of them combined, but I guess you already know that since you've seen the police reports."

"Why—?" He clamped his mouth closed, knowing the question he'd been about to ask wasn't fair in the least.

She guessed it anyway.

"Why didn't I leave?" Rachel sighed and turned away from him, walking over to the windows that looked out onto San Francisco. "I've asked myself that a million times," she said softly. "And I *did* leave at first. But I didn't have a plan, and my grandparents wouldn't take me in. I had a few friends, but I was scared to . . . it would be a lie if I said I didn't go to them only because I was scared that Preston might hurt them. That was a concern, of course, but I didn't go to them because I was ashamed."

Sebastian carefully moved to her side. He didn't touch her, not when she was holding herself so tightly that it seemed as if a feather could shatter her. "What could you possibly have to be ashamed about?" he asked as gently as he could.

Rage was flooding him, pulsing through every cell and nerve. He needed to punch something, to put his fist through a wall, to break something for no reason except to unleash this fury that was ripping him apart from the inside out.

But Rachel needed him calm, needed to excise this darkness that was bogging her down.

"Because I went back." Her hands rose, and she adjusted the low ponytail gathering her hair at her nape. "Because I was weak. Because I didn't report every time. Because I only did report him when I was forced to by the police." She dropped her chin to her chest. "Not that it mattered. Preston's father was an attorney in the DA's office. Not easy to get charges to stick there, and things were always worse after one of those reports."

Sebastian swallowed hard, trying to control himself, trying

to make his expression placid so that when she looked at him, she didn't fear him.

She couldn't *ever* fear him.

"When nothing changed after that first report, I knew it was only a matter of time before he killed me. He was too strong, too violent. It was—" Silence then a long, slow breath. "I knew I had to get out and I had to go far. But Preston controlled everything —credit cards, cash, bank accounts—so it took a long time for me to save up enough money to leave. Still, eventually I did and so I picked the place that was pretty much the farthest from home and ran."

Rachel rotated to face him, and her eyes were empty for a long moment. They were like those pictures, dead and disturbing and cold—

But then they warmed and she reached her hand up, cupping one side of his face.

"Thank you for being furious for me, Bas."

And fuck, did that break his heart.

But it also leashed it . . . only to her.

NINE

Rachel

WHOOMP, there it was.

She'd laid it all on the table, so let the man judge her or run far, far away.

That was the typical reaction when someone revealed the amount of emotional baggage she carried around, right?

But instead of running screaming out of the room, instead of calling her weak or stupid—when she struggled not to call herself those things—he placed his palm over hers, keeping her hand on his cheek.

"Confession."

Her heart stopped.

Oh God, *why* did her heart stop? It had no business stopping like this, for a man, for a man's *touch*.

Not for a woman like her, with her past.

One half of his mouth curved up. "I like it when you call me Bas."

She blinked. "What?"

"I've never had a nickname before." He shrugged, and the

slightest bit of a flush might have colored the tops of her cheeks. "That was more of my brother's specialty. Being cool enough to have a fun nickname that is."

"Did you just counter my story of abuse with a lament about you missing out on a cool childhood nickname?"

He paled. "Shit. I didn't mean it that—"

Rachel bit back a grin. "I was joking."

Sebastian—*Bas* glared. "That is *not* funny."

"So, I shouldn't joke about the bad shit that's happened in my life?"

Obviously, everything that had happened to her still hurt and, frankly, she often woke in a heart-pounding panic in the middle of the night, half-expecting to be back in that house of horror in Iowa, Preston bent over her, fists raised.

But she'd learned a lot from being lucky enough to make friends that she knew would stand by her, no matter what. Hell, she'd gone hat in hand to Bec months before, knowing that she couldn't afford the other woman's legal fees, but needing help when Preston had contested their divorce.

Bec hadn't blinked an eye and she'd refused to accept anything more than a new pair of the cozy but ridiculously expensive pajamas they all adored wearing in payment for her services.

Rachel would have bought her a hundred pairs if her friend would have accepted them, but Bec hadn't helped her for pajamas or money or even thanks.

She'd helped Rachel because they were friends.

Rachel had never been part of a group like the one she'd stumbled into after beginning to work for Heather. They'd accepted—okay, more like yanked—her into their fold and Abby, CeCe, Sera, Heather, and Bec had been nothing short of amazing. Loving, judgment-free, supportive, and . . .

They'd taught her how to laugh.

How to laugh at herself, her situation, her love life, or lack thereof.

And while she hadn't burdened them all with the exact details of what had gone down during her childhood and her marriage to Preston—Bec aside, who'd needed to know every-thing for the divorce—they all knew that she'd left something pretty shitty back in Iowa and had been looking for a fresh start in California.

"I think you should do whatever you want to do," Sebastian said, hand flexing over hers. He drew it over to his mouth and pressed a soft kiss on the center of her palm, then laced their fingers together at his side. "It's your life, Rachel. All I want for you is to live it and be happy."

She'd learned humor from her friends. They'd also shown her that sometimes life provided opportunities to leap, to live . . . to love. Her friends had grasped those chances, sometimes diving fearlessly, other times tentatively tiptoeing in.

But they'd lived and found happiness.

And in that moment, Rachel thought that she could, too.

There was just one other thing, something she'd already assumed to understand, but also she needed to know for sure.

With all the mistakes she'd made with Preston, she needed the confirmation that her instincts about Sebastian were right. So she sent a mental plea to the universe, hoping that those assumptions were right and then asked, "Why did you leave that night?"

His cheeks went pink, and he grimaced. "An intern fucked up a deal." He raised his hands, palms out, hurrying to add, "Not an excuse, at all. I know I should have woken you or at the very least I should have left a note." Regret was laced into his words. "You don't know how often over the last few months I've been kicking myself for not getting your number. Or hell, your name."

"Why didn't you?"

"Clay likes things to move and move fast. I got word that things were going south with the deal and panicked. I booked it into the office and then on a plane to L.A." He winced. "It wasn't until I got everything sorted out and was heading home in the middle of the night that I remembered . . . I did go back to the hotel the next night, but you were gone. Unless you have something to tell me and you're really into hairy dudes who answer the door in their briefs?"

Her heart squeezed even as her mind revolted against the image.

"I'm really sorry," he said. "I should have led with that. I just . . . everything else."

She nodded. "I get it, Bas."

His relieved breath was loud. "I promise it won't—"

She rose up on tiptoe and slanted her mouth across Sebastian's.

He froze, pulled back. "No, sweetheart. You don't have to do this."

Moving so that her front was more fully against his, she said. "I thought you wanted me to live my life and be happy."

"Yes, but . . . that doesn't have to involve—"

"You?" she asked, brow raised. "But what if I want it to involve you? What if you're the first person in my life who has cared what I want? What if I say that I lied before and that I'd like you to be my friend?"

Stormy blue eyes collided with hers. "Friends don't kiss." A brow lifted. "Unless Clay has something to worry about with all those girls' nights your crew of troublemakers has been organizing over the last months."

She smirked. "You wish."

A shrug. "Maybe. You are all gorgeous, but that's not my point. You've been through a lot and you shouldn't rush—"

"I'm going to interrupt you and I'm *kind of* sorry for it," she said.

"Only kind of?"

"Yes. Because again, it's my life. If you don't want me or feel pressured or uncomfortable pursuing a friendship because of Clay and Heather, I get it." She shrugged, playing at casual but knowing that if he didn't want to spend more time with her outside of work, it would hurt. For the second time in her life, she was truly trusting her gut.

The first had told her to leave.

This time it was telling her to leap.

His hands came up, weaving into her hair, sliding the strands of her ponytail through his fingers. "I'm not feeling pressured," he said and tilted his hips so that his pelvis was flush against hers.

And *oh,* how she remembered the feel of that particular body part.

"I think that tells you just how *not* pressured I'm feeling at the moment," he murmured. "But I also know you've been hurt and I don't want you to jump into something that will put you at risk."

Rachel pressed a kiss to his jaw. "And what about you? Aren't you worried I might hurt you? That I'm just using you to rebound from my marriage?"

He rolled his eyes. "I'm a big boy. I can handle myself."

Men.

She tapped his cheek. "Now repeat those words except substitute girl for boy."

His expression went chagrined. "I see your point."

"So, can we get back to kissing now?" She glanced down at her watch. "I have fifteen minutes before I need to go back and terrorize my intern."

He grinned. "I like seeing you as the boss."

She laughed. "That's Heather, but I do my part."

Fingers trailed down her nape, sliding around the slip under the collar of her shirt, to tease the delicate skin at the base of her throat. Bas chuckled, the warm puff of air on her jaw so close yet so far from where she wanted it.

"So, what you're telling me is that I need to do my part?"

Her teeth found her bottom lip, and she bit down when he nibbled at her earlobe. "You're going the wrong way," she breathed. "I'm over here."

"I see you," he said and she had the feeling that, yes, he actually did see her.

Then his mouth was on hers, and she could think of nothing but the way he kissed—like a fucking god, for the record—how his tongue felt stroking against hers—hot and wet and dizzying—and how incredible it was when his body pressed tightly to hers.

It was like that night again. One touch and she lost her mind. The only thing that made it bearable in any way was the fact that Bas seemed as crazed as she was. He groaned and pulled her somehow closer, hands running down her back to cup her ass.

And *fuck* did that feel good.

He hitched her up, and she wrapped her arms around his neck, her legs around his hips, moaning as he pressed her back to the window.

Heaven help her if anyone looked up from the street below, but *fuck* could she summon enough concern to ask him to stop. Not when his cock was hard and pressed against her, rocking in a rhythm that made her see stars.

The only thing that would have made it better was for them to both be naked and Bas inside her, but since that would require more than fifteen minutes and more privacy than her office allowed, Rachel would have to settle for this.

Not that she was complaining. *This* was damned good.

At least until her phone rang.

Bas tore his mouth from hers.

She grabbed his face, tugged him back. "Just one more minute," she begged.

"One minute," he agreed and kissed her again.

Approximately zero point two seconds later his cell began buzzing. And while she didn't mind the vibration, considering that the pocket housing it was in a very prime location, she knew their moment had ended.

Her cell cut off then immediately began ringing again. Bas's was still buzzing.

"Honeymoon's over," she said.

His lips twitched as he lowered her legs to the ground. The way he held on to her for a second, ensuring that she was steady and didn't instantly fish out his cell warmed her heart.

"Apparently," he said, wry amusement in his tone before growing serious again. "You okay?"

His phone stopped buzzing. Then straightaway began vibrating again.

"I'm great," she said and for once, felt like she'd actually answered that particular question honestly. She swept across her room and picked up her phone. "You ready for this?"

Bas slid his gaze down and back up and though the man didn't touch her, Rachel would swear to God that she could actually feel that stare. Her skin heated and suddenly her mind wasn't on her boss or the phone in her hand but back on launching herself into his arms.

"Don't look at me like that," he growled.

She released a shaky breath. "Don't *you* look at *me* like that."

His mouth quirked and the heat faded from his expression. "Only if I get a rain check for later."

She slid a finger across her phone screen to accept Heather's call.

"As if that were ever in question."

TEN

Sebastian

THE PHONE CALLS from Clay and Heather turned out to be less crisis and more work-related. Apparently, their bosses weren't great at taking time off and those two extra days he'd managed to squeeze out of their work-slash-honeymoon trip to Berlin had gone to waste.

Well not entirely to waste, since Clay had accidentally hit the FaceTime button causing Sebastian to see—

He shuddered.

A view he definitely couldn't *unsee*.

He'd quickly promised to get the ball rolling on researching a new start-up while Rachel dealt with a case of encrypted files that had somehow become corrupted.

His call hadn't taken long and he watched Rachel unabashedly as she held her cell pinned between her ear and her shoulder all while talking a mile a minute and typing furiously on her keyboard.

She was magnificent.

Her eyes flicked up and pink colored her cheeks as her gaze

quickly returned to her computer screen.

He spied a pad of Post-Its on her desk and a pen and took a moment to jot out a quick note that he propped in front of her.

Do you want me to go?

Chocolate eyes dashing up to meet his then a nod that had his gut clenching.

Damn. But he'd asked and so he obeyed. He stood, started to turn away only to halt at her hand movements.

She gestured for the pad and pen then wrote furiously when he passed them over.

I don't want you to go. But you're distracting, and I really want to finish this so we can meet up later.

He was distracting?

Sebastian felt his chest puff up. He'd take that, along with the whole meeting up later thing.

Another Post-It appeared in front of his face.

Only if you want to.

He grabbed another pen, snagged the paper back. He wrote:

To meet up later or go?

A smile.

Either. Both.

"Oh—" She jumped, glanced down at her desk. "Okay,

Heather," she said. "I'll ping your inbox once IT takes a look at those files. Uh . . . yup. Bye."

Rachel hung up and set her phone carefully beside the stack of Post-Its. "I —uh . . . I think that I just heard Clay . . . *um* . . ." This time her cheeks didn't go pink so much as fire engine red.

"Were they having sex?"

She shook her head. "No. But they definitely are going to be having it in short order."

He snorted.

She snorted.

And then they were both laughing.

Fuck, did that feel good.

Eventually they got themselves under control, and he found himself crossing around her desk again and crouching in front of her chair.

"I'm not going to kiss you again," he said, smiling. "Since we both know where we'll end up." He stroked the outside of her thighs, forcing himself to keep his hands on the outside and not in between. *Fuck it.* He allowed himself just one touch. And it was so worth it.

Rachel's breath hitched, and a moan caught in her throat.

"Did Heather sound like that?"

A nod.

"*Fuck.* I want to put my mouth on you so bad, baby." Then he groaned when she spread her legs just the tiniest bit wider.

Her lips parted.

"Don't," he said and kissed her. Just once, but enough to make it count, to hold him over until later. Only when his lungs screamed for oxygen did he pull back and cup her cheek.

She nuzzled into his palm and Sebastian's heart softened even further. This woman. God. He just liked her so much.

"Give me your number," he said.

Her eyes smiled. Which didn't really make sense, but

somehow they brightened and pure happiness radiated out of those chocolate depths.

She punched her number into his phone, pressed send. "There."

He kissed her nose, because he could and because he didn't trust himself to take her mouth again. Not when his mind was already flooded with images of him stripping off those tight little slacks, unbuttoning her blouse and undoing that tidy ponytail then bending her over her desk.

He'd drop to his knees, make love to her with his mouth until she screamed his name. Then he'd slide in deep and—

"I'll see you later?" she asked.

Sebastian clenched his hands into fists for what felt like the umpteenth time that hour, but the action did the trick. He didn't reach for Rachel and strip her naked.

Instead, he managed a semi-controlled sounding, "I'll see you later" and showed his horny ass out her office door.

But he couldn't resist sending her a new line once he'd reached his own office.

I am man, hear me cater. I can't wait to see you later.

Her response was a pert GIF and the reason he wore a smile for the rest of the day.

ELEVEN

Rachel

LUNCH BREAK MEANT that she called in the help of the Sextant . . . or at least the member who was the closest and knew the most about Rachel's particularly screwed up situation.

"Darden," Bec answered curtly.

Rachel didn't take the greeting personally. Bec was a powerful attorney whose work ethic rivaled even Heather's. She also didn't take calls from, in her words, "People she gave less than two shits for."

So if she picked up a call, and this was doubly true for an answered phone during normal work hours—which for Bec was basically six o'clock in the morning until eight at night—then it meant she'd allowed the caller entrance into her inner circle.

Jackpot.

"Molly's? I'll bring it to your office," Rachel asked.

"I would adore Molly's," Bec said.

Molly's was a sandwich and salad restaurant and pretty much the only place in the city that made vegetables and so-called health food palatable, at least according to her and the rest of the Sextants. Yes, vegetables were a necessary addition in a balanced diet, but they were also an evil one. The little cafe was one of Rachel's spots, somewhere she'd stumbled upon in the early days after arriving in San Francisco.

She'd felt lost and overwhelmed and painfully anonymous. But it had also been the best feeling in the world.

Because she'd been free.

And she could order clam chowder just because she enjoyed it and not worry later about Preston detesting the fishy smell.

She could order *anything*.

"So when are you coming by, my little born-again virgin?"

"Forty minutes work?" Rachel asked before pausing then figured why the hell not. "Also, about that born-again virgin thing . . ."

"Holy shit," Bec said. "You'd better make it thirty. I'll just take that salad thing."

Rachel rolled her eyes. "Which salad thing? The pear and brie or the apple and cranberry?"

"Either. Both. I don't care," Bec said. Rachel grinned, loving how her friend's New England accent took over when she got excited. The words were clipped and rapid, and she sounded half *Real Housewives*, half New York socialite. "I need to hear more about your vagina."

Okay, maybe more than half *Real Housewives*.

"It's—" Rachel broke off. "Well, Bec, it's pretty fucking complicated."

"A sigh and a curse word," Bec said and Rachel could swear she heard her friend rubbing her hands together in gleeful antic-ipation. "This is going to be good."

"Probably." Rachel pushed open the door to Molly's.

So, she'd already banked on Bec saying yes to lunch.

The food was really that good.

"I'm hanging up now," she said.

"Thirty minutes," Bec replied. "And you're going to spill all your secrets."

"As if I could withstand the Darden Death Stare," she joked.

"Damn right." Bec disconnected the call, and Rachel found herself smiling as she headed up to the counter to order.

Good friends. A potential beginning of something with a new guy. Maybe friendship, maybe more—friends with benefits, boyfriend?

Who knew?

But there were possibilities and those were something Rachel had lived without for a long, long time.

She would take her chances grasping at every single one of them.

"So, was he good?"

Rachel thought that her smile said it all. Especially, when Bec hooted and dropped her fork.

"Holy shit!" She clapped her hands together. "Little Sebastian really has *that* much going for him?"

Rachel smirked. "He's got enough, but better yet, he knows how to use it."

"Hot damn." Bec picked her fork back up and shoveled a bite of salad into her mouth. "I never would have guessed. So, what's the problem?"

Rachel thought about that for a long moment. "Nothing really." She shrugged. "Which I guess is kind of the problem. I thought I'd freak out the first time after . . . you know . . ."

"And you didn't?" The Darden Death Stare didn't come out, but just having Bec's gray eyes fixed on her made Rachel spill her guts.

"No," she said. "I didn't freak. I wanted more. But he'd disappeared." She scooped up a bite of her own salad. "Later I got it. I mean, I've up and left things at the drop of the hat just because Heather called. But even when I hated him for leaving, I still wanted him. *God*. Does that even make sense?"

Bec nodded, serious for once. "Yeah. I get that feeling completely."

Rachel froze with her fork two inches from her mouth. "Why do I feel like there's a story there?"

A wry smile. "Because there is, but it's not one I'm going to tell you. Or anyone, for that matter." She waved a hand dismissively. "The only pertinent thing is that I was young and stupid and naïve."

"Been there, got the freaking T-shirt," Rachel muttered.

"We're part of the same club, apparently." Bec rolled her eyes. "But no freak out. That's a good thing, Rach."

She picked at her salad, searching for another crouton. "I know."

"Then what's the real issue bouncing around that brain of yours?"

"I just—" Rachel sighed. "Ugh. I *like* him, okay?"

Bec snorted. "Woman. That's a *good* thing."

"But what if—"

"Ah." Bec nodded and pushed away her food, fixing her eyes firmly on Rachel's. "I get it now. You're scared Sebastian might be more than a quick fuck."

Rachel made a face. "He's already more than that."

"Well then, I think you already know how to resolve your problem."

"I do?"

Bec grabbed her plate back. "Sure. You see where things go with Sebastian. You keep an open mind. You prepare for either alternative."

"Either?" Rachel parroted.

"Look, Sebastian is a good guy. He doesn't have any police reports, convictions, or lawsuits." Bec ticked off the words on her fingers. "He's never even gotten a speeding ticket. His brother is a retired NHL player, his sister a brilliant engineer. His parents are still married and live in a middle-class suburb."

Rachel's mouth dropped open. "How do you know all that?"

Bec shrugged. "I had him checked out when I found out he was Clay's assistant."

Oh. Em. Gee.

Rachel bit back a giggle.

Bec had background-checked Sebastian.

That was somehow too perfect.

"What?" Bec asked, mouth full and the word sounding like "Shmut?" She chewed and swallowed before saying, "He was going to be near Heather, and no one messes with my O'Keiths."

"I love you, Bec."

"Damn right you do." She paused. "So, you either accept that Sebastian will be around for a good long while or you cut him loose now."

Rachel thought about that carefully. "I don't think I can cut him loose."

A flash of a smile. "Well then, I guess you had better get used to Sebastian being around then, don't you think?"

The thought of Sebastian being around on a potentially permanent basis made Rachel's heart feel buoyant for the first time in forever.

She grinned at Bec.

"I guess I'd better."

TWELVE

Sebastian

HE'D BEEN LOOKING FORWARD to later all day and now *later* seemed like it wouldn't be coming.

Sighing, Sebastian pulled out his cell and called Rachel.

She answered after three rings. "Hey, you." Her voice was soft and made what he was about to tell her all the more painful. "How's it going?"

"I'm knee-deep in a crisis."

"*Oh.*" She sighed. "I'm guessing that means we won't be meeting up?"

Sebastian dropped into his desk chair, head pounding, feet aching from running all over the city. "I'm sorry."

"Don't apologize," Rachel said, her voice taking on a stern quality. "Shit happens. I'm disappointed is all." Her tone softened. "I was thinking about you all day."

He liked the sound of that. "Yeah?"

"Yeah." Heels clicked across the floor and he heard a *snick*.

"Did you just close the door?"

A giggle. *God* that sound. He loved making her laugh.

"So, what if I did?"

His phone chimed and he glanced down at the screen. Rachel was FaceTiming him?

He accepted the call.

Her beautiful face appeared on his cell. She was smiling and her eyes held no small amount of mischievousness. "Hi," she said and waved.

His lips twitched. "Hi."

Brows pulling down and together, she said, almost accusing, "You look exhausted."

Sebastian rubbed his temple. "I *am* exhausted, honestly. We had a deal blow up today and the details of the offer shared with competitors." He sighed. "Then the media. Of course, it was skewed to make Steele look bad, like *we* were the ones to torpedo the contract when really the other party was the one to pull the plug."

Her lips pressed flat. "Was this for the tech center for the city?"

Shock pulsed through him. "How do you know about that?"

"RoboTech considered making an offer, but we have our hands full with other charitable projects."

"That's right. The joint venture with McGregor Enterprises. Last I heard, you guys had proceeded to some field testing?"

She nodded. "Now's my turn to ask how you found out about that." Her eyes sparkled with amusement. "I guess our bosses are sharing more than just pillow talk."

"Apparently," he said with a chuckle. Two minutes talking with Rachel, and his head had stopped pounding.

"So, I'm guessing that Steele made a good deal. Why did the city back out?"

"We got tired of the red tape. They wanted us to complete another environmental review—and we've done two already.

Then additional seismic calculations and—" He blew out a breath. "Well, it just got to be too much. So, we said they either went with our initial offers and previous reports or we would walk."

Rachel wrinkled her nose. "So, they went to the media."

"That's the game."

Her heels clicked back across the floor and he saw her computer was still on as she rounded her desk. "I'm not the only one burning the midnight oil," he said. "Why are you still at work?"

She grinned. "I was waiting for someone to call. Or text."

His stomach twisted. "Shit, sweetheart. I'm sorry. I—"

"I'm *joking*." White teeth nibbled the corner of her mouth. "But I do have something that might make you feel better."

One brow rose. "What's that?"

She lifted her hand to her collar, her fingers flicking one button open.

"Uh . . ."

Another button came loose, then another until Sebastian could see the slightest hint of black lace.

"*Fuck*," he groaned. "*That* was what you were wearing earlier?"

A trail of fingers across her chest. Her voice dropped to a conspiratorial whisper and she licked her lips. "This is what I wear *every* day."

He went hard. Just like that, his feet no longer hurt, his head didn't throb. The only thing that was aching was his cock, desperate to be back inside her. "Baby," he groaned. "You're killing me."

"In the best way, I hope." Her hand crept lower, slipping under the lace, pulling it down enough to flash him a hint of one dusky nipple.

"Why are we both still in our offices again?"

She chuckled. "I have no idea," she said and slowly extracted her fingers. He wanted to groan but didn't know whether in disappointment or relief.

Disappointment. Definitely disappointment.

Rachel nodded. "What I *am* going to do is finish up my work here then go pick up takeout. *Then* I'm going to text you my address and the code for my apartment." She glanced down at her watch. "I figure that gives you about two hours to get the crisis under control before heading to my place."

This woman undid him. He liked her so much and wanted to tell her exactly that, but what was between them was so fresh and new that it was too soon for any kind of declaration. And so he floundered, struggling to find something funny to say, something that would illustrate her importance without making her run away screaming.

And it couldn't be another line for their horrible poem.

He frowned.

"Or not," Rachel said. "Bas, if you think—"

"No, that's not it at all," he hurried to say. "It's just . . . you're too good for me, sweetheart."

She snorted. "You do remember my past, right?"

If she'd been in front of him in that moment, he would have been half-tempted to take her by the shoulders and shake some sense into her. Obviously, he *couldn't* do that, either in person or through the phone, but he still wanted to find a way to make her understand that she was perfect and incredible, beautiful and kind—

He wanted her to be his.

But she also needed to become *hers* first.

"Too. Good," he said again. "I'm just the little brother who works as an assistant when my siblings are a professional hockey player—retired now—and an obscenely smart engineer. Like insanely smart. As in Kelsey filed for her first patent at thirteen."

Rachel smiled. "That sounds like . . . a lot?"

He nodded in agreement. "Yeah. I'm the abnormal one because I'm average in smarts and drastically limited in athletic ability."

"I can think of one particularly *not* average thing you've got going for you."

He waggled his brows. "Yeah? Typing a hundred words a minute is an impressive skill, I know."

"I'm wet just thinking about it."

He choked.

"So, see you in two hours?"

Bas nodded mutely.

"Good. If you're on time, I promise you'll get to see the rest of my underwear."

He slumped back in his chair after she'd clicked off, mind spinning all sorts of dangerous and unproductive fantasies of Rachel's underwear.

That woman was going to be the death of him.

Unfortunately, he didn't know at the time how accurate that particular thought would be.

THIRTEEN

Rachel

RACHEL JUGGLED the bag of Italian food—extra garlic bread, for the win—along with a bottle of wine and her briefcase as she keyed in the code to her apartment. It unlocked with a *click,* and she nudged it open with a combination of one knee and her elbow.

Then almost dropped the bottle of wine.

"Super graceful as always," she muttered, closing and locking the door behind her.

Her phone rang just as she was setting the food on the counter.

Thinking it was Bas, she answered without looking at the number.

"Hey, you," she said.

"You've been a bad girl."

The blood in her veins froze solid at the sound of Preston's voice. "I believe there's a restraining order in place that makes it illegal for you to call me." Thank God her voice was steady, that Bec had warned her this might happen and had coached her on what to say. "I'm hanging up and calling the police."

He snorted. "You wouldn't dare."

"Do yourself a favor and lose my number, Preston. We're done."

"We are *not*—"

Rachel pressed the end button.

Her heart pounded and jumped as her phone immediately began ringing again. *"Fuck."* She jabbed at the ignore button, immediately clicking over to her contacts and pressing Bec's number.

"Twice in one day, my little not-virgin," Bec said. "To what do I owe the pleasure?"

"I—" Her cell clicked in her ear, signaling Preston trying her for the third time.

In a heartbeat, Bec's tone went from teasing to serious. "What's wrong?"

"He—" Rachel sucked in a breath, forced herself to release it slowly. "Preston called me. He's still calling me."

"Did he threaten you?"

"No. I didn't give him a chance. Just told him he wasn't supposed to call me and that I was contacting the police."

"Good. Good." She snapped out an order to someone in the background. "I'm going to call my contact at the PD, then I'm coming over."

"No. I'm okay," Rachel said. "It just shook me, I guess, to hear his voice after so long."

"You shouldn't be alone."

Rachel's gaze went to the bag of takeout on her counter, the bottle of red wine. "Sebastian's coming over."

A pause.

Then, "Good on you, Rach."

"Is this an incredibly stupid idea?"

"Trusting a man?" Bec asked. "Or trusting *this* man?"

Considering the only man she'd trusted before was currently blowing up her phone after having spent close to five years systematically destroying every good part of her.

She had finally got her shit together, finally started to feel like an actual person.

And Preston.

And Sebastian.

"Either. Both."

Bec hesitated again then said, "Trust is a tricky thing, yeah? I've only met the man a handful of times, and my gut says that Sebastian is one of the good ones. But, Rach, the more important question is what does *your* gut say?"

Rachel sighed and studied her toes. "My gut says that, too."

"That's enough for now, don't you think?"

She chuckled. "Is that your patented Darden mic drop?"

"No," Bec said. "It's already hard enough to maintain my copyright on the death stare."

"Oh, Bec," Rachel groaned. "What the hell am I going to do?"

Her friend released a puff of air that rattled through her cell. "You're going to let me handle this. Block the number Preston is phoning from, but don't delete any messages or calls. And definitely don't pick up any numbers you don't recognize." A beat, amusement slipping into Bec's tone. "And enjoy your wild night of hanky-panky with Sebastian."

"I don't even know what that means."

"Oh, you will. You. Will."

Rachel smiled despite herself. "Was that supposed to be the mic drop?"

"I'm just getting started—"

"Well, *I'm* hanging up now."

"Have hot sex—"

Rachel clicked off, somehow smiling despite her past cropping back up, despite Preston's calls still buzzing in her ear.

She really did have the best of friends.

SEBASTIAN KNOCKED BEFORE PUSHING open Rachel's door just over thirty minutes later.

He took one second to survey her apartment—a small one-bedroom because real estate prices were insane in San Francisco—then focused his gaze on her.

"What's wrong?"

She pulled out the plates of takeout she'd been warming in the oven and shrugged. "I'm fine."

Bas was by her side in a second, taking the plates and setting them onto the counter. "Bullshit. What happened?"

Rachel sighed. "Preston called. Has *been* calling pretty much nonstop for the last half an hour."

"Did he threaten you?"

She shook her head. "I didn't let it get that far."

"What should we do?" he asked when her phone lit up with another missed call. "Contact the police?"

"Bec's doing that for me."

"Darden?"

She nodded.

"Well, I don't think you could have a better lawyer."

"I agree. And we have a restraining order, so there's not much else I can do at this point."

Sebastian took the bottle of wine when she extended it toward him, along with the opener. "So, serious question now. This"—he gestured between them—"is new and . . . a lot, I guess. Is it too much? Do you want me to go?"

"First of all, that's two questions."

He cupped her cheek and her throat went tight. She sniffed.

"Second, fuck, Bas. You can't say things like that."

"For the record, I like it when you say my name."

Her lips curved. "I know you do." She stepped closer, resting her palm over his heart. "Also, would you—I mean, *could* you stay for a little while?"

He kissed her forehead. "I can stay however long you need me."

Rachel had the feeling that could possibly be forever.

FOURTEEN

Sebastian

HE HELD Rachel as she slept and it was pretty much the best thing ever. It definitely wasn't the end to the night he'd been expecting.

Sex.

He'd been expecting lots and lots of hot, sweaty sex.

Three months' worth of fantasizing, of making up for having to leave her that night . . . and he'd ended up just holding her as she slept.

But fuck if he could find the strength to care. Bas wouldn't have made love to her, even if she'd asked. No way would he force something or risk their future being tainted by her fucking asshole of an ex.

So, they'd eaten takeout and watched two documentaries and stayed up way too late, considering it was a Monday and they still had the rest of the work week to get through.

Around midnight he'd made motions to leave, not wanting to keep her up when she needed rest, but Rachel had said, "Stay."

He didn't have one single iota of strength to deny her anything.

They'd gone into her bedroom and she'd slipped into the bathroom, emerging in a pair of silky pajamas that did nothing to hide her gorgeous body beneath. He'd stripped down to his boxer briefs, borrowed a toothbrush to clean his teeth, and then had slid into bed next to her.

It was domestic. It should have felt awkward considering how short of a time they'd truly known each other.

It hadn't.

Instead, getting ready for bed, cuddling up next to her under the covers, smelling the fruity tones of her shampoo as she'd nuzzled into his neck . . . all of it had felt exactly right.

She'd fallen asleep a few moments later and Sebastian had been left thinking about everything that had happened over the last few days.

His phone buzzed and he glanced over at the screen, saw it was a text from Kelsey.

Carefully, he slipped an arm free and picked up his cell.

Coming to town. Thursday. 6 pm. Dinner with Devon and Mom and Dad.

Great, he thought and planned on scheduling a meeting during just that time. His family meant well, but God were they hard to take in large doses.

Devon would be his usual self, garnering an audience of adoring fans as his wife, Becca, teased him about it. Kelsey would have a brand-new project that would change the world.

And he'd just managed to squeeze out two extra days for Clay and Heather's honeymoon.

Streamers would fly, balloons would drop from the ceiling, so great would be his accolades.

Another buzz.

You're coming. Even if I have to drag you out of your office myself.

He sighed.

I have plans already.

As predicted her response was:

Cancel them. This is important.

Mentally, he weighed his options. Would she actually come to his office and make a scene?
Yes.
Absolutely, she would. And revel in every second of it.
Sighing, he texted back.

See you Thursday.

Her reply came half a second later.

Damn right you will.

With that auspicious ending, Sebastian set down his phone and closed his eyes. But with Rachel next to him, he found that despite the need burning through him, despite Kelsey's decree, and even despite Rachel's past refusing to stay in the fucking past, where it belonged, he was able to close his eyes and fall headlong into sleep.

HE WOKE to sunshine blinding him and Rachel's ass pressing against his cock.

Okay, he had been wrong the previous evening, waking with Rachel cuddled up to him, her warm, sleep lax body in his arms, *that* was the best thing ever.

She rolled over, her hand dropping to his chest then lower.

Well, *that* was definitely the direction he wanted her fingers to travel, though after the events of the previous evening this probably wasn't the best time.

He snagged her hand, bringing it up to his mouth to kiss her palm. "Wake up, sweetheart," he murmured. "Before I forget that I'm trying to be good."

"Mmm." Rachel rocked against him and—*shit*, why was he trying to be good again?

Sebastian closed his eyes. Because it was the right thing to do.

Fuck.

He brushed back her hair, pressed a kiss to her cheek. "Rachel, baby. It's time to get up."

She sighed and, after a long moment, opened her eyes.

"There you are," he said softly.

A smile teased her lips. "You stayed."

He shrugged. "You asked."

"I don't want to get up." Her nose wrinkled.

Bas chuckled. "Me either."

Another sigh. "So how soon until the bosses figure out we're playing hooky?"

"Sooner than we want them to, probably." The strap from her tank top had slipped down her shoulder. He fixed it.

Rachel blinked. "You know, most men would have taken that the other direction."

He slipped from beneath the sheets and stood. "Maybe." A peek under the floral patterned comforter covering her. That was followed by a stifled groan. "No, not maybe. That's a definite."

"So why aren't you in bed with me?"

He grabbed his slacks and stepped into them. "Because it's seven thirty on a Tuesday morning, and we both need to get to work."

One brown brow rose. "No, that's not it."

Bas had begun buttoning his shirt when Rachel slipped out of bed.

Fuck.

He whipped around.

Those fucking pajamas were all but transparent in the morning light.

Fingers down his sides, arms trailing around his middle, breasts pressing firmly against his back. "We should wait until you feel—"

"What?" Rachel slid around to his front and picked up his hand. Then she did something that he never would have predicted and was pretty much the hottest thing ever.

She spread her legs wider and brought his hand into the waistband of her pajamas.

Heat. Wet heat. He couldn't have stopped his fingers from flexing, from sinking into her damp center, from circling the hard bud of her clit.

And he couldn't stop himself from capturing her moan with his mouth.

Soft lips against his, a darting tongue that teased and danced, a lithe female body straining against his hand.

Sebastian stopped thinking and finally, just reacted.

He tossed Rachel onto the bed, pulling her pajama bottoms and underwear off in a single movement.

Then he all but dove for her pussy.

She groaned as he flicked his tongue over her clit then

writhed as he trailed his tongue down one thigh and up the other. "You taste so fucking good," he said and slipped one finger inside.

She bucked. "Fuck, Bas!"

He started to make a snarky comment along the lines of, "Yes, please," but then she shifted and her tank top slipped again, revealing one puckered nipple. His mouth watered to taste it, but since that was otherwise occupied, he reached up, sliding his hand over the silken skin of her abdomen, cupping the soft globe of her breast, and pinched her nipple between his thumb and forefinger.

Rachel screamed and grabbed his head, but instead of pushing him away, as he'd half-expected, she gripped his hair tightly in both fists and thrust her pussy against his mouth.

He took the hint, moving his tongue faster and with more pressure, slipping another finger inside.

She moaned again and Bas thought it was pretty much the best sound on the planet.

He couldn't resist watching her face as she rocked against him—eyes slammed shut, breath coming in gasps, pink dusting her cheeks.

She was beautiful. So damned beautiful.

And then she was . . . almost there, crying his name out on an exhale as if it were a prayer, a benediction, a curse.

He slid one more finger inside and she exploded.

Bas had been wrong again.

That was the best thing ever.

FIFTEEN

Rachel

SHE'D LOST all sensation in her legs.

Literally.

The only thing Rachel *could* feel was her vagina, and that was limited to a warm fuzzy, *good* feeling that also managed to radiate upward to her heart.

Okay, so her Bas-driven orgasm was wreaking havoc on her adjective use, but the man was a fucking god in between the sheets.

Or on top of them, since they hadn't bothered to actually slip between them.

But back to the problem with her heart.

As in Bas's ability to weasel his way past her defenses. She really should be panicking, right? This feeling, this intense longing for him, for this moment to be something that led to adjectives like long-term and permanent, not to mention nouns like future and relationship, *should* be scary.

She'd experienced nearly all the ways permanent, long-term relationships could go wrong.

And yet, this thing with Bas was different.

There weren't any warning signs, there wasn't that sinking feeling in her gut telling her to stop this before it got out of hand.

In fact, her gut was telling her to leap.

That she'd managed to live through the bad and should grab the chance for good, for *Sebastian*, firmly with both hands.

"You okay?" the man himself asked.

Rachel's eyes were still closed, but she reached a lazy hand in the direction of his face. Stubble teased her palm before he pressed a kiss there. "I'm great." She forced herself to peel back her lids. "This is where I would expound on the merits of your skills, but I can't feel my legs."

Bas jumped off her. "Shit, I'm sorry," he said.

"No." She pushed up, grabbed his shoulders, and plunked herself in his lap before he could do something stupid like get out of bed. "That's a good thing, baby. You licked me so good that I forgot I even *had* legs for a minute there."

"Oh." He grinned.

"Yeah." Rachel nipped his throat. "I figure we have maybe twenty more minutes before we risk being *really* behind today or discovered by Boss One and Two, so I think we should make the most of it."

"You don't have—"

She shifted on his lap, the hard jut of his cock both a tease and an ache . . . as in she'd be walking with an ache later today after it had been inside her. Biting back a snort, knowing that the Sextant had thoroughly corrupted her mind, Rachel leaned up and whispered, "I don't *have* to do anything. I want you inside me."

His tongue flicked her earlobe. "Sweetheart, twenty minutes isn't going to cut it. Hell, twenty *hours* still wouldn't be enough time for me to do all the things I want to do to you."

This man. *God.* He somehow managed to steal her heart,

piece by tiny piece, with his words, his actions . . . just by being him.

Rachel leaned back and took his face in her palms. "Twenty hours sounds painful, quite honestly." When he parted his lips, she kissed away his retort, sliding her tongue into his mouth to tangle with his. Her lungs were threatening to burst by the time she pulled back. "So, now we have eighteen minutes. Let's make the most of them, while we have them, okay?"

His fingers flexed on her arms, cock pulsing beneath her, breath coming in rapid gusts. "You sure?"

She reached for her nightstand and extracted a condom. "Get inside me, Bas." She ripped open the packet with her teeth. "Otherwise, I'm taking matters into my own hands."

One heartbeat, blue-gray eyes locked onto hers. Another and . . . Rachel's back hit the mattress.

Her tank top disappeared, tossed over Bas's shoulder, as she worked on the few buttons he'd managed to do up earlier. Finally, they were opened and she shoved his shirt down his shoulders. He shrugged it off then hesitated, fingers on the waistband of his slacks.

She brushed his hands aside and undid them herself. "I'm sure," she panted. "So fucking sure. Now please, Bas. Inside. Now."

Abandoning his pants at the top of his thighs, Rachel reached for his underwear and freed his cock. "God, yes," she said, wrapping one hand around its hard length. "I've missed you so, so much."

Bas groaned, thrusting into her hand. "Fuck, sweetheart. Don't talk to it like that."

She was too busy stroking her palm up and down the velvet steel to pay much attention. "Like what?"

"Like it's your favorite pet and you can't wait to take him out for a ride."

Her lips twitched and she bit back a giggle. "But what if that's exactly what I want?"

"Noted. He wants that, too, but *this* he also wants to make it good."

"It's *already* good."

Sebastian hissed out a curse as she gripped him tightly. "Insert an amusing quip here later," he said, leaning down to suck one nipple into his mouth, making her melt in pleasure, her grip faltering at least until he released it and cupped her cheek. "Fuck, sweetheart, but your hands on me . . ."

Enough teasing. Enough dancing around. Rachel rolled the condom down his length, loving how he groaned and his cock pulsed in her grip. "It's that good?"

Storm-filled blue eyes met hers. "So fucking good." She tugged, positioning him between her spread thighs, but when she shifted, trying to take him inside, Bas hesitated for a beat. "Are you—?"

Another one of those pieces of her heart slipped from her chest, headed toward Sebastian's hands. Already, he held that and so much more of her. She liked him so, *so* much.

"Twelve minutes," she reminded. "Also, I'm sure. Really, *really* sure." She thrust her hips up and *fuck*. He was big and hard and—

He started moving.

She forgot everything except how good he felt sliding in and out, how he kissed her like she was the most precious thing in the universe, how he slipped one hand between them to press firmly on her clit, how he knew that one touch would send her skyrocketing up and then over the peak into the abyss of blind pleasure down below.

"Fuck, baby," he groaned and thrust once, twice, three more times before he was calling out her name and joining her in the chasm beneath.

"Why did I think twenty minutes was enough time again?"

"Because you're nuts?" Bas said.

Rachel was in the shower while Sebastian stood by the sink. She could feel his gaze scorching her through the clear glass panes and wanted to open the door and invite him in.

But work.

And responsibilities and adulting.

Barf.

She stuck her head under the water, letting it sluice over her body and wet her hair.

Mid-shampoo, a gust of cold inundated her and her eyes flew open on a gasp.

Bas stood outside the shower, that molten stare on her.

"Fuck," he said and closed the door. "Next time, we are so doing it in the shower."

"We could—"

"Woman," he growled. "I'm wise to your ways by now. Don't you dare finish that sentence." Deliberately, he faced away from her and picked up the toothbrush she'd pulled out from her set of unopened spares the previous night.

Rachel's lips twitched.

"Stop smiling."

She smoothed conditioner through her hair. "How do you know I'm smiling?"

This snarly side of him was new, but instead of making her nervous, as she might have half-expected, she actually kind of liked it. Even bad-tempered, Sebastian still looked at her with gentleness in his expression.

"I can feel your smile from here."

"You gave me two of the best orgasms of my life. Clearly, I have something to smile about."

He whirled around, toothbrush in hand. "Only two of the best?"

"Well, you did give me a couple of excellent ones last time we were together."

One side of Bas's mouth quirked up.

"Thought you'd like that," she said.

"Your ego boosts are a thing of beauty."

She smothered a giggle, gave her hair one more rinse, then began soaping up. Sebastian turned back to the sink with a groan. "I've got to get out of here."

Rachel cranked off the water. "I thought you were going to shower."

"I need a cold one at this point."

She pushed open the door and snagged a towel, taking her time in wrapping it around her body, loving the way Bas's eyes never left her body, even though the toothbrush was hanging out of his mouth.

Stopping just in front of him, she ran one finger down his chest. "Spit."

He choked. "What?" It sounded like, "Shmut?"

"Sink. Toothpaste. Spit."

Bas followed her orders, hands clamped into fists.

"Now shower," she told him. "I'm going to get dressed."

"Thank God," he muttered. "For the sake of my sanity, I need you to not be naked—"

She dropped her towel to the tile floor.

Rachel had never heard that particular curse word combination before.

She found that she liked it.

SIXTEEN

Sebastian

HIS TUESDAY HAD CERTAINLY STARTED off right.

Unfortunately, it didn't continue that way.

Sighing at the welcome package waiting outside the Steele building, Bas steeled himself.

At least four reporters stood on the sidewalk in front of the building. Normally, he'd be able to breeze right by them, since he wasn't exactly the face of the business—that was Clay—but Sebastian had been interviewed by one of the reporters recently with regards to the project.

So instead of striding by unnoticed, Samantha's laser gaze caught him the moment he stepped out of the Uber and onto the sidewalk in front of the building.

"Sebastian!" she called, racing over.

Not idiots, the rest of the reporters rushed to join her.

Four cameras pointed in his direction and it was just perfect that he was wearing his wrinkled white button-down and giving off definite one-night stand vibes.

Shit. He started to slip on his jacket, thinking to cover as many of the wrinkles as possible then froze.

Because maybe he could swing this in his favor.

Samantha began walking next to him.

"City officials say that big businesses in San Francisco are sucking up tax breaks and resources, but not giving back as previously agreed. With Steele Technologies withdrawing from the tech and community center project, it's hard to disagree."

Bas rubbed a hand over his face. "That's not a question, Samantha, but you know all of us at Steele Technologies have been working long hours on this project that would bring tech resources to several underserved and very deserving communities." He flashed her a smile. "We discussed this very center less than a month ago."

"So, what's changed?" another reporter asked. "Why back out now?"

Sebastian didn't have to hide his disappointment when answering. "We didn't want to back out, but the city has made it nearly impossible for us to proceed. They've thrown up roadblocks every step along the way. I mean, just look at me. I've been up half the night trying to find a way to move forward."

They chuckled and Samantha indicated her cheeks. "I don't know. The stubble thing is working for you."

"Not likely, but I'm not sure how to proceed at this point." He began ticking off his fingers. "They've required three additional environmental reviews, four different structural engineers to sign off on the drawings, and two extra seismic reports. We want the project to be successful and obviously for the space to be safe for the community, but we've spent almost as much as budgeted for the entire project on pre-construction alone." Bas stopped just before entering the building. "And I don't think that it's a coincidence that the latest contractor we've been required to hire for a quote-unquote final seismic calculation is the brother-in-law of Councilman Han, do you?"

Samantha smirked, blond ponytail flicking over her shoulder. "I guess we'll find out, Sebastian."

"I hope you do," he said. "We at Steele sincerely want this project to move forward. For now, I've got to get back to work."

The reporters thanked Bas as he opened the door.

Just before it closed behind him, Samantha caught it and asked, "Any chance you can score me playoff tickets? I heard your brother has a box at the Gold Mine."

"Wait," one of the other reporters, a male with a horrible goatee and slightly pudgy middle, asked. "Your brother is *the* Devon Scott?"

Samantha nodded.

"I second the request for tickets. The Gold actually have a real shot at the Cup this year."

Bas mentally sighed. Even though he'd been retired for close to five years now, the mystique of Devon Scott lived on.

"No hookup on my end," he said. "Sorry."

And with a brisk wave, he took off for the elevators.

SEBASTIAN HUNG up the phone after speaking with Clay in depth about the tech center. Sighing, he leaned back in his office chair. He hadn't wanted to call his boss, had hoped to avoid the conversation altogether and perhaps just share the events of the fallout from the tech center when Clay returned from Berlin as a funny addendum to an otherwise uneventful trip.

But, unfortunately, that was not to be.

With the media on the trail and potentially two huge businesses—RoboTech and Steele Technologies—in their crossfire, Bas had done the prudent thing and filled in his boss.

Clay had taken it surprisingly well, pulling Heather on to speakerphone and the two of them beginning to brainstorm both a solution to the city's roadblocks and some additional ways to get the press on their side.

Clearly, both he and his wife were not good at the relaxation thing.

Heather, apparently, had walked out of the two-hour massage Clay had booked her because, "Who could sit still for that long, anyway?"

"Crazy kids," he muttered, though he was feeling more than a little jealous that Clay had found someone so perfect for him.

Not that he could begrudge his boss. He just wanted to be there with Rachel.

Patience.

They'd already come leaps and bounds and it hadn't even been a week.

And plus, with Clay taking the tech center off his plate, now Sebastian had a bit more free time to win Rachel over.

Time to bust out his wooing skills.

Snorting at his own idiocy, Bas began making a list of everything he wanted to do for Rachel. Flowers, obviously, and he needed to find out which type was her favorite. A nice dinner or *dinners*. Luckily, San Francisco had plenty of incredible restaurants, and she'd picked up Italian for them the previous night, so a trip down to Little Italy was definitely on the books. He also needed to figure out if she liked hockey, because despite his lie to Samantha, the reporter, Devon *did* have a box at the Gold Mine, so NHL games were definitely on the docket if Rachel enjoyed that sort of thing.

He wondered if there were any concerts coming up.

Bas certainly wouldn't mind spending the night cuddled next to her as she danced to her favorite songs.

Hell, he was so gone for her already that he could picture

the smile on her face and the joy in her eyes as she listened and he wouldn't even care if it was some hideous boy band or pop duo. Bas would do whatever it took to make her happy.

Sap, he imagined Kelsey saying.

Damn straight, he was.

Rachel was special, and he intended to treat her that way.

Okay, so flowers and—oh—chocolates. Dinner and some nights out. What else? A documentary showing?

He opened his inbox. He could have sworn that he'd gotten an email inviting him to a film festival recently—

The knock at the door interrupted his searching.

His assistant—yes, hilariously or not, he had an assistant as the . . . assistant. Puns or not, Keiran waited for Bas to tell him to come in then opened the door and stuck his head through the gap. "There's a delivery for you."

Awesome. He'd been waiting on several boxes of files. "Thanks, Key. Just put them on the table."

Keiran nodded and disappeared then came back into Bas's office with full hands . . . they just weren't full of what he'd expected. Instead of files, Keiran carried a black garment bag, a small silver bag from a well-known men's clothing store, and a medium-sized box.

"Uh." Bas shook himself. "Thanks, Keiran. I'll let you know if I need anything else."

His assistant left with a nod and shut the door behind him.

"What the hell?" Sebastian muttered, pushing up from his chair and walking over to the conference table that took up one half of his office.

He unzipped the garment bag first. Inside was a suit identical to the one he was wearing, except it was made from a fabric he'd never seen in the store before. Bas might drive a Toyota, but he didn't skimp on his suits. Hell, half his luxury car budget had probably gone into his closet.

Those suits were also pretty much the single thing he did to follow in his brother's footsteps. As in, he went to the same small tailor that Devon had and still frequented. It was in the South Bay and the suits that came out of that little shop were as good as any luxury store. Cost about as much, too, but Devon and later Bas both swore by them.

It had only taken purchasing one suit from somewhere else —and a really long day spent pulling at the inseam, trying to adjust the too-tight shoulders, attempting to ignore the itchy waistband—for Sebastian to realize the error of his ways.

He didn't buy anywhere else now.

Even Clay had started ordering his suits from the same shop.

And since he hadn't ordered a new suit, the person who'd sent it obviously knew and understood Bas's obsession.

It was the exact suit he favored, just in a pattern he'd never seen and probably would have never ordered for himself. An almost navy blue with a subtle brown pinstripe, the fabric was different and . . . it was awesome.

As were the soft blue tie and the crisp white button-down.

He also still didn't know who'd sent it.

Bas slipped the suit from the garment bag and hung it on the back of his door.

That was when he saw the note.

The cream envelope had his name scribbled on the front and for a second, Sebastian thought that perhaps Clay had sent the suit as a thank you or a bonus. But the note wasn't from his boss.

Bas,
Heather always keeps an extra suit in her office for just
these circumstances. I did some snooping while you were
in the shower. Hope you like this one.

-*Rach*

P.S. I like the stubble look as well. It goes with what's in the bag. (You'll see.) Let me know if you're free tonight so we can get lumbersexual.

Lumbersexual?

"What the—?" He shook his head and opened the bag. Jeans and a red plaid flannel shirt were inside, along with a pair of boots that were probably way too cool for him, but he'd rock them anyway.

Another note was stuck in one boot.

If you're free tonight . . . we get to use what's in the box.

Okay, so Sebastian could get behind the sound of that.

Then he opened the lid.

An ax was inside.

Uhhh . . .

He lifted it up, holding it by the handle. It was surprisingly light and since he felt like he could reasonably assume that Rachel didn't want to go on an ax-murdering spree . . . and that this little dinky ax wouldn't be of much use for that anyway. . .

Thankfully, before his mind could go further down that particular stretch, Bas's phone rang.

Still holding the ax, he answered it without looking at the screen. "Sebastian speaking."

"I thought you liked Bas."

Rachel's voice immediately made a smile break out on his face. "Hey, sweetheart," he said.

"Hi." Her tone had gentled. "I have to admit, and will probably need to turn in my feminist card for it, but I like it when you call me sweetheart."

His smile widened. "I'm glad."

"So," she said, now almost brusquely. "I'm guessing you've gotten my present by now?"

"They're amazing," he replied. Well, the ax was confusing, but the suit and clothes were incredible. "It's way too much, sweetheart. You really shouldn't have done that."

"It's my fault that you were caught out in the media in a disgracefully wrinkled suit."

He snorted. "Worth it." A beat. "Plus, your idea is brilliant. I'm going to start making sure that Clay has an extra suit in his office, just in case."

"And you," she said.

"And me," he agreed. "But I did have a question about—"

"Lumbersexual or the ax?"

Bas laughed. "Either. Both."

"I am woman, hear me roar. I can throw an ax like Thor."

He leaned against the table. "Um, I hate to ruin your rhyme, but Thor actually has a hammer."

"Details, details. But"—she hesitated and Sebastian's heart pulsed when her voice went tentative—"I just thought it might be fun to try that ax throwing thing?"

Ax throwing?

"I—"

"It's stupid, I know. But there's this place outside the city where you can like go throw axes at a target. You like rent a lane for an hour. There's food and beer and—" She broke off. "Never mind. This was a stupid idea."

"Rachel."

"Forget I said anything." Her breath rattled through the speaker on his phone. "And for God's sake, forget about the ax. Just forget—"

"*Rachel.*"

She stopped talking.

"Do you know what I was doing before your way too generous delivery appeared in my office?"

"No," she squeaked.

"I was planning all the ways I wanted to romance and seduce you."

"*Oh.*"

"Yes," he said. "I had dinner and flowers—what's your favorite kind, by the way?"

"Tulips," she said, almost shyly. "Yellow, if you can find them."

"Yellow tulips," he repeated. "Got it. But back to me and you for a moment. Before your package came, I'd been making a list of all the things I wanted to do for you."

"For me?" she asked. "Not to?"

He smirked. "Well, the things I want to do to you are obvious, yeah? I was trying to plan some dates to win you over and make you actually like me."

She giggled. "I already *do* like you."

"Well, that's a relief."

"So . . ." Rachel trailed off.

"So, I'd love to go chuck some axes with you."

"And you'll wear the flannel?"

"Do lumberjacks turn you on?" he asked, thinking of all the ways he could work that angle.

"Sure. But I just really want to see you not in a suit."

"Sweetheart, does this morning not count? Or were you just not paying attention?"

"Oh, I was paying attention, but flannel is sexy."

"Along with throwing axes."

He could feel her shrug. "Yup."

"Okay. Should I meet you there or pick you up?"

If she was surprised by his agreement, Rachel didn't let on. Instead, they spent a few minutes working out details before he hung up with a promise from her to not buy him any more presents.

He had a hell of a lot to make up for on that front.

Here he'd been thinking of all the ways to romance her, and she'd wooed him in return.

Wooed?

Hell, that should have made him feel emasculated, right? But Bas couldn't find that particular feeling within him. Rather, he was touched that she'd done something so thoughtful and kind without expecting anything in return.

It was all too much, but it was also certainly the nicest thing that anyone had ever done for him.

Which made him want to do the same for her.

Sebastian pulled up his text messages, scrolled down to the chain he had going with his boss, and figured what the hell did he have to lose at this point? He wasn't going to hide his feelings for Rachel. Not when she was so important.

Not work related, but can you pick Heather's brain for me? I want to get Rachel something really special that she wouldn't buy for herself.

Clay's reply came less than a minute later.

It's like that, is it?

Yes, it was. He liked Rachel—so damned much.

It's like that. And also so much more.

A minute of silence that almost killed him then Clay wrote back.

According to Heather, these.

Clay attached a link. Another buzz came before Sebastian could open it.

My wife also says that if you hurt Rachel, she will personally disembowel you.

Bas didn't have a problem with that.

If I do hurt Rachel, I'll stand still and let Heather do it.

A moment passed before:

I was going to tell you not to ruin the perfect duo Heather and I had set up to run the world, but I don't think I need to. Be open. Trust yourself. And just love her as she deserves to be loved.

Love her?
Did he?
Could he?
But how could he *not*?
Clay sent another message.

Fuck me, that was deep. But seriously, Sebastian—work less and play more.

Despite the truth circling in his brain, the obvious, yet somehow still shocking truth, Sebastian managed to find his voice.

Pot meet kettle.

Clay's final message made Bas snort.

Let's work on it together.

And he attached a video of two pigeons tag-teaming the thievery of a bag of potato chips . . . from inside a very busy store.

See, I'm working less and wasting all sorts of time on social media now.

Sebastian thought that the less work thing might actually be working for his boss.

It had found him a woman he wanted to spend the rest of his life with, after all.

And that sounded pretty damned good.

Bas opened the link and started shopping.

SEVENTEEN

Rachel

OKAY, jokes aside, the lumbersexual thing really *did* do it for her.

Rachel was seriously enjoying the view of the flannel tightening over Bas's shoulders as he lifted his arms to throw the ax.

That *thunking* sound of it hitting and sinking into the wood was hot, too.

Very manly and masculine and—

"Are you looking at my butt?" Bas asked, turning around and catching her in her obvious appraisal. His eyes twinkled in amusement.

She crossed her arms. "Yeah? And so what if I was?"

"I would say, I've been checking out your ass, too."

He smirked when her cheeks went pink then turned and made a show of bending to pick up his final ax, taking his time to aim and throw. It hit the target but didn't actually stick into the wood, just a few inches left of the bull's-eye.

Ax throwing, she'd found out, was harder than she'd expected.

Just throw a sharp object at some wood, it couldn't be that tough.

Ha.

She'd ended up missing the target completely, hitting with the wrong side of the ax totally, or not throwing it hard enough for it to bury itself in the wood.

But after her third turn, she'd started to get the hang of it, and it was actually really fun.

Or maybe that was being with Sebastian.

He had shrugged when the ax fell and walked forward to collect them from the target and the floor. He set them on the counter at the front of the lane then picked up his beer and settled next to her on the bench she was watching from.

"How's yours?" he asked, pointing at her beer. "Apricot, right?"

Rachel smiled. "Normally, I'd make fun of someone ordering a fruity beer like this, but Sera actually got me hooked on this brand."

"Really? Seraphina likes beer?" he asked and winced. "Sorry. It's just she seems so—"

"Barbie-like?"

Sebastian made a face. "I—uh—"

Rachel laughed. "It's fine. Plus, Sera would be the first to tell you that she resembles the blond-haired, pink-adorned doll, but the similarities end on the surface. She's a beer-drinking, sports-watching woman . . . who also happens to adore romance novels and *Desperate Housewives.*"

"That's an *interesting* combination."

Rachel grinned at him. "What can I say? I love all those things, too. Well, I'm a huge fan of hockey and definitely love television dramas and romance novels. And I don't mind a beer here or there, but I mostly prefer wine." She laughed. "Anyway,

I really need to shut up now, because this has to seriously be the most boring conversation ever."

Bas's voice went almost hard. "*Never* shut up. I love hearing you talk."

Her brows lifted. "You seriously want to hear me expound on television dramas."

Blue-gray irises met hers. "Sweetheart, I want to hear *anything* you have to say."

Aw. This man. Seriously. Just. This. Man.

She cupped his cheek, sliding closer to stare deeply into his eyes. "Okay," she murmured. "I won't shut up." A beat. "Also, how do you feel about curly fries?"

Bas tipped his face down to kiss the tip of her nose. "I think curly fries sound awesome. I'll order them." He stood and tugged her to her feet. "Now, go throw some axes so I can watch my sexy girl's ass."

His girl.

Yeah. She could get used to that.

———

DESPITE HER ATTEMPTS for the opposite, Sebastian left her at her door that evening.

"I'm trying to date you, woman," he grumbled when she'd tugged him inside her apartment and all but jumped into his arms. "Not get in your pants."

Worth it though, especially when he turned to pin her against the door and kissed the ever-loving sense out of her.

"But what if I want you in my pants?" she'd asked and had been thrilled when he'd groaned and dropped his forehead to the panel.

"Killing me, sweetheart."

"I think you're sexy," she'd said and been rewarded with another kiss.

But then he really had left.

And taken her heart with him.

How in the hell could a woman like her, with a past like hers, with a track record for the people she'd trusted . . . how could she have fallen in love so quickly?

She should be cautious, should be protecting herself, should be running and screaming in the other direction.

Except, she had learned to trust over the last year and a half. Rachel had made friends who supported her, who had invited her into their hearts and opened their arms to hold her tight, to help wrench her from her past.

They helped her see that there were good people, good *men* in the world.

And she *knew* that Sebastian was so, so different from Preston.

But she also knew that she was in way over her head with Bas and bound to make a mess of this.

She'd pulled out her laptop.

It was time to muster the resources of the Sextant.

Heather, despite the late hour in Berlin, was the first to answer the call. "I just knew you were going to call me," she said. "Oh my God. I've been gone all of four days, what the hell is going on with my unflappable assistant?"

"I—"

Abby logged on, baby Emma sound asleep on one shoulder. "Non-book club video-chat session," she crowed. "All the drama. Heather, what did you do now? You'd better not be divorcing Clay *again*, I don't care if he—"

"Abby," Heather interrupted. "Rachel made the call."

"What?" Abby froze, but as always managed to recover

herself quickly. Hazel eyes pinned Rachel in place through the laptop screen. "You. Drama. Dish. Now."

Bec's face appeared midway through that declaration. "Did having all those babies scramble your use of the English language?"

Abby smirked. "Probably." She bent to kiss Emma's head. "But still worth it."

Bec pretended to puke, but she was smiling. "What'd you do now, Heather?"

Heather threw her hands up. "I didn't *do* anything! Why does everyone keep asking that?"

Clay's head popped into the frame of Heather's camera as he kissed her on the cheek. He looked extra yummy in his workout clothes. "I'm out of here." He turned to wave at them. "For the record, she did do something . . . or rather *someone*."

CeCe and Sera appeared almost simultaneously, catching the tail end of Clay's statement, as well as the pillow Heather launched in his direction as he sauntered off.

And silence.

CeCe opened her mouth—

"It wasn't me," Heather snapped and pointed at her camera. "It's the quiet, steady one."

All eyes turned to Rachel's face on the screen.

She couldn't feel it considering her friends were miles to oceans apart, but she still knew all their attention was focused on her.

Which nearly made her chicken out.

But, no, dammit, she thought, lifting her chin and straightening her shoulders. She was going to do the normal—okay, *semi*-normal—well-adjusted thing. She was . . .

"I slept with Sebastian."

Going to blurt it all out, apparently.

"Well," she scrambled. "I mean, I slept with him like three

months ago. You know that night some of us met up at Bobby's. I
—uh—didn't go home early. I kind of took him back to the hotel
room I had been staying at while my apartment was being reno-
vated and then I—*we*—"

"Banged like two teenagers on prom night?" Sera supplied.

Rachel winced. "Um, kind of?"

"Word of advice, kid," Bec said. "Stop trying to be hip. You
had sex with Sebastian three months back and go." She gestured
for Rachel to continue talking.

"Well, he kind of ditched me while I was in the shower. I
came out and he'd gone."

Outraged gasps exploded out of her speakers.

"No," she hurried to say. "That's not the issue. There was a
problem at work. He had to go and I've left—" She waved a
hand. "Regardless, we didn't exactly exchange information . . .
or even names—"

Five voices began talking almost at once.

"You exchanged *something*," CeCe muttered.

"Holy shit," from Abby who promptly covered baby Emma's
ears and repeated. "Holy fucking shit."

"No names?" Bec grinned. "I told you to get un-virginized,
but damn girl, I'm impressed."

"That sounds kind of dangerous," Sera said. "Bringing a
strange man back to your hotel room." To which Abby winced
and started protesting that she'd met Jordan in that exact
same way.

Heather raised her fist to the screen. "Nice work. Honestly,
I didn't know you had it in you, kid."

"Guys!" Rachel cried and threw up her hands. "The one-
night stand was . . ."

"Outstanding?" Bec asked. "Or at least, that's what you
told me."

Abby gasped. "You told her first?"

"Oh my God," Rachel dropped her head into her hands. "Yes, it was good. *Really* fucking good, but that night isn't the point. Well, neither is this morning, I guess. It's—"

"This *morning*?" Heather repeated.

CeCe hooted. Bec and Abby grinned.

"Why did I call you all again?"

"Because you love us," Sera said. "Okay, obviously, you like him or you wouldn't have slept with him again. So, what's the real problem?"

"Is it because he works for Clay?" Heather asked. "You know, if it's important to you, we'll find a way to make it work. I want to keep you around, Rach. I honestly don't think I could do this without you."

"This, *what*?" CeCe teased. "Running your own life? Or keeping your workaholic side busy enough?"

Heather snorted. "Yes, to both."

Rachel shook her head. "It's not because he works for Clay," she said. "But thank you for being open to figuring it out. It—" And dammit, her eyes filled with tears. "It's—" A sniff. "Shit. It's because before I started working for you, Heather, my life was a fucking mess."

And then she told her friends everything.

She told them about her mom leaving, her dad and the way he used to smack her around when she'd made him angry, her grandparents and their sharp, controlling words. Then finally, she told them about Preston and his heavy fists, the blows to her body, the way he'd controlled every aspect of her life, from the food she ate to who she spent time with to the pleasure or pain she received in bed.

"I don't know how I managed to land the job with you, Heather," she said, wiping her eyes on the hem of her T-shirt. "My résumé was a mess and I hardly had any work experience at all. Plus, I felt like I was in a fog during that whole interview."

Heather shrugged. "I'll admit that you *were* lacking on the experience front, but, Rachel, there was something about you that was so determined I couldn't help but offer you the job. I wanted to see that spark inside you grow."

"Don't start up the waterworks again," Rachel said and sniffed. "But, whatever the reason you picked me, I can't thank you enough."

"Shit!" Bec's outburst drew all their gazes. She narrowed her eyes at them. "I don't have any tissues and—"

"Oh, no," Abby cried. "Are you not using that waterproof mascara?"

CeCe shook her head. "You know, you used to be a normal person who didn't worry about mascara and its waterproof qualities."

"I *used* to be a normal person before these kids rotted my brains."

"Brains?" Sera teased. "As in more than one?"

"Ugh." Abby sighed and flopped back onto the bed she was perched on. "You guys are seriously the worst."

"You love us," Heather said.

"Also, let it be noted that I wasn't complaining about my mascara at all," Bec said. "Rather that you bitches are making me have all these . . ."

"Feelings?" CeCe said with a smirk.

"Yes. Those." Bec grinned. "Pesky little things." She clapped her hands together. "I've got the Preston asshole tied up legally in a dozen different ways, and his daddy's district attorney's connection will quickly be coming to an end. As for the rest of it—"

"The feelings part?" Sera asked.

"Yes. *That*," Bec replied. "You lot had better help her. I've done all I can."

Rachel shook her head, biting back her smile. "I thought you gave me excellent advice when I talked to you about Bas."

"One time lucky girl talk session." Bec shrugged. "You need me to sue him, I'm your girl."

"I would like it noted that I feel like *I* should have been the go-to girl for Sebastian talk," Heather said.

Abby beat Rachel to her explanation. "Honeymoon."

"Pish." Heather rolled her eyes. "Plus, I'm going insane," she whined. "This is the least busy I've been on a trip in probably a decade. What am I supposed to do?"

"I don't know, *your husband*," CeCe said.

Abby cackled.

Well, okay they all did.

"Yes, yes," Heather muttered. "Clay is taking care of me in that department, but I'm bored."

"You're also taking over," Sera said.

Heather froze. "Damn. I am. Sorry, Rach."

"First, you've had three business meetings in the last two days, so still working," Rachel said. "Second. Take over all you want. I'm fine."

"If you were fine, you wouldn't have called us," Bec pointed out.

Rather unhelpfully, Rachel thought, leaning back against her couch cushions and sighing. "Okay, be logical, why don't you? I know I'm not fine, but I also—*fuck*, I don't know I *am* fine."

"Explain, please," Heather said.

"Like I feel a lot for Bas, too much for such a short time, but also like just the right amount. My gut is like this is great, he's so perfect and amazing and a little dorky and he writes me poems and actually cares about me . . ."

"He writes poems?" CeCe asked.

"Focus," Bec told them. "Poem talk later. Revelations now."

"Who's the caveman now?" Abby muttered.

Rachel laughed then sighed. "You guys. I'm so messed up. I thought it would take me forever to just trust another man to *kiss* me. Then I jumped into bed with Sebastian and it was so incredible and even this morning, he wanted to wait, to give me more time, but I was the one who really wanted to go for it."

"And?"

She didn't know which of her friends had asked that. She was too deep in her internal quagmire of thoughts that it merely spurred her on.

"All I know," she said. "Is that sex aside, when I close my eyes and picture a random day in the future—a month, a year, *more*—I see Bas with me."

"Isn't that enough for now?" CeCe asked.

"But what if I panic a month from now?" she said. "What if I'm fine now, but it's all a strange coping mechanism and then I'm going to freak out down the line?"

"Newsflash, kid," Heather said. "We *all* have freak outs."

"Right," Abby added. "Plus, if and when you do freak out, you and Sebastian will either get through it or you'll know then it wasn't meant to be."

"But what if—"

"Do you really need to have *all* the answers now?" Sera asked. "Or are you just looking for a convenient excuse to pull away?"

Fuck.

"Oh my God," Rachel said. "You guys are good." She scrubbed a hand over her face and straightened. "So, I'm doing this?"

Bec fixed her with a glance. "You tell us."

Rachel bit her lip, sighed, and then straightened her shoulders and pushed the final tendrils of her past deep down.

"I am *so* doing this."

EIGHTEEN

Sebastian

IT WAS Thursday and instead of heading over to Rachel's office to coax her away from work and talk her into dinner at his place, he was walking into a very nice, expensive restaurant near the waterfront.

Sighing, he handed off his coat to the hostess but declined her offer to take him to the table.

He could already see his family.

Bas was having Rachel withdrawals. They'd texted constantly over the last two days, sent a few business-related emails. They'd even had plans last night.

But Rachel had to cancel because a work meeting in Los Angeles ran long and she hadn't gotten back into the city until after eleven o'clock that night.

All logical reasons.

He still was almost desperate to wrap her in his arms and just smell—

Just smell her?

Fuck, he was losing it.

His phone buzzed and he pulled it out, half-expecting it to be Kelsey, telling him to get his ass in gear.

Instead, it was Rachel.

I just finished. Want to grab foods?

Foods? She was too cute. And yes. Yes, he did want to grab *foods*.

Unfortunately, he could not. But she sent another text before he could reply.

Oh shoot, I'm losing my mind. I just remembered that you're having dinner with your family and now I'm probably interrupting. Ugh. Sorry! Talk to you later.

She was fucking adorable.

He was just typing out a response to tell her that when his phone was snatched out of his hands.

"Stop working to avoid us, bro," Kelsey said.

"It's not—"

Which was pretty much the worst thing he could have said because then Kelsey glanced down at the screen and a wide smile broke out across her face. "Who's Rachel?"

"Shut up." He reached for his phone as his sister scrolled up.

"Holy shit," she said, eyes wide. "Those are either seriously dangerous HR violations or Sebastian has a *girlfriend*."

Considering she all but sang the last and held his cell out of his reach, Bas was ready to kill his sister . . . or at least tackle her to the ground and tear the phone from her cold, limp fingers.

Especially when she pressed a button on the screen.

She wasn't.

She seriously. Was. Not.

Except, she *was*. Kelsey put the phone to her ear. "Hi, is this Rachel? This is Kelsey, Sebastian's sister. Oh no, don't apologize, you're not interrupting. I just wanted to invite you to join us." A pause as she listened for all of two seconds then began talking again. "*No*. You wouldn't be intruding. Sebastian has told us so much about you. Please, come."

Kill him now.

Kelsey began walking toward the table his family occupied. Bas moved after her a beat later, but he wasn't far enough to miss her exclaim, "Great! I'm so excited to meet you."

She stopped in her tracks, so quickly that he almost mowed her down, and hung up, turning to slam the cell into his chest.

Then she hot-footed it over to the table where his parents, Devon, and his wife, Becca, sat and declared, "Sebastian's girlfriend is joining us for dinner!"

He was going to kill her.

———

IN SHORT ORDER, another chair was pulled over and Sebastian was being inundated with questions.

"How did you meet her?" Devon asked.

"What's she like?" From his dad.

"It's been so long since you've brought a girl home!" His mom's gleeful exclamation.

Thankfully, his phone buzzed, granting him a reprieve.

I'm on my way, but I definitely don't have to be.

If Rachel didn't already own his heart, that text would have done the trick.

"Aw," Becca murmured, snapping him out of his thoughts. "Look at his face. He *really* does like her."

Shaking his head, he typed out a response.

Please come and save me from the evil that is my sister.

Of course, Kelsey happened to glance over his shoulder as he sent that. "Ouch," she said. "That's mean."

"Bad things happen to people who stick their noses into other people's business," he gritted out.

Kelsey smiled. "If I didn't push, you'd just isolate yourself even more."

"Hard to isolate yourself from something you're not even part of."

She frowned. "What the hell does *that* mean?"

Fortunately, the server came at that moment to take their drink order and they put in for a couple of appetizers. Becca "awed" again when he asked for a glass of red wine for Rachel.

They'd just finished the order of Oysters Rockefeller when Rachel walked into the restaurant.

He was standing and walking toward her before he even realized that he'd moved.

And fuck, but her smile at his approach just took his breath away.

She looked a little frazzled, her hair a little windblown and her coat tied haphazardly, but she was beautiful and fuck did he love her.

"Hi," she murmured.

He crouched a little to draw her gaze when she looked around nervously. "Hey, you." Brown eyes met his and she visibly relaxed.

"Hi, sorry," she said. "I'm unreasonably nervous about meeting your family."

"They're a lot, but they mean well," he told her. "Feel free to run at any point. I'll make your excuses."

She released a shuddering breath and nodded. "Sounds like a plan."

"Come on. I'll introduce you." He handed off her coat to the hostess with a murmured thanks then slipped his arm through hers and led her to the table.

His family stood as they approached.

"Rachel," Devon said. "It's so nice to meet you. This is my wife, Becca."

She shook both their hands then extended her palm to his mom and dad. "Hi, Mr. and Mrs. Scott. I hope you don't mind me intruding on your dinner."

"Oh, not at all," his mom said. "We're happy we've had a chance to meet you. Sebastian can rarely join us for dinner when we're in town."

"He works really hard," Rachel said and turned to his sister. "Kelsey?"

"In the flesh," his sister joked. "I'm glad you came."

Rachel's lips twitched as they all took a seat. "I'm not sure I had much of a choice," she said. "But I am honored to be included."

They settled into their drinks as a few more appetizers were ordered after Bas's mom had given Rachel the fifth degree about her food preferences. Then she polled Bas, Devon, Becca, and Kelsey as if she didn't already know whether they preferred calamari or shrimp cocktail.

His mother knew all—she just wanted everyone to feel included.

Or so she claimed.

If that were the case, then why had he always been the odd man out?

Why had they never come to his school events? Or sports games? Or—

He was way too old to be holding a grudge about childhood

insecurities. His parents had done the best they could. They'd made mistakes as all parents did, of course, but he'd had food and love and—

He'd always felt left out.

Boo hoo, Scott, he sneered at himself. *You're a grown man. Get over it.*

Rachel slid her hand into his. "You okay?" she asked softly.

"I'm—"

"So," his dad said, "how did you two meet?"

Sebastian inwardly groaned, just waiting for the jokes.

But Rachel smiled and suddenly all those old hurts from his childhood didn't matter. Not when he had her and she was smiling at him like he was important.

"Funny story, actually," she said. "Bas and I met because our bosses fell in love and got married."

"Aw," Becca said and sniffed. When all eyes turned to her, she turned beet red. "Oh gosh, I'm sorry. That's just so sweet, and Devon and I met when we—"

Tears streaked down her cheeks.

Rachel looked alarmed. "I—uh—sorry if I offended—"

"No." Becca wiped her eyes on her napkin. "I'm just a mess because I'm pregnant!"

Kelsey jumped to her feet and rounded the table. "Holy shit, that's amazing! I thought the doctor said that the IVF might take a long time to—" She shook her head. "Never mind. How far along are you?"

"IVF?"

Bas didn't realize he'd spoken aloud until Devon winced. "We've been struggling for a while to get pregnant—"

The rest of the words were cut off as his dad swept Devon up into a tight hug that lifted even the six-foot-plus former hockey player off his feet. "I'm going to be a grandpa!"

"Did you know—?" Rachel began.

Sebastian shook his head, wondering what else he'd missed out on knowing since he'd kept his distance over the last years.

Something else also occurred to him.

Something more grim and decidedly much more unpleasant.

How much of his resentment toward his family was truly because he'd been excluded?

And how much was because he'd just done a really good job at pushing them away?

NINETEEN

Rachel

THE PACKAGE WAS WAITING on her desk Friday morning.

Just the symbol on the outside of the box made her breath catch. How could he have possibly known?

But she forgot all about wondering how he'd discovered her obsession when she untied the ribbon.

"Oh my," she sighed.

Inside were two pairs of her favorite—and ridiculously expensive—pajamas. They were folded neatly and wrapped in silky silver tissue paper. She rubbed the material between her thumb and forefinger, beyond touched.

Then her phone buzzed.

Do you like them?

She snatched it up.

Thank you. The pajamas are gorgeous.

A beat, then:

*What about the rest? I wasn't sure if you'd like the color .
. .*

The rest? Rachel lifted the pajamas from the box and gasped. The first thing she saw was a gorgeous purple robe. It wasn't velvet, but the material was just as soft, and beneath that was . . . a set of lingerie.

An eye-catching amethyst color, the lace set was pretty much the most beautiful set of underwear she'd ever seen.

It was also transparent and—she held up the thong—lacking in material. Smiling, she replied with:

Have plans, do you?

A buzz.

I may have seen it and then pictured a few things.

Rachel snorted.

Little things?

He replied with a GIF of a toddler plunking her hands on her hips and frowning, and Rachel laughed out loud.

Sorry. Big things. Huge things—

Her phone buzzed mid-text.

Do you really like them?

The hint of insecurity made her heart pulse. She'd seen the way he'd put up a good front with his family, but it had to be really hard being the middle sibling of the Scott trio. Older brother is model gorgeous and a professional hockey player, before retiring and starting the most prestigious athlete management company in the States . . . and abroad for that matter. Quite literally, Devon's company was named Prestige Media Group and represented more than a handful of the most popular athletes in the U.S. and abroad. And then there was Kelsey, also beautiful and young and brilliant. She'd called them all together because she'd managed to secure a government contract for her newest project and wanted to celebrate.

Add in Becca's pregnancy news and well, it wasn't surprising that Bas might be feeling the teeniest bit insecure.

Especially since it seemed as though he'd spent a lot of his early years in much the same pattern. His path had been normal —college, working his way through the ranks of a company— while his siblings' paths had been nothing short of exceptional.

Which made it sound as though she thought Sebastian was boring or ordinary.

No, he was incredible.

And while he projected a cool confidence, Rachel wondered how much of that was armor to protect his vulnerable underbelly, to prove to himself and the rest of the world that he was fine on his own, dammit.

But instead of saying any of that, she made a mental promise to make it clear to Bas at some point that regardless of the rest of the world, *she* thought *he* was special.

He was everything.

He was *hers*.

Her fingers flew across the keyboard.

I love them. Thank you, Bas. So much.

His sent an "aw shucks" GIF and she replied with a heart one in turn, and pretty soon she was giggling as they played Gif War by sending increasingly ridiculous images to one another.

Five minutes later, she still hadn't done any work.

But her cheeks hurt from smiling so much.

Yeah, Sebastian was pretty fucking extraordinary as far as she was concerned.

A WEEK LATER, she pushed open her apartment door then immediately stepped out of her heels.

"Thank God," she muttered, kicking them to the side before bending to rub her aching toes. They might be expensive, but the hefty price tag did absolutely nothing for her comfort.

Torture devices, every one of them.

But she didn't need the heels anymore. She was swapping her stilettos for sneakers, her tight business suit for a Gold jersey.

Of course, by the time she made it down to meet Bas, Devon, and Becca at the Gold Mine, she was going to be ridiculously late. Still, she'd never been to a game in a luxury box, and when Sebastian had texted her earlier that day to invite her, she jumped at the opportunity.

Those boxes had free food, right?

Which wasn't the most important part. And also, *boo*, because she'd found out that, no, the food wasn't free. However, she *was* feeling encouraged that Bas might have hit a turning point with his family.

Neither of them had discussed the dinner where his siblings had both shared huge news, but he had mentioned that he was going to try to see them more.

Rachel considered that a step in the right direction.

She was also glad that she hadn't had to badger him into the decision.

She wanted Bas to be proud of himself, not constantly comparing his path with that of his siblings.

But if she had learned anything since leaving Iowa, it was that a person couldn't find their self-worth in others. They could find friends, people to love who shored them up, who supported them when they faltered.

But that deep down worth?

That came from inside.

Yup, she'd learned that firsthand.

And so now, she'd do what she could to encourage Bas to discover his own.

Nodding at herself in the mirror, Rachel ran a quick brush through her hair and touched up her makeup. Windblown—wind-*tornadoed*—wasn't the look she was going for.

She was almost ready to leave when she thought of the box of pretty things Bas had bought for her.

They'd spent a few nights together over the last week, but it had mostly been squeezing in a dinner here or a movie there and she hadn't had the chance to *really* dress up for him.

Or, undress, if she was being truthful

The one time she'd been able to seduce him aside, he'd been sticking very firmly to his slow and steady wooing process.

It was working.

Plus, the crafty bugger had managed to keep them in public places.

Probably because he knew that the moment they were in the privacy of one of their apartments, Rachel would strip herself naked and launch herself at him again.

She was beyond pent up.

Le sigh.

So, the sexy lingerie had been staying in the box.

But . . . she bit her lip.

She was late already, how would five minutes more hurt?

As quickly as she could, she stripped down and swapped her underthings for the gorgeous amethyst lace. And, fuck, if they weren't a perfect fit.

The deep V of the bra somehow enhanced her boobs—what pathetically little of them she had, anyway—and the panties . . . well, they were practically nonexistent, but they still managed to make her lower half look both flat and curvy in all the appropriate places.

And her ass?

She smirked as she turned to view her reflection in the bathroom mirror.

Oh yeah, Bas was going to like that. A whole hell of a lot.

Jeans and sneakers went back on, followed by her long-sleeved tee and her jersey. Just wearing the lingerie made her feel different. Hell, even her clothes fit differently, and she was getting definite naughty vibes when skin that wasn't normally exposed to the elements, so to speak, met the slight rough of denim. Even her breasts were a little va-va-voom under the jersey.

Yup, Bas was definitely going to be happy with her surprise.

Grabbing her purse and cell off the counter, she hurried to the front door.

She was so excited to meet Sebastian that she didn't notice her heels.

She'd kicked them off immediately upon entering her apartment, leaving them to lie haphazardly near her front door.

But by the time she stepped into the hall, they'd been straightened—a pair of twin soldiers perched neatly on her shoe rack.

TWENTY

Sebastian

DEVON AND BECCA were sickeningly in love.

It was disgusting.

Truly revolting.

Bas only hoped that he and Rachel would be the same way.

This was the first time that Bas had been in Devon's box, and he had to admit that he hadn't even thought about coming with or asking for tickets until Samantha, the reporter, had joked about it and Rachel had mentioned that she'd liked hockey.

He liked hockey himself, had always rooted for Devon from the comfort of his own home or when dragged to the arena by his family. But he'd never asked his brother for tickets because . .
.

He sighed.

Because it was strings. Another way he couldn't compete.

Juvenile.

As in, he'd been a juvenile.

He'd never begrudged his brother his success. Or his sister

for that matter, but he'd always felt this sense of disappointment from his family.

Why wasn't he special? Why didn't he live up to the Scott legacy?

Which was, frankly, ridiculous. His dad ran a feed store. His mom stayed at home. They were normal middle-class Americans. So where in the fuck had this pressure to be great come from?

From himself.

He sighed again.

From being competitive and distant when his siblings had never been.

Becca stood up and slipped out of the suite, breezily saying something about stretching her legs.

But Bas quickly realized it had been a ploy.

Because Devon stood up and came to lean against the railing next to him. "Sigh one more time, and I'm siccing Kelsey on you."

Bas shook his head. "I'm fine," he said. "Thanks again for letting us tag along tonight."

Devon bumped his shoulder. "Anytime, dude."

Ugh. Sebastian had been such an asshole.

He sighed. Again.

And just that quickly Devon pulled out his phone and threateningly opened up FaceTime.

Bas threw up his hands. "I relent. I swear, no more sighing."

"Good." Devon pocketed his cell. "So why don't you just tell me what's going on?"

"I—" Bas stifled another sigh just in time. "I guess I spent my whole life feeling like an outsider in our family, but only just recently realized that all of that distance was of my own making."

Silence, then Devon rubbed his hand over his face. "Look,"

he said. "I was in your boat before. I didn't make an effort—" Bas opened his mouth, but Devon cut him off. "Sorry. Effort isn't the right word. I just mean I was really good at keeping people at a distance. I mean, hockey was a great excuse. Gone half the year, training for most of my off time. Then starting a new business."

"Yeah," Bas agreed.

"But I also realized that I spent a good part of my life being lonely."

Bas's gaze flashed to Devon's. "What?"

"I know." His brother grinned like the goofball he was. "With all my adoring fans, it's hard to imagine that *I* could be lonely."

Sebastian rolled his eyes. "So, what did you do?"

A shrug. "I met Becca. She was alone, and I guess just being with her made me realize how lucky I was. I only had one sister, one mom, one dad, one . . ." He sighed. "Something else."

"Brother, you idiot," Bas said, but he was smiling.

"Oh yeah, one of those." Devon's expression went serious. "I'm glad you're here tonight, dude. I felt like I kept reaching out to you and . . ."

Bas winced. "Stonewalled?" Devon nodded. "Shit. I'm sorry. I know it's not important now, but I guess as a kid I always felt like dad went to your stuff and mom to Kelsey's and I was just lost in the shuffle a lot of the time."

"I could see that," Devon said, surprising him. "Hockey was every weekend and multiple weeknights for year after year. I lived at the rink. And Kelsey, well at least, hockey had a season. Her engineering stuff never stopped."

"It's ridiculous to be upset about this as an adult," Bas argued. "Mom and dad did the best they could. I shouldn't—"

Devon cut him off by plunking a hand on his shoulder. "So, this may be a newsflash for you, bro, but you are allowed to have feelings." A squeeze. "Some even say they make you human."

"Being human sucks, sometimes," Bas grumbled.

"Seriously. And don't forget getter older," Devon said. "Hell, I'm getting pudgy around the middle just looking at those ravioli."

The ravioli in question had been demolished so quickly by the three of them that they'd ordered another plate to arrive when Rachel showed up. But also, pudgy was a relative term, considering the fact that Devon was in as good of shape now as he'd been when he was playing.

"You've got a fucking six-pack."

Devon dipped his finger into the sauce remaining on the plate and brought it to his mouth. "Used to be an eight-pack."

If Devon weren't his brother, Bas might be tempted to hate him.

There was a knock at the door and Pascal, Devon's bodyguard, poked his head in. "A Rachel Morris has arrived—"

Becca shoved past him, Rachel in tow. "Look who I found lurking around."

"Hey, Dev," Bas said as they walked over to their women. "Can you do me a favor?"

Devon glanced down at him. "Anything."

One word, but Bas knew he meant it.

"Don't stop reaching out, okay?" He shrugged then recalled a joke they'd had from way back, when Devon had first been figuring out how to curse.

Because all professional athletes *needed* to know how to curse.

The trouble was that Devon's curse word knowledge had been limited to a single word.

"I'll attempt to get my fucking head out of my fucking ass," he said.

Devon hooted as they reached Rachel and Becca. "I'd totally forgotten about that."

"Just doing my part," Bas replied and chuckled when Devon punched him on the shoulder.

"You doing your part was the problem, if I remember." A grin. "Babe," he said and laced his arms with Becca's. "I've got to tell you this story. I think Sebastian must have been six when I got it in my head that I needed to learn how to use *all* the curse words . . ."

Bas wasn't sure how his brother finished the story—or *rather* how much he exaggerated Bas's expansion of Devon's curse word repertoire. He'd added the fucking part to round out Devon's head and ass statement, something that had made his family laugh hysterically for years after the event.

He mentally shrugged. He'd always been an observer and as such, had learned many a useful thing.

"Hi," he said.

Except for suave greetings, apparently.

But Rachel didn't seem to mind. Instead, she reached up and wrapped her arms around his neck, hugging him tightly. "I missed you."

"I'm so glad you're here." He mock-glared. "Finally."

Her cheeks went slightly rosy. "It's been a crazy week, but I made it in the end."

Fingers brushed along her jaw. "Thanks for coming, sweetheart."

"Are you kidding?" She gestured to the space around them. "Look at this. It's incredible, and you've totally spoiled me for the cheap seats now."

"Me, too," he said. "I never knew it could be like this."

"Well you both do now," Devon said, coming over and herding them so they could see the ice. The third period would be starting in just a few minutes. "And Rachel, once you succumb to the power of the ravioli, you'll never watch a Gold game any other way."

"Ravioli?" Rachel asked.

"It's *ah*-mazing good," Becca said then winked conspiratorially. "We ate the first plate, but another should be up soon."

"I'm starving." Rachel lifted her elbows to the sides, as if pretending to get ready to tackle someone. "Am I going to have to fight the pregnant lady for it?" The playfulness in her tone, the giggles, and subsequent fake-trash talk she exchanged with Becca just cemented to Bas that his woman was the stuff of legend.

Fuck, but I love you, he thought.

It wasn't until the three other people in the suite whirled to face him that Sebastian realized he'd spoken aloud.

"Uhh," Becca said, taking one look at Rachel's pale face and what was probably a horrified expression on his face. "I—*we* need to go get . . . something." Then she grabbed Devon's arm and all but dragged him from the box.

He barely heard them leave, his focus was so fixed on Rachel.

She was breathing . . . rapidly and too shallow.

"I'm sorry," he blurted. "I didn't—"

She lifted a hand, half curled in on herself. But though her words were interspersed with gasping breaths, her words were fierce. "Don't," she said. "Don't . . . you . . . fucking take . . . it back."

Bas knelt in front of her. "I couldn't take it back," he said, going for gentle though his pulse was pounding and cold sweat dripped down his spine. What if she didn't feel the same? What if she wanted to end things before they really got going? What if this was too much too soon and she ran? "I couldn't take it back, sweetheart, because I love you so fucking deeply that I'd have to tear out my own heart and stomp on it to have any hope to stop loving you."

Tears leaked out of the corners of her eyes, and he hurried to wipe them away. "Even then I think I'd still love you because you're not just in here—" He brought her hand to his chest, above his racing heart. "You're in my brain, my body, my soul. And I'm sorry I blurted it out like that, but I swear I fell half in love with you the first moment I met you."

Finally, she seemed to unfreeze. Her eyes locked on his and her mouth curved. "Only half?" she asked.

Bas's lungs suddenly began working again. "The other half was reserved for you tipping over that bowl of salad dressing."

"You made me waste an entire bottle of Ranch," she groaned. Her smile grew as she tugged him to his feet and hugged him. "I'm sorry I panicked," she whispered as he held her tightly for one long quiet moment.

He pulled back, nose wrinkling. "I'm sorry I announced it in front of my brother and his wife and didn't save it for a romantic, candlelit dinner or something."

Rachel opened her mouth, but her words were interrupted by a knock.

Becca poked her head in. "Sorry to interrupt, but"—she revealed a large plate full of ravioli with a flourish—"*ravioli* are here!"

Rachel pressed a kiss to his lips. "I'd take a thousand real moments with you over one fancy candlelit dinner."

Devon sent him a questioning look, mouthed, "Is it okay?"

Bas nodded and his heart was full as they all gathered around the table at the front of the box and sat down to stuff their mouths.

Oh, and to watch the Gold trounce their opponents, there was that, too.

"For the record," Rachel whispered after they'd demolished the pasta and chatted and thoroughly joked around. "First, your brother and Becca are amazing."

He touched her cheek, kissed the tip of her nose. "And the second?"

She spoke to the group. "That ravioli is the shit."

They all cracked up and Bas couldn't help feeling that this was one of the best nights of his life.

Especially when Rachel reached laughing lips up to his ear to murmur, "Number three is that . . . I love you, too."

Yup.

Best night ever.

TWENTY-ONE

Rachel

RACHEL AND SEBASTIAN said goodnight to Devon and Becca then caught an Uber to Bas's apartment, since it was closer.

She waited until they were through the door and the panel locked behind them before she announced, "I have something to tell you."

He froze, a slice of doubt crossing his face.

Damn. She'd meant it as a playful tease, not to make him feel insecure.

"Did I—"

Acting quickly before he could hop completely aboard the unsure train, Rachel reached for the hem of her Gold jersey and yanked it up and over her head.

"Rach—?"

Her long-sleeved tee followed, leaving her in only her bra.

The very sexy amethyst bra Sebastian had bought her.

She flicked open the button on her jeans, undid the zipper,

and pushed them down, stepping out of them and her shoes at the same time.

He made a noise that sounded as if he'd swallowed his tongue.

Rachel slowly turned in a circle. "*This* is what I wanted to tell you," she said. "Or rather, *show* you."

His face was a study of lines—two brows slashing down and together, a pair of lips pressed flat, a jaw clenched tightly—and she would have almost said that he was angry if not for the heat in his eyes.

Storm-ravaged eyes slid down her body. Back up. Heat prickled everywhere that gaze traveled and . . . since it traveled pretty much everywhere, she suddenly felt as though she had been dropped inside a boiling pot and was roasting from the inside out.

She took a step toward him, but he extended a hand, one palm out.

"Turn around again?"

It was a rasping plea and one she couldn't have resisted obeying even if she'd tried.

Slowly, she spun in one more circle.

Bas's hands were clenched tightly into fists when she faced him again. "I don't care how much it will cost me, but you're never wearing anything else."

She laughed. "A G-string might not go over too well in the office."

"I disagree." A smirk. "I know I would be a hell of a lot more productive if I knew you were waiting for me."

"I *am* waiting for you," she challenged.

"There's waiting," he said. "And there's anticipation."

"I've anticipated this for weeks now," she murmured then reached up and unhooked her bra. It landed almost soundlessly on the floor.

His eyes went somehow hotter.

"How's that for anticipation?"

A slow, heated smile before he curled a finger in her direction. "Come here."

She took a step back. "No. I think I should torture you like you've been torturing me. Let's take it slow, Rachel," she mimicked. "We have all the time in the world and meanwhile, I'm dripping wet and—*oof!*"

Bas swept her up into his arms. His lips collided with hers, his tongue slipping into her mouth, tangling with hers. Approximately two heartbeats or maybe two minutes or hell, she didn't know, the man kissed her so senseless that it could have been two hours before her back was pressed against his mattress.

"Now what was that about wet?" he asked, fingers sliding under the waistband of her underwear and between her thighs.

She moaned when he brushed her clit, hardly noticed when he tugged her underwear down her legs and off. But she certainly did notice when he bent and gave her the hottest kiss of her life.

And not on her mouth.

His tongue flicked over her, settling into a rhythm that quickly had her writhing and begging for . . . what? More? Yes. But the finger he slipped inside wasn't enough.

She wanted Bas, hot and hard and *deep* inside her.

"Please," she gasped then groaned when he did something with his tongue that made her toes curl and slid another finger inside. Suddenly, she wasn't thinking about the empty, aching feeling, but rather, was concentrating on the pleasure spiraling from her center and moving outward, tightening all her muscles, tilting her head back toward the ceiling.

Sweat beaded on her skin, heat coiling in her scalp, her breasts, her—

He nipped her, a little rough but she'd needed rough,

needed something intense enough to burst through the sensations engulfing her, needed something to focus all that pleasure to a single pinprick so that it . . . would . . .

Explode.

"Fuck!" she cried and bucked hard. Bas held her in place, licking and kissing her through the peak and down the other side.

And then she just lay there, chest heaving, limbs completely limp.

It wasn't just from the pleasure either. Because, yes, that was fan-fucking-tastic, but Rachel somehow felt both completely shattered and totally intact. Almost as though Bas had taken her apart piece by piece and then carefully glued her back together again.

But she wasn't Humpty Dumpty, damaged and more fragile than before.

Bas had made her stronger.

She didn't even realize that she'd started crying until he crawled up next to her and tugged her into his arms. Rachel burrowed herself into his chest.

"I'm sorry," she said. "It's not you." A sniff. "Well, I guess it *is* you—"

He pressed a kiss to her forehead. "Since you came apart on my tongue, I'm going to assume that those were screams of pleasure, not pain."

She snorted. "Considering I was using your hair as handles to grind myself against your mouth, I'd say that was a safe bet." Her eyes slid closed, but not before she saw him smile. "I love you, Bas," she said softly. "And I guess just feeling that, knowing that you're in it with me, makes everything so much better."

Fingers on her nape, her cheekbone, her jaw. "I like that everything is better."

"Me, too. But"—her hand slid down—"I think I can save the

talking for later, don't you think? I have a *little* problem to take care of."

He groaned and thrusted into her hand as she gripped him. "Fuck, baby." A beat. "I think, normally, I'd be insulted by the term *little*, but if you're going to stroke me like that, you can call me whatever you want."

Rachel followed the path of her hand, loving the way he jerked and cursed as she took his cock in her mouth.

"Sweetheart."

"Mmm." Her tongue traced the underside of his erection.

He hissed. "Baby."

She sucked him deep into the back of her throat and matched the strokes of her tongue to those of her hand.

For all of five seconds.

"Oof!" she said again, but before another outrage noise could escape her, or hell, before she could crawl back down Sebastian's body and continue sucking him like her favorite lollipop, he'd reached over her to grab a condom from the nightstand and rolled it on.

"Please say you're with me," he gritted out.

Her only answer was to wrap her legs around his waist and tug him down.

He pushed home, and, *fuck*, but that was the absolute best feeling in the world.

"You good?" he asked.

"Stop worrying," she said. "Just love me, Bas. Love me with everything you have."

He bent, brushed his lips to hers. "Always, sweetheart."

And then he moved, stroking in and out, bringing them both higher and higher until they crashed over the peak and tumbled into orgasm.

They were lying together afterward, limbs tangled, sweat

dampening their skin, breaths in rapid gasps, when he rotated his head to face her.

Lips curved he said, "I am man, hear me roar. I'm so glad I've found the right part-*ner*."

She burst into laughter.

Somehow, she'd just been fucked into near oblivion, was lying in bed with the man who brought her there, and she was laughing.

Laughing.

"God, I love you," she said and kissed him, a long, slow, joyful kiss that filled her cells with champagne—bubbling, hopeful, and effervescent.

Perfect. Bas was absolutely, imperfectly, perfect for her.

TWENTY-TWO

Sebastian

MONDAY.

And it had been a Monday.

Clay and Heather were back from their working honey-moon, which meant that employees at Steele Technologies, and presumably RoboTech as well, were running around like crazy, readying and attempting to implement all of the ideas the bosses had brainstormed on their trip.

Rachel had texted him earlier in the day saying that she was banning Heather from any form of vacation for the foreseeable future.

No more time off. Nope. No way. No how.

He sent back:

Bad over there?

The worst. Heather has BIG ideas.

Bas had grinned.

They're probably really good big ideas.

Yes. Yes, they are. Which makes this even worse.

Considering that Clay had been on a similar warpath that morning, Bas could sympathize. He also knew how to make things better for Rachel.

Tonight. My place. Documentary on WWII, takeout, and pajamas.

Throw in a glass of wine and I'm in.

He'd agreed, of course, having already stocked his cupboards with Rachel's preferred brand. This was the woman he loved, and he wanted her to have everything she could possibly want.

Thankfully, he had that evening to look forward to when Clay strolled into his office mid-morning and dropped another project on his lap.

It was the type of project Bas had been dying to sink his teeth into.

But also one he didn't think he could do properly. Not with everything else already on his plate.

"Before you give me that look," his boss said. "Check the file underneath."

Bas flipped open the folder. "Uhh." He stared at the stack of papers, started flipping through one resume after another. "Either you're trying to fire me"—his gaze flashed up—"or . . ."

Clay's mouth quirked. "It's the *or*," he said. "I'd like you to hire your replacement so you can take on a new job title. You'll find the proposal for that in the file below." He sat in the chair in front of Bas's desk, leaned back, and crossed his legs at his ankles. "You're wasted as my assistant, have been for a long time, and I'll admit that I'm not looking forward to losing you in that role. You've been the best I've ever had."

"I—" Bas shook his head as he stared at the proposal. VP of Acquisitions. "I'm not sure I have the qualifications for—"

"Sebastian," Clay said, putting up a palm. "You've been streamlining the projects Steele pursues for months now. Think of it this way, I want to take the rest of the job—flights, schedule, email filtering—off your hands so you can focus on that."

Put it that way.

"You sure that—?"

Clay narrowed his eyes. "My future VP of Acquisitions wouldn't finish that question."

Noted.

Bas nodded.

"Good," Clay said and stood. "These are the rejects from when I hired you. One of them might be able to live up to your standards, or we might have to start from scratch." He turned for the door. "I'll trust your judgment on that."

Bas rose to his feet. "I'll narrow it down to a couple of candidates then bring you in on the final decision."

Clay paused on the threshold. "And that right there."

Bas frowned, waited for his boss to finish the sentence. When he didn't, Bas asked, "What's right there?"

"Why you won't just stop at VP."

With that, Clay left Bas standing there, mouth gaped open like a fish.

He slumped down into his chair, heart pounding, excitement racing through every nerve. Holy shit, this was actually going to happen. Picking up his cell, he texted Rachel.

I have something awesome to tell you.

When she didn't reply back within a few minutes, as was typical, he settled down to work his way through the stack of résumés. She was probably in a meeting or bogged down with Heather's grand ideas.

So, he pushed his cell to the side and got started on Clay's grand idea.

"Hey."

The female voice startled him, and he glanced up from the papers to see Kelsey standing at his office door.

His eyes flicked to his phone, saw that several hours had passed and that it was nearly lunchtime. A blip of unease settled in his stomach when he saw that Rachel still hadn't texted back.

But then Kelsey was striding into the room. "Come on, little bro," she snapped. "At least act like you're happy to see me."

Bas stood and crossed the room, phone in hand. "I *am* happy to see you," he said. "Sorry, it's just that Rachel . . ."

When he trailed off, she asked. "Rachel, what? Oh, no. Don't tell me you two broke up. I really like her and would hate to disown you." She grinned. "Because I would definitely choose her over you."

In the past, those words would have probably hurt him.

Today, he took them as intended: as a joke and nothing more.

"Hilarious," he deadpanned. His stomach churned, unable to shake the feeling that something wasn't quite right. Rachel had never gone this long without at least sending him a quick text saying she'd be out of touch.

Kelsey took one look at his face. "It was a joke," she said. "You know that, right?"

Bas pulled her into a hug. "Reading that loud and clear." He frowned. "I just—hang on a second, okay?"

He sent Rachel another text.

Sweetheart, all good?

No reply.

He shook it off. Rachel was probably in a meeting.

"Sorry," he told Kelsey. "It's silly, but I haven't heard from Rachel all morning and—"

"What?" she asked softly. "You're not exactly the clingy type, Sebastian, so I'm guessing there's another part to this story?"

"Her ex-husband is a . . ."

"Tool?" Kelsey supplied.

"Times that by about a million," he said, not wanting to reveal what the sick son-of-a-bitch had done to Rachel. That was her business. But he also wasn't about to minimize what Preston had done. "He—" Bas shook his head. "It's much better for her to not be with him."

Kelsey, apparently, read between the lines. "Is he dangerous?"

"To Rachel? Yes," he said. "But last we heard, he was still living in Iowa and she has a restraining order."

"Hm." Kelsey frowned. "Those don't always work, you know."

Bas glared at her.

"I'm just saying."

"Yeah." He sighed. "I'll give her a little more time. Her boss just got back from a business trip, so she's probably bogged down."

Kelsey nodded. "You're probably right," she agreed. "I didn't mean to bug you at work," she said as he stared at his phone screen. "But I was in town for a conference and wanted to see if you were available to grab lunch."

His eyes shot to hers, surprised. "I'd like that," he said.

Except the decision to give Rachel more time wasn't sitting well in his gut.

"But do you think we can swing by Rachel's office on the way out? It's not far."

Kelsey clapped him on the shoulder. "You know what, little bro?"

He walked over to his desk and grabbed his wallet from the drawer, sticking it along with his phone into his pockets. "What?"

"You're a good guy."

He snorted. "So effusive with the praise." But he hugged her. "Seriously, though, thanks for stopping by. I've wanted to—"

"See me?" she interrupted and fluttered her hands in front of her face. "Oh, you're so sweet, Sebastian. Just the best brother in the world."

"Dork," he said, but relief poured through him that she hadn't argued about the pit stop. He just needed to lay eyes on Rachel, reassure him that the anxiousness in his gut was an over-reaction. He was probably just on edge because they'd spent so much time together over the weekend that he was in Rachel-withdrawal or some shit.

He tugged Kelsey's ponytail. "What I *was* going to say is that I've been wanting to find out how the new job was going."

Her face softened, and he was doubly glad he'd asked. Yes, he'd already decided to put the past aside, forget the resentment, and focus on rebuilding his bonds with his family, and Kelsey's visit proved that she wanted to strengthen them, too. But it wasn't all about his family making up for perceived slights to him. He also needed to make things right by reaching out to them.

Look at him. All adult and shit.

She'd just finished telling him about her new boss when Clay met up with them by the elevators.

Bas introduced Kelsey.

"Sorry to interrupt your lunch," Clay said after shaking his sister's hand. "But Heather just texted me and wanted to know if you'd heard anything from Rachel. Are you guys meeting up with her to eat?"

Sebastian blinked. "No." His throat went tight. "She's at the office."

Or that's where she was supposed to be.

Clay frowned, held up his phone. "Apparently, she ran out to grab . . ."

Bas didn't hear the rest of the words. His heart had started pounding, a rapid *whoosh-whoosh* that drowned Clay out. He pulled out his cell and dialed Rachel's number. It rang four times before going to voice mail.

Fuck. He called again.

Same thing.

Fingers shaking, he typed out a text.

Rachel. Are you okay? Heather hasn't heard from you and neither have I. We're both worried.

He held his breath as he waited for one eternal minute.

Nothing.

He turned to Kelsey. "I'm sorry—"

"Go," she said then called, "Wait!" when he took off for the stairs. "What's her address?"

Bas rattled it off and ran.

TWENTY-THREE

Rachel

RACHEL HOPPED out of the Uber and raced through the front door of her apartment building. She had maybe fifteen minutes to grab the file she'd forgotten that morning and to stuff some much-needed sustenance in her face.

It was bizarre that she'd had to run home in the middle of the day.

She always double and triple-checked her bag, making sure she had everything she could possibly need.

And everything she *couldn't* possibly need.

But today she'd forgotten the file that Heather needed for a meeting that afternoon and, idiot of all idiots, *she* had taken it home just to make sure it was perfect.

Another reason to go solely digital, she thought, hurrying over to the elevator and jabbing the button. Of course, Trace McPearson didn't trust technology and had resisted even getting involved with RoboTech at all.

As a bone, she and Heather provided old-school Trace with actual paper files.

Which apparently, she'd left at home because her brain was rotting.

Less than a month after falling in love with a man who was sweet and sexy and so good in bed and she spent half her time dreaming about jumping Sebastian and the other half thinking about all the ways she could squeeze more time out of her schedule to see him more.

Because almost every night and weekend wasn't enough.

She wanted it all.

Smiling at that thought, because a year ago she never would have expected that a man could quickly become her best friend, Rachel stepped off the elevator and hurried over to her door.

She input the code on the keypad, waiting for the metal against metal sound of the lock disengaging then pushed inside.

And her heart stopped, bile burned the back of her throat, her knees went weak.

Then she remembered all of the self-defense classes she had gone to. She remembered her instructor's voice yelling at her, drilling it into that that she should always take the opportunity to run.

So she moved.

Whirling around, she scrambled for the door handle.

Too late.

White-hot agony ripped through her scalp as Preston grabbed a chunk of her hair and wrenched her head back.

"Did you honestly think I would let you get away with it?" he hissed.

"Preston—"

He shook her roughly and she cried out in pain. "I didn't say you could speak." He slammed her head forward and into the door. Something cracked—her nose?—and blood began gushing down her face. Then he punched her hard in the side and something else cracked.

This time, she knew exactly what had broken. Her ribs.

"You're so stupid." He breathed in her face, hot, rotten breath that made her stomach churn. "You came home for this, didn't you?" A hard *smack* of a file against her cheek. "You're so predictable. I knew, just knew, you'd come back for it."

She shook her head and received another slam of her face against the door. "Yes," he said. "I know you, darling. Know how unobservant you are. Know your patterns." He twisted the hand in her hair, forcing her eyes to his. "You used your fucking birthday as the code to your apartment, you dumb bitch."

Her eyes filled with tears. It had been idiotic to use that date.

"You didn't even notice I'd been in here, did you?"

Rachel couldn't catch her breath.

Preston didn't care. He shook her. "*Did* you?"

"N-no," she whispered.

"I even left you a clue. I never would have stood by and allowed a mess like this fucking pigsty in my house." He whipped her around. "Shoes everywhere, coats not hung up, wine bottles in the fridge. You're a slob. And a whore."

"No."

Another slam of her body against the door. This time it was her back, and the movement knocked the wind out of her all over again.

"A whore," he repeated. "Fucking another man when you used to spread your legs for me."

Just words, she reminded herself. They were just words, sharpened and aimed to defeat her before she could mount a fight, to hurt her so deeply that she'd just lie down and die.

Not today.

Preston still had a tight grip on her hair.

But her hands were free.

They were slippery, but she focused all her effort on

reaching slowly behind her for the knob, not on the hate her ex-husband was spewing, nor on the pain that had black creeping rapidly into the edges of her vision.

If she passed out now, he'd kill her.

If she didn't get out of the apartment, he'd kill her.

She knew both of those things instinctively.

So, the moment she felt the knob turn, she shifted and let her bag—which had somehow stayed on her shoulder—slide down to her wrist. Lurching forward, Rachel brought it up toward Preston's head at the same time she yanked the door open.

Preston cursed as the leather collided with his face.

It didn't knock him out, the bag wasn't heavy enough for that, but it did startle him enough that he cursed and let go of her hair.

She slipped out of the door and sprinted down the hallway, screaming for help.

Then made it all of ten steps before Preston was on her again.

"Shut up," he said and punched her in the stomach, before dragging her back toward her apartment.

"No!" she gasped and sucked in a painful breath before yelling at the top of her lungs, "Help! *Someone help me!*" She clawed at his arms, punching and kicking and biting anything she could reach.

But he was stronger.

No matter how hard she fought, he just kept pulling her down the hall. She kicked at the walls, grabbed onto the narrow indentation of a doorframe and continued screaming.

Anything. *Anything* to stop him.

Except it was the middle of the day. Everyone was at work.

She was alone.

Panic settled in as Preston yanked her over the threshold

and back into her apartment. Rachel hooked a foot over the frame then screamed in absolute agony as her ankle popped and gave way.

"Stupid, stupid bitch," he growled and threw her forward. She landed on her bag, the bulky leather jabbing her in the ribs.

The black that had been creeping in earlier was swirling now, grabbing at her, threatening to tug her into oblivion.

But Rachel knew she couldn't let it.

She knew she couldn't let Preston win.

Not like this. Not when she'd never fought back before. Not when she'd finally found people worth living for.

Gripping her bag tightly in one hand, she pushed herself up, staggering, teetering on one foot.

Preston had turned to lock the door, but when he rotated back to face her and saw she was standing, his mouth curved in a predatory smile.

"You finally found some spine?" he asked, his once handsome features transforming into something cruel and dark and sick. "Did your lawyer friend convince you you'd be safe?" Cold, *cold* blue eyes locked onto hers. "I might have let you go, you know. Thank the good Lord that my useless excuse for a wife was finally gone." He took a step toward her and laughed when she scrambled back. "But that *bitch* cost my father his job. And I cannot let that stand."

Oh God. Bec.

Rachel's knees threatened to buckle. She'd brought her friend into her mess.

How could she have risked—

But then she thought about what Bec would do in this situation, what Abby or CeCe or Heather or even Seraphina would do.

They wouldn't roll over and die.

They would fight.

Rachel lifted her chin.

"Do your worst, you fucking bastard." She spat at him, half blood from her gushing nose, half bile from her revulsion of the man.

He rolled his eyes. "You're a pathetic, scared little girl who is worth *nothing*."

"I'm not *her* any longer," she said, inching toward her kitchen counter. If she could just put some distance between them, buy herself some time—

He lunged.

She threw her bag again, but this time he dodged the leather satchel.

He came at her, would have actually gotten her if her leg hadn't collapsed, causing her to teeter to one side. She scrambled in that moment, Preston skidding past, her arms flailing to regain her balance and . . . landing on an empty bottle of wine.

She and Bas had finished it sometime last week and she'd left it on the counter, intending to drop it in the recycling bin on the ground floor.

But she hadn't gotten that far.

And now her fingers slid around the neck of the bottle and she gripped it tightly.

Preston turned, face drawn into a feral expression.

Rachel didn't think, just lifted the bottle and with every last bit of strength she possessed, brought it down onto his head.

It shattered into a thousand pieces, pain shot through her palm, up her arm . . . and Preston?

His lunge didn't halt.

He took her to the ground, landing squarely on top of her.

The agony of her ankle, her nose, her ribs, and hand . . . it was too much.

The black sucked her under.

TWENTY-FOUR

Sebastian

HE RACED into the lobby and was immediately stopped by a police officer.

"I need—" he broke off, trying to push around him. "My girlfriend—"

"This is a crime scene," the officer said. "You'll need to wait here."

Bas shook his head. He couldn't wait there. He needed to get to Rachel. "No," he snapped. "Where is she?" He shoved the officer hard. "Let me go, you fucking—"

"Cortez," a slightly accented voice Bas didn't immediately recognize said. "He's with me."

The officer nodded and with an exceptionally dirty look, let Sebastian slip under the caution tape.

A hand stopped his headlong rush for the stairs.

Bas finally turned and studied the owner of the voice. Pascal, his brother's bodyguard. In a heartbeat, he remembered Kelsey asking for Rachel's address. She must have called Devon, who'd sent Pascal. The bodyguard had connections in the police department, and the promise of more information finally had Bas's brain clearing.

"Wait," Pascal said. "Let me find out where she is."

He nodded, and Pascal went over to speak with another officer.

But it turned out that he didn't need Pascal to find out where Rachel was because at that moment, the elevator doors opened with a ding and a stretcher was rolled out.

The woman he loved was black and blue and on a stretcher.

Bas didn't think, he just ran.

Rachel was unconscious, her face covered in blood, bruises already mottling the surface, her leg was twisted in an odd direction and . . .

His woman was broken and bleeding and—

Fuck.

Sebastian's eyes stung.

Pascal grabbed his arm, tugging him after the stretcher when his feet had frozen in horror. "It's superficial," he said and pushed Bas toward the waiting ambulance. "Go with her. I'll get your family to the hospital."

Bas nodded.

The paramedics didn't complain when he jumped into the back of the ambulance. He watched as they worked on Rachel, relaxing slightly when they weren't rushing and didn't seem overly concerned.

"Three minutes to the hospital," the paramedic told Bas.

He managed another nod but couldn't take his eyes off Rachel, couldn't help but burn every single bruise and mark into his brain. The bastard was going to pay.

"I've never seen a scene like that," the paramedic said into the silence. She was a middle-aged woman, blond hair laced heavily with gray.

Bas bristled at the awe in her tone.

What the fuck was wrong with her? His woman was hurt, and she was coveting the violence?

"I've never seen someone fight so hard to stay alive." Gentle brown eyes met his. "She must have really wanted to see you again."

His anger faded, replaced with so much love that he knew if Rachel didn't wake up something inside of him would be permanently broken.

The ambulance slowed to a halt, and she reached across to squeeze his arm.

"She's going to be okay here"—the paramedic indicated Rachel's body—"but she's going to need some help here and here"—she pointed at Rachel's heart and head—"Don't let her go it alone, okay?"

"I won't."

The back doors opened and they wheeled Rachel into the Emergency Department.

SEVERAL HOURS LATER, Bas was still in the waiting room. He'd tried to follow the stretcher into the actual department, wanting Rachel to see a familiar and safe face the moment she woke, but the nurses had stopped him, redirecting him to an empty chair outside the reception desk.

He hadn't been alone long, Devon arriving within a half hour, followed by Becca and Kelsey.

His parents had called, wanting to fly out, but Bas had told them to wait.

He'd texted Clay and pretty soon, the waiting room was filled with Heather, CeCe, Sera, and Bec and their spouses. The only ones who were missing were Jordan, who was on a business trip, and Abby, who was scrambling to find a sitter so she could come down.

And still they hadn't heard a word about how Rachel was doing.

The calm assurance from the paramedic who'd wheeled her into the back had long since vanished, and Sebastian was probably only minutes from storming through the doors and risking arrest.

Because there was a new addition to the waiting room.

A pair of police officers standing, arms crossed, in front of the door that led to the actual ER.

Bec was pacing back and forth on the floor, talking softly into her cell, trying to find out exactly what had happened and not getting much of anywhere.

Rachel was back there and she was alone and—

The doors to the back opened, and a nurse came out. "Sebastian Scott?"

He was on his feet and moving before she even finished saying his name.

"I'm Sebastian," he said.

"Come with me." She led him down an anemic looking hallway and into a room.

Rachel was inside.

She had a large bandage on her forehead, several smaller ones on her nose and cheeks. Her top lip was swollen, both eyes blackened. One arm was wrapped in gauze and cradled close to her chest and her right leg was encased in a cast from foot to knee.

He'd wanted to kill the bastard before, now Sebastian wanted to absolutely eviscerate Preston Johnston.

"Hi," she rasped.

Bas rushed over to her bedside, but once there, he extended one arm and froze, not sure where he could touch her.

BAD BILLIONAIRES 2   157

She lifted her uninjured hand and cupped his cheek. "Hey, you."

There were tears in his eyes. He knew it and didn't give a damn. "I'm so sorry," he said. "I should have—" he began, even knowing there was nothing anyone could have done. That they couldn't have anticipated Preston would have come after her then, couldn't have known he'd be in her apartment waiting for her. He'd gone eighteen months without a peep, and Bas had expected the bastard would fade into oblivion.

The nurse glanced over at the police officers, who'd come to stand by either side of the door to Rachel's room. They nodded.

"You should both know that the . . . other patient"—a hint of venom in her tone—"didn't make it."

"What?" Rachel said.

"The male who arrived with you didn't survive," she said. "I thought you might sleep better tonight knowing that." A beat as she glanced at Sebastian. "That *both* of you might sleep better."

"I didn't—" Rachel shook her head.

Fingers rested on her shoulder. "He had a bleed. One that had been leaking slowly for a long time. It could have gone at any time." A reassuring squeeze. "Today just happened to be that day."

"But I hit him with the bottle so hard."

The nurse straightened, indicating Rachel's bound hand. "I think you injured yourself more than him with that bottle shattering the way it did. The coroner said he was likely gone before it even made contact."

"I—"

One of the officers handed him a card and murmured they'd need a statement at some point the next day. Bas told her they'd be in touch, and the officers left Rachel's room.

"It's over," the nurse said when they'd gone. "Just hold on to that thought for now. The rest can come later."

Rachel nodded and her eyes were misty when they met Sebastian's. "It's really over?"

He nodded. "Yes."

"Can I go home now?"

"What?" Bas said. "No. You need to stay and—"

"Actually," the nurse said. "All of her scans are clear and while she's bruised to hell and back, Rachel is very lucky. Aside from broken bones, she doesn't have any serious injuries."

"*Bones?*" he ground out.

"Just some tiny ones," Rachel said.

The nurse rolled her eyes, but she was smiling. "Several of the small bones in her foot are broken. The orthopedist has set her leg already, but she'll need several follow up appointments with her as well as an internist, just to confirm her broken ribs are healing properly."

Bas stiffened. "Why in the hell is she coming home if she has that many injuries?"

"Because she's going to be okay and doesn't need observation. Which means the best thing for her right now is to recover at home." The nurse began typing on the computer in the room. "I'll grab her discharge instructions and then go over them with you both."

Rachel glanced at him. "So my apartment is . . ."

A crime scene, probably. A horrible reminder of what had happened, definitely.

"Want to borrow mine?" he asked.

And the smile she gave him went a long way to soothing the anger and panic and absolute fury that was engulfing his heart.

A nurse wheeled Rachel out of the back and then, when she pointed, in the direction of their group.

"Fuck," Devon hissed as they came close. "That son of a bitch is going to die a slow death."

"Dev," Bas warned.

His brother ignored him, moving to kneel next to Rachel. "I'm having my car brought around. Do you know where you want to stay tonight? I can get you a hotel or you can stay with—"

"Bas?" she asked softly.

"The bed hog is staying with me," he replied.

Her lips tipped up into a small smile.

She would be okay. They would both be okay.

"You're getting a raise," Heather bawled.

Rachel frowned then winced. "What are you talking about?"

"I don't know," Heather said with a sniff as Clay tugged her into his arms. She buried her face into his chest, shoulders shaking.

Sera pressed a kiss to an unbruised part of her face. "I'm just so glad you're okay."

CeCe hugged her with extreme gentleness. "Abby wanted me to tell you that she'll make sure you get the good drugs."

Rachel snorted, then brought her hand to her middle. "Don't make me laugh, it hurts too much."

Bec had been standing in the background, but at those words, she finally knelt in front of Rachel, her eyes were wet, her nose red and dripping. "I'm so sorry. I should have—"

"Shut. Up." Rachel's harsh tone took them all by surprise. "There is not one person in this room who has any right to feel guilty"—her gaze flicked from Bec to Sebastian—"*Not* one person. Okay?"

Bec sniffed, started to shake her head—

"Bec," Rachel snapped. "Not. One. Person."

Bec shuddered but eventually nodded.

Pascal poked his head in, indicating the car was ready, and they all made their way to it, helping the nurse get Rachel settled into the back of Devon's sedan.

A few minutes later, her friends had all said goodbye and made promises to check up on Rachel tomorrow, and Kelsey was herding Becca and Devon into her rental car.

"Call me later," Devon said.

"I'd better be on that call list, too," Kelsey called before closing the driver's side door.

Somehow, despite everything, Sebastian smiled.

Eventually they would all be okay.

He'd make damn sure of that.

TWENTY-FIVE

Rachel

A WEEK LATER, Rachel finally forced Bas to go back to work.

Bas's overprotection had become both endearing and infuriating. He'd even carried her to the bathroom that morning before he'd left for the office, for fuck's sake. Her leg was broken and, *okay* so were two of her ribs, but she had one of those knee scooter things and could totally make it to the toilet.

Then there was the fact that he'd been watching her every waking moment, as though he expected her to crack.

Fine, she'd half-expected to lose it herself.

The terror of that day, of the minutes that felt like hours, an eternity, still flashed across her mind at all moments.

But . . . she'd been through it before.

She knew she'd get through it again.

And this time, she had people who loved her by her side.

That didn't mean she wasn't going more than a little stir-crazy. She was used to being busy, used to working or thinking about work during most waking hours.

It had been T-minus seven days since she'd checked her email, and her inbox was going to be the absolute worst.

Plus, she'd already watched what felt like every documentary on Netflix.

Sleep hadn't been coming all that easily, and lying in the dark was much less desirable than staying up all hours bingeing on her history and political docs.

It wasn't every time she closed her eyes, and it was definitely happening less frequently as the days went on, but Rachel could still feel the bottle colliding with Preston's head, could remember the absolute terror, the burning pain filling her body.

The police had come, and she'd given her statement. They'd confirmed that he'd had an aneurysm and had been dead before he'd fallen on top of her. They'd also revealed that she hadn't actually been alone that morning.

Three apartments down, a teenager had been home sick from school. She'd called 9-1-1 and they'd shown up seconds after Rachel had passed out.

After Preston had died.

Fuck.

Why did she feel guilty?

Because deep down, Rachel was relieved he was gone, that he wouldn't be coming back to hurt her all over again.

Did that make her a bad person?

Maybe. Maybe not.

Or maybe it just made her normal?

She'd sent the girl a thank you note but knew that she needed to meet her, make sure she wasn't terrorized by what she'd heard, what she'd seen.

The last thing Rachel wanted was for anyone else to be hurt because of Preston.

Sighing, she shifted carefully in bed, her cracked ribs still not happy with any sort of movement. Heather had forbidden

Rachel from doing any sort of work, but Abby had understood that Rachel had needed a distraction, and so she'd stolen a laptop from RoboTech and smuggled it into Bas's apartment with all the pomp and secrecy of a secret agent.

Smiling and shaking her head, Rachel knew she'd been so lucky to have found such a great group of people.

They'd had a virtual parade of visitors through the apartment, Abby and Jordan bringing the stolen laptop along with enough snacks to fill the cabinets to bursting. Sera had come bearing a new set of pajamas that buttoned on top and with legs wide enough to easily slip over her cast. CeCe and Colin had brought dinner then stayed to keep them company for several hours. CeCe had even gone so far as to book all of Rachel's follow-up appointments and then had run out to pick up the refills for her prescriptions. Even Devon, Becca, and Kelsey had come by with Bas's parents in tow, and his mom had made the most incredible spaghetti for all of them.

But as Rachel booted up the laptop and started making her way through her emails, there was one person who hadn't come.

And that was the real problem keeping her up at night.

How could she make Bec understand that what had happened with Preston wasn't her fault?

Well, she certainly couldn't do anything with one bum leg and aching ribs. Except . . . she smiled. Maybe she *could* do something.

She picked up her cell and sent a text.

I'm alone and need food. Can you bring Molly's?

Almost instantly, Bec texted her back.

I'll be there in thirty.

And so, another one fell into her trap. Rachel snorted at her own joke then got down to emails for another twenty minutes before carefully sliding out of bed. It'd take her close to ten minutes just to get to the door.

An exaggeration, yes, but only a slight one.

But it was a good thing she'd gotten up when she had because the knock came when she was still a few feet from the door. Her phone buzzed.

It's me.

Rachel rolled forward and glanced through the peephole. If she'd taken nothing else from Preston, he'd at least taught her to be more aware of her surroundings.

Bec was on the other side of the wood, bag from Molly's in hand, a tight, pained expression pulling on her face.

Rachel opened the door. "Thank you," she said and sniffed. "You brought soup, too?"

Bec shrugged. "Seemed the thing to do."

Then she just stood there, all unsure and indecisive and totally not *Bec* at all. Normally, she'd be barging in giving orders. Today, she just stared at Rachel with regret in her eyes.

"Come in," Rachel said and wheeled herself backward.

Bec nodded, stepping over the threshold then turned to lock the door. Rachel ignored how the click of the dead bolt sliding home made her gut twist. She'd get over that.

Eventually.

"Where's Sebastian?" Bec asked.

"I got tired of him bossing me around and kicked him out." Bec's brows lifted. "To the office," Rachel added. "For eight straight hours."

Lips curving, her friend walked forward to the table and

began unpacking the salads and soup. "I got you potato and leek. I thought you'd had that before, but if you don't like it, I also have butternut squash and chicken noodle." She lined up enough containers that it looked as if she'd ordered half the menu. "Oh, and tomato soup and both salads and—"

"Bec."

Her friend ignored the entreaty.

Wheels squeaking slightly as she skidded forward, Rachel closed the distance between them and placed her hand over Bec's, stilling it.

"We need to talk about it."

Bec shook her head. "That one's the peach and almond—"

"Rebecca Darden. Shut up about the fucking food and sit down," Rachel snapped. "We are going to talk about it."

Bec froze and sucked in a long breath. After a minute, she released it on a long exhale. "It's my fault," she said, sinking into a chair.

"No. It's absolutely not." Rachel sat across from her. "It's Preston's—"

"I went after him," Bec said. "You told me to leave it, to just get the divorce and forget the rest of it, but I didn't do that." Gray eyes sparkled with tears, but her words were clear. "I went after him with everything I had. I wanted to destroy everything that mattered, to *make him pay*. And I wanted to make his corrupt father to—"

She broke off and for the first time ever, Rachel saw Rebecca Darden, famed lawyer and corporate badass, cry.

"It's my fault," she wailed. "If I hadn't gone after Preston—"

Tears trailed Bec's face, and Rachel felt her own eyes water. Carefully, she pushed to her feet then limped back around the table and wrapped her good arm around her friend. "I'm glad you ignored me."

Bec pulled away.

"Look at you," she snapped. "How can you possibly be glad—?"

"Because Preston is *gone*. Because he doesn't have a hold over me any longer, because his father is no longer in a position of power. Or, at least, I'm assuming you got the asshole canned since you are Rebecca *fucking* Darden." A small smile tipped Bec's lips and she nodded. "I'm glad because they can't hurt anyone else."

Bec's chin dropped to her chest, and Rachel knew it would take time for her friend to see that she was okay, that she didn't blame her.

That it would take time for Bec to stop blaming herself.

"I know one conversation isn't a be-all-end-all, that you're a stubborn pain in the ass who likes to shoulder the burdens of everyone else and make them right," Rachel said. "But I don't blame you. I'll *never* blame you. And . . . if you forget that, I'll sit you down and yell at you until you remember."

A flash of white teeth as Bec glanced back up. "You're mean when you're on Molly's withdrawal."

"Good thing you bought half the menu, then." Moving gingerly, Rachel navigated her way back to the chair across from Bec.

Bec snorted. "I really did."

"I know." She grinned. "And I'm going to take a page out of Abby's book and say, you need to invest in waterproof mascara."

Her friend had serious raccoon eyes happening.

Bec groaned and wiped a finger under each eye, smearing the black smudges further. "This is why I hate feelings."

"This is why you hate things you can't control."

"Maybe."

They both laughed, which resulted in Rachel wincing and

forbidding Bec from any jokes or sarcasm or pithy comments on the world at hand. Which, of course, meant they both spent their whole lunch doing all three.

Rachel very quickly learned how to laugh without hurting her ribs.

EPILOGUE

Sebastian

TWO MONTHS HAD PASSED, but waking up next to Rachel was still the best thing in the world.

Especially now that she'd had her cast taken off and her bruises had faded. Of course, she was still as stubborn as ever, declaring herself completely recovered, but he had seen the shadows under her eyes after sleepless nights, caught her wincing when she coughed or laughed and her ribs hurt. Though in truth, those moments were coming fewer and further between.

Thank God, because Bas didn't know how he'd have lived with himself if she hadn't gotten better.

But she had gotten better, and she'd bounced back remarkably quickly, poking fun at her injuries, declaring that all her hours of binging on Netflix were rotting her brain.

As if. The little stink had refused to listen to him and Heather and had been working from his apartment, almost from the moment she'd been able to get out of bed.

But he had to admit that despite moving so quickly from sex

to love to living together in just a few months time, he'd really enjoyed every minute of having Rachel in his space.

It had felt right—*she* had felt right from the first moment she'd smiled up at him at Bobby's.

The touch on his cheek startled him.

While he'd been daydreaming, the woman he loved had woken up and he'd missed his favorite thing in the world. The way she stretched upon waking—arching her back, arms extended, toes pointing, the soft groan that never failed to harden his morning wood into granite.

"Morning," she said softly.

"Morning, love." He bent down to kiss her forehead. "So, my cast-free girlfriend, what do you want to do today?"

"Besides shaving this Chewbacca leg?" She poked her foot out from beneath the covers, wiggled navy blue painted toes.

He slipped his hand down her back, cupping her ass and trailing his fingers across the hip that belonged to the *Chewbacca* leg. "I kind of like you hairy."

"Ew." She wrinkled her nose.

Bas kissed that cute nose. "So besides shaving, do you want to walk by the pier?"

She shuddered. "Too many tourists."

"Shopping?"

Rachel felt his forehead. "No fever. Have you been abducted by aliens?"

"What?" he said. "I love shopping with women."

Brown brows pulled down and together. "Women?"

"You," he hurried to say. "Only you. Other women are dead to me."

"Good." She smirked. "But shopping? Seriously?"

"Seriously." A shrug. "I would never turn down a fashion show. You parading through the changing room in sexy little outfits? Taking me back and closing the door, watching you come in the mirror as I ate you out."

Rachel's cheeks went a little pink and she fanned herself. "Whew. So, you've apparently thought about that?"

Bas's lips twitched. "Just a little bit."

Okay, *a lot*. As in he'd spent a lot of time over the last two months fantasizing about all the things he was going to do to Rachel when she was completely recovered.

"Mmm," she said and tilted her head to the side, considering. "I could actually get behind prancing around in cute little outfits for you. Granted, you have to buy more of that gorgeous lingerie and prance around in outfits of your own."

"You mean this bag of lingerie?" he asked, reaching a hand out of bed as if to reach under the mattress.

Her jaw dropped open. "What?"

"I'm kidding." He kissed her. "The bag's in the closet."

She snorted. "You are such a dork. But because you're my dork, I'm keeping you."

A grin tugged at his mouth. "So, no to shopping, yes to future mutual fashion shows, and no to the touristy spots. Where does that leave us?"

"Aren't you going to ask what my fantasy is?"

Well, that was a really good point.

He rolled to his back, tugging her so she was sprawled across his chest. Her hair bounced forward, tickling his face. He tucked the strands behind her ears and laughed when they bounced right back.

"It's impossible," she said, leaning forward and shaking her head, tickling him again. "This crazy mop doesn't cooperate, especially in the mornings."

"I like your crazy hair," he said, running his fingers through the strands.

"Maybe," she said.

The blanket slid down from her shoulders to her waist, affording a very nice view of her braless state. Fuck, but his mouth watered to taste them again.

"So, are you gonna leave your guy hanging?" he asked, his voice a little rough.

"Hmm?" Her fingers trailed down his bare chest, and he had to force himself to focus, to not yank her tightly against him and kiss her senseless.

"Your fantasy," he rasped when her fingertips teased the hem of his boxer briefs. "What is it?" Not the smoothest, but fuck, her breasts were in his face, her fingers were close to the motherland, and his cock was ready to break in half.

"Oh." She leaned close, pressing her breasts to his chest, tilting her chin up so that she could whisper in his ear. "My fantasy is for you to strip me naked and then spend the entire day making love to me."

He flipped their positions between one heartbeat and the next, her legs coming up to wrap around his hips.

"You sure?" Bas asked, his mouth a hairsbreadth away from hers.

"Yes, I'm sure. Please, Bas, stop worrying about me and all the shit that happened in the past. Let's . . . not forget it exactly, because I don't think that's possible." Her hands came to rest on his shoulders. "But can we stop making it the focus and center of everything and just move forward? If something hurts, I'll tell you. If I don't like something, I'll tell you." Her eyes locked with his. "And I hope to God you'll promise to do the same." She tilted her pelvis, pressing her pussy against the erection tenting his underwear. "But today—*now*—I'm healthy, I'm horny, and I need you inside me."

"I love you," he said. "You're so deeply sewn into my being that I don't think I could ever deny you anything."

Rachel's lips curved. "Those are dangerous words to tell a

woman." She tugged him down, mouths almost touching. "Also, I love you, so, so much."

He kissed her, and then they spoke in touches and caresses, in strokes of their tongues, in nips of their teeth, in brushes of their fingers, rather than words. He stripped off her tank top, slipped off her pajama bottoms, and then traced every part of her with his lips, his fingers, his tongue.

Bas memorized every freckle and scar, teased the spot behind her ear that never failed to make her shiver. He kissed down her sides, gentle over those still-healing ribs, down over her hips . . . and in between.

She writhed against his mouth, groaned when he slipped a finger inside, but then she pushed him roughly away.

"Not now," she gasped. "Not this time. I want you inside me, Bas. Please."

As if he could deny her anything.

He reached for the nightstand and withdrew a condom then slipped it on and pushed inside.

Fuck.

That was—she was—he was beyond ready to blow and in seriously dangerous territory.

"Baby?"

Bas peeled back his lids then promptly had to grit his teeth. Rachel was flushed, her lips kiss-swollen, her brown eyes liquid chocolate. "You okay, sweetheart?"

"Can you move now?"

Fuck yes, he could move.

He laughed, but that quickly turned into a groan when she squeezed some internal muscle that had stars flashing behind his eyes.

But he moved, dammit. He moved until she bucked against him, until she screamed his name and exploded around him, until he lost his battle with control and called out her name.

Collapsing next to her, Bas rolled to his side and pulled her close. Both of them were panting and covered in sweat.

"I'm out of . . . shape," she gasped.

"I have ideas how to fix that."

She snuggled close. "I bet you do. But this is *my* fantasy." She nipped at his jaw. "So, I'm giving you fifteen minutes to recover yourself, and then we're going for another set."

He pretended to consider that. "Workout instructor and disobedient student. I can work with that."

Rachel smacked his chest, but she was smiling, and Bas found that this start to the day, just waking up next to the person he loved, joking around with her, smelling the floral scent of her shampoo, watching her eyes warm as she looked up at him when he was just being himself, not some version of Sebastian he'd thought he needed to be, but just her *Bas* . . .

Yeah, he wanted to be Rachel's Bas more than anything else in his life.

More than a job.

More than any outside approval he'd thought he needed.

More than surpassing the ridiculous standards he'd set for himself.

He wanted this woman. Forever.

"I'm keeping you," he said.

"Oh yeah?" She pushed him flat on his back and straddled his hips, then adopted a really horrible Arnold Schwarzenegger accent while flexing a bicep. "You've been a bad boy."

"When does Arnold say that?" he asked, attempting to control his laughter.

"I'm improvising, okay?" She coughed, tried again. "I'll be back? It's not a tumor? Hasta la vista, baby?"

"Stop." Bas shuddered. "I take back the workout instructor fantasy. Immediately."

"It wasn't that bad." Rachel pouted then burst into giggles

when he just raised a brow and stared at her. "Okay, fine," she said. "It was horrible." And she was so adorably perfect that he couldn't resist kissing her all over again.

Love and laughter.

Yeah, he could build a life with that.

BAD DIVORCE

BILLIONAIRE'S CLUB BOOK 5

CHAPTER 1

Bec

BEC CLOSED the file she'd been working on and stretched her arms above her head. Her shoulders ached, her eyes burned—she'd gone way over the thirty minutes of continuous computer screen time her optometrist recommended—and she was the absolute last person left in the building.

Seriously.

Security had come by her office an hour earlier, telling her they'd locked up and the high-rise was empty.

Except for her.

She probably should have been lonely, being the singular human presence around, but Bec loved this time of night. It was after one, and she'd been in the office since six the previous morning working on a case she was preparing for trial.

But fuck, did she love finding a legal loophole in a contract and being the one to decisively close it.

Nothing was better than that.

Not being made partner several months before. Not the

money or the power. Not having a slew of paralegals whose job it was to go line by line through all the paperwork pertaining to her cases and find loopholes like the one she'd just spent hours scouring for.

Those were all intoxicating in many ways.

But still, nothing topped the law itself.

The different interpretations, the way it morphed based on a court's or judge's decision, how it changed from year to year. Even finding this particular loophole after all the others before her had failed sent her pulse thundering.

One lawyer to rule them all.

Snorting at her inner SciFi nerd—not that she'd had much spare time to indulge in any form of hobby as of late . . . okay, as of the last ten years, if she were being honest—Bec knew it was all worth it. Law was her first love, and it was a constantly shifting spider's web, a fragile and intricate and complex lover.

But it also made sense to her when so many other things in her world did not.

"And now I've killed my own buzz," she muttered before logging off her computer, grabbing a stack of files from her desk, shoving them into her briefcase, and then slipping on her suit jacket and black pumps.

Down the elevator, through the locked door to the garage, and into her car.

Quiet.

So quiet.

She'd grown up in New York—or at least spent enough of her formative years in the Big Apple for her accent to reflect her time there—and felt more comfortable in big cities. San Francisco was a nice metropolis, but it had a definite sleepy time . . . or at least the district where her office was located did.

Normally, she liked that, preferred it over the way New York had always buzzed with activity.

But Bec had been . . . feeling weird as of late.

She was used to city life—the expensive rents, the exhaust fumes that hung in the air at all hours of the day, the horns and sirens and screeching brakes.

But this quiet? Fuck, did it hit her straight in the gut.

Or maybe it wasn't the quiet so much as *disquiet?*

Bec was a simple woman. She didn't censor herself, didn't trouble over hurt feelings or someone's toes being stepped on. She took care of business in the quickest, most efficient way possible.

That was Rebecca Darden. What she was famous for—at least in the legal world.

No prisoners. Decisive. Smart as hell and not a fucking pushover.

She'd spent a lifetime studying and working and losing sleep and clawing and fighting and struggling against the pressures of being in a male-dominated field to become that woman.

And yet . . .

"Fuck," she said and turned on her car, making her way through the quiet city to her apartment. "I'm losing it."

Because she couldn't help but feel that even though she'd finally met her goal of being partner, of being revered and feared and even sometimes reviled—all fine qualities in her opinion— that she was missing out on something.

There.

She'd said it.

Rebecca *Fucking* Darden felt that somehow along the way to all her success she'd missed out on *something*.

Unfortunately, she couldn't figure out what the fuck that *something* was.

A bigger challenge?

Nope. A month before, she'd taken on a case with impossible odds and had just that evening figured out how to win it.

Longer hours?

Hell no. At this point, she was paying for an apartment she was hardly ever in.

More money? No. She already had an obscene amount.

Better relationship with her father? Nope. Things were . . . well, at this point, she'd pretty much given up hope for a happy ending in that sector.

Different friends?

No fucking way. Her group of women—and now a few men —were the shit. They kept her sane and laughed at her jokes and were really incredible people.

She loved them, and *that* was saying something, especially coming from her and her limited tolerance of bullshit. She didn't like easy, let alone *love* easily.

And she loved every one of them.

So . . . *what?*

That was the fucking problem. She *didn't* know. Normally, she'd just turn a particular puzzle over in her mind until she figured it out, as she'd done with the contract that evening.

But she'd been turning this freaking enigma over in her mind for months, and Bec was no closer to discovering the exact source of her unease.

"Boo fucking hoo," she murmured, pulling into her parking spot and making it up to her floor via her private elevator. The lift went directly to her penthouse—yes, the apartment she hardly spent any time in was a ridiculously expensive penthouse that required a series of codes to access it.

Because of that private elevator, Bec didn't expect to see another person waiting for her when the doors opened with a soft *ding* and she stepped off.

But there *was* another person waiting just outside her front door.

A person she never expected to see again.

Luke Pearson.

Her ex-husband.

It was one-fucking-thirty in the morning, and her ex-husband was sitting on the floor outside her apartment.

Asleep.

Fuming, she marched over to him and kicked his shoe. Hard.

"Luke," she snapped. "Why in the ever-loving fuck are you here?"

His lids peeled back, sleepy green eyes met hers. "Becky," he murmured. "You're gorgeous as always." The drowsiness began to fade from his expression. "Did you just come from work?" He glanced down at his phone. "Do you know what time it is?"

"Of course I know what time it is—" Bec bit back the rest of her words. Fuck, but wasn't this conversation an exact replica of the broken record they'd played *way* too many times over the course of their relationship?

She crossed her arms. "Never mind that." She shot him a glare that had withered balls much bigger than Luke's. "Why did you break into my apartment?"

He stood, towering over her. Once, Bec would have said that his size made her feel petite, feminine, soft, which was atypical for a giant Amazon such as herself. Today, it just pissed her off. She was tall for a woman, almost six feet in heels, and was used to using that fact to her advantage.

No longer hunching her shoulders to appear shorter. Hell, no. She wore heels if she wanted and as high as she wanted—

And she had this man to thank for that fact.

"Stand tall, sugar pie," he used to say.

Yes, Luke had called her—world-famous, tough as shit lawyer—*sugar pie*.

But that had been a long time ago, when she'd been broken and . . .

Her heart, the one she liked to pretend didn't actually exist, pulsed with old hurt.

Because she'd merely been an entertaining side project for him, a broken toy to fix, a puzzle to figure out and one to discard when he couldn't find a satisfactory answer.

Memories.

Aw.

Motherfucking memories.

"First, I didn't break into your apartment. This is the hall. Second," he hurried to add when she opened her mouth to argue semantics, "I didn't break in. You used our anniversary as the code."

Oh, for fuck's sake.

Well, she was changing that tomorrow . . . today . . . fuck, *yesterday*, now that—

"Go away, Luke," she said, pushing past him and unlocking her door while blocking his view of the keypad that was identical to that of the elevator. Her front door's code was *not* the date of her anniversary with her ex.

But Luke probably already knew that, given that he had been sitting on the floor of her hallway rather than on her couch, beer in hand, feet making prints on her glass coffee table.

Men.

Fucking men.

She slammed the door closed behind her and secured the chain lock. The knock approximately one second later did not surprise her. Bec dropped her briefcase to the floor then opened the door just enough to shoot angry eyes at him through the narrow gap the chain allowed.

Serious green eyes fixed onto hers. "We need to talk."

"Luke," she snapped. "I'm exhausted. It's the middle of the night. I wouldn't have any patience to talk to my best friends right now, let alone my ex-husband."

"Funny story about that," he said, his lips curving. "Turns out that I'm not actually your *ex*-husband."

CHAPTER 2

Luke

HE YAWNED and rubbed a hand over his mouth, neck aching, head pounding, back stiff as shit.

Man, he was getting old if he was sore just from sleeping.

Except . . . he opened his eyes and finally clued into awareness.

His Becky had always said he was slow.

His lips twitched. Because he'd loved nothing more than when his Becky gave him sass. Luke pulled out his cell from his pocket, checked the time, and grinned as he pushed to his feet outside her apartment. He'd fallen asleep in the hallway, after listening to Becky moving around inside, probably fixing a cup of tea, slipping into a pair of those silky, stupidly expensive pajamas she loved, and finally padding on quiet feet to the door, no doubt to check if he'd gone.

Luke had shifted to the side by then, well out of sight of the peephole, so he'd heard those soft footfalls hesitate by the door before they'd retreated back into what he presumed was her bedroom.

Then his imagination had gone to work, or further R-rated work anyway, picturing Becky sliding between satin sheets, stripping off those silken pajamas, reaching a hand down between her thighs—

Yes, he was a sick bastard.

No, he didn't give a damn.

Regardless, it was early, barely six, and so Luke was in prime position to get a jump on Becky. It had been after two before she'd headed to bed, and even his workaholic of a woman wouldn't already be in the office. Plus, he'd slept here so she *couldn't* avoid him again. He'd get her to talk to him, get her good and mad so she couldn't ignore him.

Because while it might have been a decade since he'd seen his Becky, Luke had never forgotten her.

Never gotten over her.

Never regretted something as much as letting her go.

Yes, they'd been young and stupid and beyond immature at twenty-five. They'd had no business getting married, and he'd had no right to be hurt that the woman he'd loved was a go-getter.

Becky had more drive in one of her pinky fingers than most people had in their entire lives.

That work ethic wasn't common amongst their kind.

Kids with rich parents, who never wanted for anything, who always had the best clothes and cars and toys.

But they'd also been just kids.

Kids who'd wanted nothing more than their parents' attention and kids who'd been shipped off to boarding school. They craved attention and love more than anything, and they hadn't been able to find it at home.

Or maybe that was just Luke.

Except . . . once upon a time it had been Becky, too.

He rubbed a hand over his face and stood, trying to shove

those memories down. He'd been hurt, *so fucking hurt*, Becky had left—even though he'd done his best to push her away—that he'd signed the papers.

Divorce papers.

Super smart.

But that was Luke.

Make him mad enough, and he'd do stupid shit without a second thought.

Or, that was *usually* the case—a lack of second thoughts—but despite his best efforts, Luke *hadn't* forgotten Becky. Not then, not now, not ever. He'd had plenty of regrets. And when he found out the small county courthouse Becky had filed for divorce in had burned down, that their paperwork hadn't ever been fully processed, Luke had hoped.

For the first time in forever, he'd hoped.

His father was dead, his mother was busy traveling the world, and his sister was happily married.

Luke's life consisted of him . . . and the oil company. And while he'd enjoyed the challenge of running the family business, Pearson Energy, had loved spending the five years since his father's passing converting the company's focus from fossil fuels to renewable solar and wind sources, it wasn't enough.

Yes, he'd sound like a fucking pussy admitting this, but he was lonely.

And no woman could compare to Becky.

Not his former fiancée (and the reason he'd discovered he was still married to one Rebecca Darden), not the string of girl-friends and one-night stands from the last ten years.

Becky was it for him, and he'd been a fool to try to pretend otherwise.

Sighing, he reached out a hand to knock on her door. He'd let her escape the previous evening—earlier that morning—

because she'd had dark circles under her eyes and a hint of panic in her expression.

Like one of his horses.

His mouth curved, knowing Becky would definitely hate that comparison, and he shifted, readying himself to knock again.

That was the moment he heard the crinkle.

Luke glanced down and his stomach dropped.

A note.

Another fucking note.

His temper spiked as he bent to pick it up then it flared to molten, furious attention when he unfolded the paper and read the contents.

> *Go home, Luke. You know we only make each other miserable.*
>
> *-Bec*
>
> *P.S. I changed the code.*
>
> *P.P.S. Next time you try to hang out and "surprise" me, consider the fact that there's a camera in this hallway.*
>
> *P.P.P.S. Route any documentation regarding our former marriage to my office at McAvoy, Darden, and Associates.*

"Go home," he muttered, knocking once more to no answer, listening for sounds of movement inside before conceding that he'd lost this round. Becky must have slipped past him.

He headed for the elevator, punched the down button.

"Go. Home," he repeated.

He'd done that before.

And it had been the biggest mistake of his life.

Luke might be a lot of things—stubborn, stupid, and worse—

but he didn't repeat his mistakes. He learned from them, and so . . . no, he wasn't going to leave.

His lips curved into a wicked smile. Besides, in her note, Becky had all but told him to visit her at work.

Nope. Luke wasn't going anywhere.

CHAPTER 3

Bec

SHE DRANK GREEDILY from her mug of coffee, wishing her bloodstream could immediately absorb the caffeine.

No sleep made for a grumpy Bec.

Especially when the cause of her lack of sleep was Luke fucking Pearson.

Her ex-husband.

Or not, according to him.

"Bullshit," she muttered, scowling as she strode down the hall and into her office. The few enterprising interns who'd began to mirror her work schedule—in early, leave late—skittered out of her path, eyes going wide, and the non-tired, non-muddled-by-Luke portion of her brain forced herself to suck in a breath and relax the lines.

The Darden glare wasn't needed at six in the morning.

Despite Luke and despite the fact that she'd stayed up all night, watching the camera, waiting for her ex to leave or at least fall asleep so she could run.

She never ran.

Except from Luke.

Sighing, she shut the door behind her then sank down into her desk chair. Her office was plush, a visual representation of the thousands of hours she'd spent clawing her way to partner in one of the top employment law offices in the nation.

She'd focused on employment law because of an unpleasant incident at her first internship.

For lawyers, they'd been really fucking stupid.

The disparity between the hours she'd put in and the opportunities she'd been given versus those of her male coworkers had been so big it was almost hysterical.

Billionaire tech-founder for a father or not, Bec had busted her ass. And ultimately, her father didn't really matter, not when the other interns—all male, as she was the only female— each came from equally powerful families.

Yes, she was privileged to have been given the internship at a prestigious firm in the first place, but that was pretty much where any advantage had ended for her.

She'd spent the better part of three months twiddling her thumbs in her cubicle.

Until she'd watched one too many of her male colleagues be pulled into an important meeting with a higher up or invited out for drinks or given an opportunity to work on an interesting case.

She'd been invited to get coffee.

Seriously.

Top of her class at Harvard Law during her first two years, and she'd been relegated to coffee pickup.

Which would have been fine, she didn't mind paying her dues, and she'd be lying if she said she didn't send interns out for coffee regularly, but she made sure *all* her interns took a turn at the underling stuff and that they *all* got a chance with the big, interesting cases.

But ultimately, her not-so-fun internship had been a good thing. It had shifted her focus from corporate to employment law. She'd graduated number one in her class, and then passed the bar on her first try.

And because she was done with privilege, she'd applied for jobs under her mother's maiden name. No more hanging on Daddy's coattails, no more opportunities because of his connections.

Nope. She'd made her own way.

And Luke had been by her side the whole time. They'd met at boarding school, friends then lovers then, unbeknownst to both of their families, they'd become husband and wife.

He'd moved with her when she'd gotten into Harvard, had gotten accepted into the business school there, readying himself to take over his family's company.

He was driven, sexy, and he got her.

He loved that she was tough, that she didn't take any shit.

Until he hadn't.

Ugh.

"Nice, Bec," she muttered. "Nice little trip down a fucked-up memory lane." She set her coffee down and booted up her computer, shoving all thoughts of Luke deep down, back in the locked box in the depths of her heart, icing it over and throwing some barbed wire on top for good measure.

It was airtight, with more security than Fort Knox, and she knew no feelings would dare escape.

She had work and friends.

You have work. Only work. You don't care about anything else.

The thoughts were in Luke's deep drawl and thoroughly unwelcome. He didn't know her. Not any longer. She worked long hours because she loved it, but she also had a life outside the office.

She was fine.

Hell, she was even a godmother to Abby's baby, Emma.

That was something.

That was something normal, not something a cold, robotic, work-a-holic—

And damn, why, after a full decade, did those words still hurt?

Because they'd been shouted at her by the one man she'd opened her heart to, the one man she'd loved and been vulnerable to, and—

Yeah, *that*.

Sighing, she took another sip of coffee and settled down to work, pushing Luke from her mind, shoving away all thoughts that didn't revolve around their doomed marriage, and focusing on what had become her one true love over the years.

The law.

Bec dove headfirst into the safe puzzle of the law.

THE KNOCK at the door wasn't welcome.

It must still be early if someone was knocking at all, because her secretary knew that a closed door meant no freaking interruptions.

None.

None.

But before Bella was in, sometimes people forgot.

New people.

Annoying people.

"Come in," she growled, when the knock came for a second time, the idiot on the other side not recognizing that a closed door and no answer meant *go the fuck away*. She kept eyes focused on the screen, fingers hovering over the keys, typing paused midsentence as she waited for the intruder to speak.

When they didn't, she finished her sentence, sighed, and glanced up.

Then nearly knocked over her coffee.

Luke was inside her office, leaning against the closed door, paper bag in one hand, tray with two cups in the other.

That wasn't the worst part.

Nope, the really horrible, terrible, *awful* part was the expression on his face. Soft and almost gentle, with the slightest smile on his lips. It called to that part of her locked deep within, despite the ice and barbwire and steel-reinforced rebar. That paired with the curl of brown hair falling across his forehead, his biceps bulging under the sleeves of his black T-shirt, and his jeans . . . well, he'd filled out in the last decade because his thighs . . .

Thick, muscular, and *yum*. Her own thighs reacted to the sight, squeezing together, a hint of dampness in between.

Just from a look.

Fuck.

Her body still remembered his.

And he knew it, based on the way his mouth curved into a sinful—and egotistical—grin.

He was beautiful, and he also knew *that*.

Which, luckily for her, was enough for her to remember the past, to remind her who she was in the present—that she was tough and smart and didn't fall for cocky assholes.

You'd like a little cock—

Enough.

She was Rebecca Darden. She didn't cower or avoid. She faced shit head on, and she was certainly strong enough to face her ex-husband.

"Luke."

His brows rose at the icy tone, but it didn't seem to have any other effect on him. He didn't turn and leave like any other man would have done in his place. Instead, he pushed off the door, rose to his full height—still six-foot-three but no longer the lanky boy from the past—and crossed over to her desk.

After plunking the tray and bag on the wooden surface, he sank into the armchair across from her.

"Becky."

Her temper pulsed. "It's Bec."

He stared at her, raised a brow. "Bec," he repeated, and she tried to ignore the fact that it didn't sound right coming from his lips.

She wasn't his Becky anymore.

She waited for him to say anything else, perhaps to explain why he'd intruded on her at work, barreling through her office defenses, interrupting her morning.

But instead, he just sat silently in that chair.

Stifling a sigh, Bec turned her attention back to the brief on her screen, going back a few sentences, trying to remember her place so she could find her flow again. Luke was perhaps as stubborn as she was and, her lawyer skills aside, she'd never been able to pry information out of him.

Wait and see.

That was the only tactic that worked with him.

Wait and see if his disappointment grew.

Wait and see his back when he'd reached his limit and walked away.

She got it. She was a hard sell for most guys, difficult and not a woman to cut anyone any slack, but Luke was supposed to have been different.

She had been different with him.

And it hadn't mattered.

Enough.

Bec reread the sentences again, found the place she'd left off, and with another stifled sigh, she pushed on with her work. It was challenging at first, but after a few tooth-pulling sentences, she managed to find her focus, and pretty soon she was absorbed in the case again, fingers pounding across the keyboard, words filling up the screen, and . . . then she was done.

Stretching her neck from side to side, she saved the document then leaned back in her chair.

Her breath caught in her throat.

Because Luke was watching her.

Part of her brain had known he hadn't left, but that had been a distant part, and she certainly hadn't expected him to be *staring* at her while she'd worked. She could have imagined him waiting her out while scrolling through his cell phone, but studying her as though she were the most intricate, fascinating snarl of law language he'd ever encountered?

No.

Not that. *Never* that.

"Why are you here, Luke?"

"I've missed you."

Crack went the ice around her heart.

CHAPTER 4

Luke

HE'D SPENT close to an hour watching Becky work, memorizing the little frown between her eyebrows, fingers itching to smooth back the lock of her hair that had slipped free of her ponytail.

Luke used to tuck those strands behind her ear, used to trail his hand along her neck, loving the way she'd shivered at the touch.

Eventually, she glanced up at him, eyes going a little wide, lush lips parting.

"Why are you here, Luke?"

He told her the truth. "I've missed you."

For a second, he thought she might tell him that she missed him, too, that the decade apart wasn't actually a huge barrier between them being together in the here and now.

Then her face locked down. "No."

"No?" He raised a brow.

"No." Becky popped to her feet, started pacing. "No, you don't miss me. You *can't* miss me. It's been ten years without a word, Luke." She stopped at the window, facing away from him, hands on her hips. "What?" she asked, whipping around to face him. "You saw the article in the *New York Times* about my work and decided to fuck with me? Or maybe the Pearson family business needs an influx of cash? Have you managed to run it into the ground in just five years?"

God, this woman could take him from zero to livid in under one second.

A heartbeat before, he'd been admiring her beauty, the soft lines of her lips and jaw, and now he . . . well, he was still admiring her lines, except he wanted to bend her over her desk and admire the curved lines of her ass or kneel between her thighs and admire the *lines* of her pussy with his tongue.

Except, then he processed her words. *Five years.*

His temper eased.

His mouth curved. "How'd you know I've been running Pearson Energy for five years?"

Becky's shoulders went stiff. "What?"

Luke stood, walked over to her. "You've been keeping tabs on me."

"Fuck no," she snapped, crossing her arms. "I've been busy living my own life, not pining after you." But her eyes didn't meet his. Instead, they slid to the side, focusing on some point over his left shoulder.

Gotcha.

One step closer. Near enough to smell the familiar scent of her. Peaches and bourbon. The south in one inhalation, even though she was a Yankee.

"You're even more beautiful than I remembered."

Her breath caught.

He pressed his advantage. "I should have never let you go."

Lips parted, eyes went soft.

He brushed the backs of his knuckles across her cheek. "I was an ass."

Truth, but also the wrong thing to say, because the moment his words processed, Becky's face went hard and she started to turn away.

Luke caught her arm. "We were good together, sweetheart."

A scoff. "Like oil and water."

"No, like *forever*." He shook his head. "If I hadn't been such an idiot, we would still be together. We were forever, sugar pie."

Becky yanked her arm free, marched over to her desk. She scooped up one of the coffees, brought it her lips, and guzzled the now-cooled drink. Then she peered into the paper bag and froze.

He crossed back over to her, leaned a hip next to her on the desk. "I remembered."

Her sweet tooth. That she'd rather have chocolate for breakfast because it contained the same number of calories as a coffee cake or bagel with shmear or—

She rolled down the top of the bag and shoved it away. "You need to leave. I looked at my records last night. Everything was signed and filed correctly."

"Of course, it was," he told her. "That was never even a question." She was an excellent lawyer and there was never any doubt she'd crossed her T's and dotted her I's. "The issue wasn't with your paperwork, but rather that the county courthouse burned down."

Finally, her gaze rose to meet his.

"Because of the fire, the paperwork was never processed. And according to Carey County Texas"—where Pearson Energy was headquartered, where they'd gone down to his local church and had a secret wedding—"we're still married."

Those pretty hazel eyes widened. "How would you even find that out?"

And now it was Luke's turn to not look at her. His eyes skittered away, one hand came up to rub the back of his neck. "I was engaged," he admitted, daring to glance back at her.

Dimmed.

Any lightness in her expression disappeared, just flicked away as effortlessly as though someone had flipped a switch.

"Ah. And so I'm in the way of your latest conquest," she said, coolly. "What is she? Porn star? B-list movie actress? No, it had to be a supermodel."

Considering Luke *had* dated all of those over the last decade, he couldn't exactly fault her logic. There was also the fact that Tiffani—yes, Tiffani with an *I*—*had* been a model. She was also a jewelry designer and an entrepreneur, and successful in her own right.

She just wasn't Becky.

And luckily, he'd discovered that *before* the actual wedding.

Becky read the truth on his face.

"Ah," she said, a smirk curving her mouth. "I'm right. A model."

"Tiffani is very talented," he said, feeling obliged to stick up for his former fiancée. She was a beautiful woman, both on the inside and out, and incredibly sweet.

They'd gone down to pull their marriage license from the courthouse a week before their wedding, only to be informed that he was still married.

Shock. Embarrassment. Then . . . relief.

That he didn't have to marry Tiffani.

Yes, he was a fucking asshole to have felt that way, but it had also lined the pieces up in his mind, fitted them together in perfect symmetry for the first time in an eternity.

"Tiffani," Becky muttered and rounded her desk, putting the block of wood between them. "I'll put something together, make sure it indemnifies us both monetarily for the last decade."

Her gaze met his. "No spousal support, no properties to separate. It'll be quick and painless and get you back to your *Tiffani*."

"No."

One brow rose. "*No?*"

Luke strode around the desk, getting very close to her, loving that her lips parted slightly when he was near. It gave him hope that somewhere deep inside her, she might still feel something for him, that she wasn't as cool and detached as she was pretending to be.

Of course, it also made him want to kiss her.

"No," he said again. "Pushing you away was the biggest mistake of my life. Now that I have you again, I'm not letting you go."

Her hands plunked onto her hips. "But here's the thing, Pearson, you *don't* have me."

"Maybe not." He held her gaze, saw the flicker in those gray depths.

"So, I'll take care of the filing, and—"

"*No.*"

The tops of her cheekbones went bright red; fury flickered across her eyes.

"I don't want a divorce, sugar pie," he said. "I want to give us another try."

Becky exploded into motion, shoving him back, moving past him . . . or trying to anyway. He snagged her wrist. "Sweetheart—"

"No," she snapped this time. "*No.* You don't get to throw me away like trash and then just waltz back into my life. You don't get to decide that because all your other options didn't work out, you'll return for your leftovers." She jerked her wrist out of his grip. "I'm worth more. I *deserve* more. I don't need you in my life, Luke. I really fucking don't."

"I know."

That froze her in place.

"*I* need you."

Her jaw dropped open as he closed the distance between them. "But if you can convince me that you really don't feel anything for me, that your life is perfectly fulfilled without me, then I'll go." He ignored the fire in her gaze and gently touched her cheek. "I'll let that door hit me on the ass and sign whatever pieces of paper you send my way."

She lifted her chin, opened her mouth—

"*If* you can convince me that you feel nothing."

She stiffened and jerked away. "Of all the disgusting, egotistical, asinine things I've ever heard. *I* have to convince *you*? I don't *have* to do a damn thing, Pearson."

Fuck, but he loved when she called him by his last name.

But he couldn't let that distract him. Not when he had Becky where he wanted her, not when she would sense such a vulnerability and take ruthless advantage.

Luke crossed his arms. "Then, I stay."

"*Ugh!*" She threw her hands up. "What then, Luke? What do you want from me?"

"A kiss."

Becky stilled. "What?"

"One kiss. You don't feel anything, and I'll leave," he said. "But if you *do* feel something, I get to stay for a while."

Gray eyes narrowed. "How long's a *while*?"

"Ten dates. One to make up for every year I fucked up. I get to choose the days, times, and locations. I'll work around your schedule," he added when she started to protest. "But you'll have to promise to not purposely block or avoid me. At the end of it, if you decide that you've had enough of me, I'll leave. No negotiations, no fight."

Her brows pulled together for a moment before relaxing. "Fine. Not that the terms matter, since your little experiment won't prove anything. One kiss, which will be nothing, and you'll leave, sign whatever I send to you."

"One kiss," he agreed, "and I'll sign. But *I* get to kiss *you*. No cheater smack of your lips against my cheek, like you'd kiss a child."

Her face fell before she could hide it, and Luke was glad he'd thought of and closed that particular loophole.

Silence then a heavy sigh. "Fine. But when I don't feel anything, you'll go."

"Deal." He extended his hand.

She placed her palm in his. "De—"

He tugged, knowing he had to act before she had time to erect all her defenses against him. The movement brought her close, her front pressed tightly to his, her mouth mere centimeters from his. Gray eyes darkened, lips flushed pink. Wisps of her blonde hair escaped her ponytail and curled around her face. Luke watched her blink, knew he couldn't let her regain herself, couldn't let that control reappear.

Sex had never been their issue. Their chemistry was off the charts, and he was affected by their proximity himself, considering he was rocking a boner like a sixteen-year-old.

But Becky was smart and strong and stubborn as fuck. To win this battle, she'd suppress even the most overwhelming need.

In this one moment, Luke needed to be smarter, stronger, *more* stubborn.

Because this was his shot.

And he wouldn't get another chance.

He bent, flicked his tongue against her lower lip. Becky jerked, lips parting, and Luke took his chance. He pressed his mouth to hers.

Heat.

Sparks.

Right.

He angled her jaw, lining up their lips, slipping his tongue inside to tangle with hers. She stiffened, staying lax, and his gut clenched. It was a Hail Mary, pure panic on his part to snap her out of herself that prompted him to nip her bottom lip. She jumped, stiff for one long heartbeat before she melted against him, breasts flush against his chest, soft curves he was desperate to caress.

But he'd promised one kiss.

And nowadays, he kept his promises.

He slipped his tongue back between her lips, finally coaxing hers to dance intimately with his. Her hands came up, wrapping around his neck and finally, *finally* she let herself be taken over by the kiss.

Victory and relief flooded through him in equal waves.

But he knew he couldn't let himself completely lose his mind. He needed to stay sharp with his Becky or he'd lose the biggest gamble of his life.

So he pulled back way before he wanted to, loving that her eyes had slid closed, that her body listed toward his. Luke cupped her cheek and pressed one more kiss to her forehead before stepping away.

"Not unaffected," he said softly. "I win."

Lids flashed open, reddened lips parted to speak—

"I'll call you," he said and high-tailed it out of Becky's office, closing the door behind him.

This thing with Becky wasn't one battle.

It was a war. And in war, a man had to know when to make a strategic retreat.

He had ten dates to plan.

CHAPTER 5

Bec

SHE STARED, stunned and beyond turned on, at the closed
door to her office.

What in the fuck had just happened?

Bec sighed, returned to her chair on shaky legs—not that she
would ever admit such a thing to *anyone*—and sank down into
the plush leather.

"Luke Pearson happened," she muttered. "The low-down,
sneaky bastard."

Except . . . he hadn't kissed like a bastard.

"Ugh." She pounded a few keys on her computer, opening
her email and weeding through her inbox while stewing on the
problem that was her ex. She cleared everything important
before pulling up a browser and searching for the number for
the Carey County clerk.

One glance at her clock showed her that with the two-hour
time change, they should be open, and so she dialed the number.

Two rings, one ten-minute conversation with a very friendly
employee—way more friendly than her local California office—

and Luke's story had been confirmed. The courthouse had burned down, all in-house records were lost, and because they hadn't yet switched to having files backed up electronically, anything that was in the middle of being processed there had been lost.

Everything that had been stored off-site was fine and *those* documents were now in the electronic system.

Which meant that according to Carey County, they were still married.

Even though she had paperwork that said she'd filed for divorce ten years before.

Sigh.

It would really be a simple fix to push through a divorce now. No judge would deny them, not with the papers signed and the filed stamp clearly on them, but . . .

She had promised Luke ten dates.

What in the fuck had she been thinking?

She was Rebecca Darden, supposedly an intelligent lawyer. And she'd been manipulated by her ex-husband.

Husband.

Yeah, yeah. A technicality.

But why had she agreed to those terms in the first place? It wasn't like her to agree to anything that might put her at a disadvantage.

So . . . why?

Why agree to the kiss-slash-no feely-slash-ten dates plan?

Oh yeah, because she'd been overconfident and thought she could control herself around Luke. Which was a fucking joke since he'd *always* been able to make her melt. But she also couldn't deny—and dammit she really hated admitting this, even to herself—that she'd wanted to see if he *could* actually make her feel something.

And he had.

Oh boy, he had.

Her thighs clenched just remembering.

She sighed, picked up her cell, and leaned back in her chair, considering. It only took her a few minutes to face facts. She was in over her head, and that could only mean she had one recourse.

Bec needed to bring in the girls.

My apartment. Tonight at 7 pm. I'll provide wine.

A year ago, she never would have sent the text, but today, with her group of dirty best friends, she knew when she needed to call in reinforcements. They'd supported each other through thick and thin, and Bec *knew* they would have her back.

Abby replied first.

You okay?

Bec sent back:

Physically I'm fine. But I think I've just been put in an emotional blender.

Abby:

Damn. I can't believe someone got the best of Bec Darden, but I'm in and I'll bring something filled with a suitable amount of carbs.

Cecelia chimed in.

Colin and I are in Scotland. I'll conference in.

Then Rachel.

I'll bring my actual blender. I think this might call for more than wine.

Heather:

I'm in Berlin with Clay. I'll kick him out and be ready. A beat. *Who do I need to kill?*

Seraphina:

I'll bring something to soak up Rachel's booze.

After thanking her friends, Bec grinned and set down her cell. Her girls were the absolute best, and she didn't know what she would do without them.

Probably lose her mind, that was what.

But she couldn't shake the feeling that Luke might have already absconded with her brain.

Ten dates?

Fucking nuts.

THE DOORBELL RANG at a quarter to seven, and Bec hurried to answer it. She was still in her work clothes, having only made it home and inside a few minutes before.

"Hey," she said, swinging it open without looking through the peephole. "Come in. I'm—"

The words stuck in her throat.

Luke was outside her door. Again.

And he looked sexier than should be allowed in a pair of faded jeans, boots, and a fitted navy sweater.

"Hi," he said and pushed past her into the apartment, leaving her standing there, still holding the doorknob.

She let it go, grabbed his arm, and tried to shove him back out into the hall.

"I changed the code," she said. "I swear, I did."

He plucked her fingers from his biceps, clasped them in his. "You did." A shrug. "Turns out I'm good at picking your codes." He lifted her hand to his mouth, pressed a kiss to her knuckles. "Senior prom was a good night."

Her heart pulsed.

It had been.

And how in the hell had he remembered the date? Furthermore, how had he known she would use it?

"Don't think that was about you," she grumbled, tugging at their still-laced hands and trying to shepherd him out the door. "I was tired last night, and it was the first thing I thought of." She glared. "I have plans tonight. You need to leave."

Before her friends saw him.

That was a scene she really didn't want to deal with.

The verbal details would be bad enough. She didn't need to contend with the physical perfection of the specimen that was Luke.

"What kind of plans?"

His growly tone made her pause and narrow her eyes at him. "None of your fucking business, Pearson. We may still be married, but you don't have any right to know what I'm doing and when I'm doing it."

He cupped her cheek. "There's my Becky."

She jerked her head away. "*Bec*."

"Bec," he repeated. "I won't mess up your plans. I only came to give you something and to get your number. I promised to call," he added at what was no doubt a confused expression on her face.

She hadn't been confused about the number part, rather the give her something part.

Was it a sexual reference?

Because, honestly, she wouldn't mind if Luke gave her *something* along those lines.

But then he held out his hand, and her heart skipped a beat.

On his palm sat a tiny glass dolphin.

She'd always loved dolphins. And chocolate for breakfast.

And he remembered.

Another tiny fissure appeared in that icy box deep in her heart, and panic promptly spiraled out from that point, spilling into her gut, making her hands shake. Luke seemed to realize this and carefully set the little dolphin on her console table then pulled out his phone.

"What's your number, sweetheart?"

Bec shook her head. This was too much, too soon. She was too vulnerable and couldn't risk . . . her heart, her happiness, *herself*.

"415-555-2345"

It wasn't Bec's voice that'd provided her cell number. She turned, saw that Abby, Rachel, and Seraphina were gathered in the hallway.

Abby flashed her a thumbs-up.

"Thank you, darlin'," Luke said. He started to leave, paused next to Bec. "I'll call you later."

And for the second time that day, she was at a loss for words.

"It's good to see you, Abigail."

Abby smiled beatifically up at him. "You, too, Luke." Then her eyes narrowed, and that smile faded. "You hurt her again, and I'll cut you." Rachel and Seraphina nodded in agreement.

Luke blinked. He'd lifted his arms as though to hug Abby, but froze mid-reach, eyeing the three women. "I won't," he promised solemnly.

Bec snorted. Yes, it was laced with derisiveness.

No, she didn't care.

Abby glanced at her. "Time to go, Luke."

He slanted one more look at Bec, and she didn't have to be smart or a lawyer or the top of her class to see it was filled with promise. She only needed to be a woman, to be *Luke's* woman.

Luke Pearson was back.

And he wouldn't be leaving any time soon.

CHAPTER 6

Luke

HE'D JUST SAT in the driver's seat of his rental car when his phone buzzed. Considering he'd just sent a text to Bec, he assumed it would be a retort that would make his ears bleed.

The thought made him grin.

Then he opened the message.

That grin faded and his stomach twisted, because contrary to what he'd hoped, the message wasn't from his Becky, but rather from his mother.

I've given you a lot of rope, Luke.
I won't let you hang yourself with it.
-Mom

A man takes *one* leave of absence from the company he devoted a good portion of his adult life to, and everybody freaks out.

I'm fine, Mom. Enjoy your time in the Maldives.
Love you.

The " . . . " appeared on his screen, signaling a forthcoming reply, and Luke closed his eyes, praying for patience. His mom was not what one would call tech savvy—for one, she still signed her messages 'Mom'—and he knew that any message he received would be a long time coming as she typed out one . . . letter . . . at . . . a . . . time.

Sure enough, it took a solid two minutes for her to send:

You haven't been yourself since your engagement ended.

Of course, he hadn't. One moment he'd been prepared to walk down the aisle, to marry a woman he thought he loved, and the next, his life had taken a sharp right. Luke had been relieved —knees shaking, hands trembling, heart pounding relieved—that they couldn't pull the license. He'd known then he couldn't marry Tiffani. That she deserved better, more than an asshole like him.

And Luke realized how much of a fucking idiot he'd been all those years before. He'd lived in blissful ignorance for a long fucking time, pretending his marriage imploding had been Becky's fault—she'd filed the papers after all—but then he'd realized they were still married and . . . he'd allowed himself to remember everything.

How good it had been between them. How bad it had been at the end. What she'd done. What *he'd* done.

And, newsflash, his behavior had been appalling.

He'd held the thing he loved the most about Bec against her, had been jealous of her drive, of the career she was trying to build, of the early success she'd found when he'd been stuck with only two options: a shitty position, looking forward to years of paying his dues or caving and going to work for his father.

He hadn't caved, but he'd ended up in the family business anyway.

And before that? Luke had done everything in his power to push Becky away.

Not surprisingly, he'd succeeded.

*I'm trying to change that, Mom. California is good
for me.*

He'd started the car and pulled out of the parking garage before his mom's reply came.

Change things faster. The business won't hold forever.

Yeah. *That* Luke knew firsthand.

Sighing, he drove to his hotel, back to the empty suite, to his laptop filled with emails about business concerns he wasn't supposed to be tackling during his time away, back to emails he was answering anyway.

What else did he have to do?

His life was empty, and the one woman he'd truly loved in his life didn't want anything to do with him.

Rightfully so, but . . . he was still bordering on pathetic.

Sighing, he dialed his COO, Brian, and went over a few of the more problematic issues, before promising to fly back to Texas for an important meeting the following week.

After they'd dealt with the pressing business concerns, Luke mentioned an idea that had been bouncing around in his brain since he'd come to California. Brian was a flat sort of guy, limited emotions, few words, and so Luke took his, "We should definitely explore that further," as a raring endorsement.

Hell, the other man had even included an adverb, and that *never* happened.

"Do me a favor," Luke said before he hung up, "pass along the grapevine that I'm working while here, okay?"

There was a pause then, "Your mother?"

"My mother," Luke agreed. "Help me put her at ease."

"Done."

Then the call disconnected and . . . silence.

Luke was alone again, but that had been a common enough occurrence over the years, and so he was used to it.

He clicked on the TV, called room service and ordered a hamburger, fries, and, what the hell, he added a slice of chocolate cake.

Luke Pearson sure knew how to live.

CHAPTER 7

Bec

ABBY CLOSED the door and leaned back against it, staring at her with a glare that rivaled Bec's own signature Darden Death Glare.

"Put that away," Bec snapped, waving a hand through the air and turning toward the kitchen. "I'm going to spill everything, okay? That's why I called this emergency meeting for the Sextant."

Rachel followed her. "I'll grab the glasses."

"Thanks," Bec muttered, deliberately avoiding Seraphina and Abby's gazes. "Sit down and get the other two knuckleheads on the phone."

Sera stepped in front of her, arms crossed. "Why was Luke Pearson lurking in your hallway?"

"Living room!" Bec pointed.

Abby held up her cell, revealing CeCe and Heather's faces on the screen. "We're all here, so spill."

Bec grabbed a bottle and opener. "I need more wine for this."

Rachel snatched it from her. "Go, sit down. I'll do this."

"You don't know where everything is. I can—"

"*Bec.*"

A unison of voices calling her on her shit.

"Ugh. *Fine.*" She strode into the living room and plunked down onto the couch.

"Nope," Abby told her, tugging her back up and shoving her in the direction of her bedroom. "Pajamas first. We'll get everything ready."

Bec nodded and escaped to her bedroom.

Why had she invited this maelstrom of femininity into her house in the first place? Oh yeah, because she'd been trying to prove to herself that Luke's words from the past didn't matter . . . or not that they didn't matter so much as they were no longer true.

She wasn't just work, only work, all work. She wasn't a lawyer robot without a heart.

She was a living, breathing human with real feelings and emotions.

And like only seventy-five percent work.

Twenty-five, yup a solid twenty-five percent, were meaningful, important, and dare she say, significant sentiments because they did not revolve around her work.

Bec was just nodding to herself in the mirror, a confident, encouraging bob of her head she'd given herself more than once before an important case, when she heard the blender start up. And now that she was paying attention, she could also smell pizza. Or at least something equally carby and cheese-filled.

Her stomach growled as she slipped on a pair of pink fuzzy socks.

"Pizza's here!" Sera called just as Bec was pushing to her feet.

"*Yes.*" She opened the door and went out to join the girls.

Her shoulders inched higher and tighter with each step, but she forced herself to relax them. Even putting her desire to prove Luke wrong aside, she knew that calling in her friends was the right thing to do. They were there for each other, hands down, no holds barred, no judgment—okay, so maybe a *little* judgment because they truly wanted what was best for each other, and sometimes that required tough love with a dash of judgment thrown in.

Regardless, she'd handled Luke alone before, and look where that had gotten her.

She needed the Sextant, and she needed them STAT.

Rachel stuck a margarita in her hand the moment Bec crossed the threshold into the living room. "Drink first. Talk second."

Abby scoffed. "I disagree with that notion because . . . uh . . ." Her words trailed off, probably because Bec had drained the entire glass in just a few swallows. "Never mind."

Sera laced her arm through Bec's and led her to the couch. "So, Luke's in town, huh?"

Bec nodded, reaching for another glass, wine this time. Maybe the combo of the two liquors would bring her oblivion, make her forget that she'd agreed to go on ten dates with Luke. Maybe then she could pretend she hadn't been bested by the man who'd broken her heart.

"So who is Luke exactly?" Rachel asked.

"Bec's ex-boyfriend and fiancé. Sera, Bec, and I met him when we were all shipped off to boarding school," Abby said. "He went to the boys' high school next door."

"You had a *boyfriend?*" CeCe asked.

Bec bristled at the shock in her friend's tone. "I'm not asexual," she grumbled. "I've dated, had boyfriends." She gulped down some wine. "And, I like penises. I just haven't had much use for them of late."

"Sleeping with people isn't exactly dating." Sera grinned. "Also, I think the proper term is peni."

"Nope." Heather. "Definitely not. Also, *ew*, Sera. The word *peni* should never come out of your mouth."

"Why?" Sera made a face. "Why do you all get to be dirty and I can't even say *peni*?"

"It's penises!" Rachel said, lifting her own glass to her lips. "And I don't know, Sera. You're like . . . too innocent."

Blue eyes glared. "I own five vibrators!"

Silence then a collective, "*Ew.*"

"Oh my God," Sera muttered. "You guys are evil."

"It's like an innocent old lady telling me how she likes to get off." Heather shuddered.

Sera glared. "I'm neither old nor innocent."

"You don't even like to curse," Bec reminded her.

"Well, how about this? Fuck. Fuckity. Fuck."

More silence.

Then Abby shook her head and wove her arm through Sera's. "Nope. Just doesn't compute. You're too nice, Sera."

"I've decided that being nice sucks," she muttered. "But"— she sighed and straightened her shoulders—"enough about my *innocence.* I want to hear more about Bec and Luke."

One big gulp of wine to fortify herself before Bec blurted, "We're married."

Silence. And this time it had nothing to do with Sera's vibrators.

Heather was the first to regain her voice. "Well, this is unexpected."

CeCe snorted. "Because she took a page out of your book?"

Heather shushed her. But CeCe's teasing was on point. Heather and her husband Clay had pulled a Vegas cliché by getting blackout drunk and then standing up before an Elvis impersonator to exchange vows.

Enemies in the business world to husband and wife, all before they'd gone on a single date.

"I didn't take a page out of Heather's book," Bec said, setting her glass down and leaning back against the couch. A pleasant swirling feeling was circling around in her head. "We did have a secret, impulsive wedding. It was just ten years ago."

And more silence.

"I—" Abby started to speak then stopped with a shake of her head, out of words for maybe the first time ever.

Sera touched Bec's arm. "Why didn't you tell us?"

She kept her eyes closed. "I thought we were divorced."

"There's a plot twist I didn't expect," Rachel said into the quiet.

Bec sighed. "We got married right before I graduated from law school. We'd been dating for a lot longer than that, though. Since senior year of high school." A shrug. "Getting married seemed like the next logical thing to do."

Abby found her words. "But we all expected you two to get married. You were together for ages. Why hide it?"

"His parents wanted us to wait. No." She shook her head, enjoying the way her brain seemed to slosh around in her skull. "That's not entirely true. Yes, they thought we were still a little young, but there were plenty of people in our circle who'd gotten hitched." A shrug. "Luke and I had always planned to get married. I guess I pushed the secret wedding because I wanted something that was ours and ours alone."

"Then what happened?" A gentle probe from Sera.

Bec smiled. "We had a really good nine months. We'd graduated, were both working, living together. It was—" A sigh, her eyes filling with tears at the memory of late nights poring over work, ordering in pizza, getting up early to brew his favorite type of coffee, making love, and Luke holding her tightly afterward. "It was about as perfect as you could get."

"Is he hot?" Heather.

Four sets of eyes—three in Bec's living room, one through the airwaves—swiveled to glare at Heather.

"*Really?*" Sera asked.

But Bec shot Heather a grateful look, which Heather acknowledged with a nod. She might be opening up to her friends, might be sharing her sad, sad tale, but dammit, she wasn't a fucking watering pot, and she absolutely refused to cry over Luke Pearson.

Been there, done that. Got the souvenir shot glass.

"He's even hotter now," she admitted, begrudgingly.

"I second that," Rachel chimed in. "Well, I didn't know him before, but the view I got tonight . . ." She brought her fingers to her mouth, affecting an Italian chef. "Muah! The man can fill out a pair of jeans."

Abby sank down on the couch next to Bec. "Yes, he's hot, but what's he doing here now?"

Bec explained about his engagement, the courthouse burning down, and their divorce paperwork not going through.

"Is he still engaged?" CeCe asked, concern edging into her voice.

Bec froze. "I don't know."

Heather and Abby began talking, Rachel and CeCe chiming in with an occasional comment, but Sera didn't join the conversation. Instead, she snatched up Bec's phone, smiled at what she saw on the screen then began typing something, thumbs moving furiously.

"What are you—?"

"He's not engaged," Sera announced.

The girls stopped talking.

"How do you know?" Heather asked.

Sera shrugged. "I asked him, and he said, and I quote 'I couldn't marry Tiffani because I knew I was still in love with

Becky.'" She held the phone to her chest. "Aw. That's so sweet."

Meanwhile, Bec couldn't find a retort because her heart was pounding.

I was still in love with Becky.

Love.

Becky.

Finally, her brain unstuck. "Give me that," she said, snatching it from Sera's hands.

It's Bec.

A pause.

Hi, sugar pie.

She narrowed her eyes at the phone, damned stubborn man.

Bec. Not Becky. And sure as shit not sugar pie.

Barely a heartbeat before,

How about sweetheart?

"Oh, I *like* him," Rachel said, making Bec jump and look up from her cell. She hadn't realized that Abby, Sera, and Rachel were huddled around her.

"What'd he say?" Heather asked.

"She said her name is Bec, just Bec, and so then he asked if he could call her sweetheart," Abby stage-whispered.

Bec made a sound of disgust when she saw Heather grin.

"You guys are the worst."

"You love us," CeCe said, lips curved into a wide smile.

"Maybe," Bec grumbled.

"Group hug!" Abby declared, and before Bec could protest or wiggle away, three sets of arms wrapped around her.

"I'm hugging you, too," CeCe declared.

"I'm not," Heather declared. "This is just too cheeseball for words."

"Shut it," Abby said. "You love our hugs."

Heather sniffed but didn't deny that fact.

Bec's phone buzzed, and they pulled back, all looking at the screen. On it was a day and time, followed by a question mark.

They all glanced at Bec for an explanation. "I kissed him—"

Sera squealed.

"To prove I didn't feel anything for him."

If Bec had been feeling amused, she might have laughed at the way her friend's face fell.

"We made a bet," she said. "If I felt nothing, he'd go away and we'd officially get divorced."

"And if you felt something?" Heather asked.

"I'd go on ten dates with him. One for every year we've spent apart."

Sera sighed. "That's so romantic."

"And?" Abby prompted. "What happened?"

Bec made a face in answer.

"Holy shit," Rachel said.

CeCe crowed. "This man must be something to get the best of Rebecca Fucking Darden."

"Don't remind me," Bec muttered. "I made a shitty agreement, and I felt something, and now I've got to go on ten dates with the only guy who's ever broken my heart."

"But—"

"He couldn't handle me or my success a decade ago. How the fuck is he going to react differently today? My work—"

"Doesn't define you," Heather said.

If anyone besides Heather had said those words, Bec would have been able to brush them aside. But coming from Heather O'Keith, quite possibly the only other person on the planet who'd pulled as many hours as her, they weren't so easy to dismiss.

"Yeah," she muttered.

"I think the bigger question here," Abby said, "is why did you agree to the deal in the first place?"

"I—"

Abby made a slashing motion with her hand. "No. No excuses about how Luke is so sexy he made you lose your head. That's bullshit." She met Bec's stare head on. "And you know it. *No one* has ever made you do something you didn't want to, so you need to come to terms with why you agreed to this in the first place." She touched Bec's hand. "And whether your agreement means that deep down you really want this second chance with Luke."

"Damn," Rachel said, tone awe-filled. "She's good."

Sera smiled. "Yes, she is."

Bec didn't reply. She'd been too shocked to the core by the truth in Abby's words.

Thankfully, her friends seemed to recognize that, so they changed the subject to CeCe and Colin's latest travels, and then a hilarious story involving Abby's son Hunter, and then an idiotic investor who'd tried to double-cross Heather and hadn't stood a chance.

A few hours later, Heather and CeCe hung up, and Rachel, Sera, and Abby packed their things.

Hugs and goodbyes and a raised eyebrow glance from Abby punctuated their departure. Bec nodded, letting her friend know she'd truly heard her statement earlier that evening and was seriously considering it. There were some things that didn't require words after close to twenty years of friendship, and Bec's acknowledgment of Abby's insight was one of those.

With one last goodbye, she closed and locked her door.

Her cell buzzed and she wasn't surprised to see a text from Abby. Yes, there were some things that didn't require speaking, but her friend didn't often have the willpower to be silent.

Go along for the ride. You might decide you like it.

Bec sighed, sent a text back,

I did that once. Want to guess where it got me?

A beat then another buzz.

Multiple orgasms?

Yes, but that was beside the point.

Goodnight, Abs.

One more buzz.

Goodnight.

A beat. Then a GIF of a cheerleader shouting, "Go for it!" came through. Bec grinned despite herself and headed into her bedroom. Her friends had done the dishes, despite her protests, but it *was* nice to just slip between the cool cotton sheets and close her eyes.

Unfortunately, they didn't stay closed for long.

Maybe it was the alcohol. Maybe it was Abby's words. Maybe she'd just gone insane.

Or perhaps it was all of the above.

Because Bec opened the text chain from Luke, grinning when she noticed that Sera had saved his number with the name Sir Sexy Pants.

The man sure could fill out a pair of Levi's.

Not the point, but her slightly-buzzed mind still spent a good minute picturing that yummy, two-glorious-handfuls of an ass in those faded jeans.

Yup. She wouldn't mind grabbing on to that as he pounded into her—

Focus.

Bec blinked. Read back through the chain and mentally lifted her chin as she typed out a response.

*Sweetheart TBD. Depends on how good you are on
Friday night.*

A long minute passed before a reply came through.

I mean to prove to you how good I can be.

Heaven help her, but she wanted to see exactly how good that was.

CHAPTER 8

Luke

UNACCOUNTABLY NERVOUS, that was Luke.

And not only because he wasn't sure if Becky would show up for their first date, but also because . . . he wasn't sure if Becky would show up for their date.

Hilarious.

But bad dad jokes aside, Luke had a sudden case of what-if-he-was-doing the wrong thing? Not about coming back for Becky or trying to convince her that they were worth a second chance . . . but what if at the end of this she didn't want to be with him?

Then it was too late for doubts.

A car pulled into the empty lot and parked right next to his rental. He knew it was Becky even before he caught a glimpse of her through the windshield. The car just screamed Rebecca Darden, sleek and dark with just enough of an edge to make him proceed with caution.

Luke pushed off the hood of his rental, made his way over to

Becky's, but before he could open the door and help her to her feet, she'd gotten out.

That hadn't changed.

Still independent, still would force him to find creative ways to care for her.

"Hi, sweetheart."

She crossed her arms. "Don't sweetheart me," she said. "You haven't earned *sweetheart* privileges yet."

He swept in, pressed a quick kiss to her cheek. It took every bit of his willpower to not stay close, to not soak in her scent and nuzzle the spot just beneath her jaw that used to drive her crazy. The only reason Luke didn't do those things—well, two reasons he supposed—was because, first, she hadn't given him those rights and, second, she was wary. This would be a battle won with patience and small steps.

And if Luke had learned nothing else over the years, it was how to be patient.

Patient while he paid his dues in the corporate world. Patient while he helped a father who despised needing him. Patient while he dealt with a nervous board and paranoid investors.

He could be patient if required.

His Becky required it.

"Hi," he repeated, stepping so close that she had to tilt her head back in order to keep meeting his gaze. That nearness fucked with his mind, made him want to get closer, to bend and close the gap between their mouths. But only millimeters separating them also meant he could see Becky's reaction. See he wasn't the only one affected.

And that gave him hope in his plan.

Her lips parted, tongue darting out to moisten the bottom one. Just that tiny poke of pink against red had him hardening.

He wanted that tongue in his mouth. He wanted that tongue on his cock.

He wanted *his* tongue in—

Not. The. Time.

Luke sucked in a breath and took a step back. "Come on." He turned, walked away from her, even though that was the last damn thing he wanted to do.

But *patience*.

Stifling a sigh, Luke moved to the edge of the parking lot, to where he'd set everything up, pretending casualness but not actually relaxing until he heard Becky's soft footsteps trail him across the asphalt.

"What are we doing here—?" Drawing equal with him, she sucked in a breath.

"Remember senior prom?"

Becky had gone stag, even though they'd been dating, wanting to support Abby and Sera, who'd broken up with their boyfriends just before the dance, and Luke had spent the whole night drooling over her in her skintight red dress.

But it had been after the dance was over, when she'd climbed into his car and they'd driven away from the school together, that they'd created the real memories.

He laced his fingers through hers, tugging her forward and onto the plaid blanket he'd laid out. A bottle of sparkling apple cider sat in one corner, sandwiched by two glasses, and a box of It's-Its sat in the other. Vanilla ice cream sandwiched between two oatmeal cookies and dipped in chocolate, they were a treat from Becky's childhood.

Luke had been eighteen, okay? It's-Its and sparkling cider were about as romantic as he'd gotten at that age.

Hence the blanket on the grass in an empty park. Yes, the night had been pretty, the stars as bright then as they were that evening, but he hadn't considered much besides getting

Becky alone and convincing her to let him score a kiss . . . or more.

Eighteen, remember?

Her eyes hit on the box of treats and her lips curved. "Really?"

He shrugged. "It was the first time you let me kiss you, of course, I had to reenact it."

"Kissing is what got us into this mess in the first place, remember?" she grumbled, but she slipped her hand from his and sank down onto the blanket anyway, reaching for the box of treats. "A little easier to get these this time," she said.

Considering Luke had gone to close to a dozen stores back then trying to find Becky's official Bay Area It's-Its—no East Coast imposters would do—he had to agree.

Today, he'd visited one grocery store and scored the goods. Selecting a park that had been similar to theirs from that night had been a little more difficult. Turned out that creeping around neighborhood parks after dark made him look like a drug dealer, at least according to the cops who'd visited him while he was scoping one out a few nights before.

Luckily, handcuffs hadn't been involved . . . or rather, Luke hadn't ended up *wearing* them. Thankfully, the officers had taken pity on him after he'd confessed all, even giving him a hint for a good location to take her.

Not that Becky needed to know any of that, especially the almost-handcuffed part. Tonight, he just wanted her to relax, to remember the good things about them.

Or at least that Luke knew her well enough to bring her It's-Its.

She tore into the box, pulled one out. He sat next to her, waiting while she unwrapped it and devoured half. Only after she sighed contentedly, pausing her scarfing for a few moments, did Luke ask, "As good as you remember?"

Becky turned her face toward his, and he saw a hint of the girl she'd been.

Content to just sit with him, to enjoy a grocery store treat, to smile up at him like he was the answer to everything wrong in her life, in the world.

A hero because he'd bought her some chocolate-covered, ice cream-filled oatmeal cookies that had been half-melted by the time they'd eaten them, despite the cooler he'd packed them in.

Life was simpler in high school.

"I haven't had one of these in ages," she murmured. "Still the best ever."

He opened the cider, poured two glasses, and handed her one. "Still a good way to stave off homesickness?"

Becky took the glass and sipped before setting it aside. She lay back on the blanket, arms crossed behind her head, gaze on the stars. "I'm home now."

"Doesn't mean there isn't something to miss."

"Hmm." She kept her eyes on the sky. "Stop hovering over me and lie down. The stars are beautiful."

"*You're* beautiful."

"Pish." Becky waved a lazy hand. "Down."

Luke complied, lying back on the blanket, careful to keep a few inches between them, just like he'd done as a scared teenager, trying to make a good impression on the girl he was infatuated with.

He was still striving for that good impression.

Or at least a reformed one.

They stared up at the sky, silence descending between them, not uncomfortable, exactly, but filled with the tension of the past and the high stakes of the present.

"I'd half-expected you not to show up," he said after a few minutes.

Becky shrugged. "I made a promise."

"Why *did* you make the promise?" he asked, rolling to his side to study her. Moonlight gilded the lines of her face—turning her pert nose, smooth jaw, and plump lips into something reminiscent of a marble statue.

Beautiful and yet somehow untouchable.

She shifted onto her side and watched him, gray eyes almost black in the dim light. "You won the bet, remember?"

He raised a brow, waited, and . . . there it was.

The slightest flicker of emotion. She wasn't just holding up her side of the agreement, there was something more, a deeper feeling, a draw that wasn't easy for her to dismiss, and for now, that was enough.

"I had wet dreams about that red dress of yours for years." Luke had gotten his sign, and now he wanted to say something to jar her out of her worries, to see the woman who didn't take any shit, to see that sass he loved so much.

The teasing statement worked. Becky's jaw dropped open, and fire flashed in her eyes. "You're a pig."

"You knew that I was slavering over you that whole night, watching you dance with the girls, hiding a boner in my slacks, and dying to get my hands on you."

A wicked smile curved her lips. "Maybe I liked teasing you."

"All I knew is that I *loved* it." He laughed. "Spank bank material for days."

"Such. A. Pig."

"Definitely the luckiest pig around," he said.

"You were the sweetest boy around." She sighed, expression almost gentle. "I think that night—the treats on a moon-gilded blanket—was the first time in my life someone did something for me just because they knew I'd enjoy it."

And he'd ruined that. *Fuck.*

He gritted his teeth against the fury he felt at being such an idiot. "You deserved the world, and I—"

Soft fingers brushed his jaw. "You always were good at beating yourself up." She rolled back over, eyes up on the stars again. "You know what I remember from that night?"

He shook his head when her head tilted back toward him, her stare finding his.

"I remember you being upset at yourself that you'd forgotten to bring an extra blanket because I got cold in my skimpy dress. I remember you giving me your jacket and the first glass of cider. I remember the feel of your lips on mine, the heat of your tongue, the way our mouths seemed to fit perfectly together." Her voice dropped. "And . . . I remember thinking it was the best first kiss a girl could ask for."

"I—"

"The problem between us never was chemistry or romance. And it wasn't grand gestures or simple date nights. You were always way better at that stuff than I was."

He was still spinning from her revelation that he'd been her first kiss. She'd never told him that, and Luke felt a pulse of disquiet, wondering what else she might have withheld. He brushed the back of his knuckles down her arm. "So if that wasn't the issue, then what *was* our problem?"

"We weren't compatible," she said, tone less matter of fact than he'd expected, considering the plain words. In fact, it was almost gentle, at least until she pushed to her feet. "We wanted different things. We *still* want different things. Simple as that."

Luke sat up, but she sidestepped him when he reached for her hand then bent to pick up the box of It's-Its and turned in the direction of her car.

"I want you," he said. "Any or every part you want to give me."

She paused, fingers on the door handle. "What happens when you don't like what you're given?"

"That's not possible—"

Her chin dropped to her chest. "Nothing was ever enough for you, Luke. Not me. Not us. Not—"

"*You're* enough."

Wrong answer. Becky shook her head, pulled open the door, and got into her car. Luke watched her drive away, not sure if he'd blown this whole thing before it even got off the ground or if progress had been made.

The past still had its claws in them.

The plus was that Becky was actually talking to him.

CHAPTER 9

Bec

SHE WAS RAW INSIDE.

She had to take back control.

She . . . needed to focus on work.

Bec sighed and pushed her chair back. It was Monday morning, and normally she would be raring to start her work week, but . . . It's-Its and a plaid blanket, memories of tentative kisses and strong arms.

Luke Pearson had been back in her life for less than a week, and last night he'd—

What?

Made her feel something? Made her ache for their past to have been different?

Of course. But fuck, the thing about life was that they *couldn't* go back.

And so now she was scrambling, trying to find her happy in the law and loopholes and briefs, and she still couldn't change the past.

She and Luke had their chance, and it was ridiculous to try to resurrect something that had nearly destroyed them both.

Stupid, even.

Rebecca Darden wasn't stupid.

She had to end this. Now. Yesterday.

Picking up her cell, Bec began composing the text in her mind. She'd have to be firm, deliberate in pushing him away, otherwise—

Her eyes processed what was on the screen.

She hadn't even heard her phone buzz, but sure enough, on the screen was a text from Luke.

You promised me ten dates, don't back out now.

"Ugh!" She flopped back into her chair, temper spiking. If the annoying specimen of a man had gone sweet and gentle, tried to convince her to keep giving him another chance nicely, it would have been so easy to give him the kiss-off. But, dammit, he'd gone and called her honor into question.

Well, fuck honor.

She opened the text chain, started to type a reply, but another message came through.

Don't be a chicken now, Darden.

Double ugh. Now he was questioning her lady balls.

And, double dammit, she had giant lady balls. Luke Pearson didn't scare her.

Nope. Not in the least.

Then why are you looking for one of those loopholes you're so good at finding? Hmm? her brain accused.

Nine dates. Nine nights. Nine—

Oh God, she couldn't do this. Any good attorney worth her

salt knew when she needed to take a step back and regroup. She groaned, dropped her head to her desk. Because how did she regroup against the yumminess that was Luke?

Yumminess?

Had she really just used that word?

Thunk. Maybe she could use her desk to knock some sense back into her brain. *Thunk. Thunk. Th—*

"I knew you'd be like this."

Bec glanced up and saw Seraphina standing in the doorway of her office.

"What is it with everyone invading my work lately?"

Sera propped one hand on her hip, her *assets* jiggling with the movement. Really, her boobs were insane. If Bec hadn't seen them appear junior year, she would have been convinced her friend had spawned from another planet. Slender, a beautiful face, and as tall as Bec, Sera was beyond buxom and even more gorgeous than most actresses or models.

And the worst part about it?

She was *nice.*

Like, super nice. Like as nice and kind and beautiful on the inside as she was on the out.

Great. Now Bec sounded like a teenage Valley Girl.

Like this. Like that. Like—

"Why are you staring at me like I've suddenly sprouted antennae?"

"Because your boobs are superhuman."

Seraphina rolled her eyes, crossed to the front of Bec's desk, and all but threw a container of food at her. And no wonder Bec hadn't heard her phone buzz. Despite feeling off her game, she'd worked almost six hours straight.

"Molly's?" she asked hopefully.

Sera scoffed. "As if I'd bring you anything else." She dropped into the chair and opened her own container.

"Spinach, goat cheese, and apples. Plus, I got you extra walnuts."

"You're a goddess."

Sera huffed. "That's what the idiot cashier said."

Seraphina wasn't unaware that she was beautiful. She'd spent a lifetime dealing with boys and men, *and* women for that matter, fawning over her. But Sera was also the least superficial person Bec had ever met.

Many a person had said that Sera's beauty was wasted on her because she just didn't care about the way she looked.

She didn't want to be an actress or a model or an influencer.

She wanted to find Mr. Right and settle down and be a mom.

Unfortunately, all the potential Mr. Rights seemed to be blinded by her beauty. They discounted her smarts—she was a successful real estate agent—and treated her like the dumb blonde bimbo she wasn't.

"Men are idiots."

"Not all of them," Sera said through a mouthful of spinach. "Some of them are good."

Forever optimistic.

"Don't look at me," Sera added. "I know I'm naïve, but I can't help it if I'm holding out for my happily ever after. Abby, CeCe, Heather, Rachel, they've all found someone. We can, too."

Bec made a noise that could be interpreted as agreement . . . or disagreement. One of those two, for sure.

Sera pushed the container closer to Bec and continued to eat. Bec stared suspiciously at her friend, waiting for the interrogation to start. She wouldn't break under Sera's probing—she was Rebecca *Fucking* Darden, after all—but she also wasn't looking forward to an argument.

When Sera got an idea in her head, she resembled a dog to a bone.

But despite Bec opening the salad and taking a large bite—fucking delicious with the extra candied walnuts, by the way—Sera's inquisition didn't come.

They ate their salads in between Sera relating the persistent pickup attempts of the cashier at Molly's, and pretty soon her friend had her in hysterics over the much younger man's melodrama.

"I mean, I try not to be judgmental. Age is really just a number, but I'm not into college drama students and especially one who can break into a soliloquy from *Romeo and Juliet* at the drop of a hat when I politely turn him down." She raised her fork toward the ceiling, punctuating her statement. "Does he even know how that play ends? This just in: it's a freaking tragedy."

"Unbelievable," Bec said.

"The worst part?" Sera moaned. "My love life's the real tragedy."

"That's not true," Bec felt obliged to say, though if she was being truly honest, tragedy *was* a fitting word for the gorgeous inside and out Sera to have not found a man to really appreciate her.

Sera dropped her container into the trash. "It's true. *Very* true. But then again, I'm not the one who has a sexy Texan wanting a second chance with her."

There it was.

Bec sighed. "Sera—"

She lifted her hands in surrender. "I'm not going to say anything, but if *I* had a man in my life who looked at me the way Luke Pearson looks at you . . ."

"That's saying *something*."

Sera kept talking. "Further that, Luke gets under your skin,

Bec. He always has, and for a woman like you, that's critical. Otherwise, it's just too easy for you to ignore the men you date."

"I don't ignore men!"

"Scott, Steven, Sam, Sean, Michael." Sera ticked off the names on her fingers. "Also, sidenote, you date too many men whose names start with the letter S." A grin. "I think it's the perfect time to include one that begins with L. Maybe even a boyfriend"—she coughed—"or a *husband* that beings with L."

Bec lifted one brow, disregarding the L assertion and restating the important facts. "I do *not* ignore men."

Sera did some disregarding of her own. "Luke is who you're supposed to be with, don't you see? He's your chance at an HEA! It's the perfect trope—a second chance romance with your high school sweetheart."

"Sera." Bec sighed, rubbed her temples. "Things aren't that simple. Real life isn't fiction."

"I know that."

"Except, you don't. You're so sweet and innocent, and you believe that everyone has good inside of them." Bec tossed her own container into the trash. "But I've seen shit. The world isn't good. There are loads of people who don't have your best interests in mind, who don't have any qualms about breaking your heart when you give them all the pieces of yourself."

Sera leaned back in her chair. "Ah."

Bec had been ready and raring for a monologue. Sera's *ah* took the wind out of her sails. "*Ah*, what?"

"You're scared."

Now *that* was just enough. That was the second time in the span of an hour that someone had accused her of being scared. She was Bec Darden, scared wasn't in her vernacular— unless it was felt by the person on the receiving end of her death stare.

"I'm not scared," Bec said. "I'm not the one who keeps

putting my life on hold, waiting for someone who may never come. I'm living and—"

Sera stood. "I'm going to stop you right there."

Bec blinked at Sera's tone. Never, and she meant *never*, had she heard such a tone from her friend's mouth. It was sharp and reprimanding and made Bec feel about two inches tall.

"I may be stupid for holding on to hope that someday someone may love me for the person who I am inside. That may be a *fucking* pipe dream"—Bec blinked again. Sera and F-bombs rarely mixed—"but at least I'm not too scared to take a chance on something just because it might make me vulnerable. And I think that makes me the brave one of this pair, don't you?"

She strode to the door, paused with her fingers on the handle. "Also, nice try on the pushing people away thing. It's kind of your specialty."

A heartbeat later, Sera was gone, the door closing softly behind her.

Bec would have much preferred a slam.

But then again, if Sera *had* slammed the door, it would have confirmed to Bec that her friend was irrational and emotional rather than logical and smart and . . . maybe right.

So, in full Sera-rant-hangover mode, she texted Luke. Just to prove to herself that Sera *was* wrong and Bec wasn't scared or unsure or—

Shut. Up.

It didn't matter why. Only that she did text Luke and found herself committing to a date the following evening.

Name your time and place, Pearson. Only nine more dates until you're out of my life forever.

CHAPTER 10

Luke

WHY HAD he decided it was a good idea to give his woman a weapon?

His Becky stared at him, weighing the ax in the palm of her hand. Then her eyes dropped to his groin, and Luke had to resist the urge to wince and cup his dick protectively.

Her lips twitched, and she turned to face the target, throwing the ax in a near perfect arch. It hit the bull's-eye but didn't stick, falling to the floor with a clatter.

"Nice," he said, picking up his own ax without any of Becky's unspoken threats.

"Come on, Mountain Man," she teased. "Show me how to work that hard, *hard* blade."

Considering he was mid-release when she said that, Luke was unsurprised that his ax missed the target completely and crashed to the floor. "Sexual euphemisms?" he asked, lifting one brow. "Really?"

A shrug, though her mouth was curved into a smirk. "If

we're revisiting our teenage and college years, then all of the *hard* puns fit, don't you think?"

"We never threw axes in high school," he said, walking over to pick his up from the floor.

"No," she said and hopped to sit on the little half-wall that formed the back of their booth. She was wearing skintight jeans and a plaid flannel with one too many of the buttons undone for his psyche.

Hell, who was he kidding?

They'd been together all of twenty minutes, and Luke had spent most of it fantasizing about what her reaction would be if he unbuttoned the rest of the fabric, spreading it wide, kissing down the soft expanse of her stomach, slipping his fingers under the waistband of her jeans—

"But we did go camping for our senior trip, which I'm sure you remember." One blonde brow lifted. "Considering it was the night we both lost our virginity."

Luke swallowed hard as he set the ax on the table.

Their boarding schools were technically separate—all boys in his, all girls in hers—but they'd combined for events like dances and the seniors' camping trip. So, yes, he'd been thinking of that weekend when he'd seen the ad for this place, of the outdoor games they'd played, of him pretending to help Becky with her archery skills—even though she'd been better than him by far.

It had been a weekend of teasing touches, of sneaking away for a few kisses, and yes, of their first time.

Luke crossed over to where she sat on the half-wall, nudging her legs apart so he could stand between them. Becky's smile was teasing, and he wanted to kiss it off her lips. Especially when that dangerous little pink tongue of hers darted out, wetting her bottom lip, and her eyes went hot. "I think you'd like my hard, *hard* blade," he told her, somehow managing to not crack up when he said it.

Probably because his *blade* was, as Becky had said, hard, *hard*.

"Yeah?" Teasing laced with heat in her tone and so fucking tempting.

He leaned in, close enough to smell the floral scent of her shampoo, to feel her hot breath against his lips. "Yeah," he said. "I'd make sure you enjoyed it. You know that."

"Yeah?" she said again and leaned even closer, only millimeters separating their mouths and, fuck it all, he couldn't help himself.

Luke kissed that pretty mouth.

Thank God, she kissed him back. Her arms came around his neck, her breasts pressed flush against his chest, and that pert little tongue slipped into his mouth.

One hand gripped her hip, tugging her snuggly against him, while the other wove into her hair—hanging down her back in gentle waves that were beyond fucking sexy. He tilted her head, angling their mouths in order to find that perfect fit.

And then he lost himself in his Becky, kissing her the way she loved, groaning when she rose pressed closer to him, memorizing those soft, breathy moans rising from the back of her throat.

Luke's hand was sliding down to the buttons of her shirt when he remembered himself, remembered they were in a very public place.

One more stroke of his tongue, one more nip on the corner of her mouth.

Then he forced himself to step back.

And promptly almost kissed her again.

Because her mouth was swollen and reddened, and her eyes

were glazed. Because she reached for him and the feel of her hands against his chest was every-*fucking*-thing.

Fuck, but what wouldn't he give to have her back in his hotel room.

Except . . . sex was never the issue between them. They could scorch the cotton sheets right off a bed. But sex wasn't the answer now. It was everything else that needed fixing.

So he carefully trapped Becky's hands then stepped back, putting enough distance between them that he was no longer tempted.

Or rather, *less* tempted.

"Your turn," he told her and shoved an ax into those palms.

Then considered himself lucky that she didn't cut off his hard, *hard* blade and instead slowly moved to the starting line and threw.

Bull's-eye.

He stared over at his Becky and knew he was in big, *big* trouble.

But it was trouble of the best damned kind.

"You know what I don't get?" Becky asked an hour later, as they sat at a nearby restaurant chowing down on quintessential bar food. She held a half-eaten French fry between her fingers and dipped it in a pile of ketchup on her plate—or rather, she used it as a vessel to get the maximum amount of ketchup into her mouth.

She might as well just drink it straight from the bottle.

"What?" he asked when she'd swallowed, reaching for his own fry and scooping up what he considered a reasonable amount of ketchup, though Becky had already teased him more than once about his "dainty dipping."

"Why come back now?"

A reasonable question.

Though one he'd avoided discussing with any depth because he didn't really have a great answer.

How could he explain something he didn't understand himself?

How could he explain the relentless urge to make things different between them, that Becky was the piece that had been missing in his life?

"And silence," she said, picking up her beer.

Luke was aware enough to sense the edge of hurt under the droll tone.

"It would have been easier to stay away," he told her. "To have my lawyer contact you and get officially divorced, to marry Tiffani and just move on."

Bec plunked the glass down on the table. "Wow."

He snagged her wrist when she would have turned away. "I'm not going to lie. I considered doing just that." His thumb brushed lightly against her skin. "But I knew I couldn't."

She yanked her arm free, signaled their waiter for the check. "Well, you should have saved yourself the trouble and stayed away."

"Becky," he began.

"It's. Bec." She leaned close and hissed, "It would have been better if you stayed away. Instead, you waltzed back into my life on your terms, demanding my attention, and disrupting everything. I was fine, dammit. Totally fine a-and—"

Luke froze, the slight hitch in her tone telling him more than anything else could.

She might be putting on a good front, but his Becky was rattled and, honestly, he couldn't blame her. He'd shown up out of nowhere and had spent the last two weeks pressing her buttons.

"I'm sorry."

"—And you don't get to—" She froze. "You're *what?*"

One corner of his mouth ticked up. "I know they're words I haven't said nearly often enough, but I'm sorry. I'm sorry I was such an ass then . . . *now*." Her eyes softened, so he pressed on. "I'm sorry I didn't know what a good thing I had. I'm sorry I stormed back into your life without warning." He cupped her cheek. "But I'm not sorry that I'm trying to get you to give me a second chance. I spent the last decade searching for something, trying to prove myself to my bosses, my family, myself . . . and you want to know what I learned?"

A shrug.

"That the person I should have been proving myself to was you."

She shook her head. "Luke—"

"I had all this anger inside me—fury that my parents sent me away to school in the first place, that my father didn't think I was smart enough to succeed on my own and the only avenue my dumb ass had was the family business."

"You're not dumb, Pearson."

He scoffed. "You're brilliant, sweetheart. Always have been, and I was so *fucking* jealous of that, of how proud my parents were of your success. I was resentful when my father kept telling me that I should marry you because you were the best a fuck-up like me was going to get—"

"*What?*"

He released her hand, pushed his plate away. "When we moved away to school, he reinforced that. *Strongly*." Luke forced down the old frustration. "After he reminded me that the only reason I got into business school at all was because he'd donated five million for the new tech building."

"That's—"

Her sentence was cut off when the waiter deposited their check.

Eyes deliberately not meeting hers, Luke reached for his wallet to pay. When he went to drop his credit card on the bill, she covered his hands with her own. "Luke."

He pulled back.

"Look at me."

Unable to deny her, he met her gaze.

She studied him for a long time, gray eyes penetrating. Then finally she nodded, as though she'd judged what he'd said as truth.

"Why didn't you tell me?"

A soft question. One with a shitty answer.

"I was a twenty-five-year-old man." A beat. "I was an idiot."

Her mouth curved up. "Well, that was a given."

"I'm not twenty-five anymore." Luke touched her cheek. "After you left, I started a company. It did well, and in the end, it was my Dad who needed me."

"I heard about Breeze"—the company he'd sold when he'd moved back to Pearson Energy—"it did a lot more than *well*."

He shrugged. "Its success had a lot less to do with me and a lot more to do with having been lucky enough to find the right people." Breeze focused on wind technology and their R&D department had revolutionized the way batteries stored extra power on windy days, partitioning it up so it could be used on days where the weather didn't cooperate. The process was now used in most wind farms throughout the world.

"You're being modest."

Luke grinned. "Another thing I've learned over the years."

"What happened with your father?"

The urge to immediately close down was intense, but Luke knew he couldn't do that anymore. He'd wounded Becky in the past by refusing to talk about things, by shutting her down when she did ask . . . and then being resentful when she played the role of a glutton for punishment and pushed harder.

"Without getting into all the gritty details," Luke said, "let's just say my father made some bad investments."

"Your tone makes it seem like he made a *lot* of bad investments."

He nodded. "Enough that Pearson Energy was six months from folding."

Becky gasped.

"I know. Breeze licensed technology and partnered with them until they were back in the black." He turned his palms up, laced their fingers together. "Dad never forgave me. That's the irony of it all. For once, I was the savior, the one who'd been smart enough to make a difference, and he resented me for it."

"Asshole."

He squeezed her hands. "I won't disagree with you." He sighed. "Especially because he made me running Pearson a contingency of my mom and sister receiving their inheritance. Not that he asked me to step in and help him with things while he was alive. I only found out at the reading that if I didn't step in as CEO, the estate would be donated to charity."

Becky's brows pulled together. "I'm not sure that was legal."

Luke smiled. "My lawyer didn't think so either, but I was worried about what a legal fight would do to my sister and mom, and Breeze was ready for a new direction. I'm still on the board, but the new president is incredibly brilliant."

She pulled one hand free, dunked another fry. "Why do you sound so . . ." She wrinkled her nose. "I mean, that's *a lot* for anyone to compartmentalize. How are you so normal?"

"Therapy."

Her eyebrows pulled down and together.

"I'm serious. *Actual* therapy. Well, that and five years of chasing my father's demons down the halls at Pearson. Therapy.

Hallways. Both of those things helped me come to terms with a lot of stuff." He grinned. "I'm semi-well-adjusted now."

"Semi, I think is the key word," Becky said, but she left her hand in his and then changed the subject to one of her latest cases, relating a funny tale about her intern freaking out because he'd spilled coffee on an important brief. ". . . I couldn't help it," she said. "I waited until he came back in with a blow dryer he'd procured from somewhere and started blasting the sheets to tell him that I had an electronic copy on the cloud."

Luke had shifted closer as she spoke, until their sides pressed together, until he could almost pretend this was a real date, one he hadn't tricked, cajoled, *forced* her to come on.

The only thing he held on to was that she didn't push him away.

Maybe there was hope yet.

CHAPTER 11

Bec

LUKE WASN'T OUT of her life.

Not at all.

He'd somehow talked her into letting him walk her back to her apartment, and even though she'd licked her lips and sidled close to him on the ride up, he hadn't kissed her. Just punched the code on her elevator—which she'd changed again after the last time they'd ridden up together and which he'd guessed . . . again.

Bec sighed. She really shouldn't have picked the day she'd passed the bar.

Especially when memories of that night swarmed her. Of Luke struggling to open a bottle of champagne, of them giggling as they sipped the frothy beverage. He'd also brought her a chocolate cake, and because their apartment was almost completely packed up, they'd searched through the filled boxes for plates and cups—only managing to find one plastic fork— then had taken turns feeding each other bites in between drinking straight from the bottle.

Such a different time. She'd been such a different woman.

So sweet.

Both the cake and Luke Pearson.

Not her. *Never* her.

But she couldn't deny that Luke had always managed to bring out a softness in her. He'd always been able to cut through the barriers, the distance between her and everyone else.

Only Abby and Sera and Luke had been able to penetrate her defenses.

Bec didn't resent her armor. She'd needed it growing up after losing her mom in childbirth with her baby brother. Left alone with a dad who didn't really want her . . . or maybe that wasn't quite true, but she'd definitely been a poor substitute for his lost wife and son.

They'd moved from the Bay Area to New York for a few years—long enough that Bec no longer sounded purely California, long enough that she had a wide streak of New York in her voice. But then her father had moved back to California and . . . he'd left her at school.

Ten years old and stashed in an all-girls boarding school in Upstate New York.

It had been four long years before Sera and Abby had shown up for freshman year and another before Luke had been enrolled in the neighboring all-boys school.

Sera and Abby had basically friended her to death, hadn't left her alone, had pestered and bugged and bothered Bec until she'd relented and become part of a trio instead of a lonely single.

Luke, well, he'd been gorgeous with just a hint of a sexy Southern accent and piercing green eyes her heart hadn't been able to ignore.

No matter the armor and barbed wire.

He'd army-crawled his ass through, wedged himself deep inside.

It had been easier to pretend she'd evicted him from her heart all those years before, but as Sera pointed out, if Bec really *didn't* care about Luke, she never would have agreed to the deal in the first place. He'd only been able to goad her into the agreement because she felt *something*.

And it was time to stop lying to herself.

"How many times did it take you to figure the code out?" she asked as they stepped off of the elevator.

Lips curved. "Three."

She tilted her head. "What were the other dates you tried?"

"Wouldn't you like to know?"

She would. She really would. But obviously, he wanted her to ask, and she couldn't make it *that* easy on him. So, instead of pressing him further, she turned for her door.

"Did you figure out this one, yet?"

He bent, pressed four buttons on the keypad attached to the lock.

It unlatched with a soft *click*.

Oh.

Luke brushed his thumb across her lips. He leaned in, and her chin lifted, wanting his mouth, wanting him to take her into his arms again and kiss her senseless. Hot breath on her forehead, punctuated by a brush of his lips there then the same on her cheek, her jaw, just below her ear before he whispered, "I remember everything about you, sweetheart."

He nudged her over the threshold, quietly closed the door.

"Lock up," he said through the wooden panel.

She did then watched through the peephole as he strode to the elevator. Her phone buzzed just as the metal doors closed.

I can't wait to see you again.

Bec felt the same exact way.

But she was too much of a wuss to reply in kind. Instead, she pulled up her text chain with Sera and asked her friend to meet for apology salads at Molly's the following day.

The reply came in less than a minute.

You're my smartest friend.

A pause.

But just so you know, you owe me apology salads AND apology pastries.

Bec smiled.

Deal.

Her cell buzzed again.

And maybe apology soup.

She snorted.

Done.

"I'M THE WORST, and you're the best," Bec announced as she sat down in the chair opposite Sera.

Her friend had already been at Molly's for a good amount of time if the paperback, half-eaten salad, and empty glass of water were any indication, and Bec felt another pulse of guilt that she was late to apology salads.

"Well," Sera said, putting a bookmark into her paperback and closing it. "We already know that." She speared another bite of her salad.

"I'm sorry I'm late. I got—"

"Caught up in a case." Sera smiled. "I knew you'd be late. Arriving on time for lunch dates is your arch nemesis. It never fails that you're stopped on the way out of the office."

Since that was exactly what happened, Bec didn't know what to say.

"Pick a soup for us to share. I need an excuse to eat more bread."

Bec glanced at the menu. "Potato and leek?"

"And that's why we're friends." Sera reached across the table and squished Bec's cheeks, tone changing so it sounded like she was talking to a dog. "Because even though you don't like leeks, you'd still order it for me."

Bec smiled. "I don't *hate* them . . ."

"You once called them Satan's pubes of a vegetable."

"That was chives, I'll have you know. And I still stand by *that* statement."

Sera snorted. "Order the tomato, I'll get the leek and we'll live vicariously."

"Good plan." Bec got up to put in the order and then came back to the table with the triangular number placard. And in that amount of time—less than five minutes—realized why Sera had been reading earlier.

Not just because their Sextant loved reading and were ridiculously obsessed with any and all types of romance novels —even Bec wasn't jaded enough to not enjoy a fictional happy ending—but because the book had been a shield against unwanted male attention.

Male attention in the form of the Molly's employee Sera had mentioned the other day.

"Thou art—"

This was Bec's specialty.

She elbowed in between the man-child and Sera then plunked herself on Sera's lap, pressing a smacking kiss to her friend's lips. "There you are, baby."

Sera's shocked expression was worth it.

So. Totally. Worth. It.

In fact, Bec would have documented it for posterity if it wouldn't have blown the cover she was attempting to build.

She unleashed her glare on the man who was more boy than adult. "Leave."

His eyes went wide and his jaw worked for a few seconds before he spun around and left.

Bec pushed out of Sera's lap.

"What. The hell. Was that?" Sera exclaimed as Bec sank down into her own chair.

"You're welcome." Bec waved a judicious hand. "He won't bother you again."

"*Or* he'll get it in his head that he'll want a two-for-one special and then never leave either of us alone again."

Bec turned her head, sent another death glare at the boy who shrank back and hurried through a swinging door into the kitchen. "No, he won't."

Sera smacked her. "Leave poor Timmy alone."

"His name isn't *Timmy*," Bec said. "That's just too . . ."

"Tragic? Charles Dickens? Shakespearean drama?"

"That. Precisely."

A beat before they both cackled.

Sera pointed a finger at her. "I was never an asshole until I met you."

"You're still not an asshole," Bec reminded her. "You're pretty much the nicest person I know. Hence, the necessary rescuing."

Sera opened her mouth, closed it, and sighed before leaning close to Bec and whispering, "Well, I'm sorry to say your rescuing failed."

Bec frowned when Timmy appeared at her elbow. But he didn't make a pass or even risk eye contact. Instead, he dropped her salad and the two soups onto the table then all but ran away.

She smirked over at Sera. "See? Rescuing *was* successful."

"You're the worst." A shrug, a twitch of Sera's lips. "Or maybe the best. Thanks for making Molly's my safe space again." She fluttered her eyelids, dropped the back of one hand to her forehead. "Oh, Bec Darden, lawyer extraordinaire and possessor of the patented Death Stare, thank you for being my knight in shining armor. Shall I jump aboard your mighty steed and let you carry me away?"

"Sarcasm doesn't suit you." But Bec's lips twitched. "Okay, fine. I'm loving this snarky side of you."

Sera's eyes brightened. "Enough to mount me?" She waggled her brows.

"*Ew.*"

Sera huffed. "Why is it that every single time I make a dirty joke, *that's* the reaction I get from you and the girls? I'm dirty, too! I think about penises and love steamy sex scenes. I can even say"—her voice dropped—"cock."

Bec bursting into laughter. "I'm . . . sorry . . . but you can say *cock?* Oh my God, Sera you are the best."

Sera crossed her arms.

"Careful"—Bec gestured at her boobage area—"or Timmy will forget about my rescuing."

"Bec!"

"Eat, before I get called back to work."

"I need my flipping apology pastry after this abuse," Sera muttered.

Bec reached across the table, squeezed Sera's free hand, and gave her friend what she needed. "Thanks for being my friend."

See? She wasn't *always* an asshole.

Sera's eyes welled up and she dropped her spoon, clasping her hands over her heart. "I *knew* Luke was perfect for you."

Bec scoffed.

Sera stage-whispered, "You have *feelings* now."

"Shut up and eat your apology soup."

"It's *true*," Sera sing-songed.

"Don't tell anyone," Bec grumbled, shoveling her own soup into her mouth. Why had she been nice again? Assholes never had to deal with teasing.

Sera's grin was wide. "It'll be our little secret."

A secret that found its way to the Sextant's group text chain a mere half hour later.

Bec pretended to hate the attention.

But really, she was *secretly* happy that her family cared enough to tease her.

CHAPTER 12

Sera: Bec kissed me!

Abby: *Uh*, what?

Bec: She exaggerates. It was a smack, and I was in pure rescuing mode. Ask her about Timmy.

CeCe: Uh-oh. Timmy from Molly's? What did he do?

Sera: He quoted *Romeo and Juliet*.

Rachel: That sounds romantic, actually.

Bec: She turned him down, and then he began quoting lines from a Shakespearian tragedy. Definitely NOT romantic.

Heather: What does Timmy look like?

Bec: Doesn't matter, he's a drama major.

Abby: *horrified GIF*

Rachel: I second that.

Sera: He wasn't that bad.

Bec: He was worse.

Heather: He sounds worse.

Bec: Hell, yeah he was worse. Plus, he's all of twenty-one.

Sera: Too young for sure and frankly, too weird. But also . . .
Luke and Becky sitting in the tree. K-I-S-S-I-N-G.

Bec: I was wrong earlier. YOU'RE the worst.

Sera: *kissing emoji*

Abby: By my count, you've had two dates you haven't dished on.

CeCe: Exactly! I need details.

Rachel: It's my turn to host Wine Night.

Sera: Yes! Wine Night!

Rachel: :) Saturday. I'll kick Sebastian out. Bec bring all the details and the rest of you ALL the books. I need a new read. I'll provide booze and wine.

Bec: You know booze and wine are the same thing.

Rachel: Not to me they aren't.

Abby: I agree. They're two separate food groups.

CeCe: Exactly. Vodka is a veggie and wine a fruit.

Sera: *fist bump gif*

Bec: I'm friends with insane people.

Heather: I can't fault any of CeCe's logic. Stepping into a meeting, so am turning on Do Not Disturb, but I'll be there on Saturday.

CeCe: Me too. Colin and I are back from Scotland on Friday!

Abby: I'm boring and have no social life, aside from you ladies. Of course, I'll see you then.

Rachel: What she said. ^^

Sera: Ditto ^

Bec: Fine. Saturday.

Sera: Unless she has a date with Luuuuuke.

Abby: *rolling on the floor laughing GIF*

Rachel: Haha. Nice.

CeCe: *slow clap GIF*

Heather: Get back to work, ladies. *fist bump emoji* That's for you, Sera.

Bec: I hate you all.

CHAPTER 13

Luke

HE'D KNOWN this was bound to happen.

"I'm sorry," Becky said, and though her tone was laced with an apology, it also held a hard edge.

She was expecting him to be mad.

Like he used to be.

"Switch to FaceTime," he told her.

"What?"

Luke pulled the phone from his ear, pressed the button so he could see his Becky's face.

After a few seconds, it appeared on the screen.

Her blonde hair swept up into a messy ponytail, a pale blue silky tank top giving him a tantalizing view of her braless state. Fuck, she was beautiful.

"Sweetheart," he said. "Look at me."

Lips pressing together, she put what looked to be a toiletry bag down. "What?"

Ice in her voice now. Definitely expecting a fight. Or a guilt trip. He'd been good at those, too.

"It's okay."

She huffed. "I *know* it's okay. My job is important, and sometimes—"

"Sometimes it takes priority." Luke wished they were having this conversation in person rather than over the phone so he could tug her close and make her understand that this time everything between them was different. "Sweetheart, *stop*."

Gray eyes met his.

"We'll reschedule."

Hope danced across her face. "Yeah?"

"Of course, we will," he told her. "I need to fly back to Texas to take care of a few things actually."

"Oh, I didn't realize." White teeth nibbled at her bottom lip. "Is everything okay?"

He shrugged. "Yeah. I've been wanting to break into renewables in California. We've been looking for prospective sites in the Central Valley to try out some new technology our engineers have developed. I need to go back to the board with my proposals."

Becky picked up the toiletry bag again, and Luke spent a few moments staring at the ceiling while she stashed it in her suitcase. "You should talk to Heather."

"Who's Heather?"

She blew a strand of hair off her forehead, walking with the phone into the closet and pulling out a red power suit. "Heather O'Keith—"

"From RoboTech?" he asked, shocked. "We've been trying to set up a meeting with her for ages."

"Well, I think I can help you with that," Becky said. "For a price."

Luke grinned. "What price?"

"I get to plan our next date."

That grin faded.

"Becky—"

"Bec," she corrected. "And no negotiations either. You've had entirely too much control over this dating situation already."

"I don't see anything wrong with that."

Zip, went the garment bag. Up, went one of her eyebrows.

"We've had fun, haven't we?" he asked.

"I did like scoring more than you in ax throwing."

"Allegedly," he corrected.

The other brow went up. "Clearly, I won by ten points."

"You stepped over the line!" she said, lifting her suitcase to the floor and draping the garment bag on top of it before flopping onto her bed.

"Did not."

"The last throw didn't count."

"Did so."

"*Ugh.*"

"Sugar pie?"

"What?" she snapped, and Luke felt a blip of happiness when she didn't correct his use of the nickname.

"I like arguing with you."

She froze, lips curving up. "You're annoying."

"Of course, I am."

A shake of her head. "What am I going to do with you?"

"Keep me?"

Becky sighed even though her eyes danced. "Let me plan the next date, and I'll consider it."

"Relentless." A beat. "I wish you'd let me drive you to the airport."

"I have a driver," she said. "And my flight leaves at five. It's awful."

"He won't give you the goodbye kiss I will."

She tapped a finger to her chin. "Maybe. Maybe not."

"You fight dirty."

A shrug.

"Fine. You get to plan Date Three, but only if you let me come over in the morning and drive you to the airport," he added as her expression turned victorious. "I need to prove to you that I can kiss better than your driver."

Becky shook her head. "And you say *I'm* relentless." But her mouth was curved into a smile. "Fine. But be forewarned, I need to leave at three-thirty."

"I'll be there." She stifled a yawn and Luke smiled. "I'll let you get some sleep."

She snuggled into the blankets of her bed. "'Kay."

"Becky?"

"Hmm?"

Another blip of happiness as she let his *Becky* slip by.

"I like negotiating with you."

"I like *negotiating* with you too, Pearson," she said, eyes sliding closed.

Even though he'd just talked himself into getting less than four hours of sleep, when Luke hung up, he had the biggest smile on his face.

———

LUKE LIPS BURNED as he watched his Becky stride away, her hips swaying, rolling the small black suitcase behind her as she strode toward the private jet that was waiting on the tarmac. A flight attendant carried her garment bag, had tried to take the suitcase as well, but Becky had waved him off. Luke had watched the other man bend close and then laugh loudly at something *his* Becky had said.

Fucking bastard.

Luke wanted to be the man Becky talked to. The *only* man.

And that thought was staying exactly where it should, locked deep within his possessive caveman brain.

She walked up the steps, pausing just at the door. His heart leaped when she turned toward his car and waved. Luke waved back, though realistically he knew it was too dark outside for her to see through the windows.

Then she was gone, and he needed to drive back to his empty hotel room.

He missed her more in that moment than in their decade apart. Before he'd been used to not being with his Becky, had used anger to cauterize those wounds inside him. This—hope for a second chance, wishing their relationship worked out, wanting a future with her—was different.

Those old wounds ached.

His phone buzzed.

Get a move on, Pearson. I'll see you in a week.

Luke's mouth curved.

That date better be impressive.

The plane's door slammed closed, the stairs rolled away.

You doubt me?

His fingers flew across his screen.

Bec Fucking Darden? Hell, no. I'd bet on you anytime, sweetheart. Safe flight.

She sent back a GIF of a giggling movie star, and he was

smiling as he watched her plane take off, knowing his heart might as well be in the seat next to her.

This time around, Luke would wait for her, however long it took.

———

MONDAY of the next week rolled around bright and early, and Luke was beyond relieved to be meeting with Heather O'Keith.

If only because it meant he was getting out of his hotel room.

The maid had given him such a pitying look yesterday afternoon, after he'd refused a cleaning for the third day in a row. So what if he'd answered the door in a ratty T-shirt and boxer briefs, his hair a mess? He'd put all the dirty room service dishes outside in the hall. He'd taken the proffered clean towels.

Maybe he hadn't *used* them . . .

Okay, so he was a disgusting mess.

But not *this* morning because he'd caught up with all the outstanding Pearson Energy business, had put the finishing touches on his plan for what he was considering doing in California with his renewable trials, and he'd put on a suit.

Oh. He'd also showered.

And left his room for coffee that didn't come with a twenty percent markup.

Take that, judgy cleaning lady.

He'd even grabbed a coffee for Heather—pinging Becky for her favorite, so never let it be said that he wasn't going full-board with wanting to make a good impression on the CEO of Robo-Tech. He didn't typically chase connections, happy with his medium slice of the pie, but this was *Heather O'Keith*. She was a hugely successful businesswoman—her multi-billion-dollar corporation could eat Pearson Energy for breakfast—and fucking up with her wouldn't bode well for the future of his company.

But that wasn't the only reason. Luke was also putting in extra effort because she was Becky's close friend.

He didn't want to disappoint either of them.

It would also be nice if Heather liked him, at least a little bit.

He checked in at the security desk, received a temporary badge, and was told to have a seat in the lobby area. Rachel, Heather's assistant, would be down in a few minutes to collect him.

Luke's ass had barely touched the leather before a woman with warm brown hair and eyes and a lovely smile stepped off the elevator and strode toward him. He stood when it became clear he was her target and shook her hand.

"You must be Rachel."

She nodded, eyes tracing over him in a way that was completely assessing and yet also completely absent of sexual interest. "I am." A beat. "So, Luke Pearson, you're the one who got our calm, cool, and self-assured Bec so riled up."

"*My* Becky is perfectly capable of kicking anyone who riles her up straight to the curb."

One finger tapped her chin. "Hmm. Then why is she keeping *you* around?"

Luke grinned. "No clue. But I'm going to do my best to *stay* around."

"You'll do, Pearson. I just think you'll do." Rachel inclined her head in the direction of the elevators. "Come on. Heather's just finishing up with a call."

Thirty minutes later, he was packing up his briefcase with a huge smile on his face. The woman hadn't disappointed. She was brilliant and a straight-shooter, even pointing out several flaws in his project that he'd missed and would need to be addressed before the project rolled out, but RoboTech would be happy to be an investor in the venture.

Luke was glad he'd postponed his flight back to Texas until that evening. Her green light meant he could get the board to vote on the project while he was there, and then he and his team would be able to get started.

His initial thoughts had been rolling out the trials in six to eight months, but RoboTech's involvement and the infrastructure they already had in place—including several warehouses and a laboratory in the Central Valley—meant that his timeline would be less than half that.

For the first time in years, Luke wasn't in survival mode, wasn't doing something because he was obligated or trying to save his family. He was excited about work.

Heather stopped him with a hand on his shoulder. "Luke."

He glanced up at her. "Sorry, my mind was racing ahead with ideas. Did you have anything else you wanted to discuss?"

"Yes."

His gut sank. *Shit.* Maybe she was having second thoughts.

"Is it the storage numbers? My engineers truly think they can transfer it to the batteries at a rate of ninety-five percent."

Heather waved a hand. "I'll have my team confirm all the calculations before rollout. I'm sure they're competent, but . . . never mind. This isn't so much business as it's Bec." Eyes narrowing, she fixed him in place with a glare.

His gut sank further.

"You hurt my friend." She crossed her arms.

"I—" He sighed. "I was a fucking ass. I let the best thing in my world slip through my fingers."

"Hmm." Those arms stayed crossed, those eyes still narrowed.

He did some narrowing of his own. "Becky has decided to give me a second chance to prove I've grown out of my asshole tendencies, and I'm not giving it up." She opened her mouth, but he pressed on. "And if that's why you're investing in this project—to get me to walk away from the best thing in my life— well, fuck it because business doesn't mean as much to me as my Becky does."

"Hmm," she said again.

His temper spiked. Was this just a waste of his time? A way to test him and find him lacking?

"You know what?" He thrust the file with the tentative contract offer at her. "Fuck this. I love Becky. Always have, always will. I'm not leaving her." Furious, he started for the elevators.

"Luke." She caught his arm again.

"I'm not using her—"

"I don't believe I accused you of that."

Her calm tone finally penetrated his temper, and he thought back at her words. Heather *hadn't* given any indication of thinking he was using Becky for her connections. Nope. That was all him.

He winced. "I'm fucking this up, aren't I?"

A flash of white as Heather grinned. "Not as badly as you think. I like that you're defensive of Bec—or *Becky* as you call her. She deserves someone who cares enough to fight for her." She squeezed his arm. "Your Becky isn't a weakling. She'll chew up and spit out anyone spineless."

Luke raised a brow. "I'm not going to let her push me away."

"See that you don't." Heather handed him the file back. "I almost lost the best thing that ever happened to me because I was too scared to jump. Take my advice, and just dive in."

He snorted. "Good advice if I wasn't already in over my head. Fuck, if I don't love her to the moon and back—" He shook his head. "Damn, what kind of drugs did you put in the water you served me? Because I did *not* just say that."

"No drugs," Rachel teased, joining them. "Just the power of the *hmm*." Her voice dropped to a stage whisper. "It's her tactic. Gets even the most recalcitrant of peeps to dish all."

"Don't give all my secrets away." Heather smacked her. "You're supposed to be on *my* side, remember?"

Rachel smirked, leading the way toward the elevators. "This one is going to need all the help he can get if he's going to take down our *Becky*."

Oh, he was going to be in so much trouble with this Becky thing.

"True," Heather said with a nod.

They said their goodbyes, and he got onto the elevator when it stopped on their floor.

"Oh, Luke?" Heather asked.

He paused, finger on the button, holding the doors open.

"Next time you talk to Bec, ask her about the time she kissed Sera."

His brows drew together, his finger slipped off the white circle. "Did you say kis—?"

The panels slid closed to the sound of Rachel and Heather's cackling.

Well, he couldn't let that information stand without immediate action. He texted Becky and laughed out loud when her response came before he'd reached the lobby.

I'm suing the lot of them for defamation.

He strode out of the elevator, headed for his rental car.

Is this the point I shouldn't mention you've now made one of my top fantasies come true?

And instead of the sass he'd been expecting, Luke got heat.

What are the other fantasies?

He took a breath, glared down at his cock, mentally threatening it to behave.

Come home and I'll show you.

The selfie she sent in reply had his cock hardening further, regardless of his previous threat. Her hair was down, eyes sultry, lips red and lush, and her tank top positioned low enough that her nipples were almost exposed.

I thought of you just this morning.

Had she–? Did she mean—?
Luke's brain wouldn't even work in complete sentences.

Two more days.

Thank fuck for that.

CHAPTER 14

Bec

SHE WAS UNACCOUNTABLY NERVOUS.

Like stupidly nervous.

Harvard law graduate, and she was afraid of a pizza date.

But Luke was going to be there in five minutes, and . . . she was wearing short-shorts. Why had she thought it was a good idea to squeeze into them again? She wasn't twenty-one, and they weren't on the beach eating cold pizza and drinking warm beer. Things had shifted. Her legs weren't as lean, her waist not as trim.

Hell, if she sat down, she'd have rolls.

"That's life, Darden," she muttered. "Plus, real women have rolls. It's a fact of—"

"What's this about rolls?"

A masculine voice that sent a shiver down her spine.

She turned, saw Luke standing just inside her door. He was wearing those faded jeans and a tight green T-shirt that brought out the emerald streaks in his eyes. Eyes that heated as he looked her over, down and then back up. His gaze was hot, scorching her as it took in every inch of her exposed skin.

And considering she was wearing a very skimpy bikini top to go with the short-shorts, it was a *lot* of exposed skin.

"Turn around," he said, hoarsely.

"What?"

He swallowed hard. "Please, baby. If you care about me even the tiniest amount, please, *please* turn around."

Frowning, Bec rotated so her back was to him.

"Oh, thank you Jesus." She glanced over her shoulder, saw his stare go from hot to scorching. "I think you dropped something."

Bec had bent to glance down at the ground before she realized that he was messing with her. "Pig," she accused, straightening with a glare despite her lips twitching and betraying her amusement.

"Those shorts should receive a fucking Oscar."

She laughed.

Ten seconds in Luke's presence and she'd forgotten all about rolls.

She knew feeling this way—sexier, less self-conscious because of a few words and a hot look—meant she should probably turn in her feminist card. She *knew* that other people's opinions shouldn't matter and that a man appreciating her body shouldn't have any bearing on how she felt about herself, but dammit, sometimes having someone look at her and *not* see all the flaws her inner critic loved to point out felt really fucking good.

Luke wasn't worried about her legs or hips or stomach.

Luke thought she was beautiful.

And somehow, that made it easier for her to see herself that way, too.

Bec knew she projected confidence to the world, that no one

would suspect she was self-conscious or insecure, but . . . sometimes that protective armor got really heavy to carry.

Sometimes she wanted someone to appreciate the person she was . . . on the inside *and* outside.

Rolls or not.

Warm hands slid around her waist, his slightly roughened palms making her shiver. "Why aren't you wearing any clothes?"

She rested her head on his chest, cuddling close, loving the feel of his fingers skating up and down her spine. "My twenty-first birthday." His arms tightened, his body—lies, his *cock*—hardened, pressing against her stomach. "I didn't bring in any sand, but I do have the pizza and beer."

"I think I'm still finding sand in places I shouldn't," he teased.

"Hence, apartment picnicking on the 'beach'"—she made air quotes then pointed to her TV, which was displaying a screensaver of the ocean—"rather than the real beach."

"Thank you," he murmured.

She shrugged. "It's not much, but I—"

"It's *everything*. Thank you." He cupped her jaw in his palm. "I missed you."

And Bec knew he hadn't just missed her body or the skimpy clothes or even the sass she constantly threw his way.

He'd missed *her*.

Talking to her, being with her . . . *all* of her.

Click.

That locked box hiding in the depths of her heart was open —dangerously, wonderfully open.

She rose up on tiptoe and kissed him.

There was no hesitation in Luke's response. He tightened his hold and slipped his tongue between her lips, teasing her with a rhythm she remembered instinctually. They'd honed it over the years, perfected the caresses, the timing, the pressure, the speed.

And just like it had a decade before, that rhythm took her from mildly turned on to almost insane with need. One leg hitched around his waist, and she all but climbed into his arms, desperate to get closer, rubbing herself against him, groaning into his mouth.

"Baby," he said, gently clasping the tops of her arms and setting her away from him. "We should slow down."

The thing about her itty-bitty bikini top was that it was flimsy. One tug of the right string and it would end up on the floor. Bec never wore it in public for just that reason. In fact, the only time she'd ever worn it—not including this time in her living room—was with Luke.

Paired with these same shorts.

When she was skinnier (a.k.a. had yet to grow boobs).

Today? A good fifteen pounds heavier—hence, *rolls*—and she was threatening to pop right out of it.

Her intent was exactly that, of course. She'd given Luke too much power in their relationship, too much control in deciding when to come back, when to go on dates, how far they were going to go.

Bec was in this now.

She'd made peace with going for Luke and all the potential heartache that might follow in his wake.

And so, dammit, that meant she was taking some control back.

Also, she really needed an orgasm that didn't come as a result of her own handiwork, *pun intended*.

"Pearson," she said and arched her back deliberately, slipping one hand up her back and tugging. His eyes went huge as the bikini top slid to the floor. "Just in case you were wondering, I was hoping we'd celebrate with cold pizza and warm beer later."

He was frozen, jaw in a tight line, his hands still on her arms. "Becky—"

"Bec," she corrected, grabbing his wrists and placing his hands over her breasts. They both groaned at the sensation, his fingers flexing and causing little zings of pleasure to extend right down in between her thighs. "And by later, I meant *much* later, after you give me multiple orgasms and remind me how good your cock"—she reached down and squeezed the hard length of him—"feels inside of me."

"I—"

She placed one finger over his lips. "Now's the time to shut up and kiss me."

He nipped that fingertip, making her jump as more sparks of pleasure coursed down between her legs. She was wet and aching and—

Luke swept her up into his arms, carrying her over to the blanket, but when he would have set her on the square of checkered material, Bec tugged at his shoulders. "Wait."

A painful expression crossed his face. "Second thoughts," he said and gave a tight nod. "We'll wait—"

This man.

She never felt like this with anyone else—never was tender and protective, never felt her heart actually pinch with the urge to make things better for him.

She'd never *loved* another man.

Never.

The thought made her panic for a moment, to consider actually stopping, but then she remembered this was Luke, and Luke was different.

And *she* was different with Luke.

So, Bec put her lawyer mind to work. She tucked away those feelings—the panic, the relief, the hope, and the anticipation—

and promised herself she'd spend plenty of time analyzing them later. That complete, she tugged Luke's head down until his mouth met hers.

Only when her lungs burned and her heart was threatening to pound itself right out of her chest did she break away.

"I was just going to say, how about going to the bedroom?" Her head rested against his shoulder, and he still cradled her against his chest. "I'm too old to have sex on barely padded hardwood floor."

Luke's body went stiff, but before Bec had a chance to worry she'd said the wrong thing—and face it, she often *did* say the wrong thing—she realized he was laughing.

"Fuck, but I love you," he said in between breaths. "I can never, *ever* predict what is going to come out of your mouth."

That panic from before?

When she'd realized how much she still cared for—loved, okay, okay *loved*—Luke, well that panic she'd tucked away to deal with later reared its ugly head. He loved her? She loved him? How long would it last? When would she do or say something to make things change, to make Luke angry again?

Or maybe she'd run away again. Be pathetic and cowardly and—

No.

No more.

If she'd learned anything over the last decade, it was how to be fearless. She hadn't had therapy, not like Luke, hadn't been open to such a course in the past, not when every time she made herself vulnerable, things around her went to shit.

Her work had been her therapy. The one thing to not let her down. She could be terrified, but if she was always prepared, if she devoted herself and practically lived in the office, feeding off the cases, if she just worked her ass off, then she could be successful, dammit.

And it had worked.

Eventually she'd been able to weave those slender tendrils of confidence into something larger. She'd found faith in herself, knew she was smart and capable, knew she could be fucking brilliant.

And now, this was her chance.

She'd managed to be fearless in her professional life, managed to carve out happiness there, with her friends and as thus, she could damn well carry that fearlessness over into her personal life.

So, instead of pushing Luke away, Bec shoved the terror of the situation down and tugged him closer. Instead of throwing those words back at him in angry, hurtful bites, she tucked them into that empty space in her heart.

One day, she vowed, one day she might even believe them.

One day . . . she might find herself worthy of them.

One day—

Enough.

Today was here and now, and if Bec had learned nothing else through this whole painful endeavor, it was that she had to live for today.

"I love you," she said. "I don't think I've ever stopped loving you. I hated you. I loathed you. I wanted to put your balls in a meat grinder"—she grinned at his expression—"but I think I always loved you, Luke Pearson. Even when I didn't want to."

Then before he could reply, before she lost her nerve, Bec kissed him again.

"Make love to me," she murmured against his lips. "Please."

Emerald eyes met hers, warm but searching for long moments. Luke swallowed hard, eyes darting away from Bec long enough that her heart started to sink. At least until she heard his words. "Which one of those many white doors leads to your bedroom?"

Bec grinned, because she knew the hall *did* have a lot of doors. Four in one corner of her apartment, in fact—one leading to her bedroom, another to a half bathroom, there was also a linen closet and her washer-dryer.

She debated for a heartbeat, thinking of several ways to tease him.

Game show model presenting doors.

Her version of whack-a-mole, only with guess-the-door instead.

Hot-cold-hotter-colder.

Then the arm holding the upper half of her body shifted, sliding around her rib cage, calloused fingers brushing along her side, grazing the underside of one breast, rubbing over the top of her nipple.

Stars flashed behind her eyes.

Luke bent, sucked that nipple into his mouth, and made her forget about her plans to tease him. "Which door?" he asked again, releasing her and straightening.

"I—"

Another brush of that thumb and really, if driving her insane with need was a sport then Luke Pearson definitely excelled at it.

"Door, sugar pie," he said again, walking toward the hall.

"Second on the left."

He shifted her body so he could turn the knob and opened the correct door. A bare heartbeat later, she was flat on her back with him on top of her.

One long, slow drag of his tongue up her abdomen, up her sternum, and then over, back to her breast, back to the aching points of her nipples. "You're so fucking beautiful," he told her.

"It's the short-shorts," she managed to joke, even though his tongue was teasing her breasts and she was slowly going insane.

Never let it be said that Bec Darden lost her cool. She was calm and composed—

Except when Luke did that thing with his tongue.

Because any hope of composure went straight out the window.

Luckily, Luke didn't seem to mind in the least.

CHAPTER 15

Luke

HE'D BEEN SHOWN UP. He knew it. Fuck, the whole universe knew he'd been bested by a checkered blanket and a bright red bikini top.

But Luke found it didn't bother him at all.

Not when she was half-naked beneath him, skin like silken fire. He wanted to touch her all over, to stroke and kiss and lick every inch of her, but he also needed to be sure she wasn't rushing this, that she was as fully into this as he was—

Luke snorted.

Becky froze, glanced up at him. "What?"

"I was going around in my head why this both is *and isn't* a good idea." Her eyes started to dim, and he grabbed her hand, dragging it down his cock, which was threatening to break in half. "I want you. Don't *ever* doubt that, okay?" He waited until she nodded. "I was worried you were doing something you didn't want."

She raised a brow.

"Hence, the snort." He nuzzled at her neck. "My Becky doesn't do anything she doesn't want, least of all me."

"Your *Bec*," she said. "And sidenote, I'm going to get you back for all this *Becky* talk. My friends have sent me no less than a million Valley girl GIFS. I think I need to resurrect the Lucky Luke nickname."

He shuddered. "Please God, no."

She shoved at his shoulders. "Then you'd better strip me out of these short ass shorts and spend some quality time between my thighs."

"Oh, really?" Luke let his fingers drift down her abdomen, dip under the waistband of those shorts. Becky shivered, hips shifting restlessly. "You want my mouth?"

Feminine hands darted between them, undid the button, slid down the zipper. "I seem to remember you could do some really impressive things with your mouth, Pearson."

"Hmm."

A kiss just above her belly button then below.

"Now you sound like Heather."

"Shh." A nip to her hip bone. "I don't want to think about Heather. I want to think about how good your pussy is going to taste." He punctuated his statement by tugging off her shorts and underwear then dragging one finger between her wet folds.

Her breath caught when he brought it up to his mouth and sucked, closing his eyes as the sweet tang hit his tongue. She spread her thighs further, tilted her hips.

"*Luke.*"

An invitation.

One that he didn't need an engraved postcard to heed.

He tossed her legs over his shoulders, and she wove her hands into his hair, yanked his mouth against her pussy, and ground herself against him.

Suddenly, Luke wasn't thinking about teasing any longer.

Or at least not *him* being teased. His woman on the other hand . . .

He figured he had about ten years' worth of time to make up for.

Thus, he pulled out every trick he possessed, everything he knew Becky had liked in the past, every technique he'd learned and perfected since then. He licked and kissed and nipped, concentrating all his efforts on making her feel good, on driving her to the edge of reason, on propelling her straight to an orgasm.

Fingers in his hair, the grip bordering on painful, but Luke didn't give a damn, not when he had his Becky wet and hot against his mouth.

"Oh, my God—"

Thighs clamped around his head, her spine arched off the mattress, and she screamed his name.

He brought her down, slowing the movements of his tongue and fingers, helping her descend the peak, continuing to kiss her as her movements calmed . . . and not stopping until she was writhing against him again, gripping his hair, cursing him out.

And then he just used his fingers.

He kept them on her clit, circling, pressing, slipping down and inside, because his mouth was otherwise occupied.

As in he needed to get it on her breasts.

Her nipples were hard little points, and he sucked one into his mouth. "Luke— *Oh God!* Mmm, baby. I—" He switched sides, slid another finger into the heat of her, curling them up and forward, rubbing against her G-spot, feeling moisture pool around him.

"Oh *fuck*," she gasped. "Oh fuck, oh fuck, oh—"

She clamped down hard around his fingers, and Luke almost went over the edge with her. It had been *so fucking long*, and watching her come—seeing the pink spreading across her cheeks, the tops of her breasts, a sheen of sweat glistening on her forehead—was absolutely beautiful.

She was beautiful.

Especially, when her eyes opened and focused on him with lazy awareness. Swollen lips tipped upward into a smile. "You'll do, Pearson. You'll do."

He twitched his fingers—the ones still deep inside her. "You sure?" Another twitch that made her gasp and her pussy pulse around him. "Because I think"—he started moving, slow and gentle and in a rhythm that would soon have her climbing that peak again—"I might still need to prove myself to you."

His thumb drifted up—

"Touch my clit and die."

Luke laughed. He was fully dressed with a naked Becky and had a boner that could easily substitute for a hammer, and he was laughing.

Using his free hand, he cupped her cheek. "How did I ever let you go?"

Regret, and this time no pun was intended, *hammered* into him. But dammit, he'd wasted so much fucking time.

"Hey."

One sharp word of a sound, surprising his eyes into meeting hers.

"I think we've been over this already." Becky gripped his wrist, slid his fingers from her, lips parting in a silent protest before she shook her head and seemed to regain herself. "The past is the past, and we're going to move forward. Going to try and—"

"See," he said, moving up on the bed and lying down next to her. "It's not that simple—"

"Ugh." She threw her hands up. "You're ruining my orgasm afterglow."

"Uh—"

"We fucked up, okay?" she said, pushing up and jabbing him in the chest with one red-painted fingernail. "*Both* of us. That's the way this works."

"I was—"

"Oh, so are we going to play Who Was the Bigger Asshole now?" she snapped. "Really? Because I'm pretty sure we both would win that top prize." When he opened his mouth, she hurried to say, "Did you tell me to go? Yes. Did I say a lot of shitty stuff before that? *Fuck yes.*"

Luke blinked.

"Forgot about that part?" She huffed. "Yeah. Thought so. Luke, you were jealous of my success in part because I rubbed it in. I was hurt you weren't as happy for me about the job as you should have been, so I talked about it every chance I got. I made you feel inadequate and—"

He caught her hand. "That's bullshit, and you know it. If I'd been supportive like a real husband should have been—"

"And there's another *should have.*" She tugged her hand free, popped up from the mattress, and started pacing the room in all her naked glory. Or, it *would* have been glorious, if her words didn't slice to the center of him. "How convenient. You get to play the martyr and shoulder the blame for everything, and then we never work out what was truly wrong with our relationship."

His heart skipped a beat.

Because, dammit, his therapist had said much of the same thing. Absorbing blame was one way to take control of a situation, but it was also a way to push people away. To sacrifice himself for their good.

Even if such a sacrifice wasn't for the betterment of the people involved.

He cleared his throat, shoved down the urge to keep arguing

that everything was *his* fault and forced himself to ask, "What was wrong with us?"

"Communication, Luke." She stopped, stared at him. "Even now, we both have all of these feelings that are tearing us up inside and we're masking them with apologies and sex and cute date nights that only relive the good stuff." Becky crossed back over to him and sat on the edge of the mattress. "We're forgetting the hard days. The disagreements and blaring arguments, and . . . we're forgetting what made us *us*."

He slipped off his shirt then tugged it over her head. "That tore us apart. Before."

A nod. "It did."

"I'm not going to let it drag us back down," he said. "But I also can't just pretend that I didn't fuck up."

She touched his jean-clad leg. "The important point is that we *both* fucked up. That's the part you need to accept."

Luke froze. "It goes against everything in me to let someone else take the blame."

A smile. "I know."

"But it's also the truth. We both made mistakes and if we want to move forward . . ."

"We have to let that go."

He swallowed hard. "I don't want to hurt you again."

Becky curled into his side. "I understand now." A smile. "*Finally*, I get it. We can't go back and fix everything from before, but we *can* build something strong now. It's only . . ."

"I don't like the sound of that."

"I worry if we can't stop focusing on how things were and all the mistakes we made, I worry we'll be destined to—" She broke off, shook her head.

"I'm keeping you," he said. "So tough shit with the psychological stuff or the destined to fall apart nonsense. The one thing I learned in therapy was that I have never stopped loving you—"

"Then just be the Luke I know you can be," she said. "If you love me, then stop hurting yourself. Because, *fuck*, it hurts me so much when you do that."

He dropped his chin to his chest, sighed. "I hate it when you're smarter than me."

She laughed, that lovely laugh that filled him up with helium from the inside out. "Face facts, Pearson. You love me because I am smarter than you."

"Not hard to do."

Becky dropped her head to his shoulder. "I admit that I was recalcitrant at first, scared of getting hurt again, but that in and of itself was the truth of it. No other man I've met is capable of getting close enough to wound me."

His heart skipped a beat. "That's a dubious honor if I've ever heard one."

"Don't you see?" she said, pushing up with one hand on his chest so she could stare down at him. "Don't you know you're the only man to ever penetrate the armor around my heart? Don't you understand that you're the only one who ever mattered?"

Luke's throat was tight, and his eyes burned suspiciously. "Come here."

He tugged Becky close, turning them so they were lying long ways on the bed and then he held her, turning over the words in his mind, replaying their years together, studying their mistakes. He did so not as a way to flagellate himself with the multitude of regrets and *should haves*. Instead, he remembered the good times and the bad. Together. As pieces of an entire puzzle that formed a picture in color rather than black and white, rather than past equaled bad.

Instead, he saw *everything*.

Imperfect as it was.

And for the first time in his life, he wasn't worrying about measuring up to some perfect image his father or family wanted him to be. He wasn't worrying about being the perfect boyfriend or spouse.

Finally, Luke was free to be himself.

He shucked his jeans, tugged the covers up and over them, a huge weight lifted from his chest. Becky snuggled right against his side, her hair tickling his nose, floral scent surrounding him like the softest blanket.

She was wearing his shirt and as a result of just holding her, he was sporting a boner the size of Georgia and . . . he didn't care.

Because Becky was in his arms at last.

He kissed the top of her head, eyes beginning to close, her breathing slowing, evening out—

"I'm the only man to *penetrate* you?"

Without missing a beat, without even lifting her head, she pinched him just above the nipple. "Pig."

"*Ouch!*"

"Sorry," she said, her tone conveying the opposite. The fingers that had pinched him, drifted down his chest lazily. "I should—"

He caught that wandering hand, pressed a kiss to the palm.

"You should sleep and let me hold you."

She sighed. "Fine."

But Luke felt her smile against his shoulder.

"Your therapist sucked."

He laughed. "You should have seen me before."

"I *did* see you before."

"Really?" He ran his fingers through her hair. "And you say *I'm* the worst?"

"We can share the mantle." She snuggled close, traced circles on his chest.

"I'd share anything with you, sugar pie."

"Lucky Luke," she warned.

"Did you ever—" He stopped.

One eyelid peeled back. "Did I what?"

"Did you talk to someone too?" he asked. "I mean, we both have textbook daddy issues, but you're significantly better adjusted than I am."

Her mouth curved. "That's because I'm awesome. It's also not true." The smile faded. "I'm still—not screwed up exactly, and I am in a better place. But I have this hole in my heart and I'm not sure it will ever go away."

"Sweetheart." His own heart hurt for her.

"I just always wanted things to be different between my dad and me—" She blinked, her tone becoming more businesslike, less sad. "But actually, hearing that you went to therapy kind of makes me want to try it myself." She pressed her palm to his chest. "Not right now, but eventually, maybe it might be good to talk with someone."

"I think that sounds very mature."

She made a face. "Gross." But then she laughed, and he found himself chuckling along with her. "I wasn't in the right head space to talk to anyone before now. I was just lucky to have Abby and Sera and now the rest of the girls and honestly, the rest of it came from work. Work got me through a lot of the darkness. Helping other people, feeling like I had some worth in this world because I could get them some recompense. And, eventually, I was able to believe that was true."

"You're amazing."

She snuggled against him again. "Lies."

"Not lies. The truth."

A sigh, but a relaxed one rather than annoyance for a change. "If you insist."

"I do insist," he said and wrapped his arms around, letting his eyes slide closed, enjoying the feel of her next to him, the scent of wildflowers and sunshine teasing his nose. "Sweet-heart?" he asked a few minutes later.

"Mmm?"

"Thank you."

"Anytime, Pearson. Anytime."

They tumbled headfirst into sleep, waking up hours later to eat cold pizza and drink warm beer as they binged on bad reality TV. It was different from ten years ago, but Luke decided that was perfectly—*imperfectly*—fine with him.

CHAPTER 16

Becky—er Bec

INTERNAL REVELATIONS WERE EXHAUSTING.

Bec prided herself on not filtering, on being the type of person who existed without artifice. There was a reason she didn't date, why her father could barely stand the sight of her. But she'd been kidding herself when it came to Luke.

As in she'd tried to pretend that she was going to casually give their relationship another go, like one might try on a different shade of red lipstick.

But she should have known that things would get complicated.

Hell, just picking the right shade of red lipstick was really fucking hard.

Categorizing Luke was harder.

Or *had* been harder.

Because after last night . . . things had changed.

She glanced up at him sleeping. They'd tumbled back into her bed with pleasantly full stomachs, eyes burning from too much B-list celebrity drama, and had promptly passed out.

But now it was after seven. She was wide awake and needed to go in to work.

And . . . she didn't want to move from Luke's arms.

They'd each revealed something last night, and she didn't know how she'd survived the discomfort of it.

Then why did you demand complete honesty and communication?

Because, clearly, I'm a fucking idiot.

Yup. Arguments with herself at seven in the morning, she was so fucking together.

"I can smell the smoke from here."

Bec blinked, glanced up, and found Luke's gorgeous green eyes on her. "What?" she blurted and . . . *so fucking smooth.* But it was hard to be her usual calm and put together self when she felt like she should be running, pulling all those pieces of armor back around her, stitching them tightly together. It had been so easy last night to lay it all out there, but in the light of the morning?

Not so much.

Luke shifted, sliding down on the bed so their faces were level. "Good morning."

And he kissed her, ignoring all signs of morning breath—and hers was no doubt horrible, after their three A.M. booty call with pizza and beer—slipping his tongue past the threshold of her lips and giving her a thoroughly dizzying wakeup call.

Eventually, he broke away, both of them breathing hard.

"I knew you'd be doing this."

Her brows drew down. "Doing what?"

"Freaking."

She started to protest, but there was something in his expression—as though he were expecting her to withdraw—and that smug expectation gave her the courage to push on.

The bastard probably knew it, too.

Ugh.

"Fine. I *am* freaking out," she said. "But only a little bit." He snorted. "I'm not used to this. To feeling like *this*—"

Smugness faded from his face. "It would probably be better if I left you alone, let you get back to your own life—"

Just the words made Bec's heart throb. She wouldn't let him leave her, not now, not when things were different—and not even just with the two of them, but also within her.

She felt different. Inside.

Fuck all this noble shit. She wanted Luke, and even though it scared her so damned much, she was keeping him.

Sorry, not sorry. That was just the way it was—

"But I can't," he said.

She blinked, the argument she'd been whipping up inside her brain promptly fading away. "Good," she said. "Because I'm not letting you go."

His eyes warmed. "Possessive little thing, aren't you?"

"You're only a few inches taller than me, Pearson. I wouldn't push your luck."

Fingers traced down her neck, her arm, sliding to a stop on the bare skin of her hip. "I'm six inches taller, at least."

She raised a brow, doing some sliding of her own. "Sorry to say, but *six* inches isn't going to cut it." She followed the trail of hair that began at his belly button and disappeared beneath the waistband of his boxer briefs.

"It's not the"—he broke off with a hiss as she ran a fingertip over his cock—"size that counts."

Her mouth curved. "But how you use it?"

"Exact—*fuck*." She stroked him from base to tip.

"Mmm." Bec pushed up on her elbow, watching his face as she glided her hand up and down. His eyes were squeezed tight, his jaw clamped, his hips jerked off the mattress, pressing closer to her hand. Moisture pooled between her thighs as she stroked him up and down, up and down, up and—

Strong fingers on her wrist, staying her movements.

"Luke—"

The rest of her sentence was lost in a gasp of air as she was flipped onto her back. All Bec saw was a pair of molten emerald eyes before the T-shirt she was wearing was yanked over her head and Luke was all but attacking her breasts.

He sucked one nipple into his mouth, drawing on it in almost desperate pulls. His other hand was on her stomach, her hip, in between her thighs, delving into the liquid heat of her.

And he was ruthless.

Thumb pressing against her clit, rubbing in firm circles that had her crying out his name. But he didn't stop, just switched breasts and kept the rhythm of his thumb constant as he slipped one thick finger inside her.

Bec gasped, hips flying up, desperate for more than that minimal intrusion.

She wanted him pushing home, filling her to excess, the burn of his thick length mixing with her desire until she was engulfed in flames of pleasure.

"Luke—" He stole the rest of her words with a kiss, fingers continuing to work as his free hand angled her head and he replicated the rhythm of his thumb with his tongue in her mouth.

She couldn't breathe. Every muscle in her body was taut and coiled, desperate for release.

"I . . . Luke . . . *Oh God.* I need—"

He slipped another finger into her, pressed firmly on her clit.

And implosion.

Stars behind her eyes, pleasure radiating out from her core, spilling into her limbs, making them heavy and lax.

Nothing.

She felt nothing but those waves of bliss, and it could have been thirty seconds or a minute or an eternity before they slowed and finally, finally she was able to wrench back her eyelids and look up at the only man who'd ever held any power over her.

"You're beautiful," he murmured.

Her lips curved. "Condom. Nightstand. Now."

She'd almost expected Luke to laugh at her caveman instructions, but instead of teasing her, his eyes went somehow hotter. "You sure? I don't want to hurt—"

Bec reached down and gripped the hard length of him, loving the way his head fell forward and his hips thrust toward her. "I need you, baby," she murmured, knowing that the reassuring words came from some place inside her that only Luke had access to. "Please, come inside me."

One long look.

One hard swallow.

Then he reached over her left shoulder and extracted a condom from the nightstand. A few seconds later he'd rolled it on, was staring down at her with anticipation and worry and—

Bec pulled his head down to hers, kissing him this time, thrusting *her* tongue into his mouth for a change. She hitched a leg around his hips, lifting off the bed, bringing herself close enough to rub against the hard length of his cock. They both caught their breath, and she moaned into his mouth at the feel of hard gliding through silky folds, of hot meeting wet, of—

She tightened her leg, sinking back down to the mattress and bringing him on top of her. Chest against chest, hips against hips, hard against soft.

"Becky," he groaned as she wrapped her other leg around him.

"Mmm." She changed the angle of her pelvis, catching the

tip of his erection at her opening, teasing them both by allowing just the slightest bit of him inside her.

The smallest dip before retreating. Another dip. *Another.* Until she felt sweat break out on Luke's back, until she couldn't take it anymore. Until *he* couldn't either.

She shifted just as he drove home.

"Fuck," she hissed, eyes going wide, lips parting.

He paused, worry written in the lines of his face. "Shit, sorry. I—"

"No." Legs tightening around his waist, she pulled him closer. "Do that again."

He slid out, pressed back in.

Hard and deep and not particularly finessed, he drove into her. And fuck, but it was the best ever. Raw and hot, shooting her up the precipice and straight over the edge.

She screamed, actually screamed as she came, and her sore throat would serve as a testament to that later.

He pushed once, twice more, before calling out her name.

"Becky!"

In that moment, heart racing, lungs sawing, and pleasure coursing through her limp body, Luke still somehow found the energy to cradle her like she was the most precious object in the universe. The only man she'd ever loved was next to her, and she found she didn't even care that he hadn't called her Bec.

Becky.

She could live with that.

At least it wasn't sugar pie.

Her lips twitched, her eyes shut, and she forgot all about the pressing matters at work. She just cuddled closer and soaked in Luke Pearson.

Yeah, she could live with that.

CHAPTER 17

Luke

"NO," he said to his group back in Texas, interrupting the presentation they'd been videoconferencing. "That's not the right strategy. Come on, guys, this is basic science. If you roll all the variables out at once, you won't be able to pinpoint cause and effect."

The table turned to look at the camera, at him.

Years ago that would have made him uncomfortable.

Now, Luke didn't mind stepping up and being the leader they needed. In fact, he found he thrived under the pressure.

"I didn't think of it that way," Trevor, one of his leads in the R&D department at Pearson Energy said.

"*Think* about it," Luke told him before turning his attention to the rest of the room. "We have a chance at something good here, guys. The product is great, yes, but there are flaws that need to be worked out before it goes to market. That's what the site here will bring us—existing infrastructure to tie into, a huge grid to practice on." He thrust a hand through his hair. "We play this right, and this technology will be big. We fuck up, and—"

He didn't need to elaborate.

The project would crash and burn before it got anywhere.

And the years of effort, research, testing? They would be for naught.

"Go back to the drawing board," he said. "We'll discuss next week."

He clicked off and sighed, shutting off his laptop before pulling out his phone to go through his ever-filling inbox.

"You're sexy when you give orders."

Luke turned, not having heard Becky come in. It had been a week since that night—the best sleep of his life, followed up by the best *sex* of his life—and his *sugar pie* had graciously offered him the use of her apartment.

"*You already know the codes anyway*," she'd told him.

Not being a stupid man, or not *all* the time anyway, Luke had readily agreed.

No more hotel.

No more pitying looks from the maids.

Just Becky and trying to get her naked at every opportunity.

He pushed to his feet, crossed over to her, and took her into his arms. His heart pulsed, just like it did every time she allowed him to do it.

"I missed you," he said and kissed her.

"You're just trying to bribe your way into knowing what my date is," she said when they broke apart.

"I'm trying to bribe my way into *something*," he agreed, slipping his hands down and gripping the lush curves of her ass. She was wearing a black pencil skirt and fuck, did it drive him crazy with the urge to tug it up, bend her over and—

Becky stepped away from him. Started unbuttoning her cream blouse.

It hit the carpet silently.

White lace. *See-through* white lace.

"What—?"

She turned her back on him, reached up to tug down the gold zipper that held her skirt together. Slowly. So *fucking* slowly it slid down, exposing porcelain skin bisected by the tiniest white thong Luke had ever seen.

A shimmy of her hips, black fabric sliding down thighs he was desperate to get his mouth between.

The skirt hit the floor.

He was hard and aching, but watching the slow lift of one black stiletto-clad foot stepping out of that crumpled piece of clothing followed by the other, made him even hotter.

Her ass. *Fuck* her ass.

Two perfect globes that jiggled just the slightest bit as she moved. Fucking perfection. But then Luke almost swallowed his tongue when she bent to pick up the skirt and glanced back at him over her shoulder.

The pink tip of her tongue darted out, moistened her bottom lip.

"While I did enjoy playing mini-golf with you Saturday night," she said, straightening and tossing the skirt onto her couch, "I was thinking that date five could be a little more . . ." One blonde brow lifted as she waited.

His words sounded like gravel. "A little more what?"

"More sex," she stage-whispered.

His dick pulsed, threatening to tear through his zipper.

Becky closed the distance between them, cupped him through his jeans. "I'm horny and wet, and I want you, Pearson." She rose on tiptoe, whispered in his ear. "Dinner on the pier can wait."

He had enough presence of mind to file her date preference away to remember later before she undid his zipper and dropped to her knees.

"Sweetheart," he began. "You don't have—"

She tugged and his cock sprung free from his boxer briefs. Then her mouth was on him, tongue tracing the hard length of him, hand moving up and down in a rhythm that had his knees shaking and his eyes rolling back into his head.

Fingers clenching into fists at his sides, Luke focused on not immediately blowing his load.

But *fuck* it felt good.

Her mouth was hot and wet, her tongue teased the underside of him, and her hand gripped him tightly as she stroked him straight to insanity.

"Mmm." She moaned, taking him deeper.

Then she did something with her tongue that made his vision go black.

And then she did it again.

"Enough," he growled, gripping her by her shoulders and yanking her up. He toed off his shoes, yanked a condom out of the back pocket of his jeans, and rolled it on.

In one movement, he lifted Becky up into his arms and turned to pin her against the wall.

"Lu—"

Rip. Her underwear flew over his shoulder, but he didn't look to see where it landed. Instead, he shifted so he was in between Becky's thighs and pushed into her.

"*Oh,*" Becky gasped.

"*Fuuck,*" he groaned.

Pictures rattled as he set a pounding rhythm. It was too much, too fast. He was rushing, needed to slow down. A framed print of something crashed to the ground and, worried he was too out of control, that he was going to hurt her, Luke forced himself to slow.

"*No,*" she said, and her fingers dug into his nape, her legs wrapped tighter around his waist. "Don't stop. Please, *God,* don't stop."

And fuck if he could deny her that.

Not when he was riding the razor's edge already. Not when his control was all but eroded. Not when she was tight and wet and felt so fucking good clamping around him.

Thud. Thud. *Thud.*

More pictures hit the floor.

Thank God Becky's apartment was the penthouse and they were alone on this floor. But the neighbors below were going to be pissed.

Luke couldn't bring himself to care.

He kept up the rapid pace, shifting his hold so it was his hands taking the pounding rather than Becky's spine.

"Yes. Please," she said, pressing against him. "*Yes.* Oh *fuck.*"

And then she exploded.

One. Two strokes and he followed her over.

He came to sitting bare-assed on the hardwood floor with Becky in his lap.

Holy shit. Holy *fucking* shit.

"How long have we been like this?" she asked, laziness in every syllable.

Luke shook his head. "Fuck, if I know." He surveyed the damage around them, only one picture remained on the wall, the rest were scattered on the hardwood floor. Luckily, they must not have had glass in the frames, otherwise his ass would be sushi and he'd much rather *eat* sushi than have his ass masquerade as it.

"We should get up." Becky started to push out of his lap, then sighed and snuggled closer.

"I'll get us to bed," he said, wrapping his arms around her.

A good minute passed.

"Are we moving?" she asked.

He chuckled. "As soon as I can feel my legs."

Her breath was warm on his neck as she laughed. "God, I love you," she said. "Let's just stay like this forever."

And if Luke's heart hadn't already been branded with Becky's name, this moment would have burned the mark right onto it.

CHAPTER 18

Bec

SOMEHOW, Luke had managed to get them into her bed, which was a good thing because Bec knew there was no way she could have gotten there on her own.

She'd been content to curl up in the living room, Luke as her personal blanket.

But this was just as good, naked limbs intertwined, his hand snug around her waist. It was just the other thing, the reason why she hadn't felt like going out that evening.

The Phone Call.

Yes, it deserved capital letters.

Because her father had called her.

And another one of the boxes she had carefully contained in her heart, locked up and wound with barbed wire, preventing pesky feelings from escaping, had ruptured.

He'd disappointed her so much.

And he'd called.

Bec had let the call go to voicemail, not wanting to talk to the man who'd shipped her off when she'd needed him the most. She'd reached out to him so many damned times and . . .

Brick wall.

Like father, like daughter.

"What's wrong?" Luke asked into the silence.

She didn't ask how he knew to ask, was just glad that he *did* ask. And where in the past she would have brushed him off, just internalized the tangle of emotions she was feeling over the fact her father had called, today she told Luke what happened.

"My dad called me today."

He never called.

Ever.

She was *always* the one to reach out.

And the fact that he had? It terrified her. Would she turn back into that pathetic creature, striving, doing everything in her power for his approval?

Or was he sick? The thought of losing him hurt, despite everything he'd done.

But maybe he just . . . needed her? For the first time ever, maybe her father needed her or wanted to spend time with her or—

That hope was hard to stifle, especially because she knew better than to allow herself to feel hopeful when disappointment was the more likely outcome of interacting with her father.

Luke brushed a hand down her arm. "What'd he have to say?"

"I don't know."

He rose up on one elbow, rotating so he could glance down at her. And not speak, apparently, because all he did was stare at her. Then lifted one brown brow.

Bec sighed. "Don't look at me like that."

The brow went higher. "Like what?"

"Like you're all . . . I don't know, not judgy exactly, but disapproving."

"Becky, sweetheart—"

"Don't sweetheart me."

"Becky, then." He paused, giving her a chance to insert another protest, but between getting so damned used to him and her friends calling her Becky over the last few weeks and feeling so unsettled by her father's call, she couldn't even drum up a correction. "It's not like you to avoid things."

She scoffed. "I spent ten years avoiding *you*."

A smile tugged at the corners of his mouth. "Should we call it a case of mutual avoidance?"

"Sure." A begrudging agreement.

Her eyes drifted around her bedroom, deliberately avoiding his gaze as she took in the pale blue walls. Her linens were crisp white cotton because she'd always loved the way hotel sheets felt and had wanted to replicate that, but aside from one print of a Scottish seascape that CeCe had painted for her, the room was almost empty of personality.

Or empty of her personality anyway.

Even the living room and kitchen were mostly bare of knick-knacks, the only items hanging on the walls pictures of her and her friends or things the Sextant had brought back for her—more drawings from CeCe, who always teased when presenting her with original artwork by saying Bec was the only one of the group who actually had wall space to spare; a fern leaf encased in amber from Rachel, who'd visited New Zealand with her other half, Sebastian; a pencil sketch of Berlin from Heather; pictures of Bec with Abby's kids.

Bec hadn't printed the photos or framed them or even hung them on the walls.

That had all been the girls. Two months ago, they'd bullied her into running to Target for hooks and frames, and they all had spent an entire evening hanging them up in her apartment . . . and also drinking wine.

Which had resulted in a few crooked pictures. But Bec couldn't bring herself to straighten them, even after they'd gone.

Her friends had hung them for her.

Her friends had given her a gift she'd never known she wanted.

A home.

Oh, she'd long used the convenient excuse of being too busy with work, of insane hours being the reason her apartment was sterile and barely lived in. She was hardly home as it was, why bother investing any time into decorating somewhere that she spent so little time in?

But work wasn't the issue.

Not really.

It was just easier to pretend it *was* work rather than to admit the truth. Because the truth was that *she* was the one with the problem.

Why create a home when it would just be torn away from her?

"Talk to me, sweetheart."

She shook her head, blinking back tears. "I j-just . . ." She sniffed. "Dammit. I never realized how much I was missing out on until you came back."

"What do you mean?"

And so she told him everything.

Not the bare facts of losing her mom, of moving, of boarding school.

But how after her mom had died, her dad didn't come home. He didn't explain what happened. No, that dubious honor had gone to the person he'd hired to watch her while their family home was packed away and sold, any happy memories being regulated into the back of her mind.

"I lost my dad then too. He was working all the time and when he was home, he couldn't stand the sight of me." She let Luke hug her tight. "He'd disengaged, become cold and unfeeling when I needed him the most. He hired people to take me to school, to feed me, to comfort me if I had a nightmare."

"Oh, sweetheart."

Tears burned but she blinked them back. "I just thought if I could be smart enough, good enough, pretty enough that maybe he'd notice—" She shook her head. "Folly. All of it. Because I had to find that worth in myself and it took me damn near twenty years."

"But . . ." He hesitated, but she nodded, encouraging him to ask. They were baring it all, baby. Full-on honest fucking communication.

If he saw this part of her and left—

Luke opened his mouth, closed it, then hugged her again. "I can see it in your eyes."

"What?" It was a stiff question.

"You think this will make me run."

Well, yeah.

She couldn't even get her own father to stay.

"I'm not leaving," he said. "What I was going to ask is why you didn't tell me all of this before. You made it seem—"

"Like it was no big deal."

"Yeah."

Bec blew out a breath. "Don't you see? It *had* to be no big deal or I wouldn't have survived. I wouldn't have been able to cope with my father moving back to California and leaving me in New York. I couldn't have dealt with him not visiting, or flying me home over vacation." Her voice dropped. "It was easier to just pretend it was me."

"Then me."

She blinked. "Yeah." They'd created something that had

resembled a home . . . or at least, the only sort of home she knew how to create, and that hadn't exactly gone well. "I learned it was easier to put a very specific distance between myself and the rest of the world. It was safer."

"Sweetheart, I'm so sorry."

"It's okay. I'm—I had Abby and Sera."

They were the only real caveat to her plans for distance. They'd barreled on through any walls, merrily leading new— and wonderful—women along with them. And Bec? Well, she'd started to feel a bit like the Grinch, her frosty exterior hiding a heart with the potential for growth on the inside.

Now was that a millennial description of a classic children's book or what?

Fingertips brushed her bottom lip. "Why are you smiling when you're so sad here"—he touched the spot over her heart then one temple—"and here?"

"I am sad, but I realized that I have my friends, that I have you and that makes things hurt a little less." She sighed, smile fading. "I don't know why my Dad called because I didn't pick up. I haven't listened to the message. I didn't—I don't know if I even want to open that old wound back up."

Luke sank back down to the mattress, pulling her so she was tucked against his side then slowly running his fingers through her hair. "That's why you jumped me first thing when you got home?"

Home. There was that word again.

But the smugness in his tone also meant that she retained a little Darden spirit. She tugged at his chest hair, mock-glaring at the yummy expanse of muscle. "*You* jumped *me*, if I recall. *I* was just trying to give *you* a nice—"

He tickled her side, cutting off her self-righteous rant by inducing giggles. "Dropping to your knees in front of a man tends to get you jumped." She glanced up, laughing harder when she saw he was staring down at her and waggling his brows.

"See if that happens again," she muttered when she finally regained control of herself. "Not likely."

"Brutal."

"Damn straight."

He kissed the top of her head. "Tough. Beautiful. Smart. Sexy. Funny—"

"What are you doing?"

"Brilliant. Valuable. Worthy. Clever. *Sassy*," he continued, staring down at her as though just reciting character traits was a normal part of human conversation.

"I—"

Fingers covered her lips. "You're all of those things, sweetheart, and so many more. Loving. Independent. Sweet. Vulnerable. Courageous. Resilient—"

"Stop," she said. "Please, Luke. I'm not all of those things. I barely hold it together most of the time."

"And welcome to the rest of the world, Becky. So many of us are just treading water." He cupped her cheek. "But you. *You* are special. You're so much more than a grieving daughter or a ridiculously smart lawyer. You're more than just a friend or girlfriend or lover. You're—"

"Do not say special."

"Tough shit, Rebecca." He cupped the other cheek, waited until her eyes were locked with his. "Tough shit because you *are* special."

"Oh, *fuck*," she murmured.

Because her eyes burned and her throat was tight and, dammit, there were those little drops of salty liquid leaking out of the corners of her lashes. They dripped down her cheeks, pooling on Luke's chest.

He wrapped her in his arms, held her tight. "You're allowed

to cry," he said. "You're allowed to feel. You're allowed to be torn up because as much as you don't want to admit it, the wound your father inflicted on your heart isn't healed."

"Fuck off," she snapped. "I'm fine. I don't need—I'm not some broken thing."

"Of course you're not," he said, his tone soft despite her harshness. "But Becky, sweetheart, you're *human*. And that means that your feelings won't always stay collated into nice, neat files. Sometimes shit spills out and things get messy."

She pushed against his chest, but Luke wouldn't let her go.

And then *she* couldn't let him go.

She hadn't been allowed emotions. Not for so fucking long.

No. The reality was that she hadn't allowed *herself* to feel.

Because down that path came disappointment.

Warm palms brushed over her hair, glided along her spine, slow, gentle movements that soothed her as she cried and cried and cried. Tears for her mom, for her father, and Luke, and . . . for her.

She couldn't ever remember crying for her own losses, though she must have at some point.

Bec remembered her mother's funeral, how there had been two caskets, one for her mom and one for her brother, Liam. She remembered seeing the wooden letters she'd picked out on a shopping trip with her mother. They'd been displayed in front of his tiny casket, and she'd grabbed the L, desperate to have something tangible of her mother and the baby when everything in life seemed so fragile and transient.

Her father had torn it from her hands at the gravesite, tossed it down into the hole.

She shivered at the memory of its thud hitting the top of the casket.

And yet, Bec hadn't cried. She'd understood that it was her job to be strong for her father, to be tough and resilient and—

She shouldn't have had to be any of those things.

Not at seven.

Not at ten.

Not as a child.

And it made her so fucking heartbroken that'd she'd needed to be that way just because her father hadn't been able to put aside his grief enough to love her as she should have been loved.

She was livid. So fucking angry that he'd forced her into that and that he'd reached out *now?* After years of ignoring emails and texts and voicemails, after only occasionally deeming her worthy of the rare one-sentence but incredibly terse reply. After everything, he wanted to speak with her now.

Where in the fuck did he get off?

Bec's shoulders went tight as a sudden thought occurred to her.

Luke's hand stopped its soothing movement. "What is it?"

"What if . . ." She shook her head. "It's stupid that I assumed this whole thing has to do with some big behavioral or physical change of his. It's been more than twenty years, he's—" She broke off, inhaled and exhaled deeply. "Just because *I've* changed doesn't mean that he's going to be any different. He's probably just wishing me an early birthday."

Except her birthday wasn't for another month.

He'd also never called her on or near her birthday before.

This was different. She knew that as instinctively as she knew when to take on a particularly challenging case.

"You don't believe that," Luke said after a moment.

"No," she said, her voice soft, her fingers trailing over his chest, tracing nonsensical patterns on his skin that somehow soothed her. "No," she repeated. "I don't believe that. He called for a reason. One I don't know or can't fathom, but something has changed."

"He's getting older," Luke said. "He might want—"

"Don't."

Don't get her hopes up.

Don't make her feel something when she wasn't sure she could ever forgive her father.

"Okay," he said, fingers slipping through her hair again, petting her, *gentling* her.

They lay like that for a long time, their bodies intertwined, Luke's hands moving over her body, and that comforting touch had the tension leeching out of her.

"There's only one way to find out what your father really wants," he eventually murmured.

Bec sucked in a breath, knowing what was coming but still having to ask anyway. "How?"

"You listen to the voicemail."

Damn. She'd been afraid he'd say that.

CHAPTER 19

Luke

HE WATCHED the change wash over Becky.

Her shoulders stiffened, the arm that had formerly laid pliant across his chest tightened, her breathing sped, and . . . then all that tension dissipated.

"You had to go and say it, didn't you?" Forced lightness laced her tone. "I was happy to pretend to be too busy, to *forget* the message was there, and then you had to be all reasonable."

Luke chuckled. "Sorry, not sorry?"

"Hmph."

"You know I'm right," he told her. "You *hate* that I'm right, but it doesn't change the fact that I'm—"

"Right?" She pushed up to sitting. "Why don't you say it a few more times?"

His lips curved and, not deterred by the sass in the least, he tugged her back down to his side. "I'm so right. Gloriously, perfectly right—"

Her hand clamped over his mouth. "Yes, yes. Now you don't have to rub—"

He flicked his tongue out, teasing the sensitive skin on her palm. Becky jumped and tugged her hand away. "Really, Pearson?"

Luke folded his arms behind his head. "Let's continue with how I'm right."

"Ugh." She started to get off the bed. "No," she grumbled. "I've had enough of that—*ack!*" He'd snagged her wrist, yanking her to the mattress, and climbing on top of her. She was naked, a fact his body definitely noticed, but she was also running, so he focused on the more pressing issues first.

"Listen to the message, sugar pie." He bent his head, sucked one nipple in his mouth.

"*Luke!*"

"Do it," he said, kissing his way down her body. Becky's hands wove into his hair and pushed ever so discretely in the direction of her pussy. He dragged his mouth lower, brushed his tongue along the insides of her thighs. "Do it, and I'll do that thing with my fingers again."

She stilled, lifted her head up to look at him. "*Really?*"

He circled her clit with his thumb. "Really."

"I can't believe you're talking about my vagina and my father in the same sentence."

Slow circles. Gentle, teasing circles.

"Technically, I didn't put those two things together."

"You im—implied it."

"*You* inferred it." He spread her wide, bent to suck her clit into his mouth.

"*Fuck.*" Her hips jumped, her fingers went tight against his scalp, and his dick, already hard and aching, turned to granite. As usual, things with his Becky had escalated further than he'd intended. "Stop using big words," she said. "You know it turns me on."

Luke's eyes shot to hers, and he saw the mischief in those gray pools. "Stop equivocating and just listen to the message."

"Mmm. *Equivocating.*" Her head flopped back to the mattress. "So. Many. Letters."

"You're such a—" Fuck he couldn't think of another big word, not when he was between Becky's thighs, the salty tang of her against his tongue. *There.* Got one. "Such a hedonist."

She laughed. "Oh, my God," she said. "We're absolutely ridiculous."

"I'm the one trying to lick your pussy here." He circled her clit with his tongue.

"No, what you're *trying—ah—*to do is oral sex me into submission."

He paused. "Is it working?"

Laughter shook her frame, tightened her legs around him. "Yes, Pearson. It's working. Stop teasing and make me come, and I'll listen to the voicemail."

A flick of his tongue made her moan. "I understand where we went wrong now." He slid one finger through her folds, pushed it inside. "Before," he said as her breath caught and her hips tilted, trying to get him deeper.

"What the fuck are you talking about?" she snapped. "I—*oh fuck.*"

He'd done the thing with his finger.

"I should have sexed you into submission."

Hazy eyes met his. "Never would have worked."

He repeated the thing with his finger, watching as her eyes rolled to the back of her head. "If I'd known this"—more finger—"it would have worked."

"You—*ah—*act like knowing how to find a woman's G-spot should earn you a gold medal."

"I don't give a fuck about medals, so long as *this*"—another teasing touch—"has you screaming my name."

Her mouth dropped open. "Oh, *damn*. You're good, Pearson."

He grinned.

"Fine." She lifted her hips slightly. "Sex me into submission, and *then* I'll listen to the voicemail."

"I thought you'd never ask."

"Men are such—" she huffed, but her complaint was cut off when she cried out his name.

Yup. Luke definitely deserved that gold medal.

————

AFTERWARD, they showered, threw on the bare minimum of clothes, then found their way back to Becky's bed.

He picked up her cell from her nightstand. "Ready?"

"No," she muttered, but took it from him anyway, punching in four numbers to unlock the screen. They corresponded to a date in the past he was hoping to replicate at some point—four ten—the day he'd first proposed to her.

She hadn't accepted . . . because that wasn't his Becky.

She would never be an easy woman to love. She was formed of layers and layers, some soft and generous, some vulnerable and protected by sharp spikes, but if he could make his way to the core of her again?

That was the best.

If someone made it into that inner circle, his Becky loved without barriers. She would move the world to make that person happy, love them at the expense of herself.

She gave everything. He just hadn't been able to give everything back.

But he was different now. She owned him and he would give her everything down to his last breath.

Her finger hovered over the button to play the message for a moment. "I—"

"You got this."

Eyes locked with his, the finger came down, and the voice-mail began to play.

"Hi, uh, Rebecca. My name is Helen. I'm your father's . . . um, wife. I—"

A loud gust of air made them both wince.

"I'm sorry. I probably shouldn't be calling. I know you don't want to hear from us, but your father is sick and . . . I, uh, thought you should know in case. Anyway, I hope you'll come. He'd really like to see you . . ."

Helen rattled off the name of the hospital and a room number.

The message ended, and she played it again. Then a third time. But when she would have gone for a fourth, Luke stayed her hands.

She didn't fight him, just let him slip her cell from her grip and set it on the nightstand.

"He—" Her shoulders sagged the slightest bit. "He didn't tell me he'd gotten remarried." Her voice was small, too fucking small for the vibrant woman he loved. "I've talked to him once a year on his birthday. I've emailed. Texted. And this Helen thinks—" She shook her head, hands clenching into fists where they rested on the outsides of her thighs. "I *waited* for him to call me, hoped he'd remember my birthday or maybe send me a fucking Christmas present." She jumped to her feet, paced alongside the bed. "Do you know that before Abby and Sera, I was the *only* one who spent every holiday at school? *Alone.* I was so pathetic that the different teachers took turns bringing me home so I wouldn't be by myself. And he—*he* has the fucking gall to say that it was me? That I didn't want to talk to him. I—*I*—"

She stumbled to a stop, knees giving out.

But he was there before she crumpled to the floor.

Luke scooped her into his arms, carried her back to bed, and held her as his powerful, strong, courageous woman lost her battle with tears.

Sometimes the creatures with the hardest shells had the softest insides.

And his Becky, she had a really hard shell.

CHAPTER 20

Bec

SHE'D BEEN CATEGORIZING Luke in her head as the man she'd loved.

Emphasis on the past tense.

But as she looked around the living room of her apartment, the members of the Sextant who were in town gathered because of the man she loved *today*.

Luke had called them while she'd slept off her crying fit, and now it was after ten and her friends all had to work the next day and they'd still come and . . . great. Because the fact that they'd come, that Heather had FaceTimed in the middle of her workday in Berlin, that CeCe was on a beach in the Mediterranean and still had called made her feel like crying all over again.

"I don't like having feelings," she muttered.

Abby shoved a tissue box at her. "You're not the Tin Man. You've always had a big heart, *Becky*."

Bec narrowed her eyes at her friend, who just grinned unrepentantly, then turned to glare at Luke, who raised his hands in surrender and mouthed, *"I didn't know."*

"Why do you think you're usually the first one any of us call when we're in trouble, huh?"

"Because I'm single and nearby?"

Luke snorted and slipped into the kitchen, abandoning her, the jerk.

"Except, you probably have the heaviest workload of all of us, Heather aside," Rachel said.

"More," Heather chimed in. "Clay has made me slow down the last six months."

Sera's lips twitched. "What exactly is your definition of slowing down?"

"Not beach time," CeCe said, reclining back on her lounger and taking a sip of a colorful drink with a purple umbrella in it.

"Or staying in the same time zone for more than a few days at a time," Rachel teased.

Heather glared. "Considering you're the one who makes my schedule, whose fault is that?"

"Ladies," Abby said. "We've been called here for a reason."

Exactly one moment of silence before the room burst into laughter, including Bec.

"We've . . . been called . . ." Sera was bent over on the couch, clutching her side as giggles erupted out of her.

"We need cloaks," Rachel managed between laughs.

"And a boiling cauldron," CeCe added.

"Magic crystals." Heather.

"More wine," Bec said.

"Amen to that, sister," Abby muttered. "I swear, you guys, I don't even know why we're friends sometimes."

Sera tugged their reluctant friend into a hug. "Aw! You love us."

Luke walked in with a bottle of wine and filled their glasses, then sat down on the couch next to Bec. "Should I go?" he whispered. "I don't want to leave you, but I also don't want to intrude if you want to be with the girls—"

This man.

God, she loved him.

"Thank you." She cupped his cheek. "For caring. I'd like it if you stayed, at least until any talk of penises starts happening."

His brows rose. "Is that going to happen?"

Her lips twitched. "Guaranteed."

He pressed a kiss to her forehead. "Okay. Staying till talk of penises commences."

Abby waggled her brows. "So tempting."

"Shut it, you," Bec told her.

"What happened to the picture of the kiddos?" Abby asked innocently.

Bec's eyes narrowed at her friend. Luke had picked up the pictures they'd knocked to the ground before her friends had come over, and though Sera had given the naked walls a second look, no one had said anything.

Abby grinned unrepentantly.

"Becky—*Bec* is considering redecorating," Luke said.

Smiles all around, the punks. But then Sera sighed. "You've got a good one there."

Bec's mouth curved. "I do," she said. "I really do. Don't know why he puts up with me, considering I've spent this entire evening pretending to be a gigantic pile of tears."

"Well, first," Abby said. "He's lucky you let him come back into your life—no offense, Luke."

"None taken," he said with a grin. "I am lucky she decided to give me another chance."

"Second, you're fucking awesome, dude." She leaned over Sera and lightly punched Bec's arm. "What happened to the

Rebecca Darden, kickass lawyer who doesn't take any shit from anyone?"

"She got motherfucking feelings," Bec grumbled. "It sucks ass."

"I happen to like your ass," Luke said.

"I bet he does," Heather said with a cackle. "What kinds of things is he doing with that yummy ass, *Becky?*"

Bec stood, grabbed Luke's hand and tugged him to his feet as well. "And that's your cue."

He hesitated. "But there wasn't any talk of penises."

And now all the girls were cackling.

"There was yummy ass talk," Bec told him. "That's close enough."

Luke's lips were tugging up at the corners. "If you say so." He leaned in, pressed his lips to the spot just in front of her ear. "You sure you're okay?"

Bec nodded. "I am."

He rolled back on his heels. "Okay then, I'm going on an ice cream run. Orders?" he asked the room at large, typing the requests into his phone and chuckling when Heather and CeCe expressed their jealousy at missing out. After they'd all finished, he leaned in and kissed her soundly on the lips and long enough to make her head spin. "I'll be back in a bit." He started to leave, paused, and met her gaze. "I love you."

"Dude," CeCe breathed after he'd gone. "You need to put a ring on that."

They all laughed, and then Heather said, "As much as I'm enjoying this little tête-à-tête, I have a meeting in fifteen minutes and don't want to miss all the important juicy bits."

"*Juicy* bits?" Abby said with a snort.

"Yes," Heather replied. "Big ol' giant juicy bits. I like them. I want them—"

"I'm going to puke," Rachel interjected.

Sera nodded. "Let's step away from juicy bits and move onto emotions."

"I second that," CeCe said.

"I'm still semi-interested in Heather's juicy bits—" Bec stopped, made a face. "Okay, that sounded a lot less dirty in my head. I'm sorry to everyone involved."

"Bec." Sera took her hand. "For the love of God, please save us more juice talk and get to the point."

Bec took a glug from her wine glass. "My dad, or rather, my *stepmother* called me."

Silence. Only half the room—herself, Abby, and Sera— knew why that was such a big deal, and so Abby and Sera were stunned into muteness by the news. Rachel, CeCe, and Heather were quiet, as they no doubt waited for more information as to why her stepmother calling was such a big deal.

"The long and short of it," she said, "is that my mom died, and my dad shipped me off to boarding school. I was the *Harry Potter* equivalent of not going home for holidays, of being lonely and isolated, except my dad was still alive. He didn't visit or call, not even on my birthday. Every bit of contact we've had over the last twenty-something years has been because of me, because I called."

She sighed, took another sip of wine. "And even then, even after I moved back, he still never had time to meet for lunch or dinner, never wanted me to come by his house or office. Turns out he remarried and never mentioned it to me, then started another life, and other than my trust fund—which I haven't touched since I graduated from law school—he hasn't given me a second thought."

Yay for family.

Another sip from her glass as clarity dawned. "I think I reminded him too much of my mom, of everything he lost. Maybe I should have pushed harder, called more—"

"What. A. Dick." Harsh words from a source Bec wouldn't have expected.

From CeCe.

"You needed him, and he abandoned you. Good parents are good because they put their kids first." Her tone took on a bitter note. "I know because mine didn't."

"We're all on that particular train, CeCe," Heather said. "I had parents who made babies like they were going out of style but didn't want to actually spend time with them. Abby's parents are no peaches—her mom having an affair and, no offense, but your bio dad is a total dickwad—"

"None taken," Abby said.

"Let's see," Heather tapped her chin. "CeCe's disowned her because, *gasp*, she wanted to live her own life. Rachel's dad was both absentee and shockingly bad. Who's left?"

Sera raised her hand. "I don't have any of that. My parents are still happily married. But I am incredibly sorry you guys went through that."

"Girl," Abby touched her arm. "Your parents aren't peaches, either. Remember when you wanted to stop with the pageants, and they shipped you off to boarding school? Or the time you didn't want to be in that commercial, so they forbid you from eating anything except for carrots and spinach until you agreed?"

"It wasn't that bad. I was getting chunky—"

Heather raised a brow. "You'd what? Gone from a size double zero to a zero?"

"I—" Sera fumbled for a few moments to find the right words then sighed. "Okay, fine. My parents *were* pretty shitty."

"Glad you got there in the end," Heather said with a smirk. "But putting that revelation aside, my point is that none of us are the same, aside from our dirty ass minds—"

Abby snorted, thus confirming *her* dirty-minded tendencies.

Heather ignored her. "We're all very different and *still* not one of us had stellar parents. And at the risk of digressing, but something I think is also important is that the common experience of going through that is probably why we found each other in the first place. Like knows like. Pain knows pain." Heather waved a hand, probably because she was bordering on poetic, and Heather definitely didn't do poetic. "Anyway, I think the most important thing we can deduce is that their ineptitude has nothing to do with us."

Bec frowned, and she wasn't the only one in the room to do so, but Heather went on with her explanation before they could question her logic.

"I'm not saying any of us are perfect. Far from it, actually. I'm just saying our imperfections and, on the opposite side, our success and whatever happiness we've managed to carve out in our lives haven't happened because of them. We've managed to become the people we are today *in spite* of their interference and absence and general douchebaggery."

Abby nodded. "My dad definitely has a degree in douchebaggery."

"And mine," CeCe added.

"Ditto," Rachel said.

"I guess it's no wonder why we're so fucked up," Bec said dryly, and they all laughed. "Heather, I know you have to go, and I definitely feel what you're saying. But . . . I guess I don't necessarily feel comfortable blaming a sick man for my emotional problems. I've never been one to not take responsibility for my actions."

"Which makes you a much better person than your father."

Oh.

Bec's heart twisted. Not because she believed that she was the better person, but because she'd always blamed herself for her dad leaving her.

It was her fault that he'd gone.

She'd seen the pictures, knew she looked like her mother, knew she reminded him too much of her mom and that the resemblance hurt him.

But that was . . . bullshit.

It wasn't *her* fault.

And it never had been.

Strange how just thinking the words changed everything, as though a switch had flipped in her brain or maybe in her heart, or maybe Luke and her friends had finally given her the courage to understand.

She'd been a kid.

It wasn't on her.

Bec blinked back tears, though instead of crying for her past and the hurt and the painful memories, those tears were full of relief.

Relief she no longer had to carry that burden.

Relief her life no longer had to be defined by something that had happened to her growing up.

Relief she finally could be herself and that she didn't always need to be tough or impenetrable or unfeeling.

Arms wrapped around her, holding tightly as she sniffed. "Okay, fine. You win. You guys are the best," she said.

"Of course we are," Heather joked, startling a laugh out of her.

Sera broke away from the group hug. "So great, Ms. Becky here doesn't have to see her dad. She can just move on with Luke and live happily ever after."

"No." This time the rebuttal was from Bec herself. "I'm going to see my father because I have balls of steel. I'm going to clear that final hurdle and put this shit behind me. *Then* I'm going to move on with my HEA with Luke."

"Damn," Sera whispered. "You're good."

"Not exactly," Bec told her. "I just know I have to be done with this once and for all."

On the screen, Heather waved a hand—in *these are not the droids you're looking for* fashion. "I've trained you well, young Jedi." Her lips twitched. "I'm sorry that I need to run, but—"

"Go," Bec told her. "And thank you." Heather's portion of the screen went blank, and Bec looked around the room. "Thank you all. I couldn't have done this, be semi-healthy and happy without you guys. I'd still be in the office working four-teen-hour days and not enjoying anything other than the occasional book and girls' night."

"Now you're down to ten-hour days," Sera teased. "That's huge progress."

For her it was, but she also understood Sera's point. "I'm not stopping here. I'm going to grab onto my happy ending, and I'm going to fight for it and I'm never letting it go again."

"Damn straight you are," Abby said with a nod.

Rachel lifted her palm for a high five. "Fuck yeah, *Becky*."

"Give him hell, *sugar pie*," CeCe chimed in.

"I take it back. I hate you all," Bec muttered.

"I'll get more wine," Sera crowed. "And then we're talking about how Rachel and Sebastian got caught making out in Heather's office."

Rachel's cheeks went fluorescent, and Bec grinned.

God, she loved these woman.

Then Luke pushed through the front door, individual cartons of ice cream in a bag that he doled out to each one of them in turn, like some sexy, sweet treat bearing Santa Claus, and Bec's cheeks actually hurt from smiling so much.

Because she fucking loved that man, too.

CHAPTER 21

Luke

BECKY'S ALARM WENT OFF, and he reached over to shut it off. Between the news of her father, her mid-evening nap, and then the girls coming over, she'd barely gotten any sleep the night before.

He hadn't slept at all, had just held her in his arms and waited for her to pull away.

Her father. Him. The two men who'd been the closest to her had wounded her deeply. How could she possibly trust any man ever again? How could she trust *him*? Those thoughts had twisted around in his head for hours, and he knew, just fucking knew, that sooner or later his Becky was going to come to her senses and ask him to go.

Or kick his ass to the curb.

Both of which he deserved.

Fingers on his cheek startled him. He glanced down into the eyes of the woman he loved.

Fuck, he loved her so much.

"Morning," she said softly.

"Morning," he managed to croak back.

Blonde brows pulled together, gray eyes studied him intently. "I've been thinking."

They were soft words. Pitying words.

Luke's gut sank, twisting itself into knots, knowing that the moment he'd spent all night worrying about had come to fruition. He'd hoped for a few more days, maybe weeks, but perhaps this was for the best. A clean break.

Clean. *Ha.* He was about to be sliced to the core.

"I understand," Luke told her before she could give him his brush-off. "I'll go back to Texas, give you plenty of space when I'm in town—"

"What the fuck are you talking about?"

He shook himself. "Me. Your father. We're pieces of shit who don't deserve any part of you. I should leave you to your life and—"

Two palms gripped his cheeks. "Shut. Up." She tilted his face so their foreheads touched, her breath hot on his lips. "This is the first and last time I'm going to say this, okay? We both have our demons, and we're both fucked up in our own special ways, but you don't get to sacrifice yourself because you have a hero complex." She shook him slightly. "What happened to you fighting for me?"

He brushed her hands off his face, pushed up from the mattress. "Since I spent the whole night reliving all the ways the men in your life have hurt you. And *I'm* one of them, Bec. You're better off without any of us and—"

"It's Becky," she snapped. "And I didn't fall in love with you because you're really good at shouldering guilt and beating yourself up. I fell in love with you again because you're sweet and protective and make me laugh. Also, your tongue is fucking brilliant, and that thing you do with your index finger should be illegal." She stood and poked him in the chest. Hard. "So don't shit on that love by reverting back to being the martyr. We've moved beyond that. Remember?"

Fuck.

She was right.

"*Of course*, I'm right." She glared, and he realized he'd spoken aloud. "I need you in my life, Luke. You make it . . . better." A roll of her eyes. "I know that's pathetically unromantic, but the truth is that you make *me* better, you love me for who I am, and I—I'm not just going to let you go because you've developed a sudden streak of nobility." Those eyes that had rolled a heartbeat before now glistened with tears. "You promised you'd fight for me, for us. How can I trust in that if you're going to give up and walk away because you think I'm better off without you? Newsflash"—she smacked him—"I'm not. I want you in my life. But you've got to be *all* in. Because you doubting yourself and us, thinking it's best to just leave at the first sign of adversity, that's not good for either of us."

Luke dropped his chin to his chest. "I'm sorry."

"How do I know you're not going to be *sorry* again the next time something bad happens, huh? How do I know you're going to stay for—" She swallowed. "Forever. Because I want you. *Forever*. I want a future, regardless of this shit with my father and our past. I love you. I want *you*."

His heart was pounding, his throat was tight, his eyes burned like hell.

Because he wanted that, too.

He wanted Becky forever.

"Damn," he said. "I'm really fucking this up."

"Yeah, you are."

His lips twitched. "You should also know that despite this talk, I may still occasionally be a fucking idiot—"

"Occasionally?" she muttered.

"Frequently," he amended. "But I do usually learn from my

mistakes." He met her gaze. "I'm sorry, sweetheart. I wish I could say that my idiocy was from lack of sleep. But nope. It was my own mind that had convinced me I needed to leave you in peace. That and my exceedingly guilty conscience."

"Well, stop it," she said. "Stop feeling guilty for things that happened a decade ago. Let's worry about now. And our future."

Future.

Luke liked the sound of that a lot.

"You love me, sugar pie?" he asked, sliding his arms around Becky and pulling her close.

"Against my better judgment, I seem to have fallen for you again."

"My subliminal programming worked then."

She snorted. "Dork."

"*Your* dork."

"I'll take that."

"Should we go back to bed for a while?" A beat. "Or all day?"

"I like the sound"—she yawned—"of that. I'll text my boss. I've never used a sick day in my life," she said. "Today seems like a good day to start."

"I like that plan," he said, lifting her up into his arms. "I feel like I should apologize for being an idiot again."

"Please don't, Pearson," she said snuggling close to him as he tucked them both back under the covers. "Remember that whole communication thing I mentioned before? Let's chalk this up to that. You had a concern, you voiced it, and we moved on."

"And you told me that you loved me."

"Pft. As if that were ever in question. I've loved you since the night of prom."

"What? Why?" he asked. "All I was thinking about was how desperate I was to feel you up in that red dress."

"Because." She pressed a kiss to the spot just above his heart. "Most boys would have been mad I decided to ditch them the night before the dance to go with my friends. But instead of getting huffy or angry, you spent the whole night dancing with my friends, making sure we all had a good time. I knew it then."

"Knew what?"

"That you were special."

"Fuck, Becky."

She pushed up to see his face. "What?"

"You undo me."

Returning to snuggling, she said, "I know."

"And modest, too," he teased, running his fingers lightly up and down her spine. "So, are you going to tell me now?"

"Tell you what?"

He wound a strand of her hair around one finger. "What I interrupted earlier, what you've *been thinking.*"

"Oh."

A tug of that blonde lock of hair. "Oh? That's it?"

"I shouldn't tell you, just out of principle."

"Principle?" he asked.

"For making me get all ramped up and preachy at six in the morning." She sniffed. "I should make you *suffer.*"

Luke shifted his hips. As usual, just holding her had made him hard and aching.

"I *am* suffering."

Snorting, she said, "I was thinking about the dates. We have five left, by my calculations."

"Should I make some quip about lawyers being bad at math?" She glared and he lifted his palms in surrender. "Never mind. Five dates left is right."

"Well, I was thinking about just skipping to date ten." Her fingers drew nonsensical shapes over his chest. "Or to the part that came after date ten." She pressed another kiss to the place above his heart. "To the part where I say I don't want you to leave."

"Oh."

"Oh?" she teased, throwing his words back at him. "That's it?"

He laughed, stealing her lips in a kiss that he hoped conveyed how much he loved this woman. "That's it," he told her when they broke for air, chests heaving. "I don't care about the numbers. I just know I want forever with you."

"Is that so?"

"I think I've made that more than clear."

She wove her hands into his hair, tugged his mouth down to hers again. "Well, make it clear again."

Done.

He pressed his lips to hers, nipping the corner of her mouth, sliding his tongue along hers in the rhythm they both liked best. Her body was flush against his, soft to his hard, lean curves fitting perfectly into his boxier shape. He loved the feel of her in his arms, of her mouth tangling with his, the slight tug of his hair when he was kissing her exactly right.

"I don't . . . care when," he said, gasping in air and trying pathetically to make the words semi-coherent. "When . . . we do it, but I"—he sucked in a breath—"I need to give you Date Ten."

She frowned.

"Promise me."

"To do what?"

"To go on Date Ten with me."

A shrug, her brows draw together. "Okaay. I promise to go on Date Ten with you?"

"More question than affirmation, but I'll take it," he said.

Becky rested her head on his chest and, as was their habit,

they lay quietly in bed, each lost in their own thoughts. Luke liked that they were creating new habits, and he didn't hate the fact that she was close to him.

Eventually, however, she pulled away, reached for her cell, and sent off a quick text.

Then she sighed and pushed off him.

"I think it's time I see my dad."

Luke wanted to tell her, "Fuck no." He wanted to protect her from whatever the bastard might say or do.

But this was *his* Becky.

She didn't need him to fight her battles for her.

She needed him by her side, to help her if she stumbled, and to be ready with a hug—and maybe a bottle of wine and a box of It's-Its—if things went to shit.

She needed a partner, not a savior.

And Luke finally thought he could be that for her.

So, instead of telling her she shouldn't go, he held her hand on the drive over to the hospital. Instead of demanding to accompany her, he asked if she wanted him there, and when she *did* want him by her side, Luke quietly slipped his arm around her waist as they entered her father's room and saw the frail man in front of them.

Too thin, cheekbones in sharp relief, but the man's gray eyes showed him to be undoubtedly related to Becky.

A woman, thin and blonde, who would have been beautiful if not for the pale skin and reddened eyes adorned by huge dark circles, sat at his bedside. She stood when they entered, but Becky hardly noticed.

"Dad?" Becky asked, horror in the greeting.

CHAPTER 22

Bec

IT WAS TERRIBLE.

So much worse than she'd imagined.

He couldn't look like this, couldn't be *this* sick. Not when he'd always seemed larger than life, boisterous, domineering. She remembered him being able to captivate a room just by uttering a few choice words.

Now he looked as though he couldn't even squish an ant.

"Rebecca?" he asked.

"Hi, Dad," she murmured.

"Why are you here?"

Blunt words, sharpened to wound. The woman next to him, a slender blonde with a pretty face and kind eyes and who was, presumably, Helen, her father's new wife, gasped. *"Ronald."*

Luke squeezed Becky's hand.

"Good to see you too, Dad," she said, lifting her chin and crossing over to the bed. "Thanks for returning my phone calls."

Helen frowned, searching through her purse for a moment before extracting a cell phone. "I'm sorry. I didn't realize—"

"I wasn't referring to today," Bec told her, "so much as over the last twenty years."

"O-oh." Helen's gaze dropped to her hands. "I meddled." A sigh. "I shouldn't have."

Bec touched her arm. "I'm glad you did. This is a conversation we need to have, as much as *Ronald* has tried to avoid it."

"You shouldn't be here, Rebecca."

"Because you can't stand the sight of me? Or because you didn't want your new wife to know just how much of an asshole you are?"

Another gasp from Helen.

"Sorry," Bec told her. "I should have warned you, my father and I don't get along. Though that mostly stems from the fact that he abandoned me and then wouldn't return my calls for twenty years."

Helen glanced from Bec to *Ronald*, eyes searching both of them for long moments.

"Is that true?" she finally asked.

Bec's father looked away, and suddenly that anger inside her, that rage twisting and wounding and *hurting* so fucking badly was just . . . gone. In that empty cavern, resignation took its place.

She was never going to get what she wanted.

"Unfortunately, it is true," Bec said. "I'll spare you the sordid details, but know that for the last twenty-odd years I wanted nothing more than to have a relationship with my father. Ask him how many times I called or emailed, how I went to his office once a month for fucking years trying to see him, but he was always too busy. Ask him how he never wished me a happy birthday or merry Christmas—"

"We're Jewish," her father interjected.

Bec lifted one brow. "Happy Hanukah, then?"

"You haven't changed," her dad snapped. "You still want too much."

Bec's eyes dropped to the floor, hurt washing over her and making her wish for the empty feeling from a few heartbeats before.

But then Luke was there, slipping a reassuring hand around her waist, tugging her close. "No," he said. "She's never wanted enough for herself. She deserves so much more—"

"It's okay," she said, love taking the place of hurt. Love for this man that somehow made even the shittiest version of a family reunion better.

His emerald eyes darkened. "No, it's fucking not."

She squeezed his hand and he squeezed back, giving her the strength to face her stepmom. "The truth is that after my mother died, not once did my father reach out to me. I was the horrible painful secret, locked away and disapproved of. *I* wasn't worthy of Ronald's fucking attention because I wasn't my mother, was I?"

Gray eyes so much like her own drifted to the window, stared out. "No. No, you weren't her. Could never be her."

Her all-encompassing anger might have left her, alongside the emptiness and most of her hurt, but a lot of her spiked armor had flown the coop along with those emotions, and so, Bec wasn't going to lie—hearing those words stung.

"Well," she said, lifting her chin, shoring herself up. "Good to know nothing's changed. I'll leave you to your—"

Movement at the door caught Bec's gaze. Luke shifted to let someone pass by him and Bec turned fully, watching a pretty brunette walk into the room. The woman was much younger than her, maybe a college student or recent grad, but she moved with a confident grace, as though she'd been striding across hospital rooms for a long time.

And, after seeing the state of her father, Bec thought, maybe she had.

The shift in the room at her entrance was palpable.

Tension twisted the air. Helen jumped to her feet, moving to place herself between Bec and the girl.

"Mom?" she asked. "Dad? Is everything okay?"

Punch.

To Bec's heart. Her gut. Her brain.

Somehow, she'd known it was coming, and yet the blow was almost physical.

But Luke had her, his warm hand on her spine centering her, understanding in an instant that she could have withstood almost anything aside from this.

Bec's father had moved on without her.

Replacement wife. Replacement daughter.

Helen laced her arm through her daughter's and led her back to the door. "Why don't you go find your brother? Get us some coffee from the cafeteria?" She glanced at Bec. "Just some coffee and some food, okay?"

Bec had been doing okay until—

Okay, fuck it all, she'd been barely hanging on. She felt as though she'd been treading water in the open ocean for hours, and now a shark had decided to swim on up and chomp on her leg.

Brother.

Yeah, that fit.

Somehow, it all fit.

She ignored her half-sister leaving and instead turned back to her father. He *had* to feel something—shame, sadness, disappointment. But as she stared at him, Bec discovered that she couldn't find any trace of those emotions.

Instead, there was . . . nothing.

Aside from the same unique color of their eyes, they might have been perfect strangers.

And, if she were facing facts, they *were* strangers.

Bec glanced up at Luke. "I'm ready to go now."

Fury had tinged the tops of his cheeks with pink, but to his credit, he only nodded and took her hand.

"I'm sorry," Helen murmured. "I didn't know . . ."

Bec managed a half-smile. "It's—I—" She shook her head, wanting to find some absolution. This wasn't Helen's fault. She seemed like a nice woman who'd been trying to do the right thing.

But in the end, the words wouldn't come, so Bec just averted her eyes and let Luke lead her to the door.

She paused on the threshold, glanced back one last time at her dad. "I hope you found what you were looking for."

Her father's voice was still the same, even if his body wasn't.

It trailed after her into the hallway.

"I didn't," he said. "But I'll be with her soon enough."

Bec squared her shoulders and lifted her chin and walked with Luke to the elevators, but at the last minute, she tugged him into the stairwell and sank down onto the top step, resting her head on his shoulder.

She wanted to cry, but couldn't. Instead, she just sat there and sighed, despondent and aching and . . . just so *fucking* disappointed

"The people who have the most power over you also hold the greatest ability to disappoint," Luke said, and when she glanced up at him in surprise, he shrugged. "Something my therapist once told me."

"Yeah," Bec agreed. "I think he got it right on that one."

The barest hint of a smile on his lips. "You okay?"

"No." Another sigh. "But I will be. I just wanted—" She broke off.

"The perfect ending." He brushed a hand down her hair. "I'm sorry. You deserved that perfect, storybook ending. You deserved to have your family be there and—"

"He's not my family," Bec said. "I've made my own."

Luke nodded, pressed a kiss to the top of her head. "The girls *are* awesome."

"You, too, you know that, right? You're my family, too."

His lips curved. "I think you mean, I've weaseled my way back into your life, and I'm not leaving."

Her own smile teased the corners of her mouth. "More like a fungus, growing under the surface until one day it pops up and"—she clicked her tongue—"fucking mushrooms everywhere."

Luke laughed, hugged her tight. "As long as I'm a fungus without a cure, then I'll take it."

"As if you'd be any other kind." She chuckled. "Look at us, so romantic, talking of fungi and weasels after an emotional scene at my father's deathbed. If this isn't in a rom-com, it definitely should be."

"I can get behind that."

"Ew."

He squeezed her again. "Sorry, poor word choice." Then he bent and whispered in her ear. "But I thought you liked it when I got *behind* you."

She giggled.

Luke joined her for a few moments before sobering. "I am sorry, though. Sorry he couldn't be what you needed."

"Me, too," Bec said. "But what I'm realizing is that sometimes the people you need the most just don't have it in them to fulfill that role, and you either have to move on or find it in yourself."

"Sweetheart," he whispered. "That's really . . ."

"Deep?" She smirked.

He frowned. "I was going to say incredible."

"Damn, and take away my chance to insert another innuendo into this conversation?"

"Apparently." His lips twitched, and he tugged her to her feet. "Come on, let's get out of here. If we're playing hooky from work, we may as well do it right."

"Now *that* I can get behind."

And somehow, despite the last hellish half hour, Bec managed to walk out of the hospital with a smile on her face.

She knew the wounds under the surface wouldn't heal as easily, but for the first time in a long time, she was okay with that. No scrambling for armor or running or pushing people away.

She could just be.

And live.

She wanted to do that, too.

LATER THAT NIGHT, she filled in her friends, via video chat this time, since she and Luke were cuddled up in bed.

"I'm not going to lie," she said, after they'd all commiserated about asshole parents. "Aside from the dad stuff, it felt really good to not be at work today."

"And the sex," Abby said with a cackle. "I'm guessing the sex felt really *good*, too."

Luke laughed, and she smacked him.

"You," Bec said into her laptop, "are as bad as I am." A beat. "And I like it."

They all laughed.

"But seriously," she told them. "You guys mean the world to me."

"So many feelings," Heather said. "Hot damn."

Abby sniffed. "I'm sending you a virtual hug."

"We love you, Becky," CeCe said.

Rachel smiled. "I second that statement."

"We're family." From Sera and, yeah, that was exactly right.

"Thank you," she told them. "For everything."

"Thank *you* for letting us drink more wine," Abby joked. "We're using you for the free booze."

They all laughed, and then CeCe cleared her throat. "Um, actually, I'm not going to be able to partake in your free alcohol for a while." She paused, a smile growing on her face. "For seven more months, actually."

Five voices, including Bec's, rang out in excitement. Shrill excitement if Luke's wince was any indication.

"Oh, my God," Abby said. "You're going to be such a great mom!"

"I don't do the diaper thing," Heather said. "Don't forget that, m'kay?"

"Congrats, CeCe. I'm so happy for you guys," Rachel added.

Bec smiled. "I'm looking forward to you bossing McGregor around."

CeCe laughed. "Are you kidding? The man's already been hovering like a busy little bee. He'd be jumping through flame-covered hoops at the smallest sign of any bossing on my part."

"You need to take merciless advantage," Abby advised sagely.

They all giggled.

"You guys are terrible, but I love you anyway." CeCe grinned. "And I'm only taking a *little* advantage. Colin's been bringing me copious amounts of croissants since it seems to be the only thing I can keep down."

CeCe talked for a few more minutes, regaling them with humorous renditions of Colin's protectiveness before she yawned and they all bullied her off the phone with orders of a mid-afternoon nap. Abby's son, Carter, popped his face into the screen a second later, demanding a hug and consoling after a nightmare, and so she hung up. Then Sebastian came home, so Rachel signed off, and Heather was kissed off the line by Clay, who, quite literally, kissed her to distraction before pushing the button to disconnect.

"And then there were two," Sera joked ominously.

"You okay?" Bec asked.

"I'm great, actually," Sera said. "I got a new client today. He's some sort of tech genius who's looking for a new place. Wants something private and on the coast." A shrug and even through the phone line, Bec couldn't shake the feeling that her friend was sad. "Which means, expensive. Of course, it also means a better commission for me, so . . ."

"Win-win."

"Yup. Exactly." Sera smiled, but it was off.

Definitely sad.

"Salads tomorrow?"

She shook her head. "Can't. I'll squeeze myself into your calendar next week."

"Okay," Bec replied. "Get some sleep, okay? You look tired."

"Always so sweet to me." Sera reached a finger for the screen.

"Your turn's coming," Bec said, taking a stab at what was bothering her friend. It had to be hard to see everyone else happy and paired off. Even if Sera weren't jealous, exactly, it still had to sting that she was alone when her friends weren't. "If *I* could find Luke, your Prince Charming has to be just around the corner—"

"Yeah." But her tone betrayed her.

Sera didn't believe Bec.

"Hey—"

"Night." Sera disconnected.

"Damn," Bec said. "I hate that she's lonely."

"She has you guys," Luke reminded her, closing the laptop, and setting it onto the nightstand. "And she's special. Someone will recognize that someday."

"They have to see through the superficial surface layers first."

"They will." He tugged her down, kissed the top of her head.

"How do you know?"

"I saw through you, didn't I?"

EPILOGUE

Luke, six months later

IT HAD TAKEN six long months to finally get his Becky out for Date Ten.

Right after her single day of hooky, she'd taken on a huge case, and any extraneous date nights had gone by the wayside.

But, unlike the past, Luke hadn't been jealous of her career. He'd missed her like crazy, of course, but he'd dealt with her long days at the office by pulling some long days of his own. His renewable energy cells had been rolled out, and as expected with new technology, there had been plenty of problems to deal with.

There had been many nights of dueling laptops on the coffee table after he'd officially moved into Becky's place and after they'd *communicated* and figured out that she could do some of her casework at home.

Maybe it wasn't traditional couple time, but Luke just liked being with her.

And he especially liked the times that their laptops got tossed to the side and Becky straddled him on the couch.

Yeah.

Those were great times.

But now her case had wrapped up . . . or rather, the opposing lawyers had accepted her proposal and settled, and so she was taking two whole days off.

They were driving up to Tahoe to hit the slopes the following day, but tonight?

Tonight was Date Ten.

Or maybe Date Ten Thousand, but semantics didn't matter.

He'd wanted to do this for Becky forever.

He just hoped his instincts were right and she'd be into it.

"How fancy is this restaurant?" she asked, striding into the room.

And fuck him six ways to Sunday, but she was wearing the dress.

The. Dress.

The fucking red dress from prom and it was . . . everything.

She'd slipped on one of those short sweaters that just covered her shoulders and partway down her back, but the rest of it—skintight red silk, breasts spilling up and over the deep V, slit up to her thigh.

Fuck it all. He wanted to forget Date Ten.

"Uh-uh, mister," Becky said, bending to slip on a pair of sky-high black heels and nearly making his eyes bug out of his head. Her breasts. Her legs. Her *ass*. "I somehow managed to squeeze into this dress. You're not getting it off me that quickly."

Luke made a garbled sound.

Maybe agreement? Maybe disappointment?

But he did manage to get his head out of his ass long enough to pull the black velvet box from his suit pocket.

Becky stopped several feet away, glanced at the case—too large for a ring—then down at herself.

"You are *not Pretty Woman*-ing me."

Luke closed the space between them. "So what if I am?"

"How did you even know that was my favorite movie? I don't think we've ever—"

"Oh, we've discussed movies. You've just never confessed your fondness for Richard Gere."

"It's Julia Roberts," Becky said. "Her smile is incredible."

"*You're* incredible."

One hand came to her hip. "Okay, Mr. *Incredible*. Nice try. Tell me how you found out."

"I know *everything* about you." But he felt his lips curving, knew the cat would soon be out of the bag.

Becky glared. "Sera! She gave up the goods. How dare—"

He opened the box. It held a necklace and earrings. Not diamond ones like from the movie, but opals because his Becky loved opals.

Probably because they were unique and changeable and looked like they were filled with fire.

"*Oh.*" She reached a finger as though to touch the necklace then glanced up with a glare. "Nice try."

He pretended to make the lid chomp her fingers. "Gotta do it right." Then he set the box aside and carefully slipped the necklace out. He fastened it around her neck before handing her the earrings. "Want to do those?"

She nodded, and he trailed her into the bathroom as she used the mirror to swap out the earrings she was wearing for the new ones.

"So," he said, nerves making his hands shake. "I'm not saying I lied, because we *are* eating at a very fancy restaurant. It's just that *after* the eating part we're going to the symphony. Or a version of it." His words came a little faster as he hurried to explain. God, he'd been building this up in his head for so long, thinking that she would love it. But what if she didn't? What if she actually hated it? "I know it's not *exactly* like the movie, but you told me a long time ago that you always wanted to watch a movie that had a live orchestra playing the score. And they're doing *Pretty Woman* tonight, and I thought—"

She stepped into his arms, squeezed him tight. "I *fucking* love you."

Luke released a relieved breath.

"But I told you about wanting to see a movie like that a long time ago." She stepped back, met his stare. "Like *ten* years ago."

He grinned. "So maybe Sera gave up the goods a long time ago. *Like ten years ago,*" he said, mimicking her voice.

His Becky huffed and started to say something—okay, he had to face facts, it would be sass—and so Luke kissed her. He was probably smearing the sexy as shit red lipstick she wore, but he found he didn't give a damn about her lipstick when her mouth was on his, when their tongues tangled, when those gorgeous breasts were flush against him.

"You sure you don't want me to peel this dress off you?" he asked when they broke away, chests heaving.

"Nice try," she said and reached a hand up to wipe the lipstick from his mouth. "This dress is staying on." She grabbed a tissue, blotted her lips, then reapplied the color before brushing by him and strutting out of the bathroom. "At least until *after* the movie."

Yeah, he thought, watching her luscious backside sway as she strode for the front door, *he could live with that.*

"Stop ogling my ass, Pearson," she tossed over her shoulder. "I'm hungry."

Yeah, he could live with that, too.

Fire tempered with sweet and plenty of sass.

Luke knew he wouldn't want to *live* any other way.

BAD FIANCÉ

BILLIONAIRE'S CLUB BOOK 6

CHAPTER 1

Seraphina

SERA WAS GOING to lose her mind.

Or throw a fucking tantrum.

And see? There it was. A curse word.

Seraphina Delgado did *not* curse. It wasn't seemly or lady-like, and . . . she was a thirty-something-year-old woman who still saw her mother's disapproving face in her mind any time she dared utter a curse word.

Well, know what?

Fuck. Fuck. Fuckity-fuck.

There. *Ha.*

Mental diatribe somewhat satisfied, Sera turned to the source of her wannabe tantrum.

Tate Conner.

Tech genius. Real estate client—

Or, rather, *former* real estate client because he was a giant pain in her as—*tush.*

Congrats, Mom. I sound like a four-year-old.

But Tate Conner had become a *former* client because he

was such a pain. He didn't like any of the houses she'd selected, and he never showed up for appointments. In fact, she'd lost count of how many times he had *forgotten* about a scheduled showing after number twelve.

So yeah, she'd kissed away any hope of a giant commission and told Tate they would no longer be working together.

That had been four months ago.

And now he was here in her office, looking all . . . Tate-like.

Super helpful description, she knew, but it just wasn't fair. Weren't these tech guys supposed to be nerdy and unattractive? Because Tate Conner *definitely* didn't fit that description.

He was tall and lean but strong. Months ago while en route to one of the appointments he'd actually made, Sera had gotten a flat tire. She'd managed to get her car to the showing then had called AAA, and Tate had shown up while the man was struggling with her lug nut—poor phrasing, but so not the point. *Anyway*, he'd approached the tow truck driver, tweaked the angle of the wrench, and the nut had popped right off.

Again, more poor phrasing, but—

Sera mentally shook herself.

He'd claimed it was all about leverage, but she'd seen the way his muscles had rippled under his T-shirt. He was strong, and she could tell it was more of a natural strength rather than a result of spending loads of time in the gym.

Want to know the worst part?

Besides the whole strong and as tall as her—hard to do considering she was over six feet—Tate was also pretty.

Really pretty.

A chiseled jawline, a straight nose, lips that were totally kissable, and a pair of dimples that only made the rare appearance. He also had the prettiest blue eyes she had ever seen and sandy blond hair that was more appropriate on a surfer than an executive.

That hair had been her undoing. Well, that *and* his brain. He was the head of a huge tech company, brilliant, and—insert a long mental sigh here—he was also funny. Tate had a quiet wit that never failed to make her smile.

So, as she always did, Sera had fallen in love.

Fallen fast. Fallen hard.

For a man who had absolutely zero interest in her.

Her friends—none of whom had ever dreamed about finding their happy endings and several of whom had been decidedly against them, she felt required to point out—were all married or paired off. Abby had babies. CeCe was due any day, and—

Sera was alone, pining after a man who'd created the latest social media craze.

Yup. Her life was *ah-maz-ing.*

Tate cleared his throat, and Sera realized she'd been staring at him dumbfounded for a good couple of minutes.

"I'm sorry, Mr. Conner." She stood, forcing herself to shake his hand. "I was woolgathering."

Sparks. The moment their skin touched, she felt *actual* sparks.

Just like every time before.

And just like every time before, she was the only one affected.

He smiled—eliciting more sparks, because her body was a stupid jerk—and said, "I've been known to do that from time to time."

Sera indicated for him to sit in the chair in front of her desk as she sank into her own chair. He continued to stand, but she started talking anyway, desperate to get this conversation over with. "How can I help you today?" she asked. "I do hope"—*Do hope?* What was she, British? *Ugh.*—"I-uh . . . I hope you were able to find a house. The agents I passed along are very good at finding unique properties, and I even gave them a few locations to start with . . . " She bit her lip, attempting to stop the ramble.

"No."

Just no.

Um. Okay.

He lifted a hand, rubbed the back of his neck. The movement made his shirt lift, exposing several inches of flat stomach and tan skin and, oh God, a trail of blond hair leading south. Her mouth watered, desperate to trace that path with her tongue—

Sera sucked in a breath, popped to her feet.

"Ah. I'm sorry." She picked up a random file, pretending to know what was in it. "I'm actually really busy, so this will have to continue another time."

Like never.

She rounded her desk, forced a smile. "Mr. Conner," she said when he didn't move. "I'll have my assistant schedule something soon."

"Seraphina."

She shivered at the sound of her name on his lips—soft, a little raspy, and deep enough to conjure all sorts of unhelpful fantasies in her mind.

Shaking herself, she moved to open the door.

Suddenly, Tate was there, hand on hers, body inches away, spicy scent inundating her senses.

Sera's breath caught. "What are you—?"

He seemed to be arguing with himself then finally, those piercing blue eyes locked onto hers. "I need you to marry me."

CHAPTER 2

Sera

HER KNEES WOBBLED and she wavered, almost colliding with the wooden panel.

Tate placed a hand on her shoulder, steadying her. "You all right?"

She slipped from between him and the closed door, not sure if her reaction was from the physical assault of Tate on her senses or because she'd just received her first marriage proposal.

Or neither. Sera was hungry; that was all. Or she might have developed hyperglycemia.

Or both.

Or—

Her eyes stung and she turned away, blinking rapidly.

Or she was an idiot.

The truth was that she was upset because no words of love had accompanied the asking. No romantic setting. No—

So. Fucking. Stupid.

As in, *she* was so fucking stupid. How could she possibly be worrying about the fact that her childhood fantasy of a cliffside proposal at sunset, her man down on one knee as he recited a heartfelt poem he'd written just for her—

Stop.

Because how could she possibly be worrying about *any* of that when her former client had just asked her to marry him?

Delusional.

She was delusional.

And the most pathetic part was Sera thought that if all those pretty things had accompanied Tate's request, she might have actually agreed.

To get married. To a man she barely knew.

Her brain had poofed away, like so much smoke. Or maybe it had been her logic and reasoning skills that had disappeared. Or . . . perhaps she was just so fucking desperate to find her own slice of the happily ever after her friends had cobbled together.

A hand on her shoulder had her stiffening, jerking out from under the contact.

"Sera," he murmured.

She sucked in a deep breath then turned back to reach for her purse on her desk, not looking at him, not risking getting sucked into those deep blue eyes again.

"I can't help you, Tate. I'm—" Barely managing to bite back the apology—because what in the heck did *she* have to apologize for?—Sera stepped around him and yanked open the door.

Her assistant, Hector, glanced up, brown eyes concerned.

"Can you give Mr. Conner the contact information for Zedd and Associates and Brown Estates again?" she asked, slapping a smile on her face and breezing by him. "Mr. Conner lost them. Thanks."

She managed to keep her smile steady despite the knot in her stomach because she'd had a lifetime of experience in shoving down every emotion that didn't align with the bubbly little princess her parents wanted. She was excellent at tucking her feelings into a locked box in her brain. She knew how to padlock it shut, to compartmentalize it away to deal with later.

When she didn't have to worry about shattering the carefully placed mask she wore.

"Sera."

Tate saying her name again in that soft rasp of his made her shiver, but she kept walking.

"Take an early lunch, Hector," she said, ignoring Tate and reaching for the door to the stairwell. She pushed through, navigated down the three flights to the garage, and hustled to her car.

Thank God, she didn't have to unlock the door. Thank God, she only had to tug on the handle and the door unlocked itself.

Because at that moment, she didn't think that she would have been able to search through her bag and locate anything— wallet, cell, and definitely not the small key fob to get into her car—

Rambling.

She was rambling. Even in her own mind, she couldn't help the flood of words, of emotions, and . . . memories.

So much for that locked box.

She sucked in a breath, released it slowly, and focused . . . on the memories.

Because *that* was what she needed to grab on to. Not the memory of Tate helping with her tire, but the memory of him forgetting about their appointments, how it felt to be left waiting over and over again.

Because Sera had been there, done that. Got the souvenir beach blanket.

She'd grown up with parents who shouldn't have been parents. People so wrapped up in their own lives and competing with those in their social circle that they should have just stuck with designer pooches.

She'd been that fluffed up and oddly groomed poodle, hair trimmed and dyed, except instead of a crystal-studded collar—because Delgados would never wear something as uncouth as *rhinestones*—she was clad in designer clothes and shoes, one outfit that cost more than her nanny had made in a month.

In reality, that was all she knew. Clothes and looking pretty. Nannies and prep school and beauty pageants. Until she'd had enough and had refused the pageants, resisted the modeling.

Then it had been boarding school.

Devasting and freeing.

Lie.

"The second one," she muttered, buckling her seat belt and pushing the button to start her car. "I haven't been free one day of my entire life."

She was too scared to be.

If she wasn't sweet and nice and kind Sera, then who was she?

The scary . . . okay, pathetic thing was that she *didn't* know.

Was she tough and strong like Bec, one of her best friends and a famous lawyer who was incredibly smart?

Was she a talented artist with a heart of gold like CeCe?

She didn't have Heather's business acumen or the slice of softness tempered by a steel spine her friend also possessed. She wasn't a great project manager, like Abby, nor a freakishly organized woman with every aspect of her life together, like Rachel.

She didn't have a traumatic past, hadn't been hurt or abused or abandoned. Sera had been sheltered, cossetted, packed in cotton.

And she'd gone along with it, just accepted the sheltering and cossetting and the stifling cotton.

Because she was weak.

But no more.

"No. More," she promised, shifting into reverse and letting her foot off the brake. "I'm not that person any longer," she whispered furiously to herself, turning her head to glance both directions for traffic. "Everyone is happy. It's my tu—"

She broke off on a scream.

CHAPTER 3

Tate

ONE SECOND, he was reaching up to knock on the passenger's side window of Sera's car and the next, he was flying ass over teakettle—such an odd idiom, by the way—and landing hard on the payment.

He blinked, stunned at the quick turn of events, then stood, lifting a hand to touch his right temple.

It stung like a son of a bitch.

Wincing at the contact, he pulled his hand away, brought it in front of his face. His fingertips were coated with blood.

He went woozy, knees wobbling, and he found himself on his ass on the pavement for the second time in as many minutes.

Tate sucked in a breath, wiped his fingers on his jeans.

Vaguely he heard the *click* of a car sliding into gear, trailed by the slam of a door and a frenzied clattering of heels on the pavement.

Fuck, his head might be spinning, but he knew that sound. He loved the heels Sera wore, loved that even though she was only a couple of inches shy of his six-foot-three, she still had the confidence to wear them. Strappy sandals, black leather pumps, suede booties—he'd actually Googled women's footwear types until he'd discovered the correct name for those. He'd fucking drooled over every pair she'd strutted around in, showing him houses that were perfect, but that he picked apart and found unreasonable flaws in anyway, even "forgetting" appointments to draw out the process because he'd been desperate not to let his time with Sera end.

Until she'd dropped him.

He couldn't blame her either.

He'd been a pain in the ass, a waste of her time, and she'd been . . . perfect.

But Tate had resisted her allure or at least resisted yanking her into his arms and unbuttoning the fastenings on the silk blouses she wore always tucked into form-fitting black slacks or skirts. Still, he hadn't been able to resist spending time with her.

Of course, he'd justified it by telling his logical brain that spending time with someone was completely different from asking a woman out on a date.

Because he didn't do relationships.

He didn't date.

Not anymore. Not ever again.

Which is what had gotten him into this mess.

"Fuck," he muttered, remembering why he was there, why he'd sought out Seraphina, why his pathetic aversion to blood was really not going to help—

"Oh my God," Sera said, sinking to her knees beside him and cradling his face in her palms. "Tate? Oh my God. Can you hear me? Are you alive?" She leaned in, eyes searching his deeply, and he was inundated with the smell of her, strawberries and cream with a touch of floral.

Intoxicating.

Heady.

Irresistible.

His lids slid closed and he sucked in another breath. He needed to resist, needed to focus so he could find a way to convince Sera to help him.

"Oh no," she moaned, clutching his head to her chest. "I've killed you."

It wasn't a bad place to be, all things considered, cradled against those glorious fucking breasts. He didn't even consider himself a boob man, but Sera's were insane—bouncy, perky globes that had threatened his concentration *and* control.

He wanted to lick and suck and . . . he was so lost in the cradling and the mental image of what he'd do to those breasts that it took Tate a few seconds to process what Sera was saying.

" . . . need to call 9-1-1 . . . bleeding . . . oh my God, he's *bleeding* . . ."

"I'm fine," he said, gently pushing her away and meeting her concerned gaze. "Hell of a headache, but my fault for putting myself there. I didn't realize you were—"

"You're *bleeding*," she said again.

"I'm fine," he reassured her, feeling the hot liquid slowly drip down his jaw. "It's only . . ." He hesitated, suddenly not wanting Sera to know that he was such a pussy about blood.

"What?" she asked frantically, hands flying in all directions —touching his cheek, his shoulders, his jaw. "What can I do?"

"It's just that—"

"What?" Sera asked again. "Tate. Tell me. I'll do *anything*."

He leaned back, raised a brow, stomach steadying, dizziness abating, businessman coming to the forefront.

"Anything?"

Tate watched the taillights of Sera's car fade in the distance, a wad of napkins clutched in one hand.

Her one consolation, stalking over to her car, yanking open the passenger door, and reaching inside the glove box for a wad of napkins that she'd shoved at his chest, blue eyes flashing, terse words emerging from between those gorgeous red lips. "You're unbelievable, you know that?" she'd spat and then she'd gone, getting back into the driver's seat and backing out of the spot, albeit much more slowly the second time.

Tate folded several of the napkins together and pressed them firmly to his temple.

Which still stung like hell, but the pain was probably the very least that he deserved.

He was an asshole.

"Yup," he muttered, using another of the napkins to wipe at his cheek and jaw. "But what did you expect when you just blurted it out, Connor?"

Not looking at the offending soiled paper, Tate dropped it into a nearby trash can and made his way to his own car. He wasn't smooth, he knew that, but he'd always done okay with women . . . well, once he'd grown up and filled out *and* made some money, he'd done okay with the fairer sex.

If okay meant that he'd spent a lot of his time friend-zoned, then yes, he'd done that.

And the one time he hadn't been friend-zoned, had been with Priscilla.

He sighed. Fucking Priscilla.

She'd—

No. It didn't matter.

Because what *did* matter was the deal with Sam Roche. Or rather, with Roche Enterprises.

The biggest investment of his life. The one that, if he played his cards right, would mean that everything he'd worked for actually meant something.

But if he wanted the deal to go through, he had to find a wife.

And not just any wife. Because Sam Roche was a conservative, from old money, and decidedly WASPish. He had "high standards" in women, and only a select few from a select few families would do.

Unfortunately for Tate, there weren't too many single women from those families around the Bay Area, and even fewer that he had ties with.

So, when he'd found out that Seraphina Delgado was one of those, he'd lied.

He'd told Roche that they were dating, that it was serious. It hadn't been a hardship, thinking that he might have to give in to his draw to Sera for a little while, that he might have to date her or touch her or—

Well, that little white—okay, huge gray—lie had backfired.

Because Roche had run with it, demanded he take the happy couple out for dinner to celebrate the engagement. Now he and Sera were supposed to have dinner with Roche, his family, and . . . the Delgados.

Tomorrow.

The dinner was *tomorrow*.

And Sera had hit him with her car, flashing him a glare as she'd driven away that had all but told him to go to hell before he'd even managed to issue an invitation.

"Fuck," he muttered, opening his car door and slumping into the driver's seat. "You've really fucked up now, Conner."

CHAPTER 4

Sera

FLOWERS ON HER DESK.

A gorgeous man in her waiting area.

Once, that would have made Sera's heart swell with romantic thoughts of Prince Charming and singing birds. Today, it just pissed her off.

Tate wasn't her white knight and dammit, she'd given up on men anyway.

"Freaking—no *fucking* men," she gritted out, picking up the bouquet of red roses and dumping them, vase and all, into the trash. She stormed back out of her office to confront the man sitting in one of her lovely blue suede chairs. She'd spent ages carefully picking out those chairs, had gone through books of fabric samples until she'd found the perfect shade.

And *he* was sitting in it.

Thirty seconds before, having not seen the flowers that had spiked her temper and propelled her stiletto-clad feet back into the waiting area, she'd ignored Tate as she'd blown by the space to beeline—okay to *hide* in her office.

She'd pretended not to hear him say, "I can wait all day, sweetheart."

Sera was excellent at pretending, a pro at not hearing underhanded snarky comments.

But Tate's?

It had been less snark and more of promise.

Promise that had sent a little shiver down her spine.

No, she internally snapped at herself. *Sera Delgado, you will not fall for Tate again. Or—or I will throw our collection of Desperate Housewives DVDs in the trash and we will—gasp!—have to pay to stream them when we're sad. And you know how you hate paying money to stream things.*

"I do hate that," she muttered.

"What was that?"

Shiver.

"Ugh," she groaned, flapping her arms at her sides for a moment before letting them fall. That was a twofer there. One, Tate would think she was crazy because she and her inner Sera were having such a real mental conversation that she was answering aloud and two, Tate's voice was making her *feel.*

So, yeah. *Ugh.*

"Sera," he began.

"Unless, you're going to explain what the flip you were thinking yesterday, barging into my office and *proposing marriage* to me," she said, "a woman you barely know and couldn't care enough to actually show up to meetings for—"

He lifted a brow. "I've never seen you this upset before."

"Upset?" Her voice rose an octave. "*Upset?* You're kidding, right? This isn't upset. This is insanity. It's been months and you just show up here, spouting crazy and I'm supposed to what? Just say, yes?"

Tate pushed to his feet, dimples flashing. "Well, that would certainly be easier."

Smoke had to be coming from Sera's ears, but she supposed there was one thing right about Tate's words. She might not have *ever* been this upset.

"You wasted my time *for months*. You rejected every single house I showed you." She took a step toward him, poked a finger into his chest, and tried not to notice how hard it felt—because pecs, *yum*.

Not the point.

"And *that*," she said, "was when you even deigned it important enough for you to remember our appointments in the first place."

"Sweetheart," he said. "I just wanted a little more time with you. It wasn't the right way to go about it but—"

She crossed her arms. "Try again." A glare. "And ix-nay on the *sweetheart*."

He winced. "I tend to be a little forgetful when I'm working on a new project."

Now it was her turn to wince—or at least internally, because she'd had enough practice with slicing words to not let the after-effects show up on her face. *Forgetful*. Yup. Sera was absolutely, totally forgettable.

Unless a man was trying to get into her pants.

Then she was gorgeous and wonderful and amazing. While it lasted. While he enjoyed her body. Until he inevitably found someone else because she was too boring or vanilla or sweet.

Yup. *Too sweet.*

Sigh.

Unless Tate thought . . .

Her heart sank.

But it was the only explanation for why he was here now.

And somehow, the fissure in her heart, the crack this man had helped make a constant part of the topography, tore a little wider.

Typical, but still—

"There isn't any money," she said, tone icy, as she backed away and crossed her arms in front of her chest. Sera didn't miss when his eyes flashed down to her "assets," but it was clear that Tate was after assets of a different sort.

"What?" His brows pulled together.

"You might as well find some other heiress," she ground out. "I gave up my trust fund ages ago. It won't be funding whatever new project you need capital for." She turned away, started to head back to her office.

"Sera."

She stopped, didn't turn around. "What?"

"I don't need money."

A roll of her eyes, her feet moving again. "Sure, you don't."

He caught her arm. "I don't."

She sniffed. "I say again. Sure. You. Don't." Sera yanked her arm free. "I'm not an idiot, Tate. I've been through this before. I know exactly what kind of man—"

Her words cut off when he pulled out his cell and began typing on the screen.

Seriously?

"I know exactly what kind of man you are," she finished then turned away again and started walking past Hector's desk, thankfully still empty since it was way too early for her late-riser of an assistant to be in.

Yes, she was a softie when it came to Hector.

But the man was her right arm when it came to sniffing out new houses, could type up a contract faster than she could pour wine, and never failed to bring Sera her favorite salad.

So, him showing up at ten? No, she didn't care.

Especially since he rarely left her office before seven.

Thankfully, Tate didn't say anything further as she walked into her office, closing the door behind her.

If their interaction unfolded according to their past ones, he would get lost in his phone, utterly forget about her, and then eventually disappear like smoke. He'd probably forget why he'd come in the first place—

Her office door crashed open.

Tate strode into her space, all yummy six-feet-plus of him, his slightly shaggy hair bouncing like a shampoo commercial as he closed the distance between them.

And then Sera's breath caught.

Those blue eyes were focused on her.

Her.

Not her breasts or her ass or her narrow waist. His gaze was focused on hers, locking her in place, forcing her own eyes to stare deeply into his.

"I don't need money," he said, taking another step closer.

Her breath caught again.

No.

She mentally shook herself then, outwardly, her head. "Tate—"

"I don't need it." He shoved his phone in her face. She pushed it away. "This is what I was looking up." He shook it, drawing her gaze to the screen. "My bank account."

Sera sighed. "Tate. I don't even know if—"

Her words stoppered up in her throat as she took in the name on the account. Okay, if she was being *totally* truthful, it wasn't the name so much as the amount.

Had she ever seen that many zeroes?

"I—" She blinked. "I—"

"I don't need money, sweetheart," he said. "I need you."

CHAPTER 5

Tate

OKAY, he finally had her attention.

Now he needed to not fuck this up for a second time.

"Look," he told her. "I'm not saying I'm being altruistic here. When I say I need to marry you, I *need* to marry you. Not because I'm some sort of creep who's been harboring undying love for you," he hurried to add when Sera opened her mouth, no doubt to tell him to fuck off for the second time. "But because I need a wife in name, with the proper background, and I need one quickly." He slid his phone back into his pocket. "And more importantly, I need that woman to be you."

Silence.

She stared at him in silence for a long time before softly asking, "Why me?"

"Because the Delgado name brings a certain amount of . . . prestige."

A flicker in those gorgeous blue eyes that Tate might have thought was hurt, if not for the smile that accompanied her response. Her smile never failed to punch him right in the gut.

Pure sunshine in a bottle, and when she directed it at him, he got stupid.

"What are you saying?" she asked. "You only want me for my last name?"

"Yes. No. I—" He shook his head when her smile faded. "That's not what I meant."

"Yes, it is." Quiet words.

Truthful words.

And he was losing her.

Fuck, but Tate was horrible when it came to social skills. Computers and artificial intelligence he could converse with, but humans?

He got all twisted up and tongue-tied and never failed to say the wrong thing.

Like in this instance.

"Yes," he agreed like the stupid idiot he was. "It is."

Her shoulders slumped slightly, and Tate felt like the biggest asshole on the planet all over again.

Fuck. Why was he like this?

The smile came again, but this time his pulse didn't pick up, though the gut punch was still present. Because he finally got it. That smile was a shield. Just like his work and cell phone and computer were his.

Deflections.

A way to keep people at a distance.

And wholly effective.

"You should go, Tate." She turned her back on him, and he tried not to notice how fragile she appeared, as though one more stupid statement uttered might shatter her into a thousand pieces.

So naturally, he blurted one out.

"I'll make it worth your while."

Slowly, *oh so slowly*, Sera rotated to face him. Pink colored the tops of her cheeks, and her blue eyes were darkened almost to navy.

"You'll." She took a step toward him. "Make." Another step. "It." Another. "Worth." She was close enough that he could smell the floral scent of her shampoo. "My." Her finger jabbed his chest. "While?"

Tate swallowed.

Fuck, she was beautiful.

He wanted to kiss her, but Sera looked like she'd welcome that as readily as raw onion on her cereal.

Slipping his fingers around her wrist, he tugged her hand away from where it was stabbing him and said, "Yes, sweetheart. I can make putting up with me for a few weeks, maybe a month, worth it."

She tried to pull back, but Tate found his grip tightening. Not so much as to mar that beautiful porcelain skin, but enough so that she couldn't free herself.

Not yet. Not until she heard him out.

Then get to the point, fuck twit.

His inner asshole made him blink, but—and probably more importantly—it also made him focus.

"The Monroe Estate," he said, remembering how much she'd admired his house when she'd walked through it with him. He hated the cavernous wasteland of a mansion, all high ceilings and cold marble, but it had been his first major purchase once he'd made his first ten million.

That was what young, wealthy entrepreneurs did. They splurged on houses, bought fancy cars.

But it wasn't him.

And he hated living there.

Hence, his hiring Sera in the first place.

"I'll give you the exclusive listing and buy whatever house

you recommend, if you agree to be my fiancé." Maybe two huge commissions would convince her to say yes?

She sighed, shook her head, and this time when she pulled back, he let her go.

"You're not making any sense."

"I only need a wife in name," he said. "And really only a fiancé for a few weeks until this deal is wrapped up. But I can't just pick any woman . . ."

Not that he had a line of women ready to select from.

Ha. Not even close. Probably because most interactions went exactly like this . . . or worse.

He hadn't accidentally insulted Sera's mother yet.

Give it time.

"It *has* to be you."

She frowned. "Why?" she asked. "Why is it so damned important for this imaginary fiancé to be me?"

His mouth went flat.

"Tate?"

"Because I already said it *was* you."

"Oh." Sera went very still.

In contrast, Tate became a bundle of movements, pacing across the floor, running his hands through his hair, his words just as jumpy as the rest of his body. "I know it was wrong. It was so fucking stupid to even lie about being in a relationship with anyone, let alone you." Five steps there. Five steps back. "You're a goddess. So smart and funny and— Well, I know we both know I would never stand a chance with you in the real world."

She opened her mouth. Closed it. But when she didn't say anything, he kept going.

"But then Roche kept going on and on about how he only does business with 'quality' people—"

"Wait. Sam Roche?"

He nodded, waited for her to say more. When she didn't, he went on. "So look, this is a risky investment, according to my investors. But only because it's a different project from what I usually deal with—"

"What is it?"

This time, his blurting ability saved him.

"Microloans for women in the States and abroad."

Her eyes met his before drifting away. "And so, what? You don't want to dip into your social media pockets? You want someone else to fund it?"

"No," he said. "I've invested heavily in developing the app side of FundHer myself. But I need all the rest of it—marketing, infrastructure, delivery. As much as I want to, this project won't take off if I try to do it all myself. I need people with experience in this line of work."

"And Sam Roche has it."

Tate nodded. "He's got capital he can invest as well as the know-how." Roche was on the board of several nonprofits and had made his fortune in banking. And as the CEO of a large chain of banks that had revolutionized the way loans were issued to normal people (read: *not* millionaires), he was the perfect investor-slash-partner for FundHer—charity, banking, lending experience, *and* disposable income that could be pumped into the app.

"He's also notoriously conservative," Sera said, "and is known to torpedo deals for those who don't have the same 'family values' as him."

Another nod.

"So, why me?"

"I panicked and blurted, and yours was the first name that came into my mind." Her brows drew together at that admission. "Then I saw the reaction from Roche, and I knew that if I wanted the deal to work, I had to double down."

"So, you told Roche we were together?"

He nodded. The change had been instantaneous, one second Roche had been ready to dismiss Tate, and the next he'd been ready to cut a check. Or nearly so. He wanted to meet the famous Seraphina Delgado first. "I mentioned I was dating, that it was serious and . . ."

"He filled in the blank." Sera nibbled at the corner of her mouth. "Roche's string of nonprofits are some of the best in the world."

"Yes." Tate nodded again.

Sera sighed and leaned back against her desk, fingers steepled under her chin. "So, what you're saying is that you made me your fake fiancé in order to secure funding for a project that is going to provide small, low-interest loans to women who are underserved by traditional loaning opportunities."

"You know how microloans work?" he asked, surprised though he had no right to be.

The Delgados were a power unto themselves in the finance world.

One of Sera's delicate brows lifted. "I'm Francis Delgado's daughter. What do you think?"

He felt his lips curve. "I think you know how microloans work."

"Ding. Ding." She pretended to ring a bell. "That, at least, is one thing you got exactly right." Another sigh, back to steepling, her gaze hooded. "So, *all* you're asking is for me to play the role of doting fiancé in order to what? Secure the deal only? Or is it going to go further, and next thing I know you're proposing actual marriage for the sake of some new app?"

"God, no." He shuddered. "I can't ever see myself getting *married*."

Her mouth pursed.

"I said the wrong thing again."

A nod.

"I'm sorry. But if it makes things any better, my reluctance for marriage doesn't have a lick to do with you. It's all me and my inability to have normal human interactions."

"A lick?" she asked.

"I say again. I suck at humans."

She giggled. "Lick. Suck?" Sera bent at the waist, hysterical laughter bursting from her lips. "Oh my God. I've totally been corrupted, but I—I just can't with you."

Tate frowned. "Just can't what?"

"Never mind." She waved a hand, using the other to wipe the corners of her eyes. "Just that you would have had the Sextant in hysterics." Another wave. "No. Don't ask."

He didn't ask.

"Let's hammer—" She coughed, though to Tate it sounded more like laughter than needing to clear her throat. Then again, it was already established that he didn't do humans. "Let's sort this out. I agree to be your fiancé long enough for Roche's investment to clear, and I get to sell the Monroe Estate. *You* get a trophy fiancé for . . . exactly how long?"

"Until Roche agrees to the investment and the contract is signed. Then you can dump me in whatever fashion you desire."

Something happened to her expression at the word desire, but the flicker was gone so quickly that Tate wondered if he'd imagined the whole thing.

"And you'll buy *whatever* home I choose for you?"

"Yes."

"No budget restrictions?"

"You saw what was in my account," he said with a shrug. "I trust you not to use it all."

Sera went very still before her smile made another appearance.

But Tate wasn't blindsided this time, wasn't shocked to see there were different layers to that flash of teeth. He absorbed the blow, the jump in his pulse, and searched below the parting of her lips.

Trust was important to Sera.

"I think I'd have to buy you a dozen houses to do that."

Tate shrugged as he crossed over to match her position, leaning back against the desk. "That's everything," he said. "Nothing else. No blindsides, no hidden games. A simple give and take."

Head tilting, she glanced up at him. "Tit for tat?"

"Yeah."

Eyes on the floor, on the far wall, on the ceiling. Anywhere but where he wanted them.

On him.

A blip pulsed in the back of his brain, warning him that he was already in over his head. That his declaring Sera his fiancé to Roche had already been insane, especially when paired with his attraction to her.

But Tate shoved that worry down.

He was a businessman, and this was a business deal.

Easy as that.

Fingers brushed the cut on his temple and his gaze shot to Sera's. He hadn't realized that he'd been staring down at their feet, marveling at the difference between men's and women's shoes, remembering how the first loan he'd given had been to a woman at his own company who'd had a design for comfortable and affordable heels made out of recycled materials.

She'd left the company six months later and was now a multi-millionaire in her own right.

All because he'd loaned her less than five thousand dollars to get started.

Stephanie—and women like her—were only part of the reason he wanted this to work.

Tate wanted to do something good.

Something that had nothing to do with going viral or views or advertisers. He didn't want to make money.

He wanted to give it.

"Okay," she murmured.

He blinked. "Really?"

She lifted a shoulder. "I can put up with you for a few weeks."

All the stress left him in an instant. "Are you—?"

"Sure?" she finished for him. "Not in the slightest. But as unorthodox as this sounds, I can appreciate what you're trying to do." A beat. "I just have one more condition."

"Anything."

Another beatific smile, though this one with an underlying mischievousness to it. "Well, it's two things."

Tate gestured at her to go on.

"One, you donate my commission for the sale of the Monroe Estate to FundHer—"

Tate's jaw fell open, but before he could say anything, Sera went on.

"And two, I get to pick the ring."

CHAPTER 6

Sera

TATE'S EYES danced with amusement. "Really?"

She shrugged. "A girl's got to do what a girl's got to do."

"And that doesn't involve getting paid for her work?"

"That's far from the point. I don't need the money, and it will be better served in FundHer." Her brows lifted. "Or do you not believe as deeply in the app as I thought you did?"

"That's not it. I—"

"Right," she agreed. "So, take the donation graciously and know you'll be paying me a hefty commission on whatever new house you purchase *and* buying me a shiny diamond bauble."

"Graciously? I'll try." He shrugged. "But the shiny diamond bauble? That I can definitely do."

"I get to pick it out," she reminded him. "And I'm sending you the bill."

He snorted but didn't protest. "Fine."

"So, we have a deal?" She put out her hand, and he took it in his. The simple contact made her heart skip a beat, especially when those calloused fingers brushed the inside of her wrist.

"We have a deal," he murmured.

Her lips parted, breath coming out on one long, slow exhale. Tate's eyes drifted to her mouth and darkened, going almost black when her tongue darted out and moistened the skin there nervously.

"Okay," she whispered.

"Okay," he agreed just as softly.

"I'm sorry I hit you with my car."

One half of his mouth curved up. "I deserved it."

"Yeah," she said, "you did."

He laughed, finally releasing her wrist. She took a step back, sucking in air, knowing that she needed to relocate her equilibrium, especially if she was going to do this with Tate.

No falling for him.

No tender feelings.

This was for the houses . . . and the other women.

Because female solidarity and all that.

"Can you pick out a ring today?" he asked, distracting her from the guilty direction her thoughts had taken.

Which was basically something along the lines of: *Who are you kidding, girlfriend? You're dying for any kind of man, even a fake one. Throw in diamonds and a pretend wedding, and you're in heaven!*

Or hell, since Tate didn't want to get married.

But that didn't matter in the least to her. She didn't know Tate well, and the little she *did* know wasn't exactly filling up the Pro column on her Dream Man Pro/Con Chart.

He might make her laugh, but he also said the wrong thing, almost all the time. He wasn't all that charming and didn't have all the smooth words. In fact, he'd seemed to bumble his way through their interactions previously—and this "proposal" had been no different.

So, no. It would be easy to keep her distance, to remember this was a favor between acquaintances, and that was it.

"Why do I need the ring today?"

He glanced at her, guilty expression creeping onto his face. "Because we're having dinner with Roche tonight."

Sera's mouth pressed flat. "Really?"

Tate winced. "Sorry?"

"Where is it and what time?"

They spent a few minutes ironing out details before Sera rounded her desk and sat down. "Well, if I need to take off early to go ring shopping, I have lots of work to do." She picked up a folder, ready for him to leave so she could attempt to process what in the heck she'd just agreed to.

As in: What in the hell did she just agree to?

Was she insane?

Probably.

But he'd looked so earnest when talking about the microloans and female entrepreneurs, and Sera found that she couldn't turn him down.

She was a sucker for a noble cause.

"Oh," she said as he turned for the door. "And just for your future fiancé knowledge, I really can't stand red roses." She gestured toward the trash can, half the bouquet sticking out of the top. "I—" A shake of her head, not ready to tell this man why she hated them so fiercely. "They're just not for me."

He nodded.

"So, you won't send them again?"

"No problem." He waved then turned to leave again, pausing on the threshold. "Oh, Sera?"

She froze. "Yeah?"

"Those flowers weren't from me."

The door closed behind him with a small *click*, leaving Sera frowning and reaching down into the trash can to search the arrangement for a card.

There.

She extracted it and opened the flap even though she immediately knew based on the color and scent of the tiny envelope exactly whom it was from.

Her mother.

Sera,
Your father and I are thrilled to hear about your engagement to Tate Conner. He
is far better of a catch than we expected you to hook.
Congratulations and looking forward to discussing
wedding details with you this evening at dinner.
Your mother,
Sugar

Yes, her mother's actual, God-given—or rather *parent*-given —name was Sugar Delgado née Walton.

And as one might guess, she had about as much substance as the granular white stuff.

Sera sighed, pushed out of her chair. Her parents would be at dinner that evening. Her mother would make a multitude of snide comments about her outfit or how much weight she'd gained, and her father would guffaw at her "little" business— never mind that she and her team had pulled in eight figures last year in commissions.

She glanced down at her phone, saw it wasn't even nine thirty.

"Forget—*fuck* it," she muttered, leaving a note for Hector to clear her schedule and placing it on his desk. Two minutes later, she was striding down the stairs, purse on her shoulder and the empty vase in her hands.

Red roses or not, the blown glass was pretty.

A few seconds to carefully stow it in the trunk, a few more to buckle in and check, double-check, then triple-check she wasn't going to crack any gorgeous business moguls in the temple with her side mirror, and she was on the road.

Her first stop was for a new outfit, but it wasn't a *Pretty Woman* shopping montage. This was business, plain and simple.

To find an outfit her mother couldn't criticize.

Probably—no definitely—an impossible task, but Sera found herself unable to stop herself from trying.

This would be the first time she'd seen her parents in close to a year, and she wanted to feel confident in herself, even if they would find and highlight every flaw they could.

Armor was important.

And Sera had discovered long ago that clothes could serve that role . . . or at least serve to *reinforce* that role.

She exchanged her heels for the flats she always kept in her glove box the moment she parked in front of her favorite boutique then slung her purse over her shoulder and strode inside.

"Maggie," she hollered. "Help!"

The owner of the store, a recently relocated Hollywood stylist, poked her head out of a door that led to the back of the shop. Caramel curls toppled down her back, haphazardly contained in a clip. She blew one out of her face and straightened the turquoise glasses perched on her nose. "Sera? You okay?"

Sera shook her head. "No. I need a dress that my mother won't be able to criticize me in."

Brows lifting, Maggie walked toward her, pausing only to hang the armful of clothes she held on a rack. "Mothers are tricky business."

Sera wrinkled her nose. "Mine is especially so."

"Hmm." Maggie pivoted, eyeing the racks, sliding dresses to and fro. "What's the occasion?"

"Dinner. They'll be meeting my fiancé for the first time."

The hanger made a screeching noise as it slid to a stop.

Maggie rotated to face her, eyes dropping to Sera's left hand.

Since she had no secrets from the stylist, she admitted, "My fake fiancé."

Maggie's brows had never been so high.

Sera waved a hand, affecting casual even though nothing about her and Tate felt remotely casual, especially now with her parents involved. "It's nothing."

Maggie turned back around, started searching through dresses. "Does the man know?"

"About the fake part or the fiancé part?"

A shrug. "Either. Both."

Sera studied a pretty blue dress on the rack nearest her. "He knows," she said, pulling the dress off the rack and holding it to her chest in a crude determination of fit. "It was his idea."

Maggie swept toward her, tugged the dress out of her hands, and hung it back on the rack. "That's not for you." She slid away just as quickly.

Sera was used to Maggie's ways so she stayed in place and let the stylist work her magic.

"And what's in it for you?" Maggie asked.

Good question.

"He's letting me sell his house and pick him out a new one." Sera left the part off about donating her commission, knowing that wouldn't help her case.

Maggie glanced over her shoulder, fixing her in place with a look that said, "Not buying it."

"He's starting a business to donate money to women in need."

A tilt of her head that said, "That's great. But I'm still not buying it."

Sera sighed. "He was The One."

"Was?"

"Yeah," she said. "I thought he was and"—she bit her lip—"it turned out I was wrong, and so now . . ."

Maggie picked up a pale pink gown, frowned, and hung it back up again. "You've decided to torture yourself with something you just admitted wasn't meant to be?"

"No." Sera winced. "I mean, yes. I mean, *no*. I don't want Tate." Her voice dropped. "I just want to prove to myself that's actually the case."

"Prove to yourself that you don't want him or prove to him that *he* should want *you*?"

Since there was only one correct answer that didn't make her sound like a pathetic idiot, Sera just shrugged. "Do you have a dress for me or not?"

Maggie flitted over to her and handed Sera a hanger. On it hung a midnight blue gown with simple ruching at the waist and a bustline that wouldn't be obscene on a woman with her breasts. A slit on one side gave it just enough of a sexy edge without becoming parent-inappropriate.

In a word, it was beautiful.

It was perfect.

It was Maggie.

As in, Maggie always knew how to pick *exactly* the right dress.

And so, even though she gave Sera a cautioning look after she'd tried it on—perfect fit, no surprise there—even though she seemed to see right through the lies Sera was clinging to for her own self-respect, Sera knew she'd be back.

She hugged Maggie, inviting her to the next Book Club

—*cough* Wine Night—at her place, and not leaving until she'd wrangled out an affirmative from the other woman.

Okay, killer dress. Check. Now safely stowed in her trunk.

Next stop, the jewelry store.

Diamonds were a girl's best friend.

And she was going big, so Tate had better make good on his promise to pay her back.

CHAPTER 7

Tate

HE STOOD OUTSIDE THE RESTAURANT, pacing the sidewalk while trying not to look as though he were pacing the sidewalk.

Not working.

Of course, it wasn't working. Tate's mind was spinning, details for the project bouncing around his head, and interspersed with that were both feelings of guilt for getting Sera into this and fear that she wouldn't show up.

He pulled out his phone, glanced at the screen.

Ten minutes late.

"Fuck," he muttered. She wasn't going to show.

Who could blame her?

He hadn't exactly been reciting Shakespeare to her. He'd blurted, he'd verbally thrown up statements about how he was using her for her family connections only, and he—

Felt his jaw hit the pavement.

Or at least drop open.

Because . . .

Sera was there, and she looked fucking incredible.

Her heels clicked softly against the concrete as she made her way toward him, but it wasn't her heels that he was focused on, or not for long anyway. Because the black strappy stilettos encased feet that were attached to ankles that were attached to long tan legs.

They were out for all the world to see—the dress she wore had a long slit on one side—and, fuck, but that peekaboo of flesh that appeared with each of her steps had Tate's cock twitching.

Smooth, tan skin. Slender ankles wrapped around his hips. Sharp heels digging into his spine.

Yeah. All of that.

And he hadn't even gotten above her waist yet.

Tate was a legs man, and as much as he liked Sera's breasts —what straight man in his right mind wouldn't?—it wasn't her upper half that got him.

Nope. Ass. Thighs. Calves. *That* was his kryptonite.

"You alive?" she teased.

He swallowed, forced his mouth closed, and finished his perusal quickly.

Slender waist, gorgeous rack, fucking beautiful face.

She was absolutely out of his league.

"You slay me," he said, reaching for her hand and tucking it in his. It might have been the most normal physical reaction he'd had with another person in ages and one he'd just *done* without thinking through every possible angle.

There was a reason he struck out with the ladies.

He thought and thought and thought . . . then didn't act.

Or he blurted.

Nothing in between. Nothing normal.

And money aside, no woman wanted a man who swiveled between those two mediums.

Thank you, childhood. Thank you, Priscilla.

But if he'd learned nothing at all, Tate knew that at some point he had to move the blame from his parents onto his own shoulders. No, his upbringing hadn't been idyllic, but he'd had food and a safe place to stay and . . . everyone had baggage.

He could have just done without the guilt trips.

"You slay me?" Sera repeated, brows dragging together.

Tate had screwed up again. He started leading her toward the restaurant doors, preventing her escape. "I meant, you look beautiful."

Her feet slid to a stop. "Except you said *slay*."

"Uh?" He stopped too. "Is that a bad thing?"

She tilted her head to the side. "Do you even know what slay means?"

"Killed it," he said. "As in 'Beyoncé slayed her outfit at last night's Emmys.'"

Sera was silent and unmoving, her lips shaping the words he'd just said. Then she stared up at him, a perplexed expression on her face. "Why does it sound like you quoted that off Urban Dictionary?"

Because he had.

Tate had a problem . . . and that problem was an addiction to *RuPaul's Drag Race*. Look, he got it. The show wasn't the most obvious choice for a tech genius with a fat bank account. And that wasn't ego talking. It was fact.

But it was also fact that he often stayed up all hours of the night working.

Which led to plenty of opportunity to binge reality TV.

His current show of choice? Well, there was something intrinsically watchable about *Drag Race*. The colors, the costumes, the drama. He was all in. And there were so many seasons of it that he wouldn't have to find a new show for a good long while.

"Tate?" Sera stepped in front of him, face suddenly very

serious. "Is the reason you need a fake fiancé because you're gay?"

He blinked. "Um, what?"

"I have never heard a straight man use the word *slay*."

"First of all, that assumption is blatantly sexist," he said, not quite sure where his response came from. His tone had gone playful, and Tate Conner didn't do playful. But one thing hadn't changed, because his blurt ability was still on point. "Me enjoying binging *Drag Race* doesn't have any bearing on my sexual orientation. Maybe I just like the costumes, okay?"

Her expression was bewildered. "And do you? Do you like the costumes?"

A shrug. "Yeah."

"Hmm."

"We should get inside. We're late." The moment of playful had faded, and he was just normal, awkward Tate again. He knew that admitting he liked the show made him sound like a fool. Well, *whatever*. It wasn't like they were really engaged. Sera could think he was a fucking weirdo as much as she wanted so long as they went through with the fake engagement.

Too bad he didn't want her to think he was weird.

He wanted her to like him.

Danger. Danger, his internal alarm blared. There were many reasons that wanting Sera to like him was a terrible idea, not the least of which was the fact that she was way out of his league and had absolutely no interest in him. She was helping out solely for real estate and charity, and so it didn't matter if she liked him.

The other, and more important priority, he needed to remember was the project.

This was about the project.

Nothing more.

"I'm guessing I'm not wrong in thinking that you did look

up slay's meaning," she said softly. "And not on Merriam-Webster."

He sighed, nodded the barest amount to acknowledge her, then started tugging her toward the doors again. "Let's go inside."

"Tate."

He stiffened, knowing that she was going to declare that this bit of weirdness was the proverbial straw on the camel's back.

She might be able to tolerate a lot, but a man who—

"I love romance novels."

"What?"

She stepped in front of him, their eyes level because of the heels she wore. "I love the escapism, the way they draw me into a story, and I just forget about everything else around me. I love that there's always a happy ending, that good prevails over evil, that the fictional world has good in it when our real one seems on such a razor's edge."

That.

That was it exactly.

"After dealing with lines of code and business meetings and emails and financing, sometimes I just want to get lost in something that isn't real life."

"Yes," she murmured. "I know exactly what you mean."

They stood on the sidewalk, staring at each other, unaware of the people moving around them. Or at least, *he* couldn't focus on anything aside from Sera. And not just her external beauty because that obviously took his breath away, but also what was, as cliché as it sounded, inside.

Her gaze didn't hold derision or judgment.

It held understanding.

Then she licked her lips, and Tate forgot all about understanding. Her mouth was painted a glossy cotton candy pink, and he wanted to kiss it off her, to taste the sweet treat of her mouth.

Sera lifted a hand, brushing her fingers gently over the cut on his temple. The action made him shiver, but he didn't miss her wince.

"It doesn't hurt," he said.

That sweet mouth curved. "I hit you with my *car*." She rose on tiptoe, brushed a kiss to the spot.

He half-expected to feel the stickiness of her lipstick, but when she leaned back, it was still perfectly in place.

"RuPaul would be impressed with the staying power of your gloss."

She giggled even as Tate internally groaned. Why did he *always* blurt? His cheeks were hot, and he felt decidedly less like a businessman about to score a huge deal and more like an embarrassed child.

"Tate."

He brought his gaze back to her.

"I'm glad you understand."

"Lip gloss?"

"No," she said, smiling. "Though, yes, I guess. Staying power *is* important." He snorted. "But, no, I just meant that I'm glad you understand the need to escape from reality some-times." She slipped her hand into his, tugged him forward. "I got sidetracked, but look, there's something you should know before we go in there. My—"

The door pushed open, revealing a petite blond woman dressed in an expensive-looking black dress. Despite the disparity in size, her face was Sera's.

"Sera, sweetie, you're late. Don't you know how rude it is to be late?" She stepped up to Sera, air-kissed both cheeks. "What is this dress? Is that cotton? Who designed it?" Her stare shifted to him, and Tate almost took a step back. "Oh look! There you are, darling! I'm so happy to meet you finally. Sera hasn't—"

"Mother."

"—told us a thing about you. She likes to punish us, you see. Wearing dresses by designers I don't support—"

"*Mother.*"

"—then not calling me first thing upon her engagement—"

"Sugar." A man came out of the restaurant, and though he had little in common with Sera looks-wise, it only took Tate a glance to recognize Sera's bright blue eyes, to see that this man was where she had gotten her height from. He was an inch taller, and his shoulders were definitely broader than Tate's.

"—eating *organic*—"

Sera sighed.

"—and still not shedding the weight—"

That, finally, snapped Tate out of the whirlwind that was the last twenty seconds. "I love Sera's dress," he said, talking over Sera's mother when she continued to speak. "It matches her beautiful eyes."

Those eyes shot over her shoulder to meet his for a long moment, but just as her mother sucked in a breath again, Sera faced her parents. "Mother, Dad. This is Tate Conner."

He stepped forward, extended a hand. "Mr. and Mrs. Delgado. Nice to finally meet you."

Sera shot him a glance he couldn't interpret, but he was too focused on surviving the handshake with Sera's father, half-surprised when he retrieved his hand that his bones weren't crunched into a hundred pieces.

Sera's mother's hand was limp as he gently shook it. "Sugar, please," she said.

He frowned. "I—uh—I can find you some. I don't have any" —a shrug—"not much of a sweet tooth."

Sera's mom laughed, a delicate tinkling sound that sounded far too contrived.

"Oh, no, darling. My name is Sugar." She winked. "But I like to think that I'm sweet."

"Unbelievable," Sera muttered, rolling her eyes. "We should go inside," she said. "We don't want to keep Mr. Roche waiting."

"Oh, *yes*," Sugar said, slipping between him and Sera and taking both of their hands. "I can't wait to discuss *all* the wedding details—"

"Mother."

"—I was thinking white orchids. Hydrangeas are so last year—"

"*Mother*."

"Conner." Sera's dad stopped him just after they'd crossed the threshold into the restaurant then tilted his head in the direction of the wooden bar set up along the far wall of the space. "A word?"

Tate nodded, trailing the other man in silence.

In the span of forty-eight hours, he'd gone from single and pathetic to fake engaged and even more pathetic, to having what he could only imagine was going to be a Don't-You-Dare-Hurt-My-Daughter conversation.

Life.

Sometimes it was really life-y.

Sera's gaze caught his, concern in her expression or maybe that was just desperation to escape her mother since he could hear Sugar waxing poetic about the merits of organza versus satin.

Tate raised a brow, mouthed, "You okay?"

Her eyes went wide, but after a moment, she smiled and nodded slightly. *Fine*. Mouthed, "You?"

He shrugged. *Probably not.*

Mischievousness crossed her expression, which he took as affirmation to his thought that he was *probably not* okay.

A hand clamped down on his shoulder.

"Let's talk," Mr. Delgado growled.

Yup. Definitely *not* okay.

CHAPTER 8

Sera

"YOU'RE NOT EVEN LISTENING to me," her mother snapped. "We need to get this wedding planned as quickly as possible."

"Mother," she said. "Tate and I just got engaged. We're going to enjoy just being together."

Sugar sniffed. "Enjoy being *together* once he's officially locked in."

"Like a stock price, Mother?"

"Have you seen his company's stock price?" Sugar countered.

Sera sighed, mentally counting to ten before slipping in front of her mother and moving to sit at the table the host indicated. Sam Roche and his wife, Peggy, stood as she approached.

"Mr. Roche, so good to see you again," Sera said, extending her hand to shake his.

The older man had hair plugs. She probably shouldn't have noticed them, but they were so poorly done, it was hard not to do so. Plus, she'd known him for almost twenty years, and he'd never had hair until recently.

New wife. New hair.

"Sam, please," he said, rounding the table and pressing a kiss to her cheek. "You're all grown up now, Seraphina. And plus, Mr. Roche makes me feel old." His eyes drifted down then back up, and Sera was reminded again of why she stayed far, *far* away from the social circle of her parents and their friends.

Because *ick*.

He lingered too long, too close, and placed a palm on her spine, urging her forward.

What should have been a nice gesture, assisting her to her chair, turned abhorrent when his fingers drifted dangerously close to the crack of her ass. She sidestepped, putting a chair between them, and extended a hand to his wife.

Rumor had it, this new wife was thirty years his junior, but in natural light—or well, the restaurant variety—that difference seemed more in centuries.

God, could the other woman even drink?

"Peggy?" Sera said, pasting on a smile and shoving down her judgy hat. Who knew, maybe they were very happy.

A limp hand met hers, that awful weak-wristed impersonation of a shake that her mother had perfected. Sera much preferred a firm meeting of palms, but as she was quickly remembering, that wasn't their way.

Thank God, she wasn't one of them any longer.

"Pleasure," the woman said, eyes flicking over her with a dismissive glance.

Yup, she was so glad she wasn't one of *them*.

"So, where's this fiancé of yours?" Roche asked, his booming voice carrying through the restaurant. "I knew that boy had a good head on his shoulders when he mentioned he'd managed to snag you. Beauty and a brain, that's not too bad." He guffawed, reaching over and squeezing her arm, a self-satisfied smirk on his face. Never mind that Tate was probably a decade older than Peggy.

"Dad needed to 'talk' to him." She did air quotes, finding they were an excellent way to keep Roche at arm's length as she perused her seating options. Take the chair next to Peggy and hope that her mother sat next to her?

But then she risked the wedding inquisition.

Well, her only other option was to leave a seat open that Roche might slip into, and then she'd be dealing with creeping hands.

And she'd spent too long dealing with men like him to want to sit through a three-course meal next to him.

Why did the men who so often appeared to be the nicest and kindest and most philanthropic end up always being the ones who were the grossest?

Sleazy fuckers, the lot of them.

Sera smiled to herself, proud of her curse word, even if it *was* a generalization. A generalization borne of her life experience, but still one anyway. She shifted, bracing herself to be combatting wedding talk when her mother sat in the chair directly next to Peggy.

Sigh.

"Darling," Sugar said. "I need to hear all about that charity fashion show you organized. Who was the designer again?"

Peggy's eyes lit up and she began talking, rapidly discussing hemlines and models. Her mother sighed, held in rapt attention. Fashion and runways and designers were Sugar's weakness. She'd desperately wanted to model in her younger days but hadn't been tall enough.

Hence, marrying the tallest rich man she could find.

Hence, putting Sera in every pageant and in front of any model agent she could rustle up.

"There's a seat here," Roche said, pulling out a chair next to where he'd been sitting before.

"Please, sit," she told him. "I actually need to use the ladies room."

Disappointment on his face, he plunked down into his seat. "Don't be too long," he said. "I'm anxious to hear about your fiancé."

She nodded, not liking his tone. "Of course."

Fingers on her spine made her jump.

"You okay?" Tate's voice didn't sound right.

She shivered, glancing over her shoulder at him. But he wasn't looking at her. He was staring at Roche, daggers in his eyes. In fact, he appeared ready to launch himself across the table and pummel Sam into unconsciousness. She turned, rising up to whisper in his ear. "It's fine. I know how to deal with men like him."

Piercing blue eyes flashed to hers. "He made you uncomfortable."

Her father slipped past them, taking the chair next to Roche. The pair began a loud conversation about women and the various difficulties they brought into a man's life.

"Assholes," Tate muttered.

Sera took his hand. "Be right back," she told the table at large, though no one was paying attention to them, then tugged Tate past the tables until they'd reached the hall with the bathrooms.

They were in luck, they were single-use, and one was empty.

She pushed open the door, dragged him inside.

"What's wrong?" she asked.

"What's wrong?" he snapped. "I'm at the bar listening to your father threaten me not to *hurt* you, and I can see that asshole touching you."

"Roche?"

A nod. "The worst part was your father watching the same thing and not giving a damn."

She leaned back against the door, flipped the lock. "He was probably distracted by giving the don't-hurt-my-daughter spiel."

Tate shook his head. "No, I started to come over when I saw Roche, and he stopped me, said Roche was harmless and that besides, you like it."

That wasn't a slice of pain across Sera's heart. It *wasn't*.

Except, dammit, it was.

Her father thought she liked it when a man was coming on to her and making her uncomfortable? Really? And yet, why was that a surprise? Her whole life had been about pushing through discomfort, tolerating it so that it made her parents' lives easier.

"I didn't like it."

He studied her for a long moment then sighed and leaned back against the door with her. "I know you didn't."

"You didn't know?" she asked. "About Roche?"

Hesitation before the barest nod.

Damn.

"This isn't my world, Sera. Or it hasn't been. I spent the last decade keeping my head down and avoiding every connection like this I could." He shook his head. "I've never had to solicit investments. They came to me, and I could pick and choose. This—" He broke off.

"It's different."

"Yeah."

"And your investors won't take FundHer on?"

"No." He blew out a breath. "Yes, I guess. They'd throw me some money to keep the awkward boy genius CEO happy, but they don't really care if it works out. And money is only part of what I need. Roche's expertise in lending, in running nonprofits." Tate thrust a hand through his hair. "I can debug an app like no one's business, but I'm not sure I can effectively helm a company whose main goal isn't going viral or getting the most views."

"I'm sure you would do fine."

"I've—" A sigh. "I guess the truth is that I've never done anything important before. I've never been part of a project that might actually change someone's life for the better."

Her heart squeezed. He was so freaking sweet and earnest and—

She touched his arm. "You created a company that employs thousands of people."

"Yeah," he muttered. "And it's all based on cat videos and bikini shots."

"I happen to like cat videos."

He glanced up at her, smile small, dimples making the barest appearance. "I do too."

Sera's heart beat a little faster and she could almost picture herself toppling over that edge from liking him to *really* liking him. Which was incredibly dangerous for her heart. It was so much safer when she could view him as the flakey, arrogant CEO. This soft side of him was . . . well, while it was really freaking great for the world, it was also probably going to be her downfall.

She needed to find some distance and fast.

"So, you honestly thought that Roche was as clean as his public image makes it out?" Tate's expression tightened at her words. "It's not. And it's not just Roche. They're *all* like that."

"Stupid, now that I'm realizing it," he said. "I'm . . . not good at reading people. I was a fucking nerd all the way through school. I graduated from college at fourteen. Didn't have a girl-friend until I was twenty. I'm out of my league, and I know it." He paused, met her gaze. "That's why I needed you."

She ignored the past tense of *needed*. "I can help you get what you need."

He pushed off the door, paced the small space of the bathroom. "No. Not like this. I'm not tainting FundHer with an asshole like that. I'll find another partner." Carefully, he slipped his fingers around her arm, tugging her off the panel before unlocking it and pulling it open. "You're off the hook," he said, gesturing for her to go out. "The Monroe property is—"

"I guarantee she'll screw this up."

Her mother's voice preceded her appearance in the hallway.

Not wanting to deal with more wedding talk, Sera jumped back inside, quickly closing the door.

But it didn't block out the sound of her mother talking on her cell phone. "No," she snapped. "Seraphina might be beautiful, but she will never find a man who will meet her at the end of the aisle. She's too headstrong and past her prime. I guarantee if this marriage doesn't happen in the next month, then Tate will leave her as quickly as all the others did."

Her breath caught. Tears stung her eyes.

"Conner is the best catch she's ever managed to snag. He's attractive, his company is worth billions, and—"

Sera turned away, strode to the sink, and pretended to fix her hair. But she couldn't even look her own reflection in the eyes.

Leave her.

Like all the others.

Sera lifted her chin and turned back to face him, her smile fixed in place. "She just wants me settled." A giant lie, because all her mother wanted was for Sera to be her perfect little doll.

Perfect little dolls didn't talk back, didn't say no, didn't go their own way.

"You—"

"You'll secure a date," her mother said, voice taking on an

icy edge. "I don't have to tell you what will happen if you don't." An exasperated breath. "Put a deposit down first thing in the morning. You worry about the location and let me worry about my daughter. I'll make sure she doesn't screw this up."

Quiet bathrooms made for the best eavesdropping. Or at least quiet bathrooms with very thin doors. Either that or her mother was talking really loud and just didn't give a damn, Sera supposed.

Her mother sighed loudly and then the handle turned. Tate leaned back against the door, flipped the lock.

"Occupied," he said.

"Oh dear," her mother trilled in a voice that was so different from that used during her phone conversation, it should have been comical. For Sera, who'd heard that change too many times to count, it wasn't.

"My sincere apologies," Sugar added, and they heard her walk to the next room and push through the door.

Tate crossed over to where Sera stood by the sink and reached behind her to turn on the faucet.

"Better safe than sorry," he said gently, over the rush of water.

"You should just go," she whispered. "Get out of here before they manage to taint you, too."

"Taint?"

"Yeah," she said. "You're good, Tate, don't let them get to you, too."

"I think you're confused."

A huff. *Typical.*

"No," he said. "I don't mean about them, I mean about you. You're good, Sera. Anyone can see that."

She scoffed. "Sure. Great. Thanks for the compliment." She'd grown up with that, and the contamination of that didn't just fade away.

"Your mother said she hadn't talked to you in months."

"So?"

"So, I think it's obvious that you're not one of them."

He'd meant it as a compliment, and she should have taken it as one, and yet . . . it still stung. That feeling of not belonging in any world.

"That's been established time and again."

Tate crossed his arms, studied her. "I don't know what's going on in that head of yours, but Sera—"

"Just go."

The arms stayed crossed. "I'm not leaving you."

She sighed, disappointment coursing through her, but she still managed to straighten her shoulders. "I understand. Let me fix my makeup, and we'll get back out there and get your investor."

"What?"

Sera adjusted her skirt, fiddled with the straps on her dress. "I just need a minute. I c-can get through—I just need to shove it all away and—"

To her horror, a tear streaked down her cheek.

"Hey," he said, hands coming to rest on the outsides of her arms.

She dashed it away. "I-I'm fine. I've done this before."

Tate growled. Actually growled. "I'm not going to whore you out for a fucking asshole to invest in my company," he whispered hotly.

"Why?" She tried to pull back. "How is it *any* different than before?"

He froze. "I don't know."

"Exactly." It wasn't.

And she was used to this role. Used to being a pretty face, a connection, and nothing more.

So, she closed her eyes and thought of her friends, of Wine

Nights and Book Club, of a shared love of expensive pajamas and happily ever afters. She thought of the coastline overlooking the Pacific Ocean and how the crash of the waves against the beach never failed to soothe her soul.

And when she opened them again, she was ready.

"Let's go back to the table."

"No."

Sera sighed. "Tate."

"No," he said. "I meant what I said before. The Monroe Estate is yours."

Her heart sank. Which it definitely shouldn't be doing. Because the house was the only thing she wanted, right? Not Tate.

Definitely *not* Tate.

"You're leaving." Not a question. A statement, and one she shouldn't have made. It didn't matter if he left.

"Se—"

"Great," she said, shaking herself and brushing by him. "I'll be in touch about Monroe."

He stopped her by grabbing her hand.

"I'm—"

She'd started to say she was fine, that she got it, she really did. He needed to get away from the mess that was her and her family, needed to—

"Marry me."

CHAPTER 9

Tate

SERA'S JAW DROPPED OPEN. "Wh-what are you talking about?"

He laced their fingers together, tugged her around to face him, words pouring out of him, even though his mind was still spinning from having said that at all. "I know I'm not the best catch. I know I say the worst things at the worst times or nothing at all when I really *should* say something. But I like you, Sera. So much."

She shook her head in a slow swivel. "You're insane."

Tate laughed. He was insane. *This* was insane.

But not so much the proposal, but because he was so drawn to Sera in the first place. Her mother, those words, the way she'd tucked her hurt down deep and prepared to carry on.

He'd thought her beautiful and kind and sexy before, but seeing her hurt? *That* made him want to take that all away for her.

And *that*—his inner hero wanting to make a rescue—also made him remember.

His parents.

Priscilla.

He shuddered, forced his emotions to take a mental step back.

So, instead of saying any of the things he really felt, Tate affected casual and said, "We can sign a prenup, but let's make it official." A shrug. "Just for a little while. Make your mother eat her words. Show them they're wrong about you."

Something interesting happened to Sera's face.

He didn't see a blip of hurt, like the overheard conversation with Sugar had wrought, nor did he see gratitude or conflict or—

Well, he didn't see anything.

Her expression wiped clean and her eyes, which had been glistening with tears, went completely dry.

He wasn't sure if that was good or bad—though his gut had a strange feeling that told him it was probably bad—and so *The Blurt* happened. "It doesn't have to be anything romantic and definitely won't be sexual, but let's get married. That'll shut everyone up, prove that you aren't any of the things your mother said . . ." Words trailed off as he lost his steam.

A long, interminable silence.

"And what do you get out of this?" she eventually asked.

There was something in her tone that hadn't been there before.

Ice.

Tate found he didn't like it, but he also found that he didn't have the words, or at least he couldn't find the courage to say the words that described what he felt inside.

What he'd felt for this woman from the beginning.

A draw that didn't make sense, and one that he couldn't allow himself to feel.

Not ever again.

Hey, asshole, you can't shut off your feelings. No matter how hard you try.

He clenched his jaw, knowing that even though the thought might well be the truth, he couldn't afford to let it be. He'd chosen Priscilla and look where that had gotten him. Alone, heartbroken, used and then promptly discarded, all over again. "I get . . . you."

She blinked.

"Your name. Your social status," he hurried to add in case she read too much into that. "Roche is out as an investor, obviously, but if you're my wife, then I can use that connection to find someone else."

Her gaze dropped to the floor, hair swinging forward to cover that beautiful face.

She was going to tell him—and rightfully so—to fuck off.

He wasn't disappointed. He'd been an idiot to suggest they get married in the first place—

"Okay," she whispered.

"What?"

Her chin came up. "Okay."

"Oh."

Silence as he tried to formulate the right words. Not relief, because he shouldn't be relieved that she was seriously considering marrying him after the disaster with Priscilla.

Because Tate had been like this with Priscilla . . . or maybe if not exactly like this, then at least the draw was similar. He'd fallen for the tall, statuesque beauty, had been equal parts taciturn and verbose. She'd called it cute and sweet in the beginning, had loved his "little quirks," but ultimately she'd weaponized his subpar social skills, turned them into demands for apologies in the form of diamonds or expensive clothes. And Tate, having never been particularly interested or attached to a woman—or more realistically, never had the opposite sex pay much attention to him—he'd fallen hook, line, and sinker. He'd bought her the expensive clothes and the diamonds, *and* ultimately, he'd asked her to be his wife.

He'd dodged a bullet when she'd gotten so infuriated with him that she'd dumped him for the CEO of his biggest competitor and Tate had realized that he didn't particularly care.

Asshole, right?

He'd always assumed that he didn't have big, sweeping feelings for other people, that he thought in terms of code and cause and effect and pure logic, but Sera was making him wonder if perhaps, it wasn't that he *couldn't* feel, but maybe it was that he just hadn't felt strongly enough about Priscilla.

So, even as part of him was urging him closer to Sera, the other piece, the *bigger* portion, *that* was telling him he shouldn't be relieved she'd agreed to marry him, he shouldn't be feeling pleasure at the thought of her by his side.

Because that was crazy.

They hardly knew each other.

And he certainly shouldn't be feeling possessiveness, because he sure as fuck shouldn't be thinking that this woman was *his* in any way.

"Oh," he said again, clearing his throat. "Great."

As in, *great*, he sounded like a fucking moron.

A tinge of pink crossed her cheeks, and she stepped back, bumping against the door. "Unless you weren't serious or changed your mind. I just figured that I have a few friends— good people who might be interested in partnering with a project like FundHer." She waved her hand. "Never mind. This is stupid. I'll give you the names any—"

Finally, Tate got the fuck out of his own brain.

He closed the distance between them, coming close, her breasts brushing his chest, her skirt tangling around his legs.

"Sera."

She froze, eyes coming to his. "Wh—"

He kissed her.

And the moment his lips collided with hers, Tate knew *this* was what he should have been doing the entire time. Fuck talking, fuck trying to make any sense of the jumbled thoughts and feelings in his brain.

No more.

She sighed, melted against him, and . . . *everything* just made sense.

The pull he felt toward her, the feel of her mouth against his, her scent in his nostrils, the hot glide of her tongue against his.

If only he'd done this months ago.

Her hands rose, sliding into the hairs on his nape as she pressed closer, and Tate lost his head. He reached for her waist, lifted her up, and without missing a beat, Sera wrapped her legs around his hips. Her skirt was trapped between them, but he couldn't spare a moment to care, not when he was too busy pinning her against the door, kissing her harder, completely lost in the moment.

Sera was right there with him, moaning when he nipped at her bottom lip, fingers digging into his neck, tugging him closer, hips arching—

Knock. Knock.

"Sera?" her mother's voice was the harshest intrusion of Tate's life.

Nails on a chalkboard. A blaring alarm too early in the morning.

"Are you in there crying?" Sugar snapped. "What did you do to Tate? He's disappeared."

He sighed, head dropping back to study the ceiling. His dick was hard and throbbing, his mind torn between wanting to ignore Sugar and continue on with Sera, and knowing they were in the middle of a very expensive restaurant with an exceedingly *not*-soundproof door.

Tate knew that if he slept with Sera, he wanted it to be somewhere with more surface options, because getting horizontal on a bathroom floor was disgusting, and a quickie against the wall wasn't going to be enough for him.

He also knew that as frustrating as the interruption was, it was probably timely.

Because connections.

Getting too close and risking getting hurt again.

For both of them.

Avoiding crossing this line was probably best.

And so he bent close, whispered, "Marry me."

Three proposals in two days. That must be a record.

Sera's eyes were hazy when they locked with his. She nodded at the same moment another jarring knock rattled through the door before the handle jingled a heartbeat later.

Slowly, he set Sera's feet on the floor, making sure she was steady before he stepped away.

She sighed, obviously shoring herself up for another confrontation with her mother.

And so, Tate did the only thing he could think of.

He tugged her to his side, opened the door, and pressed his mouth to hers one more time.

It was supposed to be a peck, a quick meeting of lips to get her mother to shut up. But then Sera moaned, the soft vibration crawling up her throat and reverberating through Tate's mouth. That sound severed his control.

His hands wove into her hair, tilting her chin, savoring that sweet fucking mouth until—

Sugar cleared her throat.

Loudly.

And the expression on her face when he glanced over told

him that it hadn't been for the first time.

"Will you be joining us for dinner?"

He slipped his hand into Sera's, squeezed lightly. "No."

Then as Sugar's mouth dropped open, words apparently stoppering up in her throat, Tate tugged Sera forward, and they wound their way through the tables, not stopping when Roche called his name, not stopping until they were outside the restaurant.

"Which one is your car?"

She pointed, and still not stopping, he took off down the street.

Until Sera's breaths began coming in short bursts.

Concerned he'd upset her all over again, Tate glanced to his side.

The joy in her expression made his feet skitter to a stop. "Baby? You okay?"

She shook her head, chest still heaving, and he was enough of a pig to appreciate the view for a long moment . . . at least until he realized how much of an asshole that made him, staring at his future wife's breasts as she cried on the sidewalk.

Except—

She *wasn't* crying.

She was laughing.

Sera slipped her hand from his, reached up and wiped the corners of her eyes. "I'm sorry," she said, laughter pouring out of her now, and he was torn between relief that she wasn't upset and concern. Nothing about that scene inside the restaurant had been funny. It had been heartbreaking . . . well, except for the kiss.

That had been hot as hell.

"Did I—"

Another shake of her head. More laughter.

Had he broken her? Had his kiss been so bad that something

had gone wrong in her brain?

Tate froze, mentally slapped himself upside the head.

That kiss had broken *him*.

As in, it had broken his capacity for normal human interaction.

He snorted. Not that he'd had much of one in the first place.

Sera glanced up, fighting a smile, but the sight of her lips twitching made his own mouth curve in response.

"Your mother's face," he said.

And then they were both laughing.

"She was . . . horrified!" Sera gasped. "And jealous, I think." Her hand rested on his arm. "I didn't realize you could kiss like that, Conner. I might have accepted your proposal sooner if I had."

Tate chuckled, trying to play it cool even though his cheeks felt hot. "I practice on my pillow," he deadpanned.

She went still, lips parting in surprise. "I—"

He leaned in, brushed his mouth along the shell of her ear. "*I'm* kidding."

A shiver through her frame. "I knew that."

"Uh-huh. Sure. I know you were thinking that it wasn't a stretch for the nerdy tech guy to practice French kissing with his linens." Lacing their fingers together, he started them on their way again. "I'm teasing," he said when she began to protest. "But let's go before your mother decides to track us down and assault you over flower choices."

"Good point." She tilted her head to the street they were approaching. "My car's just another block over."

He frowned. "No valet?"

"No," she said with a self-conscious shrug. "I hate paying for that kind of stuff. Such a waste." Another shrug. "Plus, these heels are ridiculously comfortable. I could walk a mile in them."

He studied them for a few steps, named the brand.

Sera gaped up at him. "How in the heck could you possibly know that?"

"My first FundHer," he said, now the one doing the self-conscious shrug. "Or at least the inspiration for it." Tate explained how he'd loaned his former employee the initial money to get the business going.

"Wow," she murmured. "That's kind of amazing."

One corner of his mouth tilted up. "Kind of?" he teased. "But seriously, this is more about her than me. I've found that time and again, women have these great ideas, but they're shut down at meetings or don't have the connections or inroads that I had. Even though I wasn't from a wealthy family growing up and I was a big nerd, I was also a white male nerd, and that came with inroads other people didn't have. Especially women and people of color." He wrinkled his nose. "Sorry. I didn't mean to go all social justice warrior on you. The money I've made from my company is great," he said. "Even if it's not the key to happiness, it definitely makes things easier."

"Yeah," Sera murmured, slowing next to the hybrid sedan he recognized as hers from the real estate visits. "It does."

"But, I—it's stupid I guess, but I had this moment—"

Well, *moments*, he supposed. Priscilla wanting him to buy her something else. His board always worried about numbers. His family wanting and wanting *and* wanting.

Tate was happy to help.

But he was tired of feeling like a bank.

Which was when he'd gotten the idea.

He *could* be a bank. For those who were worthy.

Luckily, that idea—the choosing the worthy, not the bank part, because who in the fuck was *he* to decide who was worthy? —had morphed pretty quickly and he'd come up with FundHer. Microloans. Some voted on by the public via a social media component of the app, others handpicked by a board of qualified volunteers. And volunteers was the key word here, because this was about giving money away, not making it back, and Tate planned to roll back any profits made right back into the program. That fact was also why he'd had such a struggle finding people to invest alongside him.

Because it was more donation rather than investment.

And if he'd learned one thing from having money, it was that the rich didn't like to part with it. But he'd also learned that *he* had enough.

A soft hand on his arm. "You had a moment?"

Tate blew out a breath. "I had this moment when I realized that I have enough." He put up a hand. "Look, I'm not completely unselfish. Not by a longshot. I'm not planning on giving every dollar of my fortune away, but I don't need it all, and I want to make sure it goes to something worthwhile."

He blinked, coming out of his brain, realizing that he'd been staring off into space thinking about FundHer and his past and feeling so fucking vulnerable that he was ready to bolt. "I should—"

Fingers on his jaw. "If I hadn't already agreed to marry you because of your kissing ability, *that* would have done it."

His whole body stilled. "What?"

A press of her mouth to his cheek. "This is me." She stepped back. "Good night, Tate."

Then she got in her car and drove away.

Without hitting him this time.

But Tate still felt as though he'd gotten smacked in the head for a second time. Somehow, he'd gone from a fake engagement to a fake marriage to . . .

Maybe wanting to be married for real.

To a woman who'd never been far from his thoughts since the first moment he'd met her.

Why did he feel as though he were in for a world of hurt?

CHAPTER 10

Sera: I need Wine Night. I mean Book Club.

Abby: It's late. Are you okay?

Sera: Oh, gosh. I'm so sorry. I didn't realize what time it was.

Sera: Never mind. I'm fine.

Sera: I'll talk to you guys soon.

Heather: Slow your text roll, Sera.

CeCe: Seriously. Yes, it's late, but I, for one, am already up with the baby. He or she keeps sitting on my bladder and I have to pee every ten seconds.

Sera: Oh no.

Sera: —

CeCe: Do NOT say you're sorry. Babies don't like to sleep, remember? This is just practice.

Abby: Amen, girlfriend.

Rachel: Heather's my boss, so I never sleep anyway.

Heather: Hey!

Abby: I'd say you can come here, but the kids are all asleep.

Heather: Does that include Jordan?

Abby: I think we've already established the fact that your brother is NOT a child. He's a god . . .

Abby: In bed.

Abby: *waggling eyebrows GIF*

Heather: *vomiting GIF*

Rachel: ^^I second this.

Bec: I really wish I hadn't picked up my phone at the moment Abby declared her husband a god in the sack.

Heather: *shudder* Dear God, don't say sack.

Abby: Focus, ladies.

Bec: Pot meet kettle.

CeCe: Shh! No one change. I'm convening Wine Night at my house since Colin had to do a quick flight back to Scotland and I'm not fit to leave my living room.

Sera: I don't want to interrupt.

CeCe: Please save me from this parasitic lump. I love him or her already, but if this is in my future. I need wine . . . or to live vicariously through you guys drinking it.

Abby: I can do that.

Bec: Someone bring me pajamas. I'm just leaving the office.

Heather: Of course you are. What about that work-life balance you were supposed to be finding with Luke?

Rachel: I'm stealing Bec's line and saying *Pot meet kettle.*

Heather: Traitor.

Rachel: Never. Anyway, I'm on my way with wine in hand and pajamas in my trunk already for just this emergency.

Bec: Your assistant is freakishly efficient.

Heather: She's mine. You can't have her.

Abby: I'm getting in my car. I'll see you in ten minutes.

CeCe: Sera?

Sera: . . .

Abby: We go to CeCe's or you make the uncomfortable pregnant woman leave her house to come to yours.

Sera: I'll be there in twenty.

Bec: Good that gives us ten minutes to gossip about you.

Sera: Hilarious.
Abby: Damn right, we are.
Sera: Thank you, guys.
Abby: Drive safe.

CHAPTER 11

Sera

THEY POUNCED the moment she was on CeCe's porch.

"Holy shit," Abby said. "That dress—"

Bec took Sera's hand, spun her in a circle. "That is a naughty, naughty dress."

Rachel tilted her head to the side. "It's not that sexy."

Bec tugged her inside. "No. It's not. But it *is* naughty because she's covered up enough to tease, but it's still fitted enough to show every inch of our darling Seraphina's fucking gorgeous body."

Sera pulled her hand free and, self-conscious, crossed her arms over her stomach. She glanced at Rachel. "You don't happen to have emergency pajamas for me too, do you?"

A concerned look from the sweet brunette. "I'll go grab them."

Abby took her hand. "Are you okay?"

Sera started to nod, stopped. "No," she said. "I don't think I am."

Bec's expression went from teasing to deadly. "Who do I have to kill?"

Sera laughed, but then the laugh broke and her eyes filled with tears and she wasn't sure how she felt. Happy, sad, excited, terrified. Really *fucking* hurt. "I'm—" A hiccup. "—fine. I'm just—"

Her chin dropped to her chest.

"Really fucking confused."

The room went silent.

"You cursed," Abby said, surprise in her voice.

"Yes," Sera said. "I *cursed*. Big fucking deal. I curse in my head all the time, okay? And I have dirty thoughts, just the same as you all."

"That's not what I meant—"

"I know!" Sera dashed a hand across her cheeks. "I'm sorry. I'm a total jerk, but dammit, I feel like the whole world sees me as this animatron. A superficial, one-note female who should just stand there and look pretty and—"

She sighed. "And . . . Tate doesn't see me that way."

More silence.

"Sera—"

A wave of her hand. "No," she said. "I saw my parents tonight, and I'm just in a weird mood."

Abby frowned. "I don't think that's it."

Sera shrugged. "I'm just tired."

"No, you're not."

"I'm fine, dammit!"

And silence round three.

"Hmm," Heather said then, "So who is Tate?"

"He's . . . uh . . . I . . . uh—" Sera's jaw worked, trying to find the right words to explain. She glanced between her friends, but they were all staring at her as though she were an alien who'd taken over their friend's body.

Rachel visibly shook herself then held the pajamas out that she'd retrieved from her car. "Need help changing?"

Sera shook her head, grabbing the package and with a murmured, "Thank you," brushed past her friends. She hurried down the hall, pushed through the bathroom door then leaned back against it.

God, she'd spent too much of her time that evening in bathrooms.

Her phone buzzed and she jumped, having forgotten that she'd tucked it in her bra.

It was a message from Abby.

I'm sorry I pushed.

Another buzz.

Come out for wine.

Her cell vibrated again, and the GIF of a female comedian chugging a giant glass of wine made her laugh—a watery, broken laugh but a laugh just the same. She pulled down the zipper on the side of her dress, stepped out of it and her heels, then hung the former on a hook on the wall. Rachel had removed the tags on the pajamas—she was freakishly efficient as Bec had said—and so Sera just tugged the silky pants and top on.

Instantly, she felt a hundred times better.

Since there was whispering outside the door, no doubt a conclave on figuring out what they should do with this strange imposter who'd taken over their friend, Sera opened the door.

The five women she loved most were cloistered in the hall, matching concerned expressions on their gorgeous faces.

Her stomach clenched because great, she was making them worry.

And her next bit of news was going to worry them further.

"I'm fine," she said, "I've just had a hell of a few days, and"—she sucked in a breath then took a page out of Tate's book by just blurting out—"I'm getting married."

She'd expected stunned silence at her proclamation, but Sera supposed she'd shocked them into quiet too often during the last fifteen minutes, and so instead of a lack of noise greeting her declaration, she was assaulted with five voices speaking at once.

"What the fuck are you talking about?" Heather.

"To who?" CeCe.

"Are you being blackmailed? I will tie his ass up in legal paperwork so deep he won't be able to dig his ass out." Bec.

"Why don't you start at the beginning?" Rachel.

"Um. Maybe this shouldn't be my first Wine Night? Or Book Night? You know what? I'll just go," a slender brunette said, turning for the door.

Sera frowned, pulling herself out of her own brain, and said, "Wait." It had taken her a minute, but she recognized Kelsey. She belonged to Rachel, or well, technically she was Sebastian's sister—who was Rachel's fiancé. Sera had forgotten they'd invited her to join their Book Club.

This was the first time she'd made it.

Of course, it was.

Rachel winced. "I'm sorry, I didn't think. I was supposed to meet up with Kelsey and invited her to come over." She bit her lip. "I didn't realize—"

Kelsey shrugged into her jacket, smiled too brightly. "I'll come back another time." She held up a bottle of rum. "I'll just leave this here."

The girls stared at her.

Bringing alcohol pretty much cemented your way into Wine Night.

It was a fact of life, or maybe a law of nature.

Sera shook her head, pointed at the living room, since this meeting in the hallway was getting a little claustrophobic. "Please, stay. I didn't mean to take over. Why don't we all just sit down and get to know each other?"

"I don't think you need to get to know me right now," Kelsey said, voice gentle. "I think you need your friends." The barest smile. "And maybe wine."

"Amen, sister," Heather said.

Sera snorted. "You're right. About the wine that is." She sucked in a breath, released it slowly. "Okay, so you can stay if you want to witness the crazy—just know there's one rule to Wine Club."

Kelsey's face paled slightly. "What's that?"

"Never let my glass go empty."

She laughed. "I was thinking it would be something scary like, *The first rule of Wine Club is there is no Wine Club.* Filling your glass? I'm all over that."

Sera let her eyes go wide. "Never joke about alcohol."

Abby slid her arm around Sera's waist, tugged her toward the couch. "Exactly. And it sounds like we're going to need it for this conversation. What's going on?"

"Rum first."

Abby nodded, grabbing a couple of empty glasses from CeCe and filling them up as the rest of the girls poured drinks of their own. Wine for Bec and Heather, vodka for Rachel and Kelsey, and orange juice for CeCe.

"Sorry," Sera said when CeCe gave her cup a rueful glance.

"I'm not," CeCe replied, plunking down next to her. "I've been craving this stuff all nine months."

"You'd just like some in the form of a screwdriver right now," Heather quipped.

"Stop rubbing it in, 'kay?" CeCe mock-glared. "Vodka will be my friend again soon."

"Spoken like a true Wine Club member," Rachel said.

"I don't know how Book Club became Wine Club, but we really need to rethink the name. Some of our members don't like wine."

"*You* don't like wine," Heather pointed out.

"I'd like to bring up the fact that the majority of us are *not* drinking wine at the moment . . ."

Sera sank back against the couch cushions, letting the banter surround her, knowing what her friends were doing. Giving her time. Allowing her a moment to get her brain around her thoughts so she could . . .

What?

Get it all out?

She didn't even know why she'd agreed to marry Tate in the first place. Or maybe she *did*, because her mother's voice was still echoing through her brain.

"What is it about moms and their ability to hurt you in your most vulnerable spot?"

Abby had been about to respond to something Heather had said, but when Sera spoke, she clamped her jaw closed and turned to stare at Sera. "Does this have to do with the mysterious Tate? Or maybe the fact that you're getting married and none of us knew that you've even been dating someone?"

"I—" She sighed. "Yes."

"Wait," CeCe said. "Isn't Tate the Tire Guy?"

"Who's the Tire Guy?" Kelsey asked.

"Tate the Tire Guy?" Abby gasped. "Tate the Tech Guru and Tire Guy? *That* Tate?"

Bec put up her hand. "There's way too much alliteration happening here."

"Yes," Rachel said. "Let her talk."

Sera smiled at her friend. Rachel got it. They both loved their group of friends, but sometimes they were . . . *a lot.*

"Where does your mother come in?" Heather asked.

Sera sighed. "It's complicated."

"We have booze," Abby said, holding up the bottle of rum.

"More complicated than an accidental marriage?" Heather asked innocently, and the reference to her own complicated start to one Clay Steele had Sera relaxing.

"Yeah," she said.

"How about an accidental pregnancy?" Abby chimed in.

Sera lifted a brow. "I mean, technically what happened with you and Jordan was cause and effect. Sperm meets egg."

Abby wrinkled her nose. "It's weird hearing you say sperm."

Hurt sliced through her, and she shot to her feet, rum sloshing over the edge of her glass. "See? *This* is what I mean. Why can't I say *sperm* or make dick jokes or curse?" She pushed around the coffee table. "Is it because I'm pretty or I did pageants and modeling? 'Cause that's really fucking stupid! I mean, I love you guys, but I swear, I feel like sometimes you shove me into the *Sera can only be a sweet and innocent, perfect little woman* box even more fiercely than my own parents do."

She lifted her cup to her lips and drained it then all but thrust it at Kelsey, who didn't miss a beat. She refilled it and handed it back.

"I can be a nice person and still like to laugh at dick jokes. And you know what? Sometimes I can also be an asshole. Did you know *that?* Huh?"

Since that was pretty much the biggest outburst she'd had in years, the output of all that frustration made her knees weak.

Or maybe that was the alcohol talking.

She sank onto the edge of the coffee table.

"You're a nice person, Sera," Heather said.

"Well, I don't *want* to be," she grumbled, taking another sip. "Not always, anyway."

"How long have you felt this way?"

The soft question came from Abby. Sera glanced over her shoulder and let the truth show in her eyes.

Because she'd felt like this—pushed into a corner, having to hide parts of herself—for a long time.

Abby's eyes went liquid with tears. "Oh, *Sera.*"

A wave of guilt poured over her, and she dropped her gaze to her hands. Oh, she still had alcohol there. Maybe that'd make her feel better. But as she lifted it to her lips, Bec snagged it.

"Slow down there, tiger," she ordered. "And that's not me trying to control you," she added. "Okay, maybe it is, but it comes from the same place as when you wrestled the bottle of wine out of my hands the last time Luke and I had a fight and not a you-can't-like-dick-jokes place."

Sera sighed. "I love you, guys." A beat. "But I need alcohol to get through this conversation."

"Because you've been hiding yourself from us?" Abby asked. "Because the rest of us have been putting every part of ourselves out there, warts and all, and you've been hiding behind a Little Miss Perfect mask?"

Sera went from feeling guilty for hurting Abby to red-hot angry.

"That's bullshit, and you know it," she said, whipping around to glare at her oldest friend. "You know *everything* about me. And I—"

"Except the fact that you've been unhappy in our friendship for ages."

"I didn't say *that.*"

"You can't be yourself," Abby snapped, setting her glass on the table with a *plunk*. "So how can you be happy?"

"Okay, wait," Bec said. "You two need to slow down."

"*No.*" Sera glared. "You don't get it, and how *could* you? I'm not trying to attack you or say that you haven't been a good friend or—" She sighed. "The truth is that I haven't had a fucking clue of who I really am for my *whole* life. I've lived for everyone else. My parents. You guys. My job. I never stopped to ask who I was inside. I let everyone around me mold me into who I am. And it wasn't until I saw you guys find your person that I realized I couldn't do it anymore. I had to find me." Her eyes burned, but she blinked back tears. "So, I've made changes at work, changed my clothes, my hair. And . . . I've been trying to say what I really think more."

"And we've been shutting you down." Abby's expression was crushed, and Sera knew she finally got it.

"I'm not trying to hurt you." She sniffed. "I'm just trying to . . . *oh God* this sounds really fucking stupid because I'm just trying to be a fucking grown-up."

Abby moved so she was perched next to Sera on the edge of the table. "Oh shit," she said. "I am a total asshole, making this more about me than you. I'm so sorry. I won't shut you down. I'll make sure I—"

"How about you just shut up and hug me?" Sera said.

Warm arms wrapped around Sera. "That, I can do. I love you."

"I, for one," Bec said, plunking down onto Sera's other side. "Approve of more use of the word *fuck*." She gave her a brief squeeze, which was a lot for her lawyer friend, because Bec wasn't a hugger. "I'm sorry, too," she murmured.

"Me, too," Heather said, kneeling before her and touching her knee.

Rachel cupped her cheek. "I like this Sera a whole lot."

"I'd sit on there with you guys," CeCe said. "But my ass is so big I'd break the damn thing"—they all laughed—"So just know that I hope this Sera stays around. She's a lot of fun."

Sera bit her bottom lip. "Also, known as drama."

Bec nudged her. "That's fun, too."

She laughed.

"One thing." Bec's eyes narrowed. "Now that you know yourself, no more hiding, yeah?"

"That would be so much simpler if I just had all the answers," she said, exasperated at herself. "Half the time, I don't know why I do what I do. I'll be thinking something then say the opposite, like agreeing to be a man's fiancé even though I promised myself I would never get involved with him. Why did I agree to do that?"

"Oh, to have all the answers," Bec said lightly, her eyes questioning.

Sera squeezed her hand, letting her know that she wasn't opposed to equal opportunity teasing. "Shut up, you," she returned, just as lightly. Then she sighed. "He spent six months jerking me around with real estate appointments and rejecting houses and standing me up, and *I* spent six months drooling after him without one spark of interest from him. Then he shows up in my office and proposes." They gasp. "But not because he's madly in love with me or anything, but because he needs me as his fiancé to secure financing for a new project—"

"I'm going to kill him," Bec growled.

"Then I hit him with my car."

Silence. But granted, this time it was well-earned.

"That *is* more complicated than a drunken Vegas wedding," Heather murmured.

Sera smacked her. "No, it was an accident. He bent and I went and—" She waved a hand. "Never mind. The point is, he offered me a really choice listing in exchange for faking it for a few weeks—"

"Asshole," Kelsey muttered. "He thinks he can just buy you? Why are all men such bastards?"

They all froze.

"Sorry," Kelsey said, wincing. "Apparently, that's a trigger for me."

Abby pointed a finger at her. "We'll unpack *that* at the next Rum Club."

CeCe shook her head. "Give up now, Abs. It'll forever be Wine Club."

"*Never.*"

"Ladies," Heather said.

Several heads hung. "Sorry."

"Go on, Sera."

She snagged her glass from Bec, took a small sip. See? She could pace herself. "Well, obviously, I agreed. The Monroe Estate is a huge listing, and plus he gave me carte blanche to pick out a new house for him as well—"

"I like it," Bec said. "You're not a cheap date."

Sera giggled. "Focus," she told her friends. "Because the listings and houses are a definite perk, but it's all the rest of it that . . ."

"Uh-oh," CeCe said.

"He wants to start a company called FundHer," Sera said and explained about the app and the investors and the donations. She talked about the dinner and the freaking gross piece of trash that was Roche. She told them how Tate had called off the deal after seeing Roche being such a creep, how he'd been furious and ready to take a page out of the Hulk's handbook.

"I mean," Kelsey began. "I was clearly ready to condemn this dude, but honestly? He sounds kind of amazing."

Sera smiled. "He *is* kind of amazing. Well, more than kind of. He's sweet and kind and occasionally awkward, but he kisses like a dream and—"

"Wait," Abby said. "I thought you said he wasn't interested in you."

She shrugged. "He went a little caveman after Roche. We slipped into the bathroom to talk and after he called off the deal, I told him that I was going to go through with it, that the app was good and it shouldn't suffer."

"No, it shouldn't," Heather said. "But Roche probably isn't the best backer."

"Duh. That's why I was going to introduce him to you guys." She put a hand up when Heather opened her mouth to reply. "Not to hit you up to invest, though obviously, I think it's pretty much the perfect project for RoboTech, but to help Tate get some recommendations on good people to ask."

"I'm all in on this," Heather said. "Granted everything checks out, of course. I've wanted to work with Conner since his social media app blew through the roof. Then you add in women and underserved communities, and you know you're giving me an infusion of my happy juice."

Sera smiled at her friend. "Thank you."

"Pish." She rolled her eyes.

"Okay," Abby said. "Can we get back to the kissing part? Because kissing like a dream is a pretty—"

"Sera description," Bec teased, and Sera felt her cheeks go pink.

"Shut up, you."

"Tell me, did he do that twisty thing with his tongue that Luke does?" Bec brought her fingers to her lips for a chef kiss. "Muah. Remember how I described it in detail last—"

"La. La. La," Rachel sang, much to everyone's obvious relief.

"I don't know what Luke does with his tongue, thank God. However, I *do* know that whatever Tate was doing was really fucking incredible." She paused, half-expecting them to make a big deal about the curse word then went on when she realized her friends were awesome. Because they'd heard her, because they were going to respect her wish to curse and make dick jokes.

Her inner twelve-year-old snorted.

Of course, they were.

She sniffed. "I love you guys."

Abby waved a hand. "Less loving. More kiss talk. Did he pin you against the wall and go all—"

"Don't say Thor," Heather muttered, reasonably since her brother, Abby's husband Jordan, resembled the Norse god. "Don't say Thor."

"Thor," Abby finished.

Heather retched.

Sera blushed.

And the girls were off.

Cheering over Tate getting all manly, teasing each other about their spouses and fantasies, and Kelsey's apparent love of a certain hunky actor who was starring in the latest summer blockbuster.

"But none of this," CeCe eventually said, doing her part in reining them all in, "explains how you got from calling off the whole thing to actually getting married."

Sera wrinkled her nose. "My mother."

"Oh, Lord," Abby said.

"Appropriate reaction," Sera stated, pointing her finger in her friend's direction. "Because she was at dinner and said I needed to lock Tate in before he left me like all the others."

A collective inhale.

"I don't mean to overstep here, but your mother sounds like an asshole."

She turned to Kelsey and nodded. "Yeah, that's a good description. My mother hasn't had my back since. . . well, never, I guess."

"She was a Stage Mom," Abby said. "On steroids."

Sera nodded, acknowledging that statement as fact. "Delgado women are on this planet to look beautiful." She shrugged at Rachel and Kelsey's expression. "My childhood in a single statement."

"And yet *you're* not an asshole," Kelsey said.

"I like her," Bec stage-whispered.

Rachel tugged Kelsey's ponytail. "She's pretty cool. Not too much of a drag to have around."

"Not to discount Kelsey's awesomeness," Abby said, clapping her hands together and pretending to glance up at Sera adoringly. "But can we continue on with story time? Please? Pretty please?"

"I'll fill them in," Bec said, lips twitching. "He kissed her, and she got stupid. Next thing she knew, she'd agreed to a wedding."

It was Rachel's turn to stage-whisper. "She speaks from experience."

"True that."

"I did get stupid," Sera agreed. "But not because of the kiss. Or not *just* the kiss. I got stupid because he said he liked me."

Heather's brows drew together. "Why is that bad?"

"Because he followed that up with the lovely notion that nothing between us will be romantic or sexual, but instead it will be all about sticking it to the man. Or rather, the mother." She stood up from the table, unable to stand the wooden edge digging into her thighs any longer. Either that, or she was drunk and frustrated.

Or both.

Fine. Both.

Whatever.

She plunked onto the couch, moaning as she let her head drop back against the cushions.

"That's gross," CeCe said, shifting so she propped Sera's legs against her rounded belly.

"The fact that I got three proposals all equally unromantic, or the fact that I *want* it to be sexual with Tate? No. That's not the whole truth. I want it to be more with him. I want him to be The One." There. She'd admitted it. To herself and the room at large. She wanted Tate, and if she hadn't already agreed to marry him, Sera would have wanted to date him.

Not for business. Not to prove something to someone.

But because she liked him and he liked her.

Simple.

Except there was *nothing* simple about this. There was the app and the house listings, the fake relationship and her mother. Good God, her *mother*. Everything was tied up in deception and—

"This isn't how you've imagined it."

Sera blinked, not in surprise, but because Abby's statement was insightful and true, and hearing her inner thoughts expressed aloud made her eyes burn. She had spent so much of her life imagining her husband, her wedding, their happy future together with kids and kittens and puppies . . . and then it actually hadn't happened.

She'd given up on all of it.

But Tate had brought it all back.

She hardly knew him, but she still liked him more than any other man she'd been around in the last few years. Or maybe ever. He was different from all the other men, too.

And without any promise of a real future or even a kind of, maybe, *sort of* tangible happily ever after, she was going to marry him.

For all the wrong reasons.

But worst of all was the fact that he'd made her hope again.

She'd said goodbye to her dream, and he'd presented it back to her on a silver platter.

"I know a thing about noble men," Rachel said quietly. "I know he probably *does* want to rescue you, to make things easier for you. But I also think that if he's the man you describe, he's not just doing this for noble reasons. He wants you, Sera. Even if he's not willing to admit that to himself."

"I agree," Kelsey said. "A man doesn't caveman kiss a woman against a wall unless he has some connection to her."

"But what if it's *just* sexual?" she asked.

"Then he wouldn't have backed off," CeCe said. "He's got a moral code. That's a good thing. He stepped back because he doesn't want to move things along too quickly."

"We're ignoring the upcoming nuptials for this argument," Heather said with a smirk.

CeCe threw a pillow at her. "You know what I mean."

Heather nodded. "I do. I also think this is the most grounded and mature I've ever heard you when talking about a guy. It's usually white stallions and being locked away in towers—"

"I'm not *that* bad," Sera said.

"True." Another nod. "But I do think this thing with Tate is worth exploring. If only because you're different now, and he seems to be in tune with that."

Sera bit her lip. "Really? I mean the whole basis is getting back at my mother. What if at the end of it we break up anyway?"

"Well then," Bec said with a shrug. "You chalk it up to developing maturity and enjoying some really hot sex."

"We haven't *had* sex."

Bec cackled. "You will be, my darling Seraphina. Very soon, you will be."

"Okay, fine," she said with a wry smile. "You're probably right."

They all cracked up, even Sera because though the laughter was about her, the tone was different and for the first time in forever, she felt as though the person she was presenting to her friends, to the world, was the person she was on the inside.

And her friends didn't care.

They accepted her and moved on.

As the conversation turned to other things, movies and TV shows and most importantly, books, Sera wondered if perhaps Tate could accept her "as is" too.

CHAPTER 12

Tate

HIS WALKING into Sera's office was becoming a regular thing.

Three times in as many days.

Though this was the first time she greeted him with a smile.

"Hi," she said, standing up and rounding her desk. His mind took note of every detail of her appearance in a heartbeat. Blond hair tumbling down her back, white silk shirt with two buttons undone at the collar, the black pencil skirt that used to drive him to distraction as she'd climbed the stairs in front of him during the showings.

Yes, pig. Yes, she was fucking incredible.

But today it wasn't her clothes that threatened his sanity.

It was her toes.

She'd slipped off her heels and was padding toward him in bare feet. Which was sexy as hell and probably made him some sort of weird fetish-obsessed freak, but he couldn't tear his eyes from the slender lines of her feet, the pastel blue painted nails. It was like he'd been granted special access to a side of Sera that the rest of the world wasn't allowed to see.

He liked it.

He wanted to know *everything* about her.

But this wasn't about that. She was out of his league, deserved better than him.

"How are you?" she asked, coming close enough that he could smell the floral edges to her shampoo. She rose on tiptoe and kissed his cheek.

"Good."

A single rasped-out word born of longing so intense he wanted to slam her office door shut and bend her over her desk. He'd yank up that tight black skirt and—

She dropped to her heels, took a step back. "Um . . ."

Tate cleared his throat. "Hi."

Not exactly Shakespeare, but at least she wasn't running screaming from the room or searching frantically for her car keys.

"How was your day?" he asked, finally putting on his semi-normal human façade. *Go social skills.*

She took his hand in hers, tugged him to the pair of chairs in front of her desk. He found he didn't mind being led around like a puppy, so long as her fingers were laced with his and she was smiling up at him.

"Why are you being so weird?"

"I'm not—"

Blue eyes filled with mirth. Teasing him.

And somehow, he relaxed. Or maybe . . . it was just that Sera made it easy for him to relax.

"I am being weird," he admitted. "You make me nervous. Especially when I suddenly start getting phone calls from Heather O'Keith and Rebecca Darden."

Sera gasped. "They didn't!"

He chuckled. "Surprisingly, or maybe not, I suppose, they

both threatened to barbeque my balls with a flamethrower if I hurt you."

Her cheeks went pink, and he found himself unable to stop himself from brushing his thumb along them.

"But after the threats, they were very helpful. Heather wants to meet to discuss FundHer." He paused, waited for her eyes to meet his. "Thank you for that."

She shrugged. "It's nothing."

"Not to me."

There was a beat of quiet, not uncomfortable exactly, but filled with a plethora of unsaid things.

After a moment, he brushed her cheek again, her skin like silk against his thumb.

"Rebecca offered to write our prenup."

She snorted.

He laughed. "I took her up on it."

A grin that stole his breath. "Bec *is* the best lawyer around, and even though her specialty isn't in the prenup-marriage-divorce-annulment portion of the law, my friends have given her lots of practice."

"It pays to have good friends."

Her expression softened. "Yes, it does."

Tate didn't have a great response to that. In fact, he didn't know why he'd said that, exactly. He was a loner, aside from his best friend, Keith, and the bastard had gotten married the previous year, so if Tate was being honest, he was closer to his computer than anyone with real flesh and blood.

Fuck, he was going to turn into one of those weird inventors, a basement full of humanoid robots as his only company.

Or maybe you could not fuck it up with Sera. How about that?

He blinked, realized he'd been quiet for too long. Well, he wasn't doing too well with that, was he?

"Here." He thrust an envelope at her.

Startled, she scrambled to grab the manilla paper, but because he'd all but thrown it at her, the envelope fell to the floor.

"Sorry," he said, lurching for it, managing to miss it completely, *and* cracking his head against Sera's.

"Ouch," they both said simultaneously.

Smooth, moron.

"Sorry," he said again, grabbing the packet from the carpet. "I was—"

He glanced up, saw her face was very close to his, but instead of staring at him with derision in her expression, irritation that he could be such a bumbling fool sometimes, Sera's eyes were soft.

"Why do I make you so nervous?" she teased.

He relaxed, but not enough to stop his signature blurt. "Because you're so fucking beautiful that it takes my breath away."

Her lips parted on a surprised inhale, eyes sliding away—

"No," he said. "Don't do that."

Gaze back on his, the deep blue of her irises absolutely stunning. "Do what?"

"Don't look away when I give you a compliment. People always do that when they don't believe it, but if there's one thing you can be certain of, it's your beauty."

A sad smile. "Except, beauty is the one thing that doesn't really matter."

"On the outside, yes," he said. "I agree. It doesn't make one damn bit of difference. But yours is on the inside, sweetheart, and that's why it's so fucking distracting and wonderful and . . . *oh shit*," he hurried to add. "I didn't mean to imply that you're not gorgeous on the outside because—"

Fingers to his lips. "Tate."

"Yeah?" he asked, though it sounded a lot more like "Shmah?"

"What's in the folder?" She dropped her hand.

"The Monroe listing," he said carefully.

"And is that the *only* reason you came by?"

He could have lied, probably should have to keep it strictly platonic. But Tate was way beyond that now, and pretending that his being there had nothing to do with the fact that he couldn't seem to get Sera out of his mind wasn't working for him.

"No."

A stiffness he hadn't even realized was in her frame disappeared at that one word.

"I came because I wanted to see you."

Her lips curved. "Good." A nod. "I wanted to see you, too."

His smile was dopey. He knew it. He accepted it.

"So along that vein, can you do two things for me?" she asked

His grin slipped, memories of Priscilla demanding one thing and then another and another invading his brain.

"First, can you kiss—" She froze, eyes intense. "Tate?" she asked. "Why'd your face do that?"

"Do what?" he asked, shoving it all away, focusing on the fact that her first request was a kiss.

Because, of course it was.

Sera wasn't Priscilla, and he wasn't the gullible boy he'd been back then.

"Why did your face go all dark?"

"It's nothing," he muttered.

"It's *something*."

"What were you going to ask?"

She didn't deny him the answer. "For a kiss and dinner."

"Oh."

Then silence. A long halting moment before Sera said, "Look at me, Tate. Before, you wanted me to understand how you see me."

He nodded, though it wasn't really a question.

"Now, I need you to know this: I don't want your money. I can buy my own things. I don't know where we're heading or what the future holds." Her face softened. "I just know I like you and want to spend more time with you."

This woman.

Damn. How had he ever existed without this woman in his life?

"I want that, too," he said.

"Good." A pert grin. "So, where's my kiss?"

Tate didn't need to be asked a third time.

"So," Sera said, over the top of her menu. "Are we going to talk about it?"

He glanced up from his own menu. "Talk about what?"

One brow lifted. "Why your first inclination is that I'm going to ask you for something." She set the menu on the table. "I know a little of what it's like to be viewed as a meal ticket, know how devastating it can be to not know if someone likes you for you or for what you can give them."

His fingers went limp, the paper menu dropping to his plate. "How do you do that?"

"Do what?"

"Put my experience into words that make sense when I can't even begin to articulate them myself."

A corner of her mouth tugged up. "Because I'm brilliant?"

He laughed. He *actually* laughed when thinking about

Priscilla and his parents. "Yes," he murmured, reaching across the table and squeezing her hand, "you are."

Her skin was soft beneath his, her eyes gentle, and so even though he'd never admitted this to anyone, had barely admitted it to himself, he found that with Sera looking at him so kindly, he couldn't *not* tell her the truth.

"You already know I was a nerd," he said.

She scoffed.

"No," he told her firmly, "I'm not saying that to be funny or self-deprecating. I was such a nerd. I didn't fit in with anyone and when I began skipping grades, it got even worse."

"Because you were so much younger?"

"I—" The waiter came over and they spent the next few minutes ordering their food and drinks.

Sera touched his hand. "You were saying about being so much younger?"

Tate shrugged. "Just that, yes, that was tough. I was scrawny and so much less emotionally mature than the kids in my grade, but that wasn't the worst part, I guess."

"What happened?"

"Little stuff, really." Another shrug. "I got a scholarship to a great private school, one my parents would have never been able to afford to send me, and the kids, as kids do, made fun of my used uniform as well all the other stuff."

She wrinkled her nose. "Kids can be such assholes."

"Yes. Exactly that," he said, "But the teasing was easier to get over. It was my parents that made it tough." He paused as their server brought their drinks then answered the question in Sera's gaze when he'd gone. "At first it was just comments here or there, supposed teasing about them putting so much effort into driving me across town to the school because I was their meal ticket and how I'd better make a lot of money so that they could retire early."

"Ick."

"Yeah. And then I went to college, invented the app, and the comments never stopped."

"They became more?"

He nodded. "They became asks—to borrow money for a bill, a car payment. I didn't care about that. I *wanted* to help them."

"Of course, you did."

"I bought them a house, cars, then a vacation home because they'd always wanted to live on the beach." He tugged at the collar of his shirt. "I figured it was the least I could do. But it never stopped."

She reached across the table, laced her fingers with his. "I know something about parents not stopping."

Yeah, she did.

"And so what happened?"

He winced.

"That bad?"

"I was engaged before."

Both brows came up. "What happened?"

"I'd gotten used to the asks, but with Priscilla, they never stopped," he said, remembering the way she'd pouted when he didn't buy her something, how she'd given him the silent treatment for days or even weeks afterward. "She was the first girl to show any serious interest in me. I was young, stupid, too focused on thinking with my dick."

Sera lifted her glass, took a sip of the fruity cocktail. "So she was beautiful and pursued you."

"There you go again, putting my words into actuality."

She smiled. "If there's one thing I'm good at, it's talking."

He lifted her hand to his mouth, pressed a kiss to her palm. "But yes, that was it. And the asks were so small at first, so innocuous, and between Priscilla and my parents and the long-ass days, I didn't really process, I guess, that things had gotten so out of control."

A squeeze of her hand. "How did things implode?"

"I didn't want the huge five hundred guest wedding soiree with swans and gold leaf ceilings and floating handmade crystal lily pads in the aisle and she freaked. Broke every dish and vase in the house, threw my clothes in the swimming pool, and stormed out. Only . . ."

"Only what?"

"Only that time I didn't chase after her."

Sera leaned back as the server brought their dishes. "I'm guessing she came back."

He nodded. "A week later, after having been photographed with the CEO of a rival company. She begged me to start over, said she was just stressed with the wedding plans, but I'd had enough. I knew that we could never go back, that though things had mostly seemed good and normal before then, they weren't. And I . . . I just couldn't do it all over again."

"I think that's really mature."

"I pulled back from my parents, too," he murmured. "I didn't want to but—"

"You had to start fresh."

A nod. "And most of the time, computers are a lot easier to deal with than people."

She laughed then mirrored him when he picked up his fork and began to eat. "Did you—?" She broke off. "Never mind. You already talked enough heavy stuff for one night, I think."

He put down his fork. "What were you going to ask?"

"Just that . . ." She bit her lip. "Did your parents . . . ever come around?"

"No," he said softly. "No, they didn't."

They exchanged a look that spoke of difficult parents and

hurt-filled childhoods and then Sera reached over and cupped his cheek. "No asks from me, okay?" She said. "I promise."

His heart pulsed and he put his hand over hers, let her see how deep his feelings for her ran. "The thing is, sweetheart. You're so different from Priscilla that it's not even funny. I *want* you to ask. I *want* our relationship to have give and take. I just—"

"May need reassurance that I'm not her every once in a while."

"Brilliant woman." He turned, let his lips brush her palm. "Yes. Exactly that."

"Good." She popped a bite of her dinner into her mouth. "Also, this just in, Priscilla is a stupid name anyway."

He snorted, the twinkling in her eyes making his cheeks crease. "I'm not sure she'd agree with you."

"I'm not sure we give a damn what *Priscilla* thinks."

He tapped a finger on his nose. "Touché."

With that, they shifted the conversation to lighter topics, and despite how much he'd revealed, how raw the topic normally made him feel, Tate *didn't* feel flayed open.

He was starting to feel . . . put together. More whole than he'd felt in a lifetime.

Because of the woman sitting across from him.

And somehow, that wasn't terrifying.

CHAPTER 13

Sera

SHE'D BEEN BLINDSIDED.

By her mother.

And organza samples.

Organza.

Barf.

Barely more than a week of a fake engagement, and Sera was losing her mind. Phone calls. Emails. Buckets of flower samples on her front porch. Binders of stationery samples on her kitchen counter—

And how in the hell did her mother get into her house anyway?

She'd purposely never given either parent a key for exactly this reason and . . . she sighed and crossed over the threshold into her office, facing the gauntlet ahead.

"What do you think of this white for your dress?" her mother asked, holding up a swatch. "No. *This* one is better."

Sera knew weddings, had been obsessed with them for the

better part of her life, and even she could see absolutely no difference between the two samples. She also, and more importantly, had no intention of allowing her mother to have any say in the wedding.

Fake wedding. Or semi, sort of fake, sort of real.

Yeah, couldn't forget that.

She moved around her desk to stow her purse in her bottom drawer, ignoring her mother's one-sided soliloquy. Then she made a mental note to have a discussion with Hector about allowing people into her office. She was really tired of being blindsided.

Sera unlocked her computer, scanning her emails as her mother monologued her way through planning a wedding that wasn't going to happen.

Or not the way her mother wanted.

Her phone buzzed.

Still on for dinner?

Tate. She'd seen him every day over the last week—two dinners, one lunch date, three coffees, and that evening they were going to her favorite restaurant on the waterfront.

God, yes. Get me out of here.

A beat before her cell vibrated again.

Annoying clients?

Her lips twitched.

If only.

My mother.

She added an angry face emoji for good measure.

Well, this is convenient then.

Sera was staring down at her phone then almost dropped it when Tate walked in, looking ridiculously sexy in a pair of navy khakis and a burgundy sweater. He closed the distance between them and pressed a kiss to her cheek.

"Hi," he murmured.

A shiver skated down her spine.

"Hi."

"No," her mother declared triumphantly, "*this* is the perfect shade of white for your dress—" She glanced up, eyes widening when she realized Tate had come in while she'd been organza-distracted. "Oh, hello, Tate. It's so lovely to see you again. My Sera is so lucky to have a man like you in her life."

He slipped an arm around Sera's waist, but though the movement was casual, his arm was stiff. "Mrs. Delgado," he said in greeting, his tone detached, the barest hint of a nod his only deference. But what he followed that up with had her heart skipping a beat. "I'm the lucky one."

So much warmth in that sentence.

Sera reached down, squeezed the hand at her waist, wanting him to know that she felt the same way. Despite the inauspicious start, despite the deception, she'd really had a great week getting to know Tate.

Sugar's lips pressed into a flat line, probably biting back some snarky comment about Sera really being the lucky one.

"And actually," he said. "You can store your samples away. Sera and I have talked, and we're going to elope."

Her heart dropped.

They *hadn't* talked about eloping.

They'd discussed favorite shows—*Desperate Housewives* and *The Great British Bake-Off* for her, *Jack Ryan* for him. They'd talked favorite colors—blue and blue. They'd even gone down the favorite food, favorite movie, and biggest pet peeve avenues of discussion—pizza and clam chowder, *Love Actually* and *The Godfather*, and mouth-breathers and liars, respectively.

But they hadn't discussed eloping.

Because it had *never* crossed Sera's mind.

She'd been planning this wedding for almost thirty years. Her ideas had morphed as she'd grown, the princess wedding of her youth transforming into a barn wedding and then a destination wedding until finally the last few years of experience had convinced her that she wanted a small beachside affair.

A simple altar decorated with flowers—she had a unique triangular-shaped one, dotted with two gatherings of soft pink hydrangeas and sunflowers, pinned to her Pinterest board.

No bridesmaids or groomsmen—it would be too hard to pick just a few of her friends and all of them together would make too big of a bridal party for a beach wedding.

Just her in a simple silk dress, bare feet.

Her groom—hell, who was she kidding, she'd spent a good chunk of the last year imaging Tate standing next to her—holding her hand, staring down at her with warmth in his eyes.

The sun setting. Heartfelt words. The soothing crash of waves.

Not an elopement.

Tate bent and kissed her on her cheek. "Brilliant, right?" he whispered. "Now your mother can't get involved." He winked at her, his expression so proud at having solved an issue that had been plaguing Sera over the last week, that she found she couldn't do anything more than slap on a smile and go along with it.

She rested her head against his shoulder and said, "We sure are!"

Her mother's expression was classic, and it was almost worth giving up the last piece of her childhood fantasy to see Sugar look so discomfited.

"Wh-when?"

Uh. Good question.

Tate recovered first. "We can't tell you that," he said, teasing now. "Or it wouldn't be an elopement." He met her eyes. "But, sweetheart, we should go if we're going to make our dinner reservation."

She'd planned on staying in the office for a little longer since her inbox was overflowing at the moment, but doing that also meant staying with her mother.

Yeah, no.

She slipped from Tate's embrace, snagged her purse, and waved goodbye to her mother.

Sugar was still holding a square of white organza as they walked out the door.

Hector was openly staring.

"Don't let my mother into my office again, okay?" she murmured before giving him some final instructions.

"Got it." He stood, glanced through the opening, glanced back at her and Tate, then mouthed, "Elope?"

Hector had taken the news of her engagement in stride, but add a potential unplanned wedding, and he was staring at her as though she'd grown two heads. Which probably made her a pathetic sap if even her assistant knew how much she'd mooned over Tate during the months they'd worked together. But Hector followed her on Pinterest, and so he had certainly seen her obsession with all things wedding. It wasn't a stretch to think he knew how important it was for her to have it live up to everything she'd ever imagined—

Which was neither here nor there at the moment.

More important was the fact that she and Tate liked each other, that they were seeing how things went.

Yup. Those were the only important things.

All the rest of it was . . . organza in a world of silk.

She nodded at Hector.

Tate touched her arm. "Ready?"

"Absolutely," she told him.

She knew he was talking about dinner, about spending another enjoyable evening together, about continuing to explore the draw between them—because if she'd learned only one thing over the last week, it was how compatible she and Tate were.

Sera also knew Tate wasn't talking about pushing her dreams aside, that he wasn't the kind of man to want her to do that.

But . . . this wasn't a real engagement or marriage.

He was doing her a favor.

And so, what right did she have to demand that he make her silly childhood fantasy come true?

What happened to being open and honest and not hiding parts of yourself? The voice inside her brain that, fittingly, sounded a hell of a lot like Abby.

The voice also wasn't wrong.

She had committed to not molding herself into what others wanted her to be, transforming into some approximation of herself in order to please them.

But this was different.

Tate didn't want her to change. He was trying to help her, to save her from the persistence known as Sugar Delgado. And in the grand scheme of things, nothing else mattered. Not letting go of a fantasy of her spouse hiding her engagement ring in a gorgeous chocolate dessert.

Not planning her perfect beach wedding.

Not buying her dream house to raise a family in.

None of it mattered.

Because this was real life, and Sera had to learn how to live in it.

CHAPTER 14

Tate

"ACTUALLY," Sera said as they got to her car. "Do you mind if we skip the dinner reservation and go to one of our places?" She tugged the handle, opened the driver's side door. "I'm pretty tired."

"Do you want to reschedule?" he asked, worried about the trace of sadness in her eyes.

Had he overstepped in the office with her mother?

Maybe she wanted a huge affair to prove to everyone they were legit . . . or maybe, and his gut clenched just thinking about it, maybe she wanted to call off their entire sham of an engagement.

She bit her lip, and he clenched his hands into fists in order to not brush a thumb across the bottom one, to slide it free of the white teeth marring it. Or better yet, to kiss her and get that mouth distracted with something a hell of a lot more pleasurable for the both of them.

"No," she said, pulling him off that train of thought. "I was just thinking that I might prefer DoorDash and watching that new movie on Netflix."

Tate raised his brow.

He might be a giant nerd, but even *he* knew what Netflix and Chill was.

"Are you asking—" He shook his head, because—fucking moron—no man in his right mind confirmed that they were going to get Netflix and Chill. They just went with the flow, and if Netflix and Chill happened, it happened. And plus, Sera looked kind of pale. More likely, she was coming down with the flu or something and just wanted to relax.

Which meant Tate should probably stay far away, not risk getting sick when they had a big rollout happening at his company.

But the idea of staying by Sera's side, of nursing her back to health, was appealing.

Fuck, he was an emotionally stunted moron.

Because this was the first time he'd ever wanted to be with a woman *more* than his work.

And because that was scary as shit.

Yes, he wanted to take care of Sera. *Hell yes*, he wanted to do that. He liked her a lot, more than he'd ever liked any woman, ever. Priscilla included. And that should terrify him, have him calling off the sham of an engagement and running as fast as possible in the opposite direction.

But Tate wasn't terrified.

This thing with Sera felt right.

He wanted to be with her . . . always.

A warning bell blared to life in his mind, telling him he was slipping farther down the rabbit hole that was his and Sera's relationship, but then all traces of fatigue and sadness faded from her face.

She popped him on the chest. "You were *not* going to inquire about Netflix and—"

Tate kissed her.

Before she finished the sentence, before he admitted that, yes, his brain was more used to spelling out everything perfectly clear in code and not well-versed in relationships. Before he admitted that he really hoped the invitation to her place or her willingness to go back to his meant that maybe he might get to see her naked soon.

Because, fuck, he *needed* to see her naked.

"Chill," she gasped, finishing her sentence when they broke apart, sucking in air.

"Shh," he said and kissed her again.

Her mouth was *everything*—sweet and soft and not hesitant in the least. The moment their lips touched, they parted, heated breaths exchanged, slick darts of dancing tongues, his slipping into her mouth only to have hers chase his back. She stepped closer, and his brain threatened to go into sensation overload.

Breasts pillowing against his chest. Fingernails biting into his shoulders. Her pelvis pressing firmly against his cock.

Tate saw stars, felt heat snake up his spine, coat his limbs, his thoughts, his—

A car door slammed in the distance, and they jumped apart like guilty teenagers.

Sera's cheeks were tinged in red, her lips swollen and wet. The sight was too fucking much, and he leaned down to take her mouth all over again. Only this time, her hand came up, pressed against his lips.

"I think that's enough for the parking lot," she said, eyes dancing with mischief. "Also, yes." A sexy smirk. "I *am* inviting you back to my place, though not necessarily angling for said Netflix and Chill time. I really am tired, but if there happens to be some Netflixing and some Chilling, then who am I to deny my fake fiancé anything?"

He flicked his tongue out, cock tightening even further when she gasped and so he did it again, loving how her lids fluttered, her body drifting closer to his.

"Fake fiancé?" he asked, lifting her palm away. "I thought we were going straight."

She snorted. "I didn't realize we'd gone crooked."

He groaned.

"Bad, I know," Sera teased, "but I do love the banter, Conner. I hope you'll keep giving it to me."

Tate waggled his brows. "I'll keep giving you *something*."

She wrinkled her nose. "Ew."

He laughed. "Too far. Noted. So, my place or yours?"

"I thought we were business only?" Sera asked innocently.

Tate nipped her fingertips. How had he ever imagined being able to resist this woman? "Can we admit that I was an idiot?"

"Yes. That we can always do." Those beautiful blue eyes still danced, though this time with laughter. "So, whose place is closer?"

They spent a few minutes figuring that out—Sera's was closer—before he pressed a kiss to her cheek, promised to see her there, and turned for his car.

"Tate?"

He stopped, rotated to face her.

"I think it might be safer for you if you rode with me."

"What?"

She pointed to her temple, mimed a steering wheel. "Me drive you, go together. Me no hit you with my car."

He snorted and crossed back over to her, drawn to her like a magnet attracted to metal. "You're so fucking beautiful."

A non-sequitur to be sure.

But she was.

Especially with the self-satisfied smile tugging up those kiss-swollen lips.

"I think you've been concussed," she said lightly, but her cheeks were red and not from the kiss this time.

"A concussion that's developed after more than a week?"

"It's possible." She shrugged. "I can drive you back to your car tomorrow, if you want."

He pretended to consider that. "Promise I'll be safe?"

"Hmm." A finger tapped her lips. "*Hmm.* Will you consent to watching the entire new season of *The Great British Bake-off?*"

A nod. "I don't have to be into the office tomorrow until eleven."

"Words a woman lives to hear." A flash of white. "I promise you'll be safe. I'll even let you have a slice of my apple pie that I made in anticipation of Pastry Week."

"You know what?" he asked, helping her into her car and reaching over to buckle her seat belt.

"What?"

"I thought I was the bigger nerd in this relationship, but I think you just proved me wrong."

Her hand gripped his shirt when he would have leaned back.

"Is that what this is? A relationship?"

Tate lightly tugged a strand of her hair, admitted what he should have known from the start. He'd never had a chance of keeping his distance from Sera.

"Well, it sure as hell isn't business."

CHAPTER 15

Sera

TATE HAD his hand resting on her thigh as he scrolled through his phone.

He had his hand on her thigh.

And Sera was seriously worried about the whole promising to keep him safe thing because those fingers on her leg, all manly and firm and their heat soaking through the thin cotton of her slacks—

She shifted, knocking his hand off.

Not because she wanted to—she wanted *more* fingers . . . and without the fabric cock-blocking her—but because of general road safety. She didn't want to get in an accident because the tip of Tate's finger was getting close to the motherland.

"What do you feel like?" he asked, not commenting on her auto acrobatics, though the sly curve to his lips told her he'd definitely noticed. "Italian? Mediterranean? Thai?"

"I've never met a carb I don't love, so I vote Thai or Italian."

He dropped his voice to sinful, though his expression was entirely playful. "Garlic bread?" He waggled his brows.

She giggled, loving that he was like this with her, that he seemed to be forgetting his nerves and awkwardness more often than not, that these moments of joking and banter were growing more frequent.

"My panties are wet just thinking about it."

Sera's stomach clenched hard. That was *not* a nice-girl-Sera joke, not a joke she might have ever dared say aloud.

And if she hadn't felt so comfortable with Tate, that *might-have* would have been a never. As in, she would have *never* said it outside her own brain.

But Tate didn't chastise her, didn't make a snide comment about ladylike behavior.

Instead, when she stopped at a red light and dared to peek at him, Sera found his eyes had gone hot. Molten blue flames that threatened to incinerate her from the inside out.

He pocketed his cell. "You want me to do something about those panties?"

She swallowed hard, heat exploding from her center, burning through her and making her thighs clench, her breasts tingle and ache. She sucked in a breath, accelerated when the light went green, mentally calculating how long it would take to get to the house.

"Did you order food?"

Brows drawn down, he shook his head.

"Good." She returned her gaze to the road. "Because . . . I do," she murmured. "I do want you to do something about them."

His breath caught, no words filling the air between them, but not because he didn't want her, not because he was trying to hold on to that just platonic portion of their agreement.

No, the girls were right.

Tate did want her.

Despite the quiet, she could feel his need, his desire coating the air. And she wanted him just as much.

Then his hand dropped to her thigh again. Squeezed.

It took every bit of her focus to not drive them off the road.

She really wished she lived closer.

FIVE MINUTES AND THIRTY-TWO SECONDS.

That was exactly how much longer it took for Sera to get them back to her house, to pull into her garage, close the door behind her, and turn off the ignition.

They reached for each other at the same time, her grabbing for the collar of his shirt, gripping it tightly, him bringing both hands to her waist and lifting her up and over the console.

She gasped at finding herself in his lap then immediately gasped again when he shoved his seat back, giving them more space.

Their mouths found one other, molding together, lips parting, tongues sliding home. A groan that she wasn't certain if it came from her throat or his. Searching fingers and hard against soft.

As in *his* hard was against *her* soft.

"Fuck," he murmured, breaking the kiss, dragging his lips along her jaw, her throat. "You taste like—"

Sera loved his compliments, but she needed his mouth more.

She wove her hands into his hair and tugged his head up. Thankfully, he didn't fight her, just kissed her until her lungs burned and stars flashed behind her eyes.

"Inside," he panted when they finally gave into the need to breathe.

She started to nod but didn't get very far because Tate laced an arm around her back, cementing them together as he popped open the door and got out of her car . . . or tried to anyway, because he was still buckled in.

A curse. Two sets of fumbling fingers trying to unlatch the clasp.

And then finally he was free, tugging her close again, and stepping from the car. He paused for a second, but before she could worry that he was going to peruse his way through the house or ask for a tour or, well, delay a trip to her bedroom, Tate scooped her up into her arms, located the door leading to the house, and beelined for it.

They were inside a few moments later, the only illumination a couple of lights she had on a timer in her living room.

"That way," she said, pointing to the way to her bedroom.

A nod, brisk steps leading toward the stairs.

She lost focus on giving directions after that, too distracted by the heat of his embrace, the spicy masculine scent in her nose. Giving in, she nipped at his throat, lapping up the slightly salty tang of his skin.

Bang.

Sera hardly had a moment to see that they'd made it to her bedroom before Tate was tossing her on the bed and coming down on top of her a heartbeat later.

He paused, flicked on her bedside lamp, and met her gaze. "You sure?"

The growled-out question had every hair on her body rising, every nerve on high alert. By now she'd seen Tate nice, angry, and she'd even seen him tease, but this Tate? He was on razor's edge.

And Sera fucking loved it.

She was riding that fine line, too, the draw to him intense enough that she was thinking of little else aside from getting naked, sticking his cock inside her, and riding him like a fucking unicycle—

Or whatever.

Bad analogies aside, all she knew was that she had wanted Tate forever and being this close to finally having him, she wasn't thinking of stopping or how sure she was.

She *needed* him.

But that he asked the question at all, and especially when their desire made the air heavy, their passion growing by the second, and logical thoughts on the way out . . . well, that he'd asked made it mean so much more.

Reaching for the hem of her shirt, Sera said, "Yes, I'm sure." One tug and it was up and over her head.

Tate's eyes left hers, drifting down to her breasts.

Air hissed out between clenched teeth. "Baby," he gritted out. "I'm not going to ask again, but are you—"

"Don't finish that sentence."

She reached behind her, undid her bra and slid it free. His curse should have turned the air blue, should have made her embarrassed, but all that rasped out word did was make her nipples hard and pouty and desperate for his mouth.

Thank fuck, he didn't wait, didn't ask any more questions.

He bent, sucked one of her nipples deep into his mouth while his hands got busy, massaging her breasts, pinching her neglected nipple lightly, squeezing and shaping and all but driving her over the edge.

Funny how her breasts had always seemed too big, too unwieldy. She'd always been embarrassed by their size.

But when Tate stared at them, touched them?

He made her feel different. Fucking incredible and mad

with passion, of course, but also . . . Tate made her feel like she was more than just a sum of her parts.

She gasped when he switched breasts, when his slightly-roughened palms brushed over her stomach then lower, flicking open the button on her slacks, pushing them down and off her hips.

He slid down to remove her heels then tugged her pants free. The sensation of his fingers on her bare skin had her eyes drifting closed, her thighs parting in anticipation, and then . . . she jumped, those lids flashing back open.

His smile was wolfish as he licked her again through her underwear. "Just checking," he said, tongue dipping under one side of the waistband, thumb on the other.

"Mmm." Sera's head flopped back when he found her clit without a roadmap.

"This?" A flick. "Or this?" A firm circle.

And considering the second had her all but climbing the headboard, Tate got the hint. Her underwear disappeared in a flash, and a heartbeat later, his thumb was back and getting busy making those firm circles. She was absolutely soaked, throbbing and aching. Because as good as it felt to have him rub her, it also wasn't enough.

"I—" She shook her head. "I need—"

Nonsensical, but thankfully Tate seemed to know what she needed. He slipped a finger inside her, curled it up at the same time he dropped his mouth to her clit and sucked hard.

"Fuck," she groaned. "*Fuck*, that's . . . so fucking good."

Tate didn't respond to her excessive use of the f-word except to keep moving his fingers, to keep sucking, and then she wasn't even aware of the words she was using. Sera couldn't think, couldn't talk, couldn't open her eyes.

She could only soar.

Tate made her soar.

Pleasure twisted through her center, spreading out to her limbs, coiling her tighter and tighter until finally, thankfully, *finally* she exploded.

The world stopped. Or maybe that was just her heart.

She managed to lift a hand to her chest, attempted to find her pulse, but her lungs were sawing in and out as she tried to catch her breath.

"Are you okay?"

Sera shook her head. "You killed me."

Tate chuckled, and because his mouth was still against her clit, aftershocks of pleasure coursed through her. He sat up, fully dressed, eyes still hot, but she could read his expression. He was considering stopping.

Probably worried it was too much too fast.

And Rachel had been right. There was something about honorable men.

She reached into her nightstand, pulled out a condom. She did risk a quick glance at the expiration date; her sex life hadn't been what one would call *active*. But luckily, it was still good.

Tossing it on the bed next to her, she sat up and reached for Tate.

"We don't—"

"Do you want me?" she asked or rather, she blurted, pulling at Tate.

In answer, he took Sera's hand, placed it on his cock. It was hard and throbbing, and even the feel of it through his pants was enough to have her thighs quivering all over again. "I've wanted you since you showed me that house on Pacific."

Her eyes went wide.

"You were wearing that tight skirt that shows off your ass, and I spent the whole time trying not to be a giant pig." His hands dropped to the mattress, slid under the ass in question and squeezed. "You have the best ass."

She smirked, did a little squeezing of her own. "Pot meet kettle." A beat as they both laughed. "Do you really remember that house on Pacific?"

"It was fucking incredible," he said. "I wanted to buy it on the spot."

"What?" She blinked, grabbed his hand and tugged him down to the bed next to her. "You shredded that house to pieces, made me think you couldn't stand it."

He gave her a chagrined smile. "You were the first agent who seemed to get what I wanted from the beginning. But—"

"What?"

"I got one look at you, and I didn't want it to end. And it wasn't just the skirt, fuck, just seeing you made me feel lighter." He rolled to his side, facing her. "You were so excited about the house, your eyes lighting up about the inlay on the floor, the size of the kitchen island. You had this glow . . . and as creepy as that sounds, I just wanted to bathe in that."

Wow.

As in, just *wow*.

"That is creepy."

He froze then laughed. "It is. Romantic words aren't my strong suit, sweetheart, but—and I'm probably insane for this —but . . ."

"What?" she asked again, knowing that she needed to find another word but not able to.

"I want this to work out between us," he said. "I don't want it to be business or to get back at your mother. I just want you, baby."

I just want you, baby.

The most romantic words a woman could hear.

"I want that too," she said softly. Then frowned. "I mean, I don't want me, I want you. Just you. No one else. Just—"

"A blurt and a ramble in less than a minute," he teased. "I think I'm rubbing off on you."

Sera smiled. "I think I like it."

He kissed her. "I think I like it, too."

"Good," she said, reaching for the hem of his shirt and yanking it over his head. The sight of all that bare flesh had her mouth watering, so she pushed him onto his back and climbed on top. Hands tracing, tongue following suit, she took her time on that incredible chest, licking her way south until he was groaning and cursing and she'd reached the waistband of his pants.

A flick to undo the button, a few seconds to slide down the zipper, to free him from his boxer briefs.

And *God*, yes.

He was hard and hot and long, but just as she bent to take him in her mouth, she found herself flat on her back on the bed.

"Next time," he said, reaching for the condom and rolling it on.

She pouted, but that lasted all of two seconds because then his hands finished with the condom and focused on her again, teasing her breasts, slipping between her legs, winding her tighter and tighter until she was worried that she'd go over the edge again.

Normally, that was a good thing. An *excellent* thing.

Tonight she wanted to go over with him.

So she brushed his hands away, threw a leg over his hip, and used it to draw him close.

"Fuck," he hissed.

And yes, she might have hissed it, too.

Because it was perfection, a scalding brand filling her to capacity, stretching her and—

Then he moved.

Shocks of pleasure rippled through her, gathering under her

skin, sparking her nerves, heating her skin. Sweat broke out on her forehead, on the backs of her knees, and she shot up the edge of that peak.

Everything tightened as he moved in and out—her muscles, the pleasure, *Tate*.

He was living granite inside her, on top of her, under her fingertips.

"Tate," she pleaded.

He reached a hand between them. "Come for me, baby. You feel so good." A groan. "I'm so fucking close."

She was the one that was close, so close that it only took one press of his hand against her clit to send her toppling. Tate pushed in once, twice more and then cursed as he followed her over the edge.

They lay entwined for long moments, catching their breath as he rolled to the side and held her close.

He brushed his fingers through her hair, gently untangling the strands.

And it was peaceful.

So damned peaceful that she asked, "Can we do it tomorrow?"

Silence, then, "Do what?"

She risked a glance up at him, heart pounding, feeling so deeply connected to him that she didn't give one damn about the beach wedding. She just wanted him. "Can we go to Vegas tomorrow?"

His mouth curved, and he nodded. "I'd like that."

A brush of her lips against his, but just as she opened her mouth to reply, his stomach growled. Laughter bubbled up in her throat, and she grinned at him. "We forgot the *Netflix* part of Netflix and Chill."

His hand rubbed his stomach. "Does that mean snacks?"

She grinned, reaching over him to grab his pants and pulled

out his cell. "I have no clue, but I'm starving, and I think we covered the *Chill* part, don't you think?"

They had covered the *Chill* part.

At least for the hour it took for the food to come and them to eat.

Then they covered the *Chill* part again.

Just to be sure they had all the finer points perfected.

CHAPTER 16

Tate

HE GLANCED OVER AT SERA, saw her eyes were closed, her head propped against the plane's window.

He'd offered to rent a private jet, but she'd refused, telling him it was a waste of money and that she'd use points to buy their last-minute flight.

Points.

Seriously, she was so different from Priscilla.

Look, he wasn't trying to say he was some sort of damaged hero, ruined by a woman who'd scorned him or left him at the altar or even who'd irrevocably broken his heart. Tate wasn't any of that.

He'd broken things off with Priscilla because it had always been one more thing, just a little more money or another necklace or a bigger, more expensive . . . anything. Hell, that perpetual question of "Can I just have one more . . . ?" fill in the blank had led to his estrangement from his parents.

He *owed* them.

He had so much.

He . . . had felt too damned much like a bank.

And so it had been safer to keep his distance, to focus on work, especially when people made him nervous anyway.

Then FundHer. Then needing to find someone who could do what he couldn't.

Then Sera.

Her.

She was different, made *him* want to be different, inspired him to go out in the world, so long as that world had her in it.

She'd grown up with Delgado money and yet, she was so incredibly normal.

And stubborn, he thought with a smile, remembering the way she'd refused to get on the private plane he'd ordered despite her protests.

"We're not going to fly to our wedding in coach."

She'd huffed. "The flight's all of an hour."

"Sweetheart," he'd said, "Think of how much we'll save on baggage fees."

"We each get two free bags," she'd grumbled, but had gotten on the plane anyway.

Then had curled up on the couch and promptly fallen asleep.

He'd dismissed the attendant, tucked a blanket over her, and had considered taking a nap himself. They'd stayed up way too late the previous night, waiting for the food he'd ordered in . . . waiting that had led to the food going cold after their delivery driver had ended up leaving it on the porch.

Still, the best pasta he'd ever had.

Though a naked Sera cuddled up next to him probably had a lot to do with that.

Tate pushed away the urge to join his fiancé on the couch, ignored the urge to sit in silence and ponder how quickly his life had changed over the last couple of weeks—going from swearing off marriage, or at least any semblance of a real one, to shedding his recluse habits. He'd been out of his house and office more in the last two weeks than the previous two *years*.

That probably should have scared him, but instead he felt alive for the first time in forever.

So, instead of lying down next to her and pulling her into his arms like he wanted, Tate decided to clear the decks.

He'd already canceled his meetings that day, delegated the newest rollout to the person he'd hired to be in charge of them—fancy that, trusting the people he hired to actually do their job.

Dan had been shocked at the call, but also eager to prove himself.

It would be fine. Well, not *fine* since this type of rollout of new features never went completely smooth. There would be fires and crises and a plethora of problems. But in the end, his team would figure it out.

The world would go on circling around the sun, his users' experience would improve, and . . . he'd have a life.

Fancy that, he thought as he pulled out his laptop and began to go through his emails. He hadn't told Sera, but while they'd been making their respective calls to their businesses that morning, he'd also made a few not business-related calls of his own.

To Hector, to find out if Sera could slip away for a few days.

To Heather, to see if she or any of Sera's friends could meet them in Vegas.

He figured Sera might want some familiar, friendly faces as witnesses.

Unfortunately, Heather was traveling for business, but she had promised to call the crew of women that were Sera's closest friends. The Sextant they called themselves, apparently, because they'd Googled "a group of six" while drunk—which was technically a sextet, but they hadn't Googled responsibly, and so the name Sextant had stuck.

Anyway, his thought was that she spoke highly of her friends and he knew after having talked to Bec and met with Heather, how lucky she was to have them in her life.

So, he'd invited them all.

He just didn't know if they'd be able to make it, and so he hadn't told Sera.

She would have told him not to bother, to not make a fuss, but Tate found that he couldn't stop himself from *wanting* to make a fuss over her. She'd pulled him out of his careful little bubble over a year ago, and he . . .

He loved her.

It made no logical sense, this draw he had had to this woman, why she was so different from the rest of the female population. There was no explanation for why he was so different with her.

Except that he loved her.

He hadn't been able to stay away because he loved her.

Her name had been the first he'd blurted out to Roche because he loved her.

He wanted to protect her because he really fucking loved her.

Terrifying . . . or it should have been.

Instead, Tate was relieved. *This* was what had been prickling the back of his mind, the missing puzzle piece that gave him clarity. *This* was the line of code that explained every feeling and connection and—

He loved her.

It was as simple as that.

Smiling, he clicked open his email and began scrolling through the messages. Work, not important. Work, important. Work—

Not work.

Definitely not work.

The subject line read: Tate Conner, you need to see this.

The sender was Abigail O'Keith.

What he read in that email had his heart sinking, his gut twisting itself into knots.

Quietly, he rose to find the flight attendant.

He needed to speak to the pilot.

They had to turn the plane around.

CHAPTER 17

Sera

SHE WOKE up to an empty plane.

Stretching with a groan, she glanced around, confirming that she was alone. Or at least in the body of the plane. Soft voices echoed from the cockpit.

Sera pushed herself up, lifted the shade on the window to glance outside.

An airport. A quiet terminal.

So she'd slept through the entire trip, not surprising she supposed, considering how little sleep she'd gotten the previous night and how short the flight to Vegas was.

"Tate?" she called softly, padding toward the back of the plane.

Maybe he'd slipped into the bathroom.

But the space was empty.

Frowning, heart sinking, she moved to the front of the plane, to the voices she'd heard.

But though there were several people near the cockpit, none of them was Tate. The flight attendants, both men in their early twenties, were in deep conversation with the pilot, also a male.

Conversation that cut off the moment they caught sight of her.

Sera's throat burned because though the conversation had stopped, she *had* heard one thing.

"I've never seen him like this. So upset that he was all but tearing his hair out. All over a woman—"

"Have you seen Tate?"

Three heads shook.

"He said we shouldn't wake you," the first attendant said. His name was Ben, if she was remembering correctly.

"But there is a car waiting for you," the second, David, said. "And he left you this note."

She nodded, gut twisting and knowing instinctively that they weren't in Vegas, that they weren't going to elope at the chapel with the Elvis impersonator they'd chosen.

"Thank you," she murmured, taking the envelope.

"Your bags are in the car," David added.

Another nod, shaky legs as she descended the stairs.

It wasn't until she was in the back seat of the black sedan that Tate had obviously arranged that she opened up the envelope.

I can't do this.

Four words that tore her heart to shreds.

Four words that weren't a surprise.

Because hadn't her mother predicted this *exact* scenario?

Sera's eyes burned with tears, but she wouldn't let them fall. Instead, she closed her lids, laid her head back against the seat, and let the misery sweep through her.

She'd been stupid.

So *fucking* stupid.

Because she'd fallen in love with Tate again . . . or maybe she'd never stopped loving him.

And either way, all that emotion got her was another broken heart, nursing it as she sat alone in the back seat of a quiet car. She'd been living in a fantasy world for the last few weeks, but reality had decided to bitch-slap her back into real life.

How fitting.

It took Sera just over twenty minutes to figure out that perhaps her perception of events wasn't quite right.

The first clue was the scenery outside her window.

Ocean . . . and not her Northern California version.

The next was the envelope next to her on the seat. The envelope she'd failed to notice because she'd been so busy convincing herself that Tate had left like all the other men in her life.

Hesitantly, she reached for it, tore open the flap.

I couldn't just take you to Vegas when that's not what you really want.

The pointed spears of ships' masts appeared like spikes shooting out of the ground as the car drove over a bridge. White and blue and red dominated, punctuated by the deep azure of the ocean, the snowy froth of the waves cresting.

"Almost there," her driver said, glancing back at her in the rearview. "You might want to open the box."

"What—?"

But then Sera saw the third clue that she might have misjudged this situation horribly.

A small takeout box was perched on the floor.

She reached for it, opened the top . . . and then the tears fell.

Inside was an intricate dessert—a shiny dark chocolate globe topped with raspberries and white chocolate twirls and gold leaf.

"Here's a fork."

She sniffed, wiping away the tears, and used it to crack open the sphere.

Her ring was inside.

Not the one she'd bought to impress her mother, but the one that was on her Pinterest board.

Her Pinterest board.

Abby.

Or maybe Heather. Or Rachel. Or—

The car pulled to a stop, and the door opened.

Or maybe *all* of them.

As in, all of her friends were there.

Abby grinning down at her, holding a bouquet of pink hydrangeas and sunflowers. Rachel with a garment bag in her arms, Bec and Heather both with envelopes, though Bec's was of the manilla legal variety and Heather's was small and white and matched those that Tate had been leaving for her. Even Kelsey was there, holding up a cell with CeCe's smiling face on the screen, her still-pregnant friend now past her due date and not able to travel.

She grabbed the takeout box and hopped out of the car. "What the hell is happening?"

Abby took the box from her hands then tugged her toward the hotel behind them that Sera had missed initially. "Come on," Abby said. "Sunset is in less than an hour."

Her friends bustled her into a room, and the next fifty minutes were a frenzy of activity. Kelsey curled her hair, Abby did her makeup, with plenty of waterproof mascara to accent her lashes, and Bec produced a prenup that Tate had already signed.

"He let me write it up. No conditions, no complaints," Bec said then smirked. "I like him."

Last, Heather handed her the envelope from Tate.

I want you to have everything you've ever wished for.

She sniffed.

Abby snatched the little slip of paper from her hands. "Don't you *dare* cry."

"Heaven forbid she ruin her mascara," Heather teased, Abby's obsession with the running black makeup well-known.

"Shut up, she needs to look absolutely perfect in her makeup."

Rachel put the bouquet in Sera's hands. "Ready?"

She glanced at her friends, sniffed again. "Thank you."

"*Stop,*" Abby said, but she was sniffing, too. And so was everyone else in the room, CeCe included.

"No fair," she said through the phone. "I can't hug you."

They all laughed, pretending to include CeCe in a group hug before filing out the door and down to the beach.

Which was literally steps away.

The sun was making its descent, gilding the waves in gold and orange and red. And there on the beach, somehow surrounded by the gorgeous triangular altar she'd imagined—the flowers exactly as she'd pictured, stood Tate.

He was barefoot, just like her.

In navy slacks and a white button-down.

He was so gorgeous it took her breath away.

"Hi," he said, meeting her at the edge of the sand and taking her hand.

Her eyes immediately filled with tears. "Tate," she said.

"How? Why?" How had he done this all in a couple of hours? *Why* had he bothered to do it at all?

"Because you wouldn't have asked." He pressed a kiss to her lips. "Because I love you."

Her breath caught.

"Because I want you to have everything you've ever dreamed of." He tugged her forward, toward the officiant standing in front of the altar. "I know we've done this all sorts of mixed up. I know that we're new and still figuring things out together, but I've known one thing for certain in my heart since the moment I met you."

"What's that?" she whispered.

"That you were special, sweetheart," he said. "And if you'll have me, I won't be stupid enough to let something as special as you go."

Sera stared into his eyes, saw the truth there. "This is crazy," she said, hurrying to add when his face fell, "But then again, that seems to be how we roll. Because you're right about us doing this all sorts of mixed up. You're right that it's been stupidly fast. But . . . I've spent the last year wanting you, and"— she bit her lip, released it—"I think I want to spend the foreseeable ones figuring things out with you."

He smiled. "You think?"

A shrug. "Well, we do have that really good prenup from Bec, so no harm, no foul, right?"

They laughed and there under the setting sun, with her friends behind her, the man she loved at her side, and the waves and sand and salt-tinged air, Sera finally said,

"I do."

CHAPTER 18

Sera, Three Weeks Later

SHE LET HERSELF INTO HER PARENTS' house for the first time in forever, knowing that her mother always took tea in the garden at this time in the morning. Her ode to the historical romance novels Sera loved, or at least that was what Sera liked to pretend.

In reality, her mother never did anything that wasn't calculated and calibrated to bring about the biggest bump to her social standing.

In this case, her garden had become a place of envy for their circle—exotic flowers and koi fish, meandering footpaths and hidden tables topped with white tablecloths and pristine crystal glassware. All of which created a ton of work for the staff and yet if they—the gardener, the maids—weren't fanatical about the garden's upkeep, her mother would lose her shit if she saw the faintest hint of dust or fingerprints or even dead flower petals.

Her mother wanted to live in a world surrounded by perfect beauty.

She just never took into account that oftentimes the most beautiful things in life came from the imperfections.

Sera sighed and walked through the patio, along the twisting path that would lead to Sugar's favorite bench. Leaves were placed strategically so that her mother would be aware of any approaching visitors and could assume the proper position—a book she never actually read perched on her lap, hair smoothed, ankles crossed demurely.

Today was no different.

Except that when her mother saw that it was Sera, her blue eyes flashed and she jumped to her feet, book dropping to the ground with a soft *plop*.

"I've called you a hundred times," she snapped. "What in the he—"

"Mom," Sera said sharply. "Sit."

"What—"

"Sit down on the bench, shut your mouth, and for once in your life, *listen to me.*"

Sera had never talked to her parents with such a tone, even when she'd been a teenager rebelling against modeling or filming commercials, her opposition had always come in the form of something quieter.

Usually escaping to Abby's house until the opportunity had passed.

Sugar froze, mouth half-open, but the retort that was no doubt sitting on the end of her tongue never came. Instead, miracle of all miracles, she sat.

Sera sucked in a breath and held out her hand. "This is the ring I wanted."

Her mother's brows pulled together.

"Not the ostentatious diamond, not the giant wedding, not all the attention," Sera said. "I just wanted someone to see me for me and . . . to love me for me."

"That's—"

She put up a hand. "Before you tell me that's not realistic, I just want you to know that I found that with Tate. He sees me as more than a sum of my parts an-and he loves me." Sera touched her chest. "Me for me. Me without makeup or pretense. Me *with* makeup and dressed to the nines. He doesn't care that I'm obsessed with books or *Desperate Housewives*. He loves the person I am inside and—" She sucked in a breath, let the truth fall from her tongue. "And I have *you* to thank for that."

Sugar smiled.

And so Sera told the truth. She'd been thinking about this for the last several weeks, considering whether she wanted to confess anything to her mother. But in the end, Sera had wanted Sugar to know.

She hadn't wanted any shadows hanging over her and Tate.

She wanted to build a future with him.

Which meant that she wanted her mother to know her part.

"You pushed us together," Sera said, watched as Sugar's smile widened. "Just not for the right reasons. Tate agreed to marry me because he overheard you saying that I wouldn't be able to get him down the aisle on my own. He did it to save me, not because he loved me." She bent and retrieved the book, setting it on the bench. "Not at first anyway."

"What does it matter why he married you?" Sugar took Sera's hand. "The point is that you snagged *Tate Conner*. Everyone has been talking about it for weeks. You wouldn't believe how many visitors I've had asking for details."

Sera slipped her hand free. "It matters because this is the rest of my life. Because I want someone who loves me for all of the right reasons."

"Pish. Your stock is higher now. If things don't work out with Tate, you'll be able to marry—"

"Does my happiness not matter?"

Sugar rolled her eyes. "*No one's* happiness matters."

A calmness washed over Sera as she finally understood, or if not *understood* then at least she finally had clarity. Because her mother would never change. Nothing would ever be more important to Sugar than society and money and making other people jealous.

Not even her only child's happiness.

She shook her head. "Thank you for the push with Tate."

"Of course, darling," Sugar replied. "And now that you're back from your honeymoon we should plan a party to celebrate. I can get the—"

Never. Going. To. Change.

Her mother was never going to be who Sera wanted her to be.

And, know what? That was okay.

Sera had made her own family. She had her friends and now she had Tate.

So in the middle of Sugar's exposition on the perfect caterer, Sera leaned in, kissed her on the cheek. "Goodbye, Mother."

Then she turned and walked away.

And didn't spare a glance back.

Sera wasn't going to waste another moment of her HEA on the past.

Her future was ahead of her and she was going to grab on to it with two hands.

EPILOGUE

Kelsey

KELSEY PUSHED out of the door of Bobby's, the local bar she and her friends liked to frequent, and paused for a moment, enjoying the crispness in the air.

It was one of those perfect end of summer evenings, warm during the day, but the promise of fall in the air. She snuggled into her hoodie and smiled, thinking about how happy her brother, Sebastian, and his fiancée, Rachel, had been that evening at dinner.

Of course, a lot of that had to do with the fact that Rachel was sporting a diamond large enough to blind Kelsey . . . and the rest of the Earth's populace.

But, seriously, she was happy for them both.

Sebastian and Rachel were perfect for each other and they deserved all the happiness in the world.

She slipped out of the opening and let the door start to close behind her, but before she got too far, Sebastian caught it. He slid through, dropped an arm around her shoulders. "Let me walk you to your car."

"I'm fine," she said, shrugging him off. "Go enjoy your fiancée. It's not your guys' fault that my flight is ridiculously early in the morning."

He rolled his eyes. "You know you're not going to win this argument, so just accept my chivalry. It's my brotherly duty after all."

"You sell it so effectively."

"Shut up."

"*You* shut up."

"No, *you* shut up."

"*No—*"

They broke off with grins and Kels let Bas sling his arm around her neck, tugging her into a hug. "I love you, brat," he told her.

"Well, I don't love you."

"Rude."

"You know it." But she hugged him back before leading him to her car. "I am really so happy for you both, you know that right?"

"Of course I do, Kels," he said.

They spent the next few minutes discussing the wedding—the date and location were set, as was the food—and the whole crew of females, including Kelsey were going dress shopping the following week.

"It sounds like you've got it pretty much sorted."

Bas smiled. "Rachel's a force of nature," he joked. "Seriously, though, she wanted to ask you this, but I preferred to do it myself."

Kels frowned. "Ask what?"

"To be a bridesmaid. We were hoping you'd be in the bridal party." He lifted his hands, palms up. "No pressure, of course, but we'd love to have you in the wedding."

Her lips curved. "I'm happy to play whatever role you want, Bas."

"Flower girl?"

She shot him a glare. "Really?"

"So bridesmaid then?"

Since they'd reached her car, she unlocked the passenger side door and tossed her purse on the seat. "I'd be honored. As long as that's what you guys want."

He nodded. "It is."

"Great." She pressed a kiss to his cheek. "Then count me in. Thank Rachel for me?"

"Done."

Kels rounded her car, paused with her hand on the driver's door handle. "Oh, besides Devon"—their brother—"who are the other groomsmen?"

"We're keeping it small." He shrugged. "Heather is going to be the maid of honor, you a bridesmaid, and Devon is going to be my best man."

She smiled. "And Clay is going to be the other groomsman."

Bas shook his head.

Kelsey had opened her mouth, ready to tease Bas about choosing to include Rachel's boss over his when her gut sank.

Small bridal party.

Two on each side.

One of which was *not* Clay.

And her brother had only had a few close friends growing up. None of whom she could see in the wedding party.

Except one.

Fuck.

But she was worrying for nothing. Bas hadn't talked to Tanner in years as far as she knew. They *hadn't* talked in years. They couldn't have—

"Who is it then?" she asked through stiff lips.

Because it couldn't be. Her brother didn't know about them. She'd made sure of it. They'd kept things on the down-low and . . . then she'd nursed her broken heart two thousand miles away in college.

"Tanner."

Her gut twisted.

Double fuck.

And a shit for good measure.

"That's fine, right?" Bas asked. "You guys seemed to get along great." Concern rippled across his face. "Is there something wrong. Did—"

"No," she said quickly. "That's great. I'm sorry. I'm just preoccupied with my new project."

He grinned. "Always work with you."

She blew him a kiss. "You know it."

"Great. So you'll be paired up with him. And I know it's been a while, but he's coming into town next week to catch up." He tapped the roof of her car, took a step back. "You want to grab dinner with us?"

"I'd love too," she lied before getting into her car and with a wave that hopefully didn't show her dismay, Kelsey drove away.

Paired up with Tanner.

Been there, done that.

Got the souvenir broken heart.

Triple fuck.

BAD TEXT

A BILLIONAIRE'S CLUB NOVELLA

CHAPTER 1

Lorelai

BUZZ. *Buzz.*

Lori groaned and rolled over, scrambling for her cell and hitting the side button to shut it up. Then she burrowed her head into her pillow and tried to go back to sleep.

Her eyes slid closed. Her breathing slowed—

Buzz. Buzz.

"Ugh," she muttered, scrabbling for her phone again. Her fingers closed around the case, bringing it up to her face, and glancing at the too-bright screen with scrunched up eyes.

Fuck, that was intense.

Buzz. Buzz.

Squinting, she looked at the home screen, saw a trail of three texts.

Hey, baby, the first one read. *I'm so glad I met you tonight.*

I hope that you really DO want this, the second one said.

The third one . . . was a picture.

Call it stupidity, or perhaps it was just because she'd been woken up in the middle of the night and her brain was mush, but for whatever reason, Lori touched the text bubble with the picture.

A second later, the screen unlocked.

And then—

"Um . . ." She blinked, looked again. "Um. *Wow*."

There on the screen was . . . holy balls—no pun intended—but there were . . . well, *balls* and a penis and abs and—

Look, she'd seen her fair share of dick pics, being a single woman in her early thirties. They seemed to appear in her inbox in uninvited droves and while this one was definitely *not* invited, it was also . . . kind of the best she'd ever seen.

Her phone buzzed again, and she glanced at the screen.

You there?

Lori froze, eyes glued to the picture and knowing she had a choice to make. One to pretend to be whoever *you* was in order to obtain more photos. Gross, but it had been a long time since she'd . . . fine, here was her inner perv talking, seen a penis in the flesh.

Ick. Not the best thought.

But it was two in the morning, she'd been an idiot to not have her phone on Do Not Disturb, and . . . it had been A. Really. Long. Time.

However, even being pent-up sexually, she still had enough of a moral center that she felt the need to respond to the man and tell him he had the wrong number.

But maybe if she waited long enough, she might get another pic?

Just one to look at—briefly—before she'd promptly delete it and—

Her eyes drifted back down to her phone, to the words this time, and her pesky conscience reared its head. Sighing, she let her fingers work on the keyboard.

You have the wrong number.

Silence.
Several long minutes of silence.
Then,

Oh, fuck. I'm so sorry.

She couldn't help it—she laughed, but sent back,

It's . . . not okay, I guess. But don't worry. I'll delete it and we can pretend it never happened.

A beat.

Thank you. And again, I'm so sorry.

Which was the point she couldn't help herself from replying with,

Next time you send a dick pic, leave off your head.

Lori winced.

The head attached to your neck, not the one on your . . . well . . . *finger pointing down emoji*

There was no response for a long time. But eventually her cell vibrated again and—

Noted.

Sighing and sending out sad, pathetic thoughts to the universe for having to be a good person and noting that she'd better get some good karma for being nice about an unsolicited dick pic in the middle of the night, she deleted the photo. Then sent a screen shot of their chain—sans pic—as proof to the mysterious, albeit gorgeous man with the yummiest cock she'd ever laid eyes on that she had, in fact, deleted the photo.

A buzz.

Thanks.

She wrinkled her nose and flopped onto her back, wide awake and huffy about it. Then made huffier when her phone vibrated again.

Um. Does that thing happen a lot?

Me receiving unwanted photos of penises? Or the man sending them apologizing?

Either. Both.

She grinned.

Yes to the first. No to the second.

Fuck. Men are assholes.

At least the latest one had a pretty face.

And a pretty something else, but that was beside the point. Lori set her cell on the bedside table again and started to lie back.

Buzz. Buzz.

"Oh my fucking God," she muttered and scooped up her phone, glaring at the screen as she read.

Then her lips twitched.

How about you send me your pretty face?

The man either had the slickest game on the planet or he was seriously horrible at reading the opposite sex.

That's a no.

Though, she was the one who kept engaging, so what did that make her? Rolling her eyes, she turned on Do Not Disturb, placed her cell on the bedside table—for the *final* time—and then cuddled back under the blankets. She had to get up in four hours. She was going to sleep, and that would happen *right* now.

Right. Now.

Right—

Fuck it, she was going to look.

Flipping to her side, she reached for her phone, tilting it up just enough to see the screen. A response was there. Of course, it was. But nope. She was not opening it. No way. No how. No—

Oh, look. Her Face ID magically unlocked the screen and loaded her messages.

Please?

She snorted.

Nope.

Pretty please with sugar on top?

What are you? Five?

I'm thirty-five, actually. And totally helpless when it comes to women.

I can see that.

Ouch.

A beat before he sent,

So now will you show me your face?

She shook her head. This man was persistent, if nothing else.

Going into the creepy territory, Mr. Thirty-Five.

Victory!

thinking emoji

I'm no longer helpless. I'm creepy.

Lori couldn't help it. She outright laughed. Oh boy, this man was something else.

You do realize it's almost three in the morning, right?

You're the one responding to my messages.

You're the one who sent the filthy dick pic in the first place.

She asked for it!

Her lips curved. Now, *this* was a story she had to hear. Lori sat up, tucking her fuzzy purple comforter under her arms as she went. A moment later, she'd fluffed the pillows up behind her back and then flicked on the light. Only once she was comfortable did she send a reply.

How exactly did she "ask for it?"

The little ". . ." bubble appeared at the bottom of the screen. Then disappeared. Then reappeared and stayed there for a while. The reply that buzzed into her cell made her understand why it took a while. He'd sent a dissertation.

Well, there was this girl in the bar. Hannah. Okay, I'm not the type of person to go to bars usually, but I'm new in town and jet-lagged and I figured it was better than just staying in my condo staring at the empty walls since only half of my furniture arrived and none of that arrived furniture included my TV. Also, I have no internet because they're coming tomorrow.

There was a pause here where she assumed he was waiting for her to respond and so she did.

Tell me more.

More bubbles appearing and disappearing until her cell vibrated.

So I went out looking for a diner or coffee shop or what-ever, but the only place that was open was a bar—

She snorted. Sure, it was.

I had a couple of drinks—

Another snort. A couple, right.

Next thing I know, Hannah came over and we spent a few hours eating, drinking, and talking but then she had to go. Before she left, though, she wrote her number on my hand—

How very high school.

—and told me to text her something she could use to relax her later—and here, she patted my crotch—

Wow.

I mean, who does that? She could have just put the number in my phone. Anyway, by the time my drunk ass got over the feel of her hand on my cock and I'd really processed what she'd done, she was gone, and I was paying a big bill.

She pressed her lips together.

You seem awfully sober now.

A beat then,

Being the type of asshole to send an unsolicited dick pic will do that to a man.

She snorted.

I'm not sure that's true.

Well, true or not, I obviously got played.

Lori considered all that then sent,

Pictures, or it isn't true.

There was a long silence before she got a reply.

Um, isn't that what got us into this problem in the first place?

She grinned.

I meant of the number this Hannah wrote on your hand.

Oh.

A few seconds later, her cell buzzed, and another pic appeared on her screen. This one was also naked, but because it was a picture of a naked palm, it was less exciting. Though those thick fingers, yo. And . . . she was an idiot, but it was now after three in the morning, she was texting a stranger, and so she was allowed to be a bit delirious. Shaking her head, she focused on the photo.

Sure enough, there was a scrawling phone number on his skin.

Except—

That's not a 1.

What?

At the end. That's a 7.

Lori's stomach was clenching tighter than during her Pilates class. Okay, bad analogy, but the point was that she was trying not to laugh. Trying didn't mean she succeeded. In fact, she failed miserably and missed the next three texts her mystery man had sent.

That's a 1.

Oh my fucking God, that's NOT a 1.

Kill me. Now.

By the time she could breathe again, or at least by the time her laughter had been reduced to giggles, several minutes had passed.

Then her phone buzzed again.

It's a 7.

Lori grinned, almost able to hear the defeat in his tone, even though all she had was words on a screen. But this man, whoever he was, had personality.

I'm going to go throw myself off a bridge.

She paused, concern now mixing with amusement.

Is this joking or are you actually suicidal? Because, in the grand scheme of things, a dick pic isn't the end of the world. I'm not emotionally scarred and plus, I deleted it.

A beat, then,

Too bad you can't delete my unending shame.

But seriously, I'm sorry . . . about everything. The picture. The comments—that was insensitive. I'm not that kind of guy.

Hmm. Well, *that* was interesting.

Why type of guy are you?

No reply. For a solid three minutes. For long enough that Lori realized she'd clearly pushed the wrong button and no matter how pretty his dick or how interesting his text personality was, they were done. An hour of texting and strangely, she found that disappointing.

Sighing, she plugged her cell back in.

Well, another one driven away. Somehow that wasn't surprising in the least. Too bad this time she hadn't even known his name.

Her eyes slid closed, sleep finally welled up and surrounded her, and she fell head-long into darkness.

And missed the final *buzz-buzz* from the mystery man.

Missed him saying,

I'm . . . I don't know who I am.

CHAPTER 2

Lorelai

OH GOD, she was late.

Late.

Normally, that wouldn't matter. Her boss, Heather O'Keith didn't really care what hours her engineers kept, so long as the deadlines were met. The trouble was that today she had a meeting.

With her boss.

A meeting she was going to be late for.

"Shit," she muttered, shrugging on her backpack and snatching her phone from the charger. She'd somehow turned down the volume on her cell and hadn't heard the alarm until it had been going off for forty-five minutes.

That was why she didn't stay up all night anymore.

Her sleep-hangover was deadly when it came to hearing alarm clocks.

"Fuck," she hissed, stubbing a toe and hopping around on one foot for a few moments before throwing on her "fancy" sneakers. Sneakers, since no one in her department dressed in anything more formal than jeans, tennis shoes, and a tee, but nice because she still had a meeting with her boss.

Classy, she was.

Okay, so backpack, check. Phone, check. Jacket, check. Clothes on all pertinent portions of her body because she really didn't want to live her nightmare of showing up at work pantsless, check. Coffee . . . she wanted. Badly. But she would have to wait.

Ugh.

Regardless of her inner, ugh-ing, Lori hurried to her front door and fumbled through it in her daily struggle of heavy wooden panel meets a bulky jacket and a giant backpack with a phone in one hand.

It wasn't pretty.

Ever.

And also why she didn't realize that her new neighbor was standing in the hall, thoroughly entertained by the process until a hand landed on the door above her head, stopping it from swinging closed on her leg.

"Thank—"

She glanced up and *every single muscle* in her body locked in place. It was—

She shook her head, tried to clear it, because it couldn't possibly be . . .

No. No fucking way.

Warm fingers wrapped around her arm, tugging her gently forward so the door could shut. Absently, Lori checked the knob to make sure it had locked.

She reached for the fingers on her arm, not necessarily to push him away, but to flip over his palm and see—

"Are you okay?"

Hot sunshine burning into her skin, drifting down her spine, slipping between her legs. Her pussy clenched . . . because she knew *exactly* what this guy was packing.

"What's your name?" she whispered.

A pause then, "Logan."

"Are you still jet-lagged?"

"Um. Yes?" He stepped back, head tilting and drawing her focus to deep brown eyes and sun-kissed olive skin. If he'd told her the reason he was jet-lagged was because he had just stepped off a yacht in the Mediterranean then Lori would have absolutely believed it.

"It's not a 1," she murmured.

And waited.

Luckily, it didn't take long.

His eyes went wide, and he took another step back, gaze flicking from her apartment door to her neighbor's—or well, now *his* apartment door.

"When did you move in?" she asked.

Logan blinked, focused back on her. "Yesterday."

"Cool," she said, suddenly realizing that she should be feeling awkward because she'd seen this man's business parts and not focusing on how much her body was telling her that it had been a really *long* time since she'd seen said business end of a man. Oh, and that there wasn't any time like the present to remedy that fact, might not be the best strategy moving forward.

But he has a great cock—

Focus.

Great. Now she was mentally arguing with herself.

That was the surest sign of sanity. Totally.

She turned to leave.

He snagged her arm. "What's your name?"

Figuring she owed him that much based solely on the fact they were neighbors but also reinforced by the fact that she'd seen his penis, she said, "Lorelai. But mostly everyone calls me Lori."

"Lori," he murmured.

Her phone buzzed, and she glanced down at the reminder that she had five minutes to make it to her meeting with her boss.

"Shit!" she exclaimed, dashing toward the elevator. "I've got to go."

"Wait—"

"I'm late!" She jabbed at the elevator button, thankful that, for once, she didn't have to wait forever for the doors to open.

"Lori—"

"I've got to go!" She pressed the floor for the garage repeatedly. "My boss. I need to go."

"Can I—"

The elevator doors shut before he could finish his question

CHAPTER 3

Logan

THE SILVER PANELS slid shut before he could finish asking Lori if he could make up for the unfortunate dick pic situation by buying her dinner.

Or maybe a year's worth of dinners.

Fuck, what had he been thinking?

He *hadn't* been thinking. Which was precisely the problem. He'd been near delirious from not sleeping fully for days and add in four, no *five* beers and he'd been blitzed out of his mind.

Stumbling back to his apartment, thinking of that little smirk Hannah had sent him before she'd gone. *"Send something to relax me later."*

None of that meant a fucking picture of his cock.

With his face in it.

No, he didn't go around sending random photographs of his private parts to women he'd just met—or as it turned out, women he'd never met who turned out to be beautiful and funny and smelled incredible . . . *and* lived next door.

Fuck.

Okay, so he didn't have a *lot* of experience sending dick pics. None, actually.

But even drunk, he should have had some fucking sense.

Moron.

He hit the button for the elevator, waited a godawful long time for the car to come, then got on and headed out to explore the new city that was going to be his home.

Logan was going to beat this jet-lag, dammit.

First stop was to take a Lyft down to the waterfront and see Pier 39. He'd never been to San Francisco before, having grown up in the Midwest before joining the military and spending most of his time in Germany, Japan, and then various bases across the States. But he'd never been to San Francisco. So, when his brother had moved out of his apartment in the city and had needed to sublet the space, Logan had jumped on the opportunity to spend his first few months out of the military somewhere new.

Somewhere to reset.

To figure out what the fuck he was going to do with his life.

He had some technical skills, but what he actually enjoyed? He was . . . drawing a blank.

That was the confusing and frustrating part.

He'd been competent for fifteen years and now he had to figure out the next chapter of his life. No pressure, no big deal.

Sighing, Logan thanked the driver then got out of the car. Immediately, he was blasted with surprisingly cold air, the wind whipping through his coat and hair. It wasn't as frosty as a German winter, but it was a damn lot colder than he'd expected for California.

Fog curled around the buildings, the bay was churned up into heavy waves, and even though it was relatively early on a weekday, the pier was busy.

He wove his way through the crowded boardwalk, taking in

the myriad of shops with racks of sweatshirts lined up in front of their doors—a smart business move as far as he was concerned, based on the wind and fog. But there weren't just T-shirt and souvenir and sock shops, there were also galleries and candy shops with huge drums full of salt-water taffy and root beer barrels and ribbons of colorful, twisted sugar.

But it didn't take long for him to reach the end of the shops and slip through an opening that led to a wooden walkway surrounding the perimeter.

Here was the part he liked.

Actually being able to hear the waves crashing against the support posts, the barking of the sea lions as they alternately lounged and jostled for prime position on the floating platforms in the water. There were only a few other people walking or taking in the view, mostly older folks or couples sneaking in an early lunch.

Here he could smell the tang of fish.

Here he could hear the waves.

Here he could feel a bit more like himself.

Logan stood for a few moments, watching the sea lions, enjoying the breeze and the fact that he didn't have anything pressing on his time.

He could binge bad TV all day, wander around the city for hours, go to bars, get numbers from beautiful women, and . . . send random dick pics.

Groaning, he pulled his cell from his pocket and took a photo of the sea lions, then one of fog-enshrouded Alcatraz in the distance, which made him suddenly have the urge to watch that old Nick Cage movie, *The Rock*. Well, know what? Once the cable guys came that afternoon, he *could* watch it. He had *all* day to watch. He had *six* months to watch it. He—

Was going to go absolutely insane unless he found something to do.

For nearly all of the last fifteen years, he'd been told when to get dressed, what job to do, when to eat, when to go to bed.

Now five days of freedom, and he was losing his mind.

But all Logan could picture were endless blank days of waking up and wandering around or watching TV until the sun set and he got tired enough to sleep.

What a prime catch he was, having this much of a pity party.

Deliberately, he pulled up the app on his phone and scheduled a ride to take him back to the apartment. It was time he pulled his shit together and began figuring out what the rest of his life would entail.

He strode to the front of the pier, just as his car pulled up, and got in, making small talk for a minute or two before the driver went quiet.

That quiet was what did him in.

Though this time, it didn't involve nudity.

Or, well, of the human variety.

Though the object in the shot wasn't wearing pants. Thankfully, the pant-less state wasn't illegal, as it was a sea lion that was making a comical face as it was knocked off the platform.

He pulled up his text chain with Lori, added the photo, then sent,

Sorry I made you late.

Then he rode back to his apartment, vowed to never send another dick pic, and immersed himself in the want ads.

BY THAT AFTERNOON, still Lori hadn't texted back. Not to his picture, nor the message from the night before. Which, in fairness, he hadn't really expected, considering she was both at work and their first go at texting hadn't exactly been great.

Well, for her.

For *him*, he couldn't get her out of his mind.

She'd been so fucking cute when he'd deserved a verbal thrashing. Then funny enough to make his drunk ass laugh, then sober up rapidly when she'd rightfully called him out after that. Beyond all of that, she was gorgeous. And . . . she was his neighbor.

Fucking hell.

He'd sent a dick pic to Brandon's neighbor.

His brother was going to kill him. Especially, when he'd gotten an email just that morning telling Logan to keep it in his pants and give Lori her distance.

Thrusting a hand through his hair, Logan pushed up from the sofa and set his laptop to the side.

He'd spent several hours going through the online classifieds, trying to find anything that might excite him enough to want to spend the second half of his life doing it.

And . . . nothing.

Plus, it wasn't like the sniper skills he'd learned in military were particularly useful, unless he wanted to be a police officer or private security.

Did he want to be a cop? Not really. Private security? Even less appealing.

Firefighting? Maybe, but he'd need to go back to school—

School.

Maybe that was the answer.

If so, what would he study?

Another question.

Because even if he did want to be a firefighter, he didn't think he'd pass the physical. The piece of shrapnel in his hip ensured that.

He'd recovered, mostly, but he couldn't make a day-to-day career out of lifting people or dragging hoses around. A year ago, before the IED had gone off, then sure. Now, not so much.

Logan shook his head, not letting the memories take him back under.

He was in a good place finally. He'd been lucky when several others hadn't.

And so he had a duty to move on.

Sighing, he continued pacing and found that the movement didn't give him any answers.

School.

Yes. That felt right. He should focus on that.

Figure out what he should study, use it as an opportunity to move forward.

Good. Great.

But *what* to study?

Only one thing came to mind. One subject he'd always enjoyed. Biology.

But he was going to be downright elderly sitting in those chairs surrounded by eighteen-year-olds.

And what else did he have to do that was better?

Sit around his brother's place for days on end brooding?

"Fucking hell, man," he muttered, striding to the window and deliberately ignoring both the pain in his hip and his heart. Both would abate. Move on.

Move *forward*.

Because that was what this was about.

He needed to move forward when all he wanted to do was look back.

He went back to the computer and started filling out college applications.

CHAPTER 4

Lorelai

LORI CAME out of the elevator at the end of the day a hell of a lot slower than she'd left. Her backpack felt like it weighed a hundred pounds, her brain was fuzzy from the lack of sleep, and . . .

Logan had texted her another picture.

She was scared to open it.

Snorting, she knew she was less scared to see the picture and more frightened that if she looked at it and liked it then she'd suddenly find herself next door, sampling the goods she'd seen in that first picture, and thus, ending her very long celibacy streak.

Not that she was opposed to ending it.

Just the reason she *hadn't* was because normally she was extremely picky.

Who was she kidding?

A man who looked like Logan? No red-blooded, straight, single female was going to turn him down, photo faux pas or not.

Still, she'd had a day. Heather had been understanding, albeit not pleased to be kept waiting, and throughout their meeting Lori had felt like a misbehaving child in the principal's office.

Thankfully, the program she'd been working on had demonstrated beautifully, with absolutely no hitches on her part.

The rest of the day hadn't gone smoothly though.

She'd spilled coffee on herself, accidentally and permanently deleted several important lines of code for a different project, whose deadline was rapidly approaching. At which point, she'd christened everyone within earshot with her favorite set of curse words. Unprofessional, yes, but uncommon? No. Unfortunately for Lori, Heather O'Keith's nephew, Hunter, had been visiting the office. He'd heard her then had joyfully repeated the slew of f-words the entire way down the hall, much to his mother, Abby's, displeasure.

Pissing off *all* the O'Keiths today.

Way to go, her.

She reached the front door of her condo and wrestled her key into the lock. The damn thing always stuck, and then add in the heavy wood and her oversized backpack, and it was a struggle to get into her place on a good day.

Today, with her fuzzy brain, it was not her finest moment.

And it got worse.

"Here," Logan said, "Let me help you."

One arm reached down to snag the keys from her hand, and suddenly she was ensconced in yummy, spicy male.

Come on, universe. Throw me a bone here.

It did, her brain reminded her. *Last night.*

She snorted as Logan easily twisted the key in the lock—big hands—and then effortlessly pushed open her door, holding it wide so she could slip inside.

"Thanks," she said, dropping her bag on the floor then leaning back against the heavy wooden panel.

"No problem." He let go and turned to leave. Randomly, she noticed he had a jacket on. Was he going out to another bar to find another beautiful Hannah who rattled his brains enough to send her naked pictures?

Lori bit her lip, indecision warring within her before she just decided to go with her gut.

"Oh, hey, Logan?" she asked, not wanting him to leave even though she didn't exactly understand the reason why. "How did you end up in Brandon's condo?"

Logan grinned. "Brandon's my brother. When he got the contract to work in Germany, he threw me a solid and let me stay since I've never been to San Francisco."

Two thoughts went through her mind.

First, how in God's green earth were Logan and Brandon related?

Second, *he was Brandon's brother?*

Okay, so really, they were just one looping thought, but still.

How was that possible?

Not that Brandon wasn't attractive. He was. But he was also five-seven, maybe a hundred and fifty pounds on a good day, had white-blonde hair, pale blue eyes, and—

"Are you the milkman's baby?" Lori blurted.

Then immediately gasped and threw her hands over her mouth.

Logan grinned. "Nope. Full related by blood."

"I'm sorry," she said, and the apology was muffled by her fingers, so she peeled them back and tried again. "I'm sorry. That was exceptionally rude."

"Not the first time I've heard it," he said, leaning back against the door frame and pulling out his cell. "And it won't be the last. If I didn't know my mom as well as I do, I would definitely think I was adopted or hatched out of an egg or something. See?" He held up the phone and instinctively, she jerked back.

He dropped his hand, smile chagrined. "I deserved that."

Lori shook her head. "No, sorry. That was my fault."

"Want to see my family?"

"Are you all clothed?" she asked tentatively.

He glared.

"Okay," she said. "They're clothed. Why don't you come in for a second? My feet are killing me."

Logan glanced at her shoes. "Um . . ."

Her fancy sneakers. She shrugged, tone a little defensive. "They're my special tennies, and not broken in."

One brow came up.

She got irritated and let go of the door. "This, sir, is a judgment-free zone." Lori spun and started down the hall of her condo.

The day had been a day, and so now she was going to put on her pajamas, order a pizza, and watch a movie. Her cell would be on Do Not Disturb and she was going to get a full night's sleep so tomorrow wouldn't be as life-y as today.

There.

Good plan.

Done.

The door closed as she was shoving her fancy sneakers into the closet in her hallway.

"I hope the offer to come in is still good," he said from a few feet behind her.

She sniffed, brushed by him and hefted her backpack, taking it to the kitchen counter and going through her usual post-work process of plugging in her laptop, unloading the snacks she'd hoarded home from the office, and then extracting her cell.

"Do you like pepperoni?" she asked.

Logan's face warmed. "Yup."

"Good," she muttered and spent the next half minute putting in an order for pizza before setting her phone on the counter. "Drink?"

He nodded. "Sure, thanks."

She walked to the fridge and handed him a beer. "I'm putting on my pajamas and this is *not* an opportunity for you to get a real-time view of anything that I might sext."

There. Told off.

"Lori?"

She paused in the doorway to her bedroom. "Hmm?"

"Did *you* want a drink?" he asked.

Oh. That was nice. She wrinkled her nose, not wanting nice, wanting to hold on to her irritation, however unreasonable it was.

And let it be stated for the record, that she knew it was incredibly unreasonable to be annoyed because someone had misjudged her fancy sneakers.

It was just . . . the day had been a *day*.

"I have wine back at my place, if you prefer that."

Ugh. Fine. That was nice as well as sweet.

She sighed, let go of her irritation. "I'd love a beer. I promise I'll be more human by the time I put my pajamas on. It's just been a . . ."

"Day?" he finished when she trailed off.

Her lips twitched. "Yup. *That*."

"Okay, well, I'll attempt to make your day better by opening you a beer." He paused, head cocking to the side. "I can also leave, if that's better for you."

More nice. More wrinkling of her nose.

"No," she said. "I'd like for you to stay. Brandon and I used to hang out a lot. I've missed that." Lori pushed into her bedroom. "I'll be back in five minutes."

Closing and locking the door behind her, she headed to her closet. The very day-y day was going to get better.

She knew it.

CHAPTER 5

Logan

HE SPUN to the fridge and pulled out a beer for Lori, thinking that the contents inside mirrored what he'd filled Brandon's with, although his had more vegetables.

Lori appeared to only have an assortment of beer, ketchup, and mustard.

Logan pulled open the freezer. And ice cream.

A *lot* of ice cream.

He grinned and shut the freezer then went to sit at the dining room table where she'd dropped a mound of protein bars, bagged popcorn, freeze dried fruit, and several small cans of Diet Coke.

Quite a haul.

No wonder her backpack had been weighing her down.

Or maybe that was just her day, because he'd gotten her started off on the wrong foot.

Fuck. Guilt sucked.

But then again, after having come out of the IED mostly

unscathed when several of his friends hadn't, Logan knew all about guilt.

He heard the lock on the bedroom door just before it opened and Lori walked out. How in the hell she made a baggy sweatshirt and pink printed unicorn pajama bottoms look sexy was a feat of nature. But she did.

His cock twitched. Pathetic.

"Beer?" he asked, holding it out.

She nodded and took it, leading them over to the couch and sitting down. He sat on the opposite end.

"Can I see that picture of your family?"

Logan grinned. "Sure that's the one you want to see?"

A huffed-out laugh. "Yes, I'm sure."

He pulled out his cell, unlocking it to show her the photo of him, Brandon, and their parents the last time they were all together. Logan towered over all of them, and his coloring was completely different.

Which is why he wasn't the least bit offended when Lori lifted her eyes from the screen and said, "Can we circle back to the milkman's baby?"

"No." He laughed, flicked a finger so another pic came up on the screen. "My grandfather," he said when she glanced up at him, question in her eyes.

"Oh."

"Yeah."

"I'm an only child," she said. "My parents retired to Florida, but I grew up here." A shake of her head. "Sorry, that was a weird transition. I feel like my brain works in tangents some-times. A line heading toward infinity then jumping onto a completely other one, heading another direction."

Logan smiled. "I have to admit, I'm kind of digging the zigzags."

She giggled. "That is almost verbatim what Brandon used to say."

Which was the moment he realized she'd mentioned Brandon several times now, and he didn't have any understanding at all of what Brandon was to her. Had they been dating? Friends? Was Brandon interested in her?

Shit. What if his brother wanted Lori?

He couldn't—

"It's also one thing my fiancé hated about me," she said and sighed, taking a long swig of the beer. "Obviously, he became my ex." Her smile was tight. "But because he became my ex, I also got to meet your brother."

Logan's gut tightened. "Oh. Did you two—"

"No." She shook her head. "God *no*."

Now his gut tightened for a different reason. His brother may not be the most built or outgoing guy in the world, but he was good and smart and—

"Brandon's girlfriend Cassie is absolutely perfect for him. In fact, things got so serious right before he moved that I went from having two buddies most weeknights to no buddies." Her lip stuck out. "Both of my best friends moved to Germany. Brandon for work. Cassie because she decided—rightfully—she couldn't be without Brandon for a year."

"I—Cassie?"

She frowned. "You didn't know your brother had a girlfriend?"

More tightening. And who was the asshole now?

"No," he said. "Brandon never said anything."

"Hmm."

Familiar guilt reared its head. "Not his fault," Logan said. "I've been . . . out of contact for a lot of the last year."

Lori set her beer down. "What does that mean?"

He sighed. "I was in the military. Last year, I was in an accident. An IED went off near—"

She gasped. "Oh my God. Are you okay?" She patted his arm, pulled back. "Of course, you're okay. I'm sorry. I—"

Logan covered her hand with his. "I'm fine. I had some friends who aren't."

Her eyes dropped to her lap, but not before he saw them fill with moisture. "I'm sorry. That's horrible."

"It is," he said. "It's our job. It's part of the risk we accept, but it is also really hard to lose people you consider family." He sucked in a breath, released it slowly, tucking those memories back down. "I was hurt, and it took me some time to recover in Germany."

She nodded. "So, that's why he applied for the job."

"Brandon?" Another nod. "Yeah, I think so. We just didn't think by the time his German visa was processed that I'd be home. I think we overlapped for all of a week and most of that was filled with my appointments and debriefings."

"Cassie didn't leave to join him until a few days ago. I'm guessing that's why—" He nodded as Lori did that nose-wrinkling thing that was absolutely adorable. "I wonder why he didn't tell me about you, though."

"My fault," Logan admitted. "I didn't want anyone outside our family to know. Stupid, but"—he sighed—"it felt like my whole life had been determined by the military and then suddenly I was injured and forced to be discharged. I didn't want to be someone's pity case of a brother. I just wanted to be left alone and—"

She tugged her hand back. "And now I'm forcing you to rehash it."

"No," he said. "The psychologists did that. My parents and Brandon did it. I'm in a better place than I was six months ago, but I still definitely feel like my life has taken a sharp left I hadn't prepared for."

"Did you always want to be a soldier?"

He nodded. "Joined the army straight out of high school. Been in ever since." A sigh. "Thought I'd retire in uniform."

"I'm sorry."

Logan picked up his beer. "Stupid to be upset about something I can't change. Especially when that something isn't loss of life or limb, like—"

He cut himself off with a sip.

Lori touched his arm, pretty eyes locked on his for a long moment. She didn't tell him she was sorry again, or give any other platitudes. Instead, she leaned up, wrapped her arms around his shoulders, and hugged him tight.

Everything inside Logan relaxed at the contact.

The past disappeared. The hurt faded to an ache.

The only thing that mattered was how good Lori felt against him, how incredible she smelled, how nice it felt to have someone to hold him.

"My bad day suddenly seems less life-y," she murmured.

He grinned, leaned back when she dropped her arms. "*This* is what I was looking for last night in the bar."

"A hug?"

He shook his head. "A distraction. Some comfort. Someone to talk to."

Lori had tears in her eyes, but he watched her blink them back and smile up at him. "Well, anyone who knows me, knows that I can talk with the best of them. So, for as long as you're around, you'll be stuck talking to me."

Logan opened his mouth to say that being stuck with anything—talking, hugging, texting, whatever—with Lori wasn't a trial in the least, but then the buzzer rang, and she popped off the couch to answer it.

Then spent the next five minutes bringing the pizza and plates and napkins in, dishing up slices, then consulting him on what movie to watch.

Eventually, they settled on an action flick they'd both already seen.

But that worked for him, because Logan got to hear her commentary on why the hero was failing, ask questions to get her fired up enough to go off on one of those tangents her ex had supposedly hated, but that he found extremely charming, and he got to spend time with a beautiful—where it mattered most, on the inside—woman.

By the time he went back to Brandon's condo, he was happy and relaxed and so full of pizza and beer that he didn't have any problems falling asleep.

And because of that, he didn't see Lori's reply to his picture until the morning.

I think I like the first pic better.

But he did see it first thing in the morning.

And because of *that*, for the first time in more than a year, he went about his day with a smile on his face.

CHAPTER 6

Logan: You're not late today are you?
Lori: Nope. No a-holes made me sleep through my alarm.
Logan: Maybe you need a louder alarm?
Lori: *eye roll emoji* Nice try, buster.
Logan: Want to have dinner at my place tonight? I saw your fridge. It's in desperate straits.
Lori: Does that mean you're buying?
Logan: If you steal some more of those chocolate-covered pretzel things from your work then, yes, I'm buying.
Lori: Good. Pick what you want to eat and get two. I'll eat anything except for mushrooms.
Lori: *shuddering GIF*
Logan: Anything?
Lori: Anything aside from fungi.
Logan: Anchovies?
Lori: Sure.
Logan: Oysters.
Lori: Both raw and Rockefeller.
Logan: Olives.

Lori: Yup. I especially like putting them on all my fingers and then eating them off one by one.

Logan: Lori.

Lori: What?

Logan: That's worse than my picture.

Lori: Um. No. Nice try.

Logan: I'm imagining you sucking them off and—

Logan: I'm stopping there.

Lori: . . . I. Can't. Breathe.

Logan: I didn't mean it like that.

Lori: Uh-huh. Sure.

Logan: Stop laughing or no pasta for you.

Lori: Carbs?

Logan: If you behave yourself. I was also going to get dessert.

Lori: Chocolate carbs, please.

Logan: Will you be on your best behavior?

Lori: No promises. But I won't send you naked pictures.

Logan: Not going to live that down ever, am I?

Lori: Nope. But I promise to keep it a private joke between us.

Logan: Good. Then I'll get you chocolate and carbs.

Lori: And chocolate carbs?

Logan: *sends photo of the dessert case at the bakery* Keep it between us and you can pick your poison.

Lori: All of them.

Lori: Just kidding. That chocolate cheesecake on the left.

Logan: Done. 6pm work?

Lori: I'll be there with bells on.

Logan: All I'm asking is for you . . . and your fancy sneakers.

Lori: *glarey eyes emoji*

Lori: Gotta go back to work. See you later.

CHAPTER 7

Lorelai

LOGAN DELIVERED ON THE CHEESECAKE, and she came wearing pajamas paired with her fancy sneakers. The pasta he'd had DoorDashed was delicious, and they put another movie on, but same as the night before, they spent more time gabbing than actually watching it. She'd gone home late and then crashed headlong into sleep. No more mid-night wake-ups, no more sleeping through her alarm.

They'd done the same thing at her place the next night.

Then back to his after that.

Then repeated the pattern, trading off with hosting dinners every night for the next few weeks.

Lori loved every minute of their time together. It was mostly like having Brandon back, the easy rapport between her and Logan making her wonder if conversation skills ran in the Smith family or if Logan and Brandon had both just lucked out.

Of course, the *mostly*-like-having-Brandon-back part stemmed from the fact that Logan was his brother.

And also because she didn't want to jump Brandon's bones, like she did Logan's.

Not that Brandon was unattractive, because he was certainly good-looking. But there wasn't a spark, and the entire time they'd known each other, she'd been with someone, or after The Dumping that had left her crying in the hall and had provoked Brandon to have her over for the first time, she'd been in recovery mode. Then by the time she'd able to end her hiatus of self-imposed social distancing, he'd been with Cassie.

No opportunity. No interest.

That was mutual.

But he was a damned good friend, along with Cassie.

Although, he was also damn good friend who hadn't shared the information about Logan's injury and recovery.

Though, based on what Logan had said, it hadn't been Brandon's information to share.

Sigh.

She'd need to talk it out with Brandon.

Hard of late, with the time difference. Every time they got a few minutes on the phone, he'd had to run off to bed or she'd been blearily just awake. She was going to have to put her concerns in email form, but for now, she'd just focus on the fact that it felt nice to have a friend next door again and not that Brandon hadn't shared, or that she'd dreamed about his brother the night before.

Lie. She'd dreamed about him for *all* of the nights before.

Or rather, a very specific part of Logan.

Pervert.

As in, *she* was the pervert this time.

But it had been a very good dream, one that involved her having multiple orgasms courtesy of that giant cock.

Yum.

If only Logan had been giving her signals that he might be interested.

Instead, he'd seemed to step into Brandon's role and been carefully keeping distance between them.

Which proved he wasn't the huge dick—no pun intended—that his text messages had first presented him as . . . but she already knew that. He'd shown that within a few minutes of them meeting in person. He didn't need to keep proving he was a good guy.

In fact, she'd like some of that dick to—

Stop.

She'd been missing Brandon and Cassie, now she had Logan. Maybe he simply wasn't interested in her as more than a friend.

Well, that wasn't a maybe.

That was a certain.

He'd held doors for her, occasionally touched her arm. He texted funny stuff, saw her every night. He knew about her ridiculously happy parents, her double major in math and computer science. She knew about his favorite movies, that his injury had been to his hip, that he'd decided to go back to school and study biology.

But there wasn't an undercurrent of heat between them.

She might have longing, but he wasn't carrying a torch for her.

Stifling a sigh, she reached to pick up her plate, but Logan nudged her away. "I got them. It's late and you've got that that important work meeting tomorrow."

It was true she was meeting with Heather again the next day, but—

"I can help—"

He nodded to the door. "Shoo."

"I should—"

The plate dropped to the table. "Lori." He sighed.

Her brows drew together. "What's the matter?"

His chin dropped to his chest, a long, slow breath escaped his lips. "Lori, honey," he murmured. "You need to go."

Her heart skipped a beat at the endearment. "I can wash—"

Hot brown eyes flew up to meet hers. "Go."

She shook her head, not certain why he was upset—

"Lori." It sounded like it was ground out between his teeth.

"What? What did I do?"

"Fuck." He thrust his hands into his hair, turned and paced away, eyes on the window. She crossed to him, placed a hand on his arm. His head whipped around so fast that she took several steps back. He looked absolutely furious. "I'm trying to be good here, Lori. I've spent the last few weeks dreaming of you, wanting you, jerking off to the mental image of stripping those ridiculous pajamas off your sexy body. I get that you don't want me, but—"

"*What?*"

"I know you want me to be a friend, like Brandon was," he said, turning around to face her. "But I can't just be around you all the time and not want to—" Logan paced away again.

"You want me?"

Brown eyes over his shoulder. "Go, Lori."

"But I thought you didn't want *me*." She strode around in front of him, shoving him back lightly. "I've been over here every night in my fancy sneakers and you've been friend-zoning the shit out of me."

"Um, no," he said. "You've been friend-zoning *me*."

"Uh, no. I'm the one having wet dreams about you every night."

He frowned. "Can girls have wet dreams?"

She rolled her eyes. "That's your response to me telling you that?"

Lips twitching, he said, "I take it back."

"Good."

"Good." His eyes bored into hers, and it was as though he'd finally pulled back a veil, revealing heat he'd kept banked over the last few weeks. "I don't want to be your friend, sweetheart."

She nibbled at her bottom lip. "What *do* you want to be?"

"More."

Lori dropped her gaze to her feet for a moment. "A boyfriend?"

"Yes."

"*Friend* friend?"

"Yes, that, too."

Her heart rolled over in her chest, exposing itself. Could she do this? She wanted to, but should she? She glanced up, saw the warmth in his eyes, and figured if she didn't, she'd regret it for the rest of her life. "How about a provider of chocolate carbs?"

Amusement crept into his tone, and he said, "Yes."

"Good."

She launched herself into his arms and slanted her mouth across his.

CHAPTER 8

Logan

HER MOUTH MET HIS, and heat exploded down his spine. He didn't think, just reacted, wrapping his arms around her waist, hauling her up against him, and kissing her exactly as he'd been dreaming up for weeks now.

It was better than he could have imagined.

Her lips were soft, her mouth was slick and hot, and her tongue met his stroke for stroke.

Eventually, though, he had to pull back to breathe.

"Logan," she murmured, when their lips parted.

He knew the feeling. His lungs were screaming, but his mind was demanding *more, now.*

"Lori," he groaned, dragging his mouth along her jaw, tracing it along the shell of her ear, noting that she shivered when he made it to the spot just behind it. Then her fingers were in his hair, and she was yanking his head so their mouths met again, and they kissed and kissed and kissed.

Her hands slipped under the hem of his T-shirt, nails dragging along his back. "Off," she demanded, yanking it up and because it was fewer clothes rather than more, he broke their mouths apart and tugged it over his head. Hers was next, Lori grabbing the bottom and pulling it off without ceremony. It landed on the floor next to his, but when she made to reach for the button on her jeans, he stopped her.

"Hey," he murmured. "I don't think—"

"I want you, Logan Smith," she said. "So, I guess the question is do *you* want to stop?"

He froze for a heartbeat before his lips curved. He didn't think he would ever be able to predict what this woman was going to say. "I don't want to stop."

"Good." A beat. "Do you have a condom?"

"Yup."

"Good." Her fingers flicked open the button on her jeans, tugged at the zipper, and shoved them down her legs. They tangled at her ankles and she teetered, but Logan lurched forward to grab her, sweeping her up into his arms. "The one time I don't change into pajamas," she muttered.

"I happen to like that ass in jeans," he murmured, shifting her weight as he walked so he could help her untangle the denim from her ankles.

"Pajamas would make for easier access."

"Sometimes easy access isn't everything."

She paused, eyes coming up to meet his, lips curving. "True."

He got the jeans off the other foot and let them fall to the floor, and then he had his arms full of beautiful woman, breasts encased in black lace, pussy in . . .

"Are those unicorns?"

Her cheeks flared red, but she didn't look away. "Unicorns happen to be very sexy," she grumbled.

Considering they were on the woman he was crazy about, Logan wasn't going to argue. Instead, he tossed Lori onto the bed, followed her down, and let his mouth tell her exactly how much he enjoyed them.

She tasted of honey and sunshine.

Her skin was silk.

Her breasts . . . well, he lost his mind for a bit there, kissing and sucking at the pebbled tips, kneading the round globes, licking and tasting and laving every inch of them. And then every inch of *her*.

Her pussy tasted like honey, too.

And he couldn't get enough, using his tongue on her labia, pressing and flicking it against her clit, slipping a finger inside her until he found a rhythm that had her hips jerking up and pleadings escaping her lips in gasped exhales.

"Logan— *oh*. Fuck," she groaned, head writhing on the pillow. "Yes. Like that. No, faster. Yes. That. Don't stop. Don't stop. Don't—"

She broke off with a long keening moan, pussy convulsing around his fingers.

Logan's head was spinning, the taste of her on his tongue, her scent in his nose, his cock ready to break in half, but he paused, waited for her eyes to flutter open.

"Are—"

Lori reached for the button of his jeans . "Inside me. Now."

He didn't need to be told twice, extracting the condom from his wallet, brushing her hands away, unbuttoning and pushing his jeans down before rolling it on. Twenty seconds later, he was between her thighs and pushing home.

Fucking. Best. Thing. Ever.

She was tight. She was hot. She was—

Lori kissed him.

—everything.

He moved, thrusting in and out, desire spiraling out from his cock and shooting down his spine. It was absolutely the best thing he'd *ever* felt. In fact, it was so good that he didn't even register the fact that his hip was twinging.

Logan couldn't feel anything except him, Lori, and the magic they were making.

He didn't last long.

But luckily, neither did she.

Thirty seconds later, he slipped a hand between them, finding a spot that made her arch and cry out, pussy clenching around him as she toppled over the edge.

He was right behind her.

He'd started the night thinking he'd be getting nothing more than friendship with Lori and trying to convince himself that it was all she was willing to give, and so he needed to be content with it.

He ended the night pulsing inside her.

Life had dealt him another sharp left.

But this time, he didn't mind.

The morning, however, wouldn't be so kind.

"I'm LATE!" Lori shot out of bed, completely naked, hair an absolute mess, and ass shaking in his face.

Best. View. Ever.

But then he processed what she'd said.

Shit. *Fuck.*

He'd screwed her over again with another meeting for her boss.

"Here," he said, leaping out of bed and making a mad dash for her clothes. "Get dressed, get to the office. I'll go next door and get your laptop and drop it with a change of clothes later."

The panic disappeared, relief taking its place. She leaned

toward him, pressed her mouth to his for a brief second. "You're the best, Logan Smith."

"Go," he said. "There's a spare toothbrush in the drawer next to the sink."

He threw on a pair of sweats as she ran into the bathroom then hustled to grab her purse and her cell, putting both where she couldn't miss them by the front door. A moment later, he grabbed the spare key to her place that Brandon had hanging in his hall closet, and was out in the hall.

And running straight into Brandon.

Who had a beautiful blonde standing behind him, one who was apparently madly in love with his brother, but who Logan hadn't known about until Lori had mentioned her.

Secrets. His brother was all about the secrets.

"Whoa, Log," Brandon said.

"Hey," Logan said. "I'm happy to see you, but just a second. Lori needs—"

Hip twinging, he'd definitely overdone it on round two the previous night, he darted across the hall, opened Lori's door then spent the next few minutes dashing around her place and shoving things into her backpack. Clothes, underwear, fancy sneakers, laptop. All check.

Then he hustled out, thinking maybe he could catch her before she'd gone.

Instead, when he came out, the elevator doors were closing, Lori presumably within them, and his brother was glaring at him from his condo's door with crossed arms. "What the fuck, dude?"

Logan sighed and pushed past him, heading toward the bedroom to put on a shirt and shoes.

Cassie, or at least that was who he assumed the blonde was, was standing uncomfortably in the hall, and he paused.

"Hi," he said. "I'm Logan. Come in."

"Cassie," she murmured as she and his brother trailed him into the condo.

"I'll be right back," he said, moving toward the bedroom.

She nodded, glanced uneasily from Logan to Brandon.

A few minutes later, Logan was dressed, teeth brushed, and facing a pissed off older brother.

"What in the fuck are you doing with Lori?" Brandon snapped

Logan stifled a sigh, decided to counter-attack. "Why didn't you tell me about Cassie?"

Brandon's teeth clicked together.

"I know you two are friends," Logan said. "But I like Lori, a lot."

Brandon sniffed. "Sure, you do. I know all about how you *like* women," he muttered.

"Because you saw me trying to cope when the worst shit of my life happened. Yes, I was drinking. Yes, I was fucking. Yes, I was absolutely out of my mind." He sucked in a breath. "Look. I know we both hold a lot of stuff to our chests, but I'm not the asshole I was a year ago. I fully admit I was a fucking mess then. I didn't know what I was doing. Who I was any longer. My friends were severely injured or dead and—"

Cassie gasped.

Logan dropped his chin to his chest. "I'm sorry. I shouldn't have said it that way—"

She crossed over to him. "Logan. *No.* Oh my God, I'm sorry. I—"

Brandon touched her shoulder, tugged her back. "Hey, I get it. You were running." He glanced down at Cassie. "That seems to be a Smith trait, but that doesn't mean you're good enough for Lori. She's my best friend, and her ex was an asshole. She deserves someone who isn't bogged down by the past, who can live in the present. No offense, Log, but you've got a lot of baggage."

He did.

That much was true.

"And I know Lori is beautiful and convenient but—"

"I love her."

Both Cassie and Brandon's mouths fell open.

But it was the gasp in the hallway that set his heart sinking.

Lori was there, Brandon's condo door wide open, her face pale, keys dangling from her fingers. "I-I sh-shouldn't have heard t-that," she stammered. "I'll g-go." She spun around and ran .

The backpack hit the ground as he chased after her, snagging her arm just as she made it to the hall.

"Shit, Lori," he said. "I didn't mean for you to hear that. It's too soon, I know. I—why are you here?"

She shakily held up her cell. "Heather had to cancel. I figured I'd come back and change." A shuddering breath. "Did you mean it?"

Fuck.

But he couldn't lie to her.

"I did," he said and hurried to add, "I know it's insane. I know we're just starting to learn each other, but Lori, you're the most incredible woman I've ever met. Hands down. I want to learn you more, for us to spend more time together, for you to forget you heard me declare my love so that I can take you somewhere romantic in a reasonable amount of time and tell you then." He cupped her cheek. "I want to do this right with you and—"

"I love you, too," she blurted. "I agree this is insane and too fast and—well, you can just forget you heard it, too"—a smile—"so I can tell *you* again later."

His heart had been pounding out of his chest, but at her words, it relaxed. "Really?"

Her finger came to his lips. "Shh."

"Tell me again."

"Later," she admonished.

And then she dropped her hand to his shoulder and rose on tiptoe. He didn't need any further encouragement. Logan bent his head and kissed her. Then kept on kissing her until Cassie and Brandon came out of the apartment and caught them.

"You boys will talk the rest of this out later," Cassie said, waving as she tugged Brandon toward the elevator.

And Cassie was right.

Brandon and Logan did talk it out later.

In fact, they talked it out so much that Brandon decided that this new Logan, the one who'd decided to go back to school, the one who didn't get drunk in bars any longer, who didn't hide beneath painful memories to keep the world at a distance, was absolutely perfect man for Lori.

EPILOGUE

Lorelai, Two Months Later

SHE WALKED into her condo to find candles on every surface, rose petals on the floor, and . . .

Logan asleep on the couch.

In fairness, she was the one who'd fucked up.

She was supposed to have been home two hours before, but she'd had a problem with one of her programs and had sat down to troubleshoot for *just one minute*.

Well, one had turned into a hundred, and now she was obscenely late.

Two plates were on the table, along with an entire chocolate cheesecake. Her heart pitter-pattered. The man had brought chocolate carbs.

Aw.

She turned, walked over to where Logan was sleeping, the textbook from one of the classes he was taking sprawled across his chest. Carefully, she slid it from him and set it on the coffee table then burrowed her way under his arm.

Even asleep, he still let her in, still hugged her close, still murmured, "I love you."

Just like he did every single time she came to him when he was sleeping.

Whether it was on the couch, like this—though sans candles, cheesecake, and rose petals—or in bed when she worked late. Or even if she got up to get a glass of water or go to the bathroom.

Every time she came back, he whispered, "I love you."

And every time, she whispered back, "I love you, too."

Someday, they would manage to say it again when both of them were awake, or at least *semi*-conscious.

Until then, Lori was just going to let Logan have his moment.

Just hopefully next time she wouldn't be late and ruin it.

Or those glorious chocolate carbs.

Kels

Kelsey pushed out of the door of Bobby's, the local bar she and her friends liked to frequent, and paused for a moment, enjoying the crispness in the air.

It was one of those perfect end of summer evenings, warm during the day, but the promise of fall in the air. She snuggled into her hoodie and smiled, thinking about how happy her brother, Sebastian, and his fiancée, Rachel, had been that evening at dinner.

Of course, a lot of that had to do with the fact that Rachel was sporting a diamond large enough to blind Kelsey . . . and the rest of the Earth's populace.

But, seriously, she was happy for them both.

Sebastian and Rachel were perfect for each other and they

deserved all the happiness in the world.

She slipped out of the opening and let the door start to close behind her, but before she got too far, Sebastian caught it. He slid through, dropped an arm around her shoulders. "Let me walk you to your car."

"I'm fine," she said, shrugging him off. "Go enjoy your fiancée. It's not your guys' fault that my flight is ridiculously early in the morning."

He rolled his eyes. "You know you're not going to win this argument, so just accept my chivalry. It's my brotherly duty after all."

"You sell it so effectively."

"Shut up."

"*You* shut up."

"No, *you* shut up."

"*No—*"

They broke off with grins and Kels let Bas sling his arm around her neck, tugging her into a hug. "I love you, brat," he told her.

"Well, I don't love you."

"Rude."

"You know it." But she hugged him back before leading him to her car. "I am really so happy for you both, you know that right?"

"Of course I do, Kels," he said.

They spent the next few minutes discussing the wedding—the date and location were set, as was the food—and the whole crew of females, including Kelsey were going dress shopping the following week.

"It sounds like you've got it pretty much sorted."

Bas smiled. "Rachel's a force of nature," he joked. "Seriously, though, she wanted to ask you this, but I preferred to do it myself."

Kels frowned. "Ask what?"

"To be a bridesmaid. We were hoping you'd be in the bridal party." He lifted his hands, palms up. "No pressure, of course, but we'd love to have you in the wedding."

Her lips curved. "I'm happy to play whatever role you want, Bas."

"Flower girl?"

She shot him a glare. "Really?"

"So bridesmaid then?"

Since they'd reached her car, she unlocked the passenger side door and tossed her purse on the seat. "I'd be honored. As long as that's what you guys want."

He nodded. "It is."

"Great." She pressed a kiss to his cheek. "Then count me in. Thank Rachel for me?"

"Done."

Kels rounded her car, paused with her hand on the driver's door handle. "Oh, besides Devon"—their brother—"who are the other groomsmen?"

"We're keeping it small." He shrugged. "Heather is going to be the maid of honor, you a bridesmaid, and Devon is going to be my best man."

She smiled. "And Clay is going to be the other groomsman."

Bas shook his head.

Kelsey had opened her mouth, ready to tease Bas about choosing to include Rachel's boss over his when her gut sank.

Small bridal party.

Two on each side.

One of which was *not* Clay.

And her brother had only had a few close friends growing up. None of whom she could see in the wedding party.

Except one.

Fuck.

But she was worrying for nothing. Bas hadn't talked to Tanner in years as far as she knew. They *hadn't* talked in years. They couldn't have—

"Who is it then?" she asked through stiff lips.

Because it couldn't be. Her brother didn't know about them. She'd made sure of it. They'd kept things on the down-low and . . . then she'd nursed her broken heart two thousand miles away in college.

"Tanner."

Her gut twisted.

Double fuck.

And a shit for good measure.

"That's fine, right?" Bas asked. "You guys seemed to get along great." Concern rippled across his face. "Is there something wrong. Did—"

"No," she said quickly. "That's great. I'm sorry. I'm just preoccupied with my new project."

He grinned. "Always work with you."

She blew him a kiss. "You know it."

"Great. So you'll be paired up with him. And I know it's been a while, but he's coming into town next week to catch up." He tapped the roof of her car, took a step back. "You want to grab dinner with us?"

"I'd love too," she lied before getting into her car and with a wave that hopefully didn't show her dismay, Kelsey drove away.

Paired up with Tanner.

Been there, done that.

Got the souvenir broken heart.

Triple fuck.

Thank you for reading! I hope you loved diving into Rachel and

Bas's, Bec and Luke's, and Sera and Tate's happily ever after! The next book in the Billionaire's Club series is BAD BOYFRIEND. Find out how Kels for fell for her brothers' best friend...and what her protective brothers do when they find out.

CLICK HERE TO READ BAD BOYFRIEND NOW >

And if you enjoyed BAD BOYFRIEND, you'll love the small town of Stoneybrooke, its swoony heroes, and the klutzy, lovable heroines who steal their hearts. The first book in the series, TRAIN WRECK, is free to download!

"I laughed out loud all the way through the book, except perhaps during the sexy scenes. I'm not telling you what I did during those." —Amazon reviewer

The more she falls for Stefan, the more she risks her career... Don't miss the Gold Hockey series. It begins with the over 400 five-star-reviewed BLOCKED!

"Off-the-charts hot, smexy scenes with one of the best book boyfriends I have come across!" —Amazon reviewer

DOWNLOAD BLOCKED FOR FREE >

I so appreciate your help in spreading the word about my books, including sharing with friends! Please leave a review on your favorite book site!
You can also join my Facebook group, the Fabinators, for exclusive giveaways and sneak peeks of future books.

SIGN UP FOR ELISE FABER'S NEWSLETTER HERE:
https://www.elisefaber.com/newsletter

Want a free bonus story? Hate missing Elise's new releases?
Love contests, exclusive excerpts and giveaways?
Then signup for Elise's newsletter here!
https://www.elisefaber.com/newsletter

And join Elise's fan group, the Fabinators https://www.
facebook.com/groups/fabinators for insider information, sneak
peaks at new releases, and fun freebies! Hope to see you there!

BILLIONAIRE'S CLUB

Bad Night Stand
Bad Breakup
Bad Husband
Bad Hookup
Bad Divorce
Bad Fiancé
Bad Boyfriend
Bad Blind Date
Bad Wedding
Bad Engagement
Bad Bridesmaid
Bad Swipe
Bad Girlfriend
Bad Best Friend
Bad Billionaire's Quickies

BILLIONAIRE'S CLUB

Did you miss any of the other Billionaire's Club books? Check out excerpts from the series below or find the full series at https://www.elisefaber.com/all-books

---

Bad Night Stand
Book One
https://www.elisefaber.com/bad-night-stand

Abby

"I'M THE BEST FRIEND," I said and lifted my chin, forcing my words to be matter-of-fact. I'd been through this before. "You might be fuckable to the nth degree and perfect for Seraphina, but I refuse to set her up with a liar."

In a movement too quick for my brain to process, my stool was shoved to the side and I was pinned against the bar, heavy hips pressing into me, a hard chest two inches from my mouth.

Seraphina whipped around at the movement and I could just see her over Jordan's shoulder, her blue eyes concerned.

"Hi, Seraphina, I'm Jordan," he said, calm as can be, gaze locked onto my face then my eyes when mine invariably couldn't stay away. "I'm going to borrow your friend for a minute."

"Abs?" she asked, and I knew she'd go to bat for me right then and there if I needed her to.

"Weasel or no?" I managed to gasp out. For some reason, I couldn't catch my breath.

Not that it had anything to do with Jordan.

No, it had *everything* to do with him.

"Weasel?" he asked.

I shook my head, focused on my best friend. Weasel was our code name for the men trying to weasel, quite literally, their way into my pants and then into hers.

I was just about ready to say fuck it—or me, rather—even if Jordan was a Weasel. He smelled amazing. His body was hard and hot against mine.

And it had been way too long since I'd had sex.

"No chemistry on my part—" Seraphina began.

"Your friend isn't who I'm attracted to," Jordan growled out. "You are, and it's fucking pissing me off that you don't believe that."

—Get your copy at https://www.elisefaber.com/bad-night-stand

Bad Breakup
Book Two
https://www.elisefaber.com/bad-breakup

CeCe

"You're even more beautiful than I remember," he said, and the rough edges of his accent hacked at the words, making them more of a growl rather than a soft sentiment.

Her breath caught, and she found her eyes drawn to the stormy blue of Colin's.

And she stared again, utterly entranced before she remembered how it had all ended.

Her in a white dress.

Alone, except for the priest who'd given her a pitying look and invited her to stay as long as she needed.

But it had always been like this, Colin's gruff words winning her over. They were unexpected from him—he was typically so reserved and taciturn. And that compliment, freely given as it was, chipped away at any defenses she managed to erect.

The problem was that his words weren't always followed up by action. In fact, they were typically trailed by pain for her and fury for him.

The hurt of those memories—of Colin so angry, her so broken—helped shore up her resolve.

"Don't say things like that," she snapped and started to pop her earbuds back in. Her friends at home had filled her phone with a slew of romantic audiobooks and she decided that she much preferred fictional heroes at the moment.

At least if they broke their heroine's heart, it was only once.

Colin had already broken hers twice.

She wasn't looking for a round three.

—Get your copy at https://www.elisefaber.com/bad-breakup.

Bad Husband
Book Three
https://www.elisefaber.com/bad-husband

Heather

"I'm getting drunk," he said, but allowed her to pull him inside the car so that her driver could shut the door behind them.

"You're already drunk," she said.

He stiffened. "*More* drunk."

"Fine," she said, half-worried he was going to launch himself from the sedan. She'd never seen Clay like this. Usually he was so cold and uncompromising, impenetrable even under the toughest of negotiations. He was . . . well, he was typically as *Steele*-like as his last name decreed.

She wrapped her arm through his in order to prevent any unplanned exits from the vehicle and gave the driver the name of her favorite bar. "If you really want to drink, let's do it right."

And *then* she'd drop him at his hotel.

Except it didn't happen that way.

Yes, they hit the bar.

Yes, they drank.

Yes, they got plastered.

But then they woke up . . . or at least, *Heather* woke up.

Naked.

With a softly snoring Clay Steele passed out next to her in bed.

That wasn't the worst part.

Because Heather woke up naked and with a softly snoring Clay Steele in her bed *and* she was wearing a giant diamond ring on her left hand.

Still not the worst part.

That came in the form of a slightly crumpled marriage certificate tucked under her right cheek.

And not the one on her face.

She pulled it from beneath her, a cold sweat breaking out on her body, dread in every nerve and cell.

She *still* wasn't prepared for the horror she found.

The marriage license had been signed by . . . Heather O'Keith and Clay Steele.

Holy fuck, what had she done?

—Get your copy https://www.elisefaber.com/bad-husband.

Bad Boyfriend
Book Seven
https://www.elisefaber.com/bad-boyfriend

Seraphina

SERA WAS ALONE, pining after a man who'd created the latest social media craze.

Yup. Her life was *ah-maz-ing*.

Tate cleared his throat, and Sera realized she'd been staring at him dumbfounded for a good couple of minutes.

"How can I help you today?" she asked. "I do hope"—*Do hope?* What was she, British? *Ugh.*—"I-uh . . . I hope you were able to find a house. The agents I passed along are very good at finding unique properties, and I even gave them a few locations to start with . . . " She bit her lip, attempting to stop the ramble.

"No."

Just no.

Um. Okay.

He lifted a hand, rubbed the back of his neck. The movement made his shirt lift, exposing several inches of flat stomach and tan skin and, oh God, a trail of blond hair leading south. Her mouth watered, desperate to trace that path with her tongue—

Sera sucked in a breath, popped to her feet.

"Ah. I'm sorry." She picked up a random file, pretending to know what was in it. "I'm actually really busy, so this will have to continue another time."

Like never.

She rounded her desk, forced a smile. "Mr. Conner," she said when he didn't move. "I'll have my assistant schedule something soon."

"Seraphina."

She shivered at the sound of her name on his lips—soft, a little raspy, and deep enough to conjure all sorts of unhelpful fantasies in her mind.

Shaking herself, she moved to open the door.

Suddenly, Tate was there, hand on hers, body inches away, spicy scent inundating her senses.

Sera's breath caught. "What are you—?"

He seemed to be arguing with himself then finally, those piercing blue eyes locked onto hers. "I need you to marry me."

—Get your copy at https://www.elisefaber.com/bad-boyfriend

Bad Blind Date
Book Eight
https://www.elisefaber.com/bad-blind-date

Trix

REGARDLESS, she was back in California for the time being, ready to begin a new chapter in her life.

Apparently, that meant starting by dating.

At least, that was Heather's logic.

Or maybe Trix's own brand of stupid.

Still, whatever it was that had convinced her to come, she was there now and was going to make the best of it.

Or at least that *had been* her thought until she recognized who was approaching the table.

Him.

Trix slammed her eyes closed and counted to five.

It could *not* be him.

Could not—

She opened her eyes.

Clay was on his feet, shaking the man's hand, shaking *Jet's* hand, and making introductions all around. Heather looked thrilled, probably because Jet was gorgeous and funny and smart—

"And this is Heather's sister, Trix. She's a nurse."

Jet knew that.

Because he knew her. *Intimately.*

The doctor and the nurse. So cliché. So stupid on her part to think that things in her life might have turned out differently.

He'd been smiling as he turned to meet her, and it was almost comical to see his expression darken to fury. Or it *would* have, if that fury hadn't been directed at her. By then his hand was already in hers, mid-shake and *fuck* if his touch didn't still make sparks shoot down her arm.

She went to pull back, but he held fast then jerked her forward, as though he were giving her a hug in greeting.

No one at the table could see that he was hissing in her ear.

"What the fuck are you playing at, Trixie?"

—Get your copy at https://www.elisefaber.com/bad-blind-date

Breakaway

Breakout

Checked

Coasting

Centered

Charging

Caged

Crashed

A Gold Christmas

Cycled

Caught

Breakers Hockey (all stand alone)

Broken

Boldly

Breathless

Ballsy (April 26, 2022)

Love, Action, Camera (all stand alone)

Dotted Line

Action Shot

Close-Up

End Scene

Meet Cute

Love After Midnight (all stand alone)

Rum And Notes

Virgin Daiquiri

On The Rocks

Sex On The Seats

Life Sucks Series (**all stand alone**)

Train Wreck

Hot Mess

Dumpster Fire

Clusterf*@k

FUBAR (March 29,2022)

Roosevelt Ranch Series (**all stand alone, series complete**)

Disaster at Roosevelt Ranch

Heartbreak at Roosevelt Ranch

Collision at Roosevelt Ranch

Regret at Roosevelt Ranch

Desire at Roosevelt Ranch

Phoenix Series (**read in order**)

Phoenix Rising

Dark Phoenix

Phoenix Freed

Phoenix: LexTal Chronicles (**rereleasing soon, stand alone, Phoenix world**)

From Ashes

In Flames

To Smoke

ABOUT THE AUTHOR

USA Today bestselling author, Elise Faber, loves chocolate, Star Wars, Harry Potter, and hockey (the order depending on the day and how well her team -- the Sharks! -- are playing). She and her husband also play as much hockey as they can squeeze into their schedules, so much so that their typical date night is spent on the ice. Elise changes her hair color more often than some people change their socks, loves sparkly things, and is the mom to two exuberant boys. She lives in Northern California. Connect with her in her Facebook group, the Fabinators or find more information about her books at www.elisefaber.com.

facebook.com/elisefaberauthor

amazon.com/author/elisefaber

bookbub.com/profile/elise-faber

instagram.com/elisefaber

goodreads.com/elisefaber

pinterest.com/elisefaberwrite

www.ingramcontent.com/pod-product-compliance
Lightning Source LLC
Chambersburg PA
CBHW031022030726

47497CB00004B/956